LILLEY
&
CHASE

LILLEY & CHASE

TIM WATERSTONE

HEADLINE

First published in 1994 by
HEADLINE BOOK PUBLISHING

10 9 8 7 6 5 4 3 2 1

British Library Cataloguing in Publication Data

Waterstone, Tim
Lilley & Chase
I. Title
823.914 [F]

ISBN 0-7472-1129-9

Typeset by
Avon Dataset Ltd., Bidford-on-Avon, Warks

Printed and bound in Great Britain by
Mackays of Chatham PLC, Chatham, Kent

HEADLINE BOOK PUBLISHING
A division of Hodder Headline PLC
338 Euston Road
London NW1 3BH

'For all my family.'

PART ONE

Prologue

The irony of it all was that Hilary told Sam what had happened almost on a whim. She was sitting up in their bedroom, trying to collect herself sufficiently to go downstairs and talk to him in the kitchen, aware that she had not so much as asked him about his week in London. But before she got herself ready to do so, Sam came in and, sitting on the bed, asked her what she was upset about, and whether he could help her. Almost casually, but with a growing sense of relief as she discharged the shadow of guilt that hung over her, she found herself telling him about Dan Galetti, and a rather generalised version of the events of the last few weeks. The guilt sprang from Hilary's inherent desire for faithfulness and seriousness as a wife and mother, in which the act of adultery was painfully out of character; the casualness from her assumption that Sam loved her to the extent that he would always forgive her any transgression – even this.

'I'm so sorry, Sam. These things happen. I didn't mean it to turn out the way it did. It's all over now. He's gone off to Leicester, and we won't see each other again. I absolutely promise you that we won't see each other again. It was an absurd misjudgement on my part. I realise that, and I'm extremely sorry about it. I know something of why I did it, though that hardly helps. I really am so sorry. Let's put it behind us, Sam.'

She reached across the bed and stretched her hand out to him, but he left it there and turned away. She was immediately frightened. She had threatened her marriage so stupidly. She recognised some of what had happened. It had been a chance for her to close the circle on a part of her life that had been left so painfully unreconciled. The loss of her virginity to Dan in that humiliating episode at university was still such a raw memory for her. That nothingness. That void of response. That complete disinterest. She had been given a second chance to make something of the relationship. It was no longer left as a squalid, trivial, meaningless affair. She had had the opportunity of giving it a significance, and a mutuality, and a conclusion, and she had taken it.

'For Christ's sake, Hilary. We can't just dismiss it as easily as that. We can't just have a nice hug and cry together and pretend nothing has happened.'

And yet the truth was that, although this was exactly what Sam would have liked to do, he had a compulsion to pick away at the bone, to expose as much pain in himself as he could. He needed to hear it all, and as brutally as possible. The more it hurt, the more it needed to hurt. There was a grotesque element of unexpectedness and incongruity in what he was hearing. This was not Hilary. Hilary was the happy, affectionate, laughing girl he was in love with, and had been in love with for all these happy years. The radiant young wife whom he had driven off to St Thomas's at three o'clock in the morning to have her baby; he so excited that he had found it difficult to drive the car with safety. All those Cambridge memories, and the wedding day at Chewton Mendip, all the love-making on the carpet, and on the bed, and on the bathroom floor, the walks to Grantchester, the meals in the little local Italian restaurant, and his arm around her waist, and Annabel lying suckling at her breast that first night home from the hospital.

This was a nightmare. This was not Hilary. This had to be heard out. Every bitter, cold, agonising detail had to be heard out. All the pain had to come. All of it. It wasn't really true. This couldn't have happened. This wasn't his wife. This was some absurd game. But it had to be played. He had to go on.

'I can't understand what you are saying, anyway. What on earth are you saying to me? Just be clear. Was it all simply lovely kisses and cuddles? Or did you go to bed with him? Make love with him? Or, putting it in Galetti language, did he fuck you?'

The use of the word was quite exquisitely painful. The image it conjured up both aroused and sickened him; the white, raw, defined

4

picture of Hilary's body naked, her thighs excitedly raised and open, her pubic hair and vagina revealed to another man, Dan above her and entering her, the crude sounds of sexual coupling.

There was a pause.

'Yes. I told you. Yes. I'm sorry. Yes.'

Sam got to his feet, and went across to look out of the window at the gardens below, and the fields and woods beyond. He turned around and looked at Hilary as she sat on the bed, her expression grim and taut.

'You stupid bloody woman. You stupid bitch. You stupid fucking bloody whore.'

He was puce in the face, and his whole body was shaking. He began to shout, and the voice carried both the rage of the humiliated cuckold and a hysterical sexual tension. Hilary had never seen him like this before. Or anything remotely like this. Her kind, crumpled, lovely Sam. Now shouting and shaking and roaring at her like some sort of crazy, deranged psychotic bully.

'How many times, for Christ's sake? How many times? Tell me, for Christ's sake. How many times? And where? Where did you do it? *Where* did you do it?'

He strode across to the bed, put his hands up her skirt and started to try to wrench her pants down her legs. He was still shouting, his voice cracked and shrill.

'Tell me. How many times did he fuck you? And how did he fuck you? How did he fuck you? Tell me. Tell me.'

He was weeping now, but aggressively and with a terrifying, bull-like hysteria. Hilary kicked and rolled away from him, managing to shake his grip free so that she could escape to the door and out on to the landing. She too was sobbing now, the tears streaming down her face as she ran down the stairs.

He shouted after her. 'Don't bloody run away. You've ruined everything. Everything. You've ruined it all.'

Chapter One

The Lilley & Chase (Publishers) Limited offices were tucked away rather uncomfortably in a cramped and dark mews near Cheyne Row in Chelsea. They were close to the river, and perpetually slightly damp.

The building stood at the head of the mews, occupying a small courtyard fronted by railings, of which some were broken, and all needed painting. Inside the railings there was invariably a heap of plastic bags and bundles of cardboard, the bags overfilled and inadequately tied, the cardboard wet and flaccid.

An elderly rose, mysteriously leafless, climbed a side wall, on it sporadic blooms of faded yellow. Around its base there were clumps of dried dung, placed there the previous year by Sam Lilley. He did this in a sudden round of enthusiasm, fresh from lunch in a particularly lovely Hampstead garden with a late-middle-aged English actress of great fame, whose autobiography was on the Lilley & Chase autumn list.

The little courtyard was greatly in need of sweeping. Albert, the office odd-job man and van driver, was asked at least once every six weeks to do it but rarely did, and Sam would attack it himself in occasional bursts of furious activity.

The yard would be brushed down, and then he'd turn his attention to the offices; his personal secretary's filing cabinets were sorted and largely emptied, and the kitchen swabbed. Bewhiskered coffee mugs discovered behind chairs and boxes were flung into bins, together with the entire contents of the staff noticeboard, plastic shopping bags containing dismembered and unidentified manuscripts, various parched and terminally ill pot-plants, miscellaneous cardboard dump-bins, and old copies of trade journals, all out of sequence, ringed with coffee stains, and sticky and grimy with dust.

Sam's office was at the top of the building. It was a large room, bounded by bookcases whose shelves were jammed full of Lilley & Chase titles published over the twenty-eight years of the firm's life. The floor was covered by a worn and fraying Persian carpet, and there were leather chairs of various sorts bought by Sam in a job lot at the Lots Road auctions some years before. The desk was piled high with manuscripts, box files, letters and envelopes, spreadsheets, book jackets, printers' proofs and newspapers.

The untidiness of the place, and its aura of bustle and engagement and disorder, was, to some eyes, a reflection of the character and presentation of Sam Lilley himself. For Sam was, on occasions, quite spectacularly ill-kempt, with a penchant for baggy trousers, worn with a sports jacket rumoured by the staff to be the same age as the firm, and cotton shirts, always blue, too tight in the neck, frayed at the cuff and curling at the collar. He was well built, if perhaps a little overweight, and had he held himself more erect might have been considered tall. His hair, curly and wiry, the chestnut brown now flecked with grey, was worn short when he could remember to have it cut. And if his pleasant face, habitually smiling, always warm, was not perhaps conventionally handsome, the features were good, and the brown eyes alive. He was, by anybody's count, an agreeable-looking man.

The desk was at one end of the room, and at the other a rectangular mahogany table was pushed back flush against a bookcase. On this table were further heaps of papers and files, together with silver-framed photographs of Sam's most important authors, each with a message of varying warmth scrawled across it.

'Darling Sam', on the photograph of Dame Celia Smith, the Hampstead actress. 'Kind and lovely Sam', wrote Callum Kelly, the late-middle-aged Irish author, ex-civil servant, twice short-listed for the Booker Prize. 'Still waiting for the cheque, darling!' scrawled across the rather full-lipped, louche face of Anthony Ruges, a waspish, wildly prolific novelist, now well past the brilliantly worldly early middle age into which he had privately locked himself in perpetuity. 'Sam Lilley – most sincerely yours', neatly and firmly inscribed by Lord Harper, the Labour Party ex-Home Secretary, whose memoirs, bland, complacent, self-justifying, humourless, Sam had published the previous year. There had been a battery of reviews so scathing and sales so poor that Sam had not as yet dared to reveal them to Lord Harper's agent.

He felt particularly guilty about this book as he had paid far too much for it, and was uncomfortably aware that he had done so in the vague hope of a knighthood. The fact that he had made a point of insulting everybody else's knighthoods all his life served only to increase his discomfort.

The maroon plush curtains were never drawn. The sash-windows, frames painted a dull cream, overlooked the mews and gave glimpses of the river beyond. On the floor were overflow piles of books and loose manuscripts, and two large wicker wastepaper baskets, jammed full with papers and cardboard.

Sharing the top floor with Sam, and beside a tiny lavatory with a wooden seat that had been broken and askew for at least ten years, was the office of Sam's personal secretary, Hazel Walters. Hazel had joined the firm in its opening weeks as a pert, bright-eyed, slight girl of twenty-one, and was now, at forty-nine, still pert and bright-eyed, if not perhaps quite so slight. Her office was tiny, neat, and plastered with 'things to do' lists, which Sam always found an irritant. She had a tendency to hoard papers and letters indiscriminately, but typed with deafening speed, had faultless shorthand, and was treated with God-like respect by the dozen or so office juniors who found it impossible to get to see Sam without her consent. Appointments made with him direct by a member of staff were always cancelled immediately as soon as Hazel spotted them in the office diary.

She was flirtatious with the more libidinous male authors, coldly correct with Lord Harper, and glacial with agents pursuing their authors' royalties. She gave a hint of sexual ambiguity to a lesbian feminist author of international fame. She was witheringly dismissive to unknowns trying to retrieve their unsolicited, unread and mislaid manuscripts. She was a mother confessor and cuddly aunt to all but one of the office staff and sales people, the exception being Birdie Jones, publicity director, a new recruit to the firm from Secker & Warburg, who, Hazel felt, treated her like a junior copy-typist.

Most of the staff knew the form exactly, and approached Hazel with just the right mixture of deference and sauciness that she liked. She knew of every intrigue, and every affair. She was the authority on who was in, who was out, who was drinking too much, who quarrelling with their wives, who leaving their husbands. She had her favourites for whom she would do anything bar allow direct access to Sam's diary. Perhaps the greatest of these was a freelance reader/freelance editor by the name of Aubrey Giles, gay, seedy, and of an elaborately courtly manner, who festooned her desk with immense bouquets of flowers each birthday.

For Richard Chase, Sam's co-founder and chairman of the firm, she had guarded respect. She was frightened of him, and tried to strike a balance between the familiarity of twenty-eight years of working together, and a stilted professional correctness. She had never been able to say a single word to him that did not sound forced and uneasy. Her greatest dread was to find herself beside him at the Christmas party or the summer outing.

Richard Chase's office was on the floor below, directly underneath Sam's. Bookcases lined the walls, and there were manuscripts on a side table, but where Sam's office was a jumble of half-opened correspondence and half-read contracts, Richard's had an order and a tidiness about it that spoke of a different man and a different mind.

Richard had gone up to Cambridge in the same year as Sam, and both had been at Queens', though they had been acquaintances there rather than friends. He was as an undergraduate a celebrated intellectual, extravagantly good-looking, ambiguous sexually, a multi-linguist, a scholar and, in due course, a double first. A tall, dark-haired man, his angular face was dominated by eyes of a startling light blue, which carried a look of apparent pain and melancholy even when he smiled. These eyes were of a transfixing quality and they gave his whole appearance a strange and, to some people, an unnerving sense of remoteness and detachment. A famous English novelist in his seventies, a fellow of King's, fell in love with him. His Hamlet with the Marlowe Society was praised by Harold Hobson in *The Sunday Times*. Faber & Faber had published his first novel when he was nineteen. He was president of the Union, played the cello in his own string quartet, dined with F. R. Leavis in his rooms at Downing, and with C. S. Lewis at Peterhouse. Professor Henn had him to tea, talked Yeats, and tried to recruit him as a spy. The *Economist* nominated him as one of the six most promising Englishmen of his generation. He joined neither the Labour Party nor the Conservatives, but was courted by both, with murmurings of candidacy in winnable seats.

Richard and Sam both read English, but were paired separately for supervisions. Sam was joined in his first year with a small, neat Welshman named Gareth Morgan, who drank quite extraordinary quantities of beer each night, following which he would vomit into his bedroom basin. He was sent down after four terms, became a bank manager, and died ten years later or so in Newport, falling down an open manhole outside a working men's club. Richard was joined with the son of a famous actor-knight, who worked elegantly but selectively, wrote exquisite verse, was editor of the undergraduate newspaper *Varsity*, president of the Cambridge University Dramatic Society, and a leading light of the Cambridge Marxists. They were the two most famous undergraduates of their year. They disliked each other profoundly.

It was in the last two terms or so of their Cambridge years that Richard and Sam became a little better known to each other, largely because they found themselves with rooms on the same staircase, and had dined together one evening with the President, a Natural Historian of uncomfortable social ease and manner. It had been a notably difficult occasion, which Richard, who was a very good mimic, lampooned for Sam as they walked back to their rooms.

Neither of them had quite been able to remember since how Lilley & Chase had first been conceived, though it was certainly the case that Sam's parents had died just before this time, leaving him a house, which he sold for twenty thousand pounds, together with a small amount of cash, and that from this the firm was started, with Richard's mother matching Sam's investment in Richard's name.

Sam was overawed by Richard's reputation from Cambridge,

and embarrassed that his own name had somehow managed to precede Richard's on the letterhead. They took the offices in the Chelsea mews, and Richard's second novel was rescued from Faber & Faber who, in truth, having greatly overprinted his first, were not entirely unhappy to see it go. The book was published in Lilley & Chase's first list, together with four other first novels by various writers they had acquired from an agent in a job lot.

They followed with some reprints of First World War novels and short stories which had fallen out of print, binding and jacketing them as a single series called *Cries for Peace*. This series was a notable success, well suited to the pacifist, flower-power flavour of the times. They bought from an author's widow, for scandalously little, the rights to a series of literary travel books called *Yellow Guides*, which they cannibalised, re-edited and relaunched in elegant cream jackets. They published the memoirs of a homosexual Member of Parliament, salacious for their time and probably libellous. They had a great success with the early novels of Anthony Ruges and Callum Kelly. They cherished and fussed over an unhappy English lady minimalist, who later won the Booker Prize and promptly left them for a larger firm.

There was also a New York Jewish writer, completely indifferent to money, who took a liking to Sam on meeting him at a party at Shakespeare and Co. on the Upper West Side, and subsequently insisted to his agent that he should be published in England by Lilley & Chase. He won the Nobel Prize as he lay on his deathbed, and his name in the catalogue had served to encourage others. Further American authors followed. The beginnings of a strong Jewish literary flavour to the Lilley & Chase list began to emerge.

The company's Christmas lollipops each year were reprints of books and pamphlets from the days of the British Empire. These comprised works such as guides to etiquette, English-Swahili phrasebooks, health handbooks for young Englishwomen in tropical climates, and – their particular triumph – a supposed reprint of a 1910 work entitled *The White Man's Burden – Memoirs of an English Gentleman in Black Africa*. This Sam had spent several happy weekends surreptitiously rewriting; to his delight he found one of his bolder interpolations quoted verbatim by the *Guardian* in an article of shocked liberal sentiment.

Lilley & Chase lived in those early years in a state of permanent financial panic. They paid their printers as late as they dared, staff worked for salaries that were notoriously inadequate, and all were trained by Sam in the technique of ensuring that the other party always paid for lunch. Rather than fly with the rest of the British publishers to the Frankfurt Book Fair each year, they drove: Sam and Richard in the front of the 1960 Volvo estate car, and three editors, five suitcases, sundry manuscripts and boxes of advance bound copies squeezed somehow into the back. Sam and Richard stayed at the Frankfurter Hof for appearances' sake, and the others shared one room in a pension in the red-light district behind the railway station.

Sam charmed bank managers, moved their account at least once every twelve months, and the firm's harassed chief accountant did little else but compile monthly cash-flow projections. These were always over-optimistic, usually substantially so, but, rather like sucking his thumb, gave the poor man sufficient comfort to allow him at least partial rest at night.

The firm's bookseller debtors were pursued with a concentrated and self-righteous fury. Royalty statements were produced as late as possible, and settled even later. Authors were cherished and flattered and hugged and lunched, in the latter case always with their agents, who were expected to pick up the bill. Advances were charmed down to a fraction of their market value. Sam drove the rights department with singular intensity. The firm was particularly good at working on the jealousies of the broadsheet newspapers to extract large sums for serialisation rights – paid in advance – and on the basis of usually absolutely phantom competitive interest.

Lilley & Chase had once been bought out entirely. In 1971 a California conglomerate called MegaMedia Inc. had decided that they needed to have access to English language material direct; they called it 'pan-international sourcing facility'. They had clearly taken only the slightest of glances at the Lilley & Chase list, but long enough at least to recognise the name of the famous New York Jewish writer. They approached Sam, and on his hint that a rival

California multi-media conglomerate, MultiMedia Inc., had almost closed a purchase deal with them, produced an incomprehensibly large sum themselves on the basis that the sale had to be completed within forty-eight hours.

The deadline was met, the money paid over, the overdraft cleared, and Richard's mother repaid. The vast sums borrowed on their houses, on life insurance policies and on a wing and a prayer were discharged, and Sam and Richard contemplated their new world with complete amazement.

Formal board meetings were arranged for each fourth Tuesday, and they were sent a folder, at least four inches thick, entitled 'MegaMedia Inc. Planning Directives'.

With the chief accountant, who had until this point been wreathed in pink, beaming smiles ever since the sale had gone through, the three of them were introduced to a mysterious world of Strategic Plans, Operational Plans, Planning Cycles, Action Plans, Personnel Models, Unique Selling Propositions, Discounted Net Worth Analyses and the Wombat Test, which appeared to have something to do with the productivity of executive directors, expressed as a multiple of the simple average of the work co-efficients of the ten most junior members of staff, seasonally weighted and adjusted for maternity leave.

There were four board meetings under this régime, and these proved to be of agonising embarrassment.

Trying to please, Sam and Richard had put up a list of Lilley & Chase properties eligible for the MegaMedia Inc. pan-international sourcing facility programme. This included Sam's *The White Man's Burden*; the complete works of the unhappy lady minimalist; both Richard's novels (which had sold between them in aggregate rather less than one thousand five hundred copies in hardcover, and had never been published in paperback); some vegetarian cookery books; a handbook on colonic irrigation; the *Yellow Guides*; and a masterly translation of the New Testament by a Hebraic scholar.

Finally, Hermann Diefenbaker, the MegaMedia Inc. vice-president for European Diversification and Development, called Sam and asked if he and Richard might consider it best if Lilley & Chase was resold back to them. A price was agreed, their two houses went back into mortgage, Richard's mother wrote another cheque, a young and rather susceptible bank manager of romantic literary aspirations was discovered by Sam and brought in, mercilessly, for the overdraft, and Lilley & Chase re-emerged once more on the London scene as an independent house.

Nothing much had changed. Albert, the odd-job man and van driver, had still not swept the courtyard and the accountant went back to his cash-flow schedules and his insomnia a happier and wiser man. And so did Sam and Richard, whose lives reverted to exactly the pattern of the pre-MegaMedia Inc. days.

Sam worked endless hours. He worried about everything, and was always trying to do sixteen things simultaneously. He had long conversations on the telephone trying to wheedle books out of agents, he massaged his authors' hurt sensibilities, he persuaded literary editors to put his books in the hands of kindly reviewers. He ran sales conferences, called on the major bookshops, and rushed his authors around the country doing signing tours. There were literary luncheons at Foyle's, and happenings in left-wing booksellers' in Camden Town, and all-night read-ins at Trinity College, Dublin. He harassed printers, approved every jacket design, and sold rights to foreign-language editions. He worried about the annual Frankfurt Book Fair, and he agonised over the firm's selections for Booker Prize submission. All the energy and the drive of the firm came from him. Without him, Lilley & Chase would certainly never have developed in the years following the MegaMedia Inc. affair in the way that it did.

Richard's life was almost the direct antithesis of this. His office – sparse, ordered, contained – was a reflection of a personality that had, in reality, developed and matured only marginally since his Cambridge days, but whose professional success moved seamlessly on.

He was cold, cerebral and extremely private. His own novels were surprisingly weak, but he was an excellent critic. He reviewed regularly for *The Times Literary Supplement* and the *New York Times Review of Books*. He was frequently on radio, and a standard source of instant comment on any literary matters for 'Kaleidoscope' or 'Bookshelf' or the World Service. He became a regular guest on

'Any Questions', and an intimate of Lord Rumbado, the chairman of the Arts Council. He dined now with the Sainsbury family and Lord Goodman. On television his good looks and intense, focused intelligence were bringing him increasing invitations to appear on 'Question Time' and 'The Late Show'. There was talk of him hosting a new Sunday night arts programme in direct competition with Melvyn Bragg.

Jeremy Paxman treated Richard with caution and deference when he appeared on 'Newsnight' to discuss arts funding. Lord Rees-Mogg nodded to him at the Garrick Club. He had been seen at the Ivy with Steven Berkoff, and at the Wigmore Hall with Alfred Brendel. David Frost embraced him at the Savoy Grill. Jeffrey Archer tried to sell him the Playhouse Theatre. He had become over the course of the nineteen-seventies and -eighties a man of status, influence and position, and London – or, more precisely, media-London – was at his feet.

But as Richard's fame grew, at Lilley & Chase he became more and more withdrawn and remote. He had his own stable of authors, many of them people who were on the television and radio circuit with him. He tended now to work from his home in Onslow Square, coming to the office for half days in the middle of the week, his correspondence and messages guarded by his assistant. He corralled his own authors around him in a private world, quite unlinked with the affectionate, noisy eclecticism that surrounded Sam.

Richard's contacts were immaculate, his sources of information impeccable, his tastes unchallenged. He read Spanish, Portuguese, Italian, French and German. He found untranslated jewels before any publisher in London or New York had so much as heard of the author. His elegant, softcover *Living Fiction of the Twentieth Century* series, mostly of translated work, but including some previously unconsidered English writers whom Richard rescued from oblivion, was amongst the most prestigious publishing anywhere. His love affairs were discreet, the women intellectuals, and always married. The closing of the affairs was gentle, sophisticated and calm. His dinner parties, cooked exquisitely by him, were famously exclusive. He was on the Board of the Royal Ballet, and a Trustee of the National Gallery.

His relationship with Sam was always cordial, but even after more than a quarter of a century together as colleagues, and colleagues who had together been through so many financial crises and disasters, they had never become intimates. They never quarrelled, they communicated courteously and well with each other; there were no secrets, no intrigues, no jealousies. They never went to each other's houses or exchanged any personal confidences, but when required to host a Lilley & Chase function, or attend together a Foyle's luncheon or a Booker dinner, they did so easily and charmingly.

Richard had never married, and Sam had been divorced from Hilary for twenty-three years, so neither had a spouse who might have encouraged and fostered more social contact and warmth between them. But the world understood perfectly clearly their respective roles and acted accordingly. And as partnerships go, it went as well as most, and the lack of any hint of overt tension between the two founders was a major component in the reputation Lilley & Chase held as a nice firm – perhaps the nicest firm – to be published by. You would certainly wait for your money, but your telephone calls would be returned, your views would be respected, and your friendship would be genuinely and warmly sought.

Lilley & Chase was really a very congenial publishing house indeed.

Chapter Two

Camellia Mansions is one of the better kept of the long line of mansion blocks that runs the length of Prince of Wales Drive, which acts as the entire southern perimeter of Battersea Park. On the north side the park is bounded by the River Thames, across which stands the handsome presence of Chelsea Hospital at the head of its grounds.

The mansion blocks rise four or five storeys high, and are faced in pleasant pink brick. They have good late-Victorian sash-windows, wide stone entrance halls, and mature and reasonably tidy privet hedges curve round the front of each individual building.

These mansions were built around the turn of the century for the lower-middle classes, and have perhaps marginally improved their status as the decades have rolled on, Battersea itself becoming more fashionable as property in Chelsea across the river became prohibitively expensive. Noël Coward lived in one of the blocks for some of his early childhood, and hated the memory of it.

Some of the mansion buildings are better than others. The most scruffy are at the lower end of London private housing: the staircases unswept, the rooms dank and dark, cooking smells everywhere, and half-washed empty milk bottles – waiting in vain for collection – standing outside the two front doors that abut on to each staircase landing.

Camellia Mansions was pleasantly clean and cared for, however. There was bright and cheerful carpet on the stairs, fresh paint on the walls and front doors, flowers on the windowsills of each landing and an embargo on empty milk bottles. The hallway was swept, the glass in the front doors shone, the privet hedge at the front was clipped and neat, and tubs of wallflowers – gold, deep red, copper, bright yellow – stood by the door. Everyone living in the block knew each other, and made a point of doing so.

There were a couple of young families with babies, but very few young children. There was an actor or two, a history teacher at the Francis Holland School in Graham Terrace near Sloane Square, a young bassoon player in The London Philharmonic with his flautist wife, a diplomat's widow, an unsuccessful merchant banker, a South African journalist and, on the top floor right, overlooking the park, the Reverend Christopher Howard.

His flat was full of books, and overcluttered with heavy Victorian furniture. The sofas and armchairs in the sitting room were deep and comfortable, and the quite generous-sized rooms were informal and untidy without being dusty or unkempt. Some happy-looking family photographs stood around on tables and perched on the bookshelves; from the evidence of the dress, most had been taken some decades before.

Christopher's bedroom was dominated by a large bed with good comfortable blankets and coverings, an armchair, a small reading table and a grand piano, on the lid of which lay piles of music. These included several sheets of Victorian music-hall songs, Duke Ellington's 'Mood Indigo', some Elgar salon pieces, an omnibus collection of Jerome Kern, and another of Vivian Ellis. There were letters, several copies of *The Times*, and some curling editions of the *Spectator*, the *Tablet* and the *New Statesman*.

There were two further bedrooms at the back, much smaller and darker, though both most attractively wallpapered and decorated, their aspect over the gloomy yard that separated the mansion building from a matching block that faced away to the south.

The kitchen was modern, neat and bright, copper pans hanging from hooks, sharp butchers' knives standing in a jar, a cheerful Matisse print hanging on the pristine white walls.

There was a single bathroom, freshly hung with creamy-yellow-striped wallpaper, the room dominated by a colossal Victorian bath with great thick taps and curved cabriole legs, installed no doubt at the time the mansion blocks were built. A comfortable blue carpet covered the floor, and a large hot-towel stand, with huge, rather threadbare towels hanging across it, stood against the wall. The room carried a pervading smell of Imperial Leather soap and sandalwood shaving cream.

It had been a soft and lovely early summer that year, and Christopher was sitting as he did most evenings at the French windows leading on to the narrow verandah. A slim, ascetic-looking, white-haired man in his eightieth year, he had a countryman's dislike of city airlessness and stuffiness, and whenever it was warm enough the windows were thrown open so that he could catch the coolness of the breeze, and hear the rustling of the huge old London plane trees in the park across the road, as tall as the mansion blocks themselves. Their leaves had only just come out, a fresh, lovely lucent green which would soon be lost as the summer coarsened and muted their colour.

Christopher could hear Mark in the kitchen. Curly-haired, small, slender, angel-faced, a man who looked considerably younger than his age of thirty-five, Mark Ryder lived with Christopher as his lover. Although both an author and a notably successful BBC radio producer, he made time to organise and run all Christopher's domestic life, and he particularly enjoyed cooking, which he had taken up when he and Christopher had come to London ten years before. He had taught himself entirely from newspaper cookery columns and books, and was joyfully enthusiastic and experimental. Meals were prepared at furious speed, with much banging of saucepan lids and cupboard doors, obscene curses when ingredients were found to be missing or eggs dropped, and shouts of triumph at the tasting of a sauce or the rising of a soufflé.

'What time are they coming, Chris?' Mark shouted out. 'Please God not before eight-fifteen. I'd completely forgotten how long these things take to cook. And, you forgot to get the chives, so the vichyssoise is going to be totally repellent.'

Christopher reflected that part of the pleasure of living with Mark was being exposed to his vocabulary. His descriptive structures dealt only at the extremes. Food was 'quite wonderful' or it was 'totally repellent'. People were 'absolute heaven' or they were 'hell on wheels'. Mark's moods were 'terminal' or they were 'ecstatic', his day's work at Bush House either 'blissful' or 'raw purgatory'. Mark had the conversational style of the clever metropolitan

21

homosexual world. His conversation flowed in a constant charming stream, rich with anecdote, fluent in description, and with a humour based largely on self-mockery. There was a campness certainly, but above all there was an exuberance and good nature in Mark that defied dislike. He would criticise himself, but seldom others, and certainly never those whom he did not consider strong enough or egotistical enough to be fair game.

By this logic, of those whom Christopher and Mark both knew, the Bishop of London was absolutely fair game, as to a lesser extent was the Dean of St Paul's, but the Archbishop of York was not. The vicar of St Barnabas's, King's Road, where Christopher gave some occasional help, was absolutely not, though there were some members of his congregation who very definitely were. It depended on ego rather than rank. Mark's immediate boss at the BBC World Service – an ex-deputy editor of the *Economist*, who had had at least two major nervous breakdowns in the seven years that Mark had known him – was not within the rules. The head of his department very certainly was, however, and Mark's assistant, a raw lad from Manchester, greatly intelligent, but given to bouts of extreme intellectual arrogance, probably was. Mark never lampooned him with much enthusiasm, however, as he felt uncomfortable as a Southerner at any suggestion of assuming superiority over a Northern boy.

'And, Chris – talk tonight, old love, for heaven's sake, talk. If you can't hear, then say so. I absolutely can't go through another evening like last Tuesday.'

Mark resumed singing – the Victorian music-hall songs on the piano were his, and he was fond at the moment of 'Don't Go Down The Mine, Daddy', of which he had made Christopher sing the chorus the previous night so many times and so loudly that The London Philharmonic bassoonist had telephoned through and asked if he could move them on to another song, and did they know one called 'The Eve Is Here, The Long Night's Falling, For Christian People Now It's Sleep'?

Mark and Christopher had started on a series of post-Easter small dinner parties for members of the St Barnabas's congregation. Christopher was at an age when his clearly declining vitality gave him the option to do as little or as much as he wanted. Partly through habitual reticence, and partly through his personal circumstances, he tended to use his age as an excuse to lead as reclusive a social life as possible. He did feel remorse, however, about Andrew Boot at St Barnabas's. Andrew had been the only person in the church community to put out an immediate and unwavering hand of friendship to Christopher when he came to London to live, after The Fall, as he and Mark put it, some ten years before. Christopher helped him at the church, but knew perfectly well that he could do more. The dinner parties were his latest attempt to ease his guilt.

The previous Tuesday had been the first of these evenings. Christopher had asked a widow, Mrs Hinds, who lived in Lowndes Square, and attended High Mass at St Barnabas's regularly and with a certain theatrical piety. With Mrs Hinds had been invited a Major Johnston, also now part of the congregation, who lived near her in Marsham Street, and whom the verger had claimed to have found in her embrace one summer evening in the vestry.

The evening had not gone well. Christopher had been struck by hopeless shyness from the moment that they had arrived, and – Mark was quite right – as his unease increased, so did his deafness, or his fear of deafness, with the result that he said practically nothing at all.

Halfway through dinner he had tried in desperation to follow what he had thought was a comment from Major Johnston about Eton, with a reminiscence of preaching in the chapel there some years before. The story he told was that he had suddenly developed a sensation halfway through the sermon that almost every word he employed carried for the boys the sniggering delight of hidden sexual innuendo. He found to his embarrassment, however, that the major had actually talked momentarily of Eastbourne, the extremely minor public school he had gone to, and of which he was deeply ashamed.

The gaffe so humiliated Christopher, who hated above all things to appear a snob, that he retired into a shell of miserable reticence until the end of the evening, made the more acute by Mrs Hinds's arch little attempts to charm him out of it.

Tonight they had a married couple coming, Mr and Mrs Rankin, who between them ran everything at the church, from the annual Flower and Music Festival to the parish pilgrimage to Walsingham. He was church warden, she was treasurer of the PCC. They led the prayer groups, the Mission to the Poor League, the Wednesday Quiet Evenings, the St Barnabas's Music Society, and the St Barnabas's For Peace Committee. The vicar was frightened of them both, particularly as they were intimates of the verger, who had been at St Barnabas's for almost forty years. The verger's scorn if any one thing went wrong, were it the calling of banns, the loss of the Poor-Box key, or the underprovision of service sheets, frightened Andrew Boot very much indeed.

Mark knew no one at St Barnabas's very well, but the Rankins a little better than most, and what he did know of them did not encourage him to believe that a comfortable evening lay ahead. He reflected that Chris was so delightful when he was in familiar company and amongst friends; funny, self-deprecating, gentle in his judgements, and yet perfectly capable of sudden little bouts of waspishness, always delivered blushingly and with a habit of biting down on his lower lip at the end of the comment. Delightful also, of course, when paralysed by shyness, but – goodness – how hard Mark had to work to make up for it.

He suddenly remembered that Christopher had been to see his Harley Street doctor that day, and cursed himself for not asking him about it earlier. He shouted from the kitchen, 'Chris – I'm sorry I forgot to ask. What did Morgan have to say?'

Christopher got up from his chair and went into the kitchen. 'Oh, not much. The heart's not too strong, as we all know. The blood pressure's not that good either. Kidneys pretty moderate. What does it all matter? I'm very fortunate to be as fit as I am.'

Mark was wrapped in a large blue apron, his sleeves rolled up, and was stirring away at some chicken and some rough-cut vegetables. He smiled at him and put his arms for a moment around Christopher's back.

'Stay with me, Chris,' he said.

Before The Fall and After The Fall.

Mark and Christopher had met ten years before. Christopher at that time was principal of a religious community at Hunstanton in

Norfolk, and Mark was a graduate student reading philosophy at the University of East Anglia. Christopher was sixty-nine, Mark twenty-five.

Christopher, who was unsanctimonious, clever, unambitious, and totally uninterested in Church politics, had been a popular figure to the young men passing through the community for the twenty-three years that he had been at its head. He considered himself a happy man on the few occasions he thought about it. He had spent his life untroubled by any great strains of temptation. He had no particular sense of pride, nor any great pride in its absence. He was a good raconteur, but he was perhaps rather pedantically precise with the literal truth, which took from his stories that spice of hyperbole which gave Mark's conversation so much of its charm. He was seldom angry, and invariably courteous, if somewhat vague. His appetite was cheerful but moderate, and he had a notably plain taste. He drank very little. He displayed no extravagances of any kind, envied nobody, and was content with his position and his achievements. He was fond of his friends. He had been an affectionate and dutiful son to his parents, both now long dead, and was devoted to his twin sister Norah, who had lived for years an eccentric life buried in the Yorkshire countryside. In all, his life was that of a generous, simple, good man, blessedly free from the excesses of human temperament.

He was aware that there were Churchmen of his generation who disliked him, resenting the pleasant ease and security that his long career tucked away at Hunstanton had given him. But he bore them no malice for it, and indeed seldom thought about it or them.

His sex drive as a young man had been mild. By the age of forty he had had only the occasional heterosexual experiences, and these mostly in his early to mid-twenties when he was a research student at Oxford. He had had no physical homosexual experiences since he had been a schoolboy, nor had he ever been tempted to do so.

He knew that some of his colleagues in the community where he had spent his whole career were tortured by physical desire. He was not. He thought of himself as vaguely bisexual, had enjoyed the few sexual encounters he had experienced, and was grateful that he was as he was. He sometimes had dreams of an overt nature, but their absurdity amused him rather than aroused him, and after the age of forty-five or so these became less and less frequent, and eventually faded away altogether.

And then, nearing seventy years of age, he met Mark Ryder, who was at Hunstanton on a summer course in Contemporary Metaphysics in pursuit of his doctorate. In the way these things happen, Christopher fell in love immediately and overwhelmingly, and knew that he was about to embark on a journey that was perilous and undefined.

There was no great struggle of conscience, and no wrestling with temptation. He had fallen in love for the only time in his life, and now that he had done so he had no intention of letting love, or Mark, go. The concept of sacrifice never entered his head. Meeting Mark had closed the circle of his life, and to deprive himself of him now would be an insanity.

He was, however, painfully indecisive as to how to tell Mark what had happened. He was a fastidious man, and accustomed to hiding any emotional exposure behind an instinctive wall of shyness. There were several occasions when he could have spoken to him of it, but did not do so. And then suddenly he did. He had found Mark reading on a bench under the great sycamore tree that stood beside the long lawn stretching in front of the main buildings. Christopher went up to him, his heart pounding, stood in front of the bench, looking absurdly awkward, and in a strangled voice asked him to go for a walk.

They followed a path that ran down to the river, and then along to the dairy farm that the community ran for its kitchens. To his astonishment, Christopher found himself directly, and without qualification, shyness or reserve, telling Mark that he was in love with him. He told him that it had never happened before, that he had no idea where it was going to lead, and that wherever it led he had no fear and no regret. Sentence tumbled after sentence, as he tried to avoid the possibility of Mark interrupting him. He was deeply frightened of rejection, and he was rational enough to know the absurdity of what he was saying. The flow only stopped when Mark eventually held up both his hands, as if in surrender, moved in front of him, and put his arms around him.

They became lovers. They were too obviously and frequently seen in each other's company, and their indiscretions became open and careless. Within two weeks, Christopher received a letter from the Archbishop of Canterbury, an old friend from the days when he had been taught by Christopher at Hunstanton, ordering an immediate meeting. A week after that, Christopher resigned.

The Fall. He left the community immediately, within a matter of hours making the steps that closed a lifetime. He packed his books, threw his few clothes together, and left little handwritten messages of farewell to the community's servants.

He went first to Norah in Yorkshire, and then the following day to the Prince of Wales Drive flat, which Norah had owned since her twenties. He was shown that evening on national television, foolishly allowing himself to be quoted as saying that he had been treated ungenerously by the Church. This led to a volley of letters to *The Times*, the *Daily Telegraph* and the *Guardian*, of which the great majority were sharply critical of Christopher's behaviour and judgement.

The *Guardian* carried an article on homosexual repression in closed male communities, and the consequent manifestations of this. The *Spectator* regarded the whole affair as the final nail in the coffin of the Church of England. The *Daily Telegraph* thundered disagreement. *The Times* placed the incident in the context of the discreet contribution of Anglicanism to Christendom, with emphasis on the Church of England's particular grace of serenity, tolerance and absence of judgementalism.

Fellow members of the Hunstanton community appeared on television in a special programme two or three days later. Every one of them was angry with Christopher, and all condemned with a brutal candour every aspect of his behaviour. The Archbishop of Canterbury made a cold, formal statement of censure and regret. Within two weeks or so the story and the correspondence in the press had died.

Mark had terminated his summer course at Hunstanton, and, after spending a month hitch-hiking and backpacking alone in Europe, joined Christopher at Camellia Mansions. He abandoned his prospective last year as a graduate student at the University of

East Anglia, and almost immediately joined the BBC as a management trainee.

They had lived together ever since, at first in some financial strain, but as the years passed they found they had sufficient for the sort of lives they led. Christopher had a small annuity from his family trust, Norah would take no payment of any kind for the use of the flat, Mark's career at the BBC moved ahead very well, and the three novels he had written for Lilley & Chase over that time – dark, intense, elliptical novels of love and urban loneliness – had sold increasingly well, if still modestly. Reviewers had become more respectful of his work, however, and Mark nursed private hopes that his new novel, now nearing the completion of its agonisingly painful first draft, would break through with wider recognition than he had as yet achieved.

They holidayed in Italy each summer in Mark's little car. There were some acquaintances to visit and trips to be made, but The Fall had taken Christopher away from his friends, and he was reluctant to contact anyone for fear of rejection.

After an interval of two or three years, the Archbishop of Canterbury began to send Christmas cards, but they were formally worded and made clear by their tone the depth of the breach between them. There was no contact of any sort with his former colleagues at Hunstanton, some of them of forty years' standing. Some kindly little approaches were made by people Christopher hardly knew, to which he responded courteously but always dismissively. Only Andrew Boot at St Barnabas's, whom Christopher knew not at all well but remembered with mild affection as a pleasant but unremarkable pupil of his some thirty years before, was so persistent, and clearly generous and open in his approaches, that Christopher was in time responsive to them.

He and Mark dined with the Boots in their quite unnecessarily sparse and uncomfortable Victorian vicarage adjoining the church. (Mrs Boot was a physiotherapist at the Royal Free Hospital, and there was perfectly adequate income in the family for them to live less spartanly than they did.) Christopher promised to preach, cancelled twice but, in the face of Andrew's perseverance, did so in the end. And, as he always had, he gave his congregation – and at

St Barnabas's the ninety or so that Christopher attracted was considered to be a very satisfactory congregation indeed – ten minutes of simple, direct spiritual vision. He spoke informally from jotted handwritten notes. His clarity and anecdotal, narrative style brought rapt attention.

Andrew then secured a promise that he would preach not less than four times a year, and Christopher had honoured the agreement ever since. In time he agreed to help with some confirmation classes, and also to take Mass once a month at the early eight o'clock Sunday service. Andrew rested at that, and Christopher recognised his kindness; he knew that, without the little disciplines of organisation that his activities at St Barnabas's brought him, limited as the work was, there was a real danger of his physical solitude at Camellia Mansions bringing him a final few years of acute loneliness.

There was always Norah to telephone, of course, but Mark spent long days at the BBC, building a career that was showing promise of being very successful indeed, and Christopher was beginning to accept a life for himself with too little human contact in it. It was sometimes difficult for Mark when he was at home, for he was deeply aware of Christopher's need for his company, but he was the most studied and conscientious of writers, and he took such elaborate care over his books that he did need long periods on his own at his desk in his bedroom, without which he grew very fretful. Christopher, knowing full well that he was being irritating, but quite unable to stop himself, would repeatedly come into the room to talk to him, as a child would, until Mark would bustle him out, shut the door and tell him not to reappear until tea-time.

Mark's religious faith had always been erratic, and since The Fall he had found it accelerating away in rather sharp reverse. He would describe himself as an agnostic to Christopher, but privately wondered if he was even that. Whilst personally increasingly uninterested in any church matters, he recognised in Andrew and Lizzie Boot real goodness, and was fond of them both, particularly Lizzie, an awkward woman whom Mark charmed by teasing. He understood what they had done for Christopher, and acknowledged it to them at every opportunity he had.

The dinner parties had been Christopher's idea, and Mark enthusiastically responded. Mark saw them as an unspoken gift to the Boots, and enjoyed the prospect of one or two bizarre little matchings of St Barnabas's couples that sprang to his mind. Apart from anything else, he so loved cooking that he saw the Tuesday evenings as an opportunity for some amusing little experiments from the *Italian Provincial Cookery* book that Norah had given him for Christmas, with the firm proviso that he never attempted any of it on her.

'Tell me about your day, Mark. Forces of Darkness?'

'Forces of Darkness' was the Mark and Christopher shorthand for the head of Mark's department at Bush House, a homophobic red-haired Scotsman nearing retirement who greatly disliked Mark and had done whatever he could to dampen the growing reputation that he was developing. Claiming problems of budget, he tried at the last minute to cancel Mark's recent series of four programmes on China – 'China, the World, and the Twenty-First Century' – but Mark had corralled support, including, fatally for his relationship with his head, that of the controller of the BBC World Service, the programmes were made, and the reviews excellent.

On the other side were the Angels of Light; pretty well everybody else in Mark's department except for the Glaswegian, but primarily Mark himself and his co-producer Angie Morris.

'Oh, such a jerk. We had one of those simply agonising conversations you're trapped into as you stand side by side in the pissoir. He tried a sort of mumbled compliment on "China", which I pretended to mishear. Otherwise OK. Angie and I are quite a long way forward on developing a shape for the Africa idea. Actually, she's got a much better feel for it than I have, but there we are. I do find it difficult to see any very identifiable linkages in their culture that we can make much of. If we get it wrong, and make the wrong emphases, we run the danger of sounding patronising in a sort of inverted colonialistic way, and I'm so anxious to avoid that. We'll see.'

The doorbell interrupted them. The Rankins were indeed very punctual, and there was a certain amount of awkwardness over the fact that drinks were not laid out ready for their arrival. And, despite Mark's instructions before he left that morning, Christopher had forgotten to buy any whisky, which was all Mr Rankin ever wanted to drink. He had also forgotten to buy a new corkscrew, Mark having broken theirs the previous evening. There was a trip to the flat below to borrow one, and then five minutes later another one for some Perrier, also on Christopher's list, before they could settle down.

Amanda Rankin, tall and conventionally pretty, was a slightly uneasy woman but, although awkward, was distinctly warmer than her husband Edward. He had a temperament that could swing from noisy good humour and affability towards those to whom he felt superior and dominant, to suspicion and a sense of brooding menace towards those by whom he felt disadvantaged. He had thick grey hair, and glasses perched permanently and theatrically on the end of his nose, and was a lawyer in a small firm in Bloomsbury, having previously been a senior partner in a large firm in Leeds. He had been prominent there in local affairs, until his first marriage broke up in circumstances which Leeds society found inappropriate, and he had left for London.

He had come across St Barnabas's soon after he and Amanda arrived. He found Andrew to be an accommodating man, and used the church as a main focal point for his energies and ambitions. But it was a poor substitute for the life he had led before his own Fall, and he missed Leeds very much indeed.

It proved to be a taut party that evening, and the Rankins' conversation had strayed too easily towards the malevolent for Mark's taste, as he watched and listened to Christopher trying to cope with it all. He was making such great attempts to be talkative, after the disasters of the previous week, that Mark largely, and thankfully, left him to it. And as he did so, he thought to himself what little interest he had in these people, and their tittle-tattle about their draughty, under-attended church and its dreary, commonplace congregation. But at that he made himself pause; clearly, were he not with Christopher, he would never have gone near the place, but that was not the point. He was involved in it because of Christopher, and in those circumstances it was not a high price to pay.

'Life's not just a bed of roses, young man.' How often, he thought, had he heard that ridiculous statement from his mother when he was small. 'When you make your bed, you have to lie on it.' She had only seemed capable of addressing him in these volleys of aphoristic clichés, made the more absurd by her own tendency to complain about every aspect of her personal circumstances.

And, anyway, she was lecturing the wrong person. I've never had the remotest difficulty, Mark thought as he speared a piece of chicken, in accepting the consequence of my actions. It's a smug piece of self-analysis, but it's true. I knew when I went with Chris it was not going to be a bed of roses, as my mother would have put it. I knew he would be lonely and oppressively dependent on me as he grew older, and that's exactly what's happened, of course. It was bound to turn out to be repressive and irritating at times. And it certainly has. I thought also that in taking on Christopher I would be casting myself off from my own age-group. In some ways I have, I suppose. But not from anybody I really cared about, for I simply haven't wanted to be emotionally involved with someone of my own age. Sexually, possibly, but not emotionally. And I underestimated the fun I would get from being at the BBC. And the friendships made there. Not all of which have I shared with Chris. Very far from all of which have I shared with Chris. It's not really a very desirable thing to parcel up one's friends into separate groups like that. And I suppose there are too many areas of my life in which he has no part to play. But all that was inevitable. And I do depend on him, too. There's no doubt about that. The dependence has become unexpectedly mutual. Thank God. It needed to be to make things hang together. Heaven knows what would have happened otherwise.

Mark looked up at Christopher across the table and listened as he was paying an agonisingly laboured compliment to Amanda Rankin about her Flower and Music Festival at St Barnabas's the previous summer.

'It was quite the best festival of its sort I can remember going to,' he said. 'Quite wonderful. You couldn't have done it better. Mark and I were overwhelmed by it.'

Amanda Rankin turned her head and smiled in mock self-deprecation at Mark, who nodded at her and smiled too.

The old humbug, Mark thought. He never went near it. Actually, I tried to get him to go to it one afternoon, as I was so desperate to finish my rewrite of the last chapter, and he absolutely wouldn't leave me alone. Even when I was on the bog he insisted on continuing the conversation through the door.

He could hear that the Rankins were talking now to Christopher about Rupert Henley, a member of the St Barnabas's congregation, but, rather more interestingly in Mark's eyes, a notably good journalist, who had died a month or so previously after a sudden heart attack. Christopher had very much enjoyed his company, and Rupert had been around to Camellia Mansions on one or two occasions for dinner. He had been gay, but his circle of friends was very wide, and he was one of those men whose sexual orientation was never obviously expressed.

'He was a very discreet man, of course. Most discreet and private.'

As Edward Rankin said this he smiled encouragingly at Christopher, then continued: 'I respect that, I'm sure we all do. It's so absurd, this convention nowadays that one has to make a public display of one's entire private life. There's a great indignity in it. I'm sure you would agree, Father.'

I've got to rescue him, Mark thought. This bloody man's having the time of his life with him. He is playing with Christopher's loathing of the very suggestion of 'coming out', or making a heroic statement of it all. How exposed poor Chris found himself in The Fall.

'When is your next book out, Mark?'

Mark turned hastily to Edward Rankin beside him, guilty that he had made such little attempt to talk to him during the meal.

'I'm still trying to complete the first draft, I'm afraid. I work so painfully slowly. But I would hope April or May next year, if all goes well.'

Despite everything, Mark thought, I must make an effort to be as pleasant and forthcoming as I can to him over the rest of the evening. And get him away from the life and times of St Barnabas's to something else. Anything else.

He turned on Edward his most winning smile, and soon they

were on the comparatively more promising grounds of books Edward had recently read, and plays he had seen, and at eleven o'clock Mark was able to spirit them away and sit with Christopher for a few minutes before getting him off to bed.

He soaked in the bath before going to bed himself. I love Chris, he thought, and that is why it's worked. I didn't know that I was going to love him. I thought I was going to be making great sacrifices for him, but I haven't. I'm not an idealist. I'm pragmatic and I'm rootless, and I made the decision to go with him when he wanted me to because I wanted to belong to somebody, and I wanted somebody to belong to me. And it worked. I needed that, too. Not just Christopher. I couldn't have borne for myself to be a failure in this. Once we did it, it really had to work.

Chapter Three

Annabel Lilley, now twenty-eight – though Sam always said she was twenty-six – worked at the advertising agency Monk Grolsch Parsons as an account supervisor, though Sam told everyone she was an account director.

She had arrived at the agency shortly after coming down from Oxford at twenty-two. She was an attractive, exuberant, vivacious girl. Her honey-coloured hair was swept off her face and held behind her ears, and her smile, so open and warm and beaming, very reminiscent of her father's, gave her slightly irregular features the appearance and illusion of a greater beauty than was really there. Her teeth were almost absurdly perfect, however, and there was about her a physical self-confidence that gave her a considerable sexuality.

In joining the agency she felt a little guilty at the time, as Sam had been a friend of all three of the founders since their Cambridge days together, and Matthew Monk, Peter Grolsch and Julian Parsons were recurrent figures at Sam's dinner parties throughout her childhood.

But the truth was that she had at the time no particular leaning to any profession, and advertising seemed to be an amusing choice of occupation for a year or so until something else came along.

She thought about going into the City, but had no very clear picture about what the City actually did. She went for an interview with the civil service graduate recruitment body, but they thought her immature and she thought them dull. She had worked at Lilley & Chase for one long vacation as a secretarial assistant in the editorial department, as much as anything to decide whether publishing should be her career, and she had made some good friendships there with both staff and authors, particularly with Mark Ryder. It was at the time when Mark's first novel had recently been published, and he was sent off on a forlorn signing session at a bookshop in Camden Town. Sales since publication date had been modest, but the signing had been arranged some weeks before by the publicity department, perhaps unwisely, as some sort of attempt to show Mark how enthusiastic everyone was about his book.

Annabel had been assigned to him as a minder. Mark was extremely nervous, and he sat there at the signing table for thirty minutes, fiddling miserably with his pen, and gazing at a bookshop devoid of any customers whatsoever, save for two elderly men in old mackintoshes browsing in the Sexual Hygiene section.

She and Mark abandoned the whole exercise as soon as the half hour struck, went straight around to the pub nearby, where Annabel bought Mark several drinks on what she hoped would prove afterwards to be her Lilley & Chase expense account, and the two of them had been friends from that day. And not simply friends, but confidants too, and the relationship had grown into one of real intimacy over the years that followed.

In every way Annabel had enjoyed an amusing summer at the firm, but she decided not to return there for her career, feeling that she was leaning too heavily on her father's patronage. Some of her friends were going to barristers' chambers, and she quite nearly decided to change direction and take a law degree in order to follow them, but at the last moment decided not to. She felt uncomfortable at the thought of personally judging anybody for anything, having far too many memories of her own transgressions. These included shoplifting a packet of condoms for a bet at the age of eight, altering her Post Office book by adding the suffix '3' on the deposit entry of a Christmas cheque for six pounds when she was eleven, and stealing eggs from her headmistress's chickens and selling them to the village shop at thirteen.

She might have been a schoolteacher – and nearly was – and, after being in advertising for almost seven years, now felt she very much meant to be. She could have been a journalist, and had in fact sold several rather racy articles under *noms de plume* when impecunious at Oxford. But advertising had sounded fun, and from a child she had loved the triumvirate of Monk, Grolsch and Parsons, particularly Peter Grolsch, whom she found delightfully louche. They in turn were attracted to her – she was exuberant and amusing, wrote well, thought well and articulated well, and so in she went.

Monk Grolsch Parsons was not a large agency, but was ensconced in pretty offices off Berkeley Square, and carried the self-confidence of a firm very much bigger than it actually was. They were profitable, actually extremely profitable given the generous nature of the three founders' 'compensation'; they had a small number of immovably devoted clients, and the work atmosphere was collegiate, happy and eccentric.

The grand advertising agencies despised them for their informality and their apparent lack of gravitas and respectable professionalism, and resented their client list. There had been attempts to buy the agency out, all rejected; and there were frequent predatory approaches to the MGP clients, invariably in vain.

The MGP staff were famously bright. Inter-office memos tended to be written in any one of the major European languages, which were treated in the agency as broadly interchangeable. A 'ladder' on the staff notice board – which everyone on the staff had compulsorily to join – had a role of extreme importance in the life of the agency; its purpose was to set a riddle for the name immediately above to solve. If that person was unable to solve the riddle within ten working days, then the places on the table were reversed. The rules of the game were set and policed by Julian Parsons, who had invented it and who umpired it. The top six names on the Feast of the Immaculate Conception were presented with red lapel ribbons, resembling those of the *Légion d'Honneur*, which they then wore for the full year. The bottom six names on St Mewan's Day – who was much Julian's favourite saint, having been an asthmatic and eczema-plagued child – were subjected to traditional and painful humiliations at the staff summer party, which lasted for at least a long weekend.

Matthew Monk, Peter Grolsch and Julian Parsons had spent almost all their lives together. They first met at the Dragon School in Oxford, as little boys of seven. From there all three made their way to Eton, then Trinity College, Cambridge, and then the agency, which they started immediately after they came down.

They had opened with a single client, Mackintosh's Butter Biscuits, Oliver Mackintosh having been up at Trinity with them, inheriting his family business at the age of nineteen. The TV commercials which appeared that first Christmas were a direct lampoon of the market leader, who was furious and complained to the Advertising Standards Board, but too late to stop a marked rise in the Max Butter Bix market share.

For their second client, a manufacturer of bubble-gum, they ran a campaign featuring a bishop with a wooden leg and an eye patch, which became a cult hit. Milton Garden Sheds followed, and the pet food Kittikake next, for whom the son of the actor-knight, Richard Chase's rival at Cambridge, did the voice-over in the TV commercial.

Slowly the client list built: an insurance company, a health food, a toothpaste, a Japanese car, a brand of London gin, a clearing bank, the prestigious magazine the *Financier*, and the Rothley grocery chain.

Matthew supervised almost all the client presentations, took them extremely seriously, and presented research findings and advertising recommendations with a cerebral simplicity and clarity. Peter did most of the running around, lunched furiously, was used by the agency in the role of the corporate charmer, and was known in the office as 'The Teeth', in deference to his startling smile and dissolute good looks. Julian ran the Ladder, was chairman of the agency, wrote much of the copy, and was remarkably astute with their finances. He also did most of the recruitment interviews, and made a point of rejecting any candidate who was impertinently familiar with him about the agency's style of working life, which was famous by reputation in the universities, scorned publicly by all MGP's rivals, and envied by all.

Sam Lilley had met Matthew first of the three. They had come across each other at the Cambridge University Film Society, of which they had both been members from their first term up. In time he got to know Peter and Julian also, and they all became friends in a casual, undergraduate way, but he remained closest to Matthew. As an outsider, Sam was initially surprised by the affinity between the three of them, as they appeared to him to be of radically different dispositions.

Matthew was a serious, quietly academic boy, and a busy member of various clubs and societies, all of them totally unfashionable. His clothes, rather like Sam's, were the corduroys and duffel coats of the time; quite unlike Peter's, which were Pitt Club and flamboyant, and reflected the womanising, party-giving, sports-car life he led. Julian lay somewhere between the two; self-confident, socially prominent and an active undergraduate, there was an aura of genuine academic seriousness and purposefulness about him as well, and Sam frequently found him tucked away all day at the university library, where he was researching a work on Macaulay which was published shortly after he came down.

It was a surprise to almost everybody when the three of them started the agency. Julian seemed bound for a career at the Foreign Office, though there were rumours at the time of a position at the Conservative Party Research Unit. Peter looked to most to be an obvious man for the City, and one of the smarter merchant banks, and Matthew for a teaching career, possibly at one of the emerging provincial universities.

Perhaps there was a certain triviality in all three personalities. Perhaps they were unusually reluctant to break their bonds of childhood friendship. Maybe they had planned it for longer than anyone had realised. However it came about, the agency Monk Grolsch Parsons was born the summer they came down from Cambridge, and with it all the eccentricity, the Ladder, Top Six, Bottom Six, the *Légion d'Honneur* lapel ribbons and the rest of it. Before long, the three of them had a very successful business on their hands, and they were delighted by their achievement. And it has to be said that behind it all lay an aggregate intelligence beyond that of the common experience of clients and advertising agents, and that behind the mask of languor and cynicism, good commercial decisions were made and effective advertising placed.

Annabel was in her own way perfectly content at MGP, working mostly with Matthew and his immediate subordinate initially on the health food brand Wholetone, and then on Milton Garden Sheds and Kittikake as well.

Wholetone was her favourite, and she particularly liked the market research in which they undertook attitudinal studies into health food consumption. For this, Annabel recruited panels of heavy buyers, found by offering a year's free supply of Wholetone to volunteers who could provide proof of purchase of at least three canisters in the last few weeks.

The client wanted information on consumer attitudes to pricing, to packaging design, product appearance, product taste, product density, competitive brands and content claims. Annabel kept her panels hard at work for hours at a time, and wrote up her findings with painstaking care and responsibility. But she knew full well of course, and rather sadly, that at the end of the day Julian and Matthew would take one glance at the research findings, decide what would work best, present the research in the light of their own judgement, the client would be delighted, and all would be well.

She travelled to Japan for the car company, there were shoots in Antigua and Cape Town and Rome, and she slept rough in Lincoln's Inn Fields for three nights when Matthew put her on a housing-aid charity account, which the agency supported free of charge. She designed processed-cheese wrappings, launched Snugglies, the American diapers, and sold garden sheds by direct mail. She was good at her job, excellent company, full of self-mockery, liked most people at the agency, and was popular in return. She told herself that one day she would leave to do her schoolteaching, obliged herself to feel guilty that she had not done so already, and was aware that she would have done had she been anywhere less congenial.

And congenial it was. The atmosphere of the agency was pervaded by an odd mixture of the lightheartedness and humour and triviality that reflected the low boredom threshold of the founders, and a certain quite ruthless, professional, unbending determination to succeed. It was the combination of this raw drive of the three founders with the fun of it all that gave MGP its particular flavour. Like Lilley & Chase, if in a quite different style, Monk Grolsch Parsons was very good indeed at its job.

Chapter Four

Annabel saw Sam every week or so. Her relationship with her mother, Hilary, who had largely brought her up, was pleasant and unthreatening, but her relationship with Sam was more complex altogether. They always met at Sam's house for supper, never at her flat, because Sam said he did not trust her cooking. He would cook huge suppers for her, as if she was still a child who needed filling up before being sent back to school. They would sit together in the kitchen of Sam's house in Priory Grove, or in the garden in the summer, drink wine, and he would tell her of the Labour ex-Home Secretary's disastrous book and Celia Smith and Anthony Ruges and Callum Kelly, and she would tell him of the agency, and of what Matthew had said, and whom Peter had been rumoured to bed, and the story of the *Financier* editor, and the time that he had worn a Ladder lapel ribbon at a French embassy banquet when sitting next to their Minister for the Arts, to the latter's considerable confusion.

At some point in the evening Sam would ask after Hilary, almost as if it was a point of honour to do so, and Annabel would always, as her point of honour, get out the ironing board and do some of his laundry while the dinner was cooking and the first glasses of wine drunk.

'Bells,' he said, his private name for her which no one, including Hilary, trespassed upon. 'Bells – do you know why I call you that? Partly because it's short for Annabel, of course. But mostly because it was the first word you ever said. Your first word, honestly and truly. "Bells." You were sitting on Hilary's knee one evening by the kitchen window at your grandfather's house in Chewton Mendip. The church bells were ringing across the meadow, and

43

you looked up at Hilary and you said, "Bells." And you kept on saying it and grinning, "Bells. Bells. Bells." You had never said a single word before. How on earth you even knew the word, God only knows. Least of all what it meant.'

Hilary's family house in Chewton Mendip was an important memory in both their lives. For Sam the house brought memories of Hilary's father, of whom he had been very fond; a retired military man whose later career had been blighted by whispers of cowardice under fire at the Normandy landings. For Annabel there were half-remembered recollections of picnics by the river, and Sam and Hilary playing croquet on the lawn together, standing there hugging each other in their laughter, and tea in her loving grandmother's kitchen with little Marmite and cucumber sandwiches and chocolate cake, and bath-time, and her grandfather's laboured awkwardness as he kissed her goodnight. For them both the Chewton Mendip house was a crystallisation of much that had been good in Annabel's early childhood.

On the same evening as Christopher and Mark were at Camellia Mansions with the Rankins, Sam and Annabel were sitting out in the Priory Grove garden side by side on the garden bench, jerseys thrown across their shoulders, their wine and the remains of dinner in front of them on the big rectangular wooden table. At the end of the garden the rambling old 'Mermaid' rose in the crab-apple tree had just come into full bloom, and the borders that ran the length of the walls were packed with phlox, lupins, delphiniums, dahlias, roses, asters, lilies, clumps of cornflowers and peonies, and lily-of-the-valley peeping in its season through early sprays of mint and thyme. Sam loved his garden, and enjoyed the physical act of planting things, so that in mid-summer the beds were packed tight and not a bare patch of earth was to be seen, the colours tumbling into each other and the foliage dense and jumbled.

'You're an odd child, Bells. In all these years I don't think you've ever asked me why I left Hilary.'

'Why did you leave Hilary.'

'I can't remember.'

Annabel laughed. 'Don't worry about it now. I'm not sure I remember very much either. But I do remember Mummy talking to me the day you had gone, and that it was a very painful thing to face up to. I don't think it lasted for long. Perhaps the pain went on, I don't really recall. It's all so long ago. She and Jack got married and you know how nice to me he was. And I saw you a lot, and I always loved that. I don't know – perhaps I'm making it all sound too easy. I love you so much, you know that. Of course I missed you when you'd gone.'

She put her arm through his, and Sam looked away over the crab-apple tree to the lights shining from the back of the houses in The Boltons.

He really had blocked out so much of what had happened at that time. There had been some fairly dispiriting quarrelling, of course, when he and Hilary had first come down from Cambridge. There was the sort of quasi-sibling pressure of two young people fighting to make their initial marks in their professional lives, privately competitive with each other, secretly envious of each other's successes. And always worries about money. Never enough, and always bills to pay and things to buy.

But that was just the preamble to what followed. The raw, biting physical jealousy. The horror in the realisation that she had been unfaithful to him. The torture and rapier pain of knowing that her body had been looked at by her lover. And aroused. And possessed. She was so pretty then, and still was. He remembered suddenly their honeymoon, and the memory almost knifed him in its acuteness – Hilary getting out of the bath, and towelling herself, and laughing with him, and then the dash to the bedroom and her wet body on the bed.

And her awkwardness. The way she sat on her hands like a schoolgirl. Her ears were a little too big, and she had a habit of tucking loose strands of her hair behind them like a child, in a gesture which touched Sam with its heartbreaking vulnerability. Her walk, with her feet at a ridiculous angle. Why is it that you love first the physical imperfections in someone, never the beauty? It's not the orthodox that you fall in love with, not the things that work. You search out and beam love on the point of weakness. The back of the neck, the ears that protrude, the angle of the foot, the mark on the thigh. The yearning is to protect and shield, and it is the things that are flawed which need your protection.

'Get some coffee, Bells. And some Armagnac – you'll find a bottle around somewhere.'

God – the pain of that break-up. That moment of raw horror when he told Annabel he was leaving home. Those first months on his own, at first numb with the shock of what had happened in his life, then deeply, impenetrably unhappy. The journeys down to Hilary's house to see Annabel, so eagerly looked forward to, and so bitterly distressing. The agony of the parting each time it happened. The intensity of the love.

He remembered driving her back to Hilary's a year or so later, and Hilary suggesting that he bathed her and put her to bed before he left. And Annabel's joy at being bathed by Sam in Hilary's house – for a moment the family all together again – and then being put in her bed, and reaching out for Sam and holding him tightly to her, her arms wrapped around his neck.

And the trip to the zoo at about that time. Hilary had not yet met and married Jack, and her parents, in the most well-meaning way, were hoping to put Sam and her together again. The five of them all went to Bristol Zoo, Annabel frenzied in her excitement, alternately clutching her grandparents' hands and then both her parents'. And at the end Hilary's parents drove Hilary and Annabel back to their house, and Sam stood in the car park to wave them off, and as they drove away he could see Annabel's face pressed against the back window, first smiling broadly, then suddenly collapsing into weeping as she saw that Sam was waving with tears streaming down his face. Oh Christ. Christ. Christ. Christ.

Annabel came out with the tray.

'I love you, Bells.'

'You too.'

'Forgive me, Bells.'

'Nothing to forgive.'

'Yes – there are things to forgive. Forgive me.'

She put her hand in his, and they sat together silently for a moment or so. 'It's all worked out in its own way. I'm fine. You're fine. Mummy's fine. Jack's fine, perhaps – I never quite know. I say that there's nothing to forgive because I don't think there is.

Whatever happened all those years ago happened and nothing can be changed. Mistakes are made. All I really care about is that I'm sure you were happy together once. That's all I want to think about.'

There was a sudden sensation of void in Sam's stomach as he remembered a tiny, inconsequential moment when he and Hilary were at Cambridge; Hilary playing in the Newnham lacrosse team, Sam watching the match in his duffel coat standing on the damp, heavy grass at the side of the pitch, and Hilary falling flat on her back immediately in front of him, and lying there helpless with laughter.

'Yes, of course we were happy together once. I've never forgotten it. And I don't want to forget it. It just came to an end. There was some bad luck, and some bad judgement. And it came to an end.'

There was a moment of awkwardness as they sat there. Annabel knew that they were at the point where they might, for the first time ever, truly explore what happened between her parents. Neither Sam nor Hilary, at any moment, had ever allowed her to look with them at the real memories and the real truth.

But Sam, after a long pause, drew back, as he always had.

'And what about your life, Bells? All well? Love-life all it should be?'

Annabel looked across at Sam, and made herself smile. 'Love-life's fine. As if I'd tell you anyway. But everything is all right, I promise you. I must run now. Look after yourself. Lovely dinner. Love to everybody at Lilley & Chase. See you soon.'

'Goodnight, dear heart.'

He walked to the front door with her, and there was an awkward moment while he tried to give her some money, which as usual she wouldn't take, and then she found that she had left her jersey in the kitchen, and went back for that, then the customary little rituals of hugs and embraces.

Sam smoothed the hair back from her face, in a gesture of his familiar to her all her life. 'Eat an apple every day. When you're on a spree. Take good care of yourself. You belong to me. And, Bells . . .'

She was already at the gate.

'Bells . . . You're what I've got.'

She smiled, shrugged her arms and shoulders in a gesture which had always melted Sam's heart, raised her hand, and set off up the street. Sam watched her to the end, and reflected as he always did that her walk was so like Hilary's, with her feet turned out at that odd angle, her body leaning slightly forward, the arms almost motionless. Then she turned the corner into Gilston Road and was gone.

'God save us, Bells. You're what I've got.'

He said this to himself slowly and just audibly, then went back again inside the house.

As Annabel walked away from the house and up the street, her mind turned, as a response to Sam's questioning, to what had happened in her personal life since she had first grown away from adolescence. In her Oxford days she had been cheerfully promiscuous and, although as she matured she was much less casual about it all, there had been a number of partners, if few genuine lovers. There was the occasional relationship that looked serious enough to last, but none did, and whether it was Annabel who terminated the affair or the boy, Annabel always came out hurt and wounded.

Those early sexual experiences at Oxford had been child-like and exploratory, and extremely frequent. She went to bed with almost every boy who asked her to, sometimes because she was attracted to them, mostly because she found sex an easy and comfortable thing, and it was easier to agree to it than go through the rituals of refusal and explanation.

She enjoyed making love, sometimes very much indeed, and, even when only moderately, felt kindly disposed to whomever it was that lay beside her. She had occasional lesbian experiences, grudgingly but affectionately, and always with the same girl, a missionary's daughter of extreme plainness, who pursued Annabel with desperate and dogged devotion throughout their three years together at Oxford.

Her post-Oxford love affair had been with an Indian boy named Vikram Singh, a year or so older, whom Annabel had met several times at college, found attractive, but never got to know. When they came down he went into his father's shipping firm, and called her at the agency when he was in London for a few weeks on business. He was a tall, thin, very beautiful boy with unusually light brown eyes for a Punjabi, and a gentle, courteous manner.

Annabel went to the National Theatre with him twice, they ate together in Soho, they made love, and they fell in love. For six or seven months they lived together at Hammersmith Grove, they were in each other's company every minute they were able, and Annabel was happier than she had ever been. Then Vikram said that he wanted to marry her, but Annabel knew that she would not be happy to leave England and live the life in India of a shipping magnate's wife. She was desperate not to lose him, but she knew what had to be done. She said goodbye to him at Heathrow Airport, putting in his hand as he went a little silver oval frame holding her photograph. She drove back to the flat in Hammersmith, where she sat alone for that whole weekend. On the Monday morning she got up at seven o'clock, went to the office and worked all day with Matthew on the agency's corporate plan. She kept one memento of Vikram, a tiny piece of jade set in a gold clasp that they had bought together in the Portobello Road. She threw away his letters, prayed for him, and had never seen him since.

For all the closeness of her relationship with Sam, she had never told him of Vikram, nor indeed of any lover. It was as if she wanted to keep the two parts of her life separate, knowing that for Sam she was the focus of his entire emotional life. Annabel knew that there was a lack of completion in their relationship, a missing balance and wholeness that would have allowed Sam to accept a lover as a natural development of her life as a mature woman. He talked to her as if she was still a teenager, naughtily exploratory with the boy next door. He asked about her love affairs, but always in the same jocular, meaningless way, as part of the rituals of badinage that they had developed between them. When Annabel finally had to brush this badinage away, and make Sam accept that she was loved sexually and emotionally and maturely by someone, and that she returned that love, she was going to have to do so very carefully indeed.

The problem was, though, that Annabel's emotional life had failed for her since she had broken with Vikram, and she felt that failure very deeply. Few would have suspected that anything was amiss. She was twenty-eight, attractive, sexually experienced and warm, and a clearly intelligent and successful woman. She was sociable and popular, and she had as wide a circle of friends as she could possibly have wished. Professionally she was one of the best-known young women in the advertising world, and she was probably higher paid at this point in her life than any of her New College contemporaries. In her social life she looked to be as active and as busy as any of her circle; forever at parties at the Groucho Club, or having supper with friends at Orso's or San Lorenzo, or going in groups to art movies at the Lumière or the National Film Theatre.

It all looked so successful, and Sam was certainly one of those who assumed that all was as well as could possibly be. From what he heard it seemed that the whole world was in love with her, and he was frequently told by the MGP trio how well she was doing at the agency. But the truth was that there was beginning to build within her an incessant sense of fear and anxiety; Annabel was at heart a marrying woman, and she was at an age now when she wanted to be a mother, and a conventional wife to a man she loved. One part of her very much regretted that she had sent Vikram away, and she thought about him a great deal, though she knew in her heart that a marriage with him would have been unlikely to have succeeded. But she had loved Vikram, and he had loved her, and that was what she wanted now. She wanted love with a man who wanted that too. Simple, requited, uncomplicated, devoted love. And instead of that what she was now having was a series of relationships with attractive, articulate people of her age and group, who would provide sparkling company and amusing times for two or three weeks, then wander on their way.

Twenty-eight was not so old, she would tell herself. But Sam and Hilary were married at twenty-two or -three, and their marriage could so easily have been successful. And twenty-eight was fine nowadays, perhaps, but thirty . . . ? Thirty-five . . . ? That trap was looming in front of her and she feared it; the trap of missing marriage in one's twenties, when it was easily available, and then finding that the men of one's circle, now in their mid-thirties, were turning to girls eight or ten years younger.

It was not marriage for marriage's sake that Annabel craved. It was what a good marriage would bring to her: the chance of motherhood, and nursery bedrooms; and the care and protection of someone of her own blood and image; and emotional interdependence with a man who would be there for her always, and who would share with her and grow with her in mutual, reciprocated love. She didn't look it, but she was, in this sense, a most deeply conventional woman. She had a longing for order, and dependency, and fulfilment in her emotional life, and she was frightened now that it would never come.

And Sam too, as he sat alone in the kitchen, was thinking about love. His mind turned, as it so often did when he had been with Annabel, to childhood memories of his dead sister. He had never spoken very much of Sally to Annabel, or indeed to Hilary or to anyone else, rather as if the recollection of her was too precious a thing to be dispersed and trivialised by anecdote or description. Sam recognised to himself of course that he idealised both his sister and his daughter in a way that, in reality, dehumanised them both. But he needed the fantasy in the way that it was. Sally and Annabel. Sam's key to a private, unsullied, crystalline world.

Chapter Five

Lilley & Chase's board meetings, held just six times a year, were deeply ritualised occasions, dreaded by Sam and Richard, but most keenly anticipated by the other directors, who used the intervening weeks setting alliances, preparing to spring traps, and falsifying evidence.

Since the MegaMedia Inc. débâcle, Richard and Sam had reorganised the share structure of the company, the two founders now owning one-third of the shares each, the balance being in the hands of the other directors and certain senior members of staff.

The object of this distribution of the shares was to build a sense of shared responsibility and democratic decision-making in the executive team, but the truth was that the changes were but cosmetic in so far as the operating style of the firm was concerned, which remained totally dominated by Richard as chairman, and Sam as managing director. Sam continued to have his hand in every pie, and was also currently overseeing the sales and marketing departments, the director previously in charge of these functions having recently left the firm, complaining, quite accurately, that Sam would never allow him any control whatsoever over the divisions he was supposed to be responsible for.

The meetings began at ten o'clock, invariably too early for one of the two non-executive directors, who arrived each time huffing and puffing and muttering excuses and at least ten minutes late. The two non-executives were men of the same generation, and both very well known. They were guarded and distrustful with each other.

Arthur Hill – the late arriver – was a Cambridge don of raffish appearance and notorious drinking habits. He was a Modern

Historian, a prolific and internationally admired author, a journalist of the radical right, and a frequent performer on television. He spoke eight European languages, all fluently, and read at least two more. His lectures were standing room only. He taught with a radicalism all of his own, turning his position full circle when he found that he was no longer on the rock on his own, which was where he liked to be.

Arthur Hill had written four books for Lilley & Chase, each a substantial bestseller, and all aiming quite specifically to destroy the reputations of his opponents of the moment. His most vociferous enemies were at Oxford, the most persistent at University College, London, the most dangerous at Harvard.

Arthur was a director of Lilley & Chase because the firm, anxious to satisfy their bankers' pressure that there should be some non-executives on the board, knew that he had been conspicuously faithful to them over the years, and felt that he would be a safe pair of hands. It had, however, been a relationship full of drama. Arthur Hill's authorship attracted writs like bees to honey, and there were occasions when Lilley & Chase might have wished for a quieter life. But his loyalty and commitment to the firm, and particularly to Sam personally, had been a source of great strength over the years. Other publishers had waved large cheques in front of Arthur from time to time, but, having found Lilley & Chase, and having liked what he had found, he was immovable.

The other non-executive director was Walter Lynne Thomas, a life peer, and at the epicentre of the British Establishment. His progress through life carried the appearance to the outside world of serene inevitability. His father was a bishop, and he was at preparatory school at Summerfields, where he was captain of cricket and head boy. He took a scholarship to Winchester, where he was captain of cricket and, again, head boy. He took a scholarship to Balliol College, Oxford, where he was president of the Union and, to the amazement of all, failed to get his First. All Souls', to Lynne Thomas's agonising disappointment, was no longer an immediate possibility, but he went to London, initially to the Treasury, then to the *Daily Telegraph*, where in due course he became editor. Then back to Oxford as Rector of Exeter College, from where he wrote a weekly column in the *Spectator*, and in due course another in the *Independent*.

It all looked so successful, and was, of course, but to Lynne Thomas the failure of his degree left a deep scar. For the rest of his days he would gnaw away at the wound, and, with a pedantic determination, exposed his failure at every conceivable opportunity. Of all the people in *Who's Who*, Lynne Thomas alone insisted on his entry showing a description of himself as BA (second class).

Lynne Thomas was on every royal commission, and a confidant of the Prime Minister and the Archbishop of York (if not perhaps of the Archbishop of Canterbury, with whom he had a brief amorous flurry at preparatory school; this leading them rather to avoid each other as their respective fames grew in adulthood). He dined at Buckingham Palace, he lunched with the Chief Rabbi, and he was on terms of intimacy with Cardinal Hume, as he was with all the surviving ex-Prime Ministers, bar one that he had decided to drop. He was a scourge to the philistine, a saviour to the oppressed, and a beacon of light and hope in the deteriorating fortunes of his class and his country.

Walter Lynne Thomas and Arthur Hill were not friends.

Hazel had brought in trays of coffee and – a firm Lilley & Chase tradition – doughnuts, which she laid out on Richard's desk. Directors started to assemble from about a quarter to ten onwards, all heading straight for the coffee. Richard would not allow the interruptions to the board meetings that inevitably occurred if trays were set down on the board table halfway through the meeting, with all the resultant passing of milk jugs and whispering for sugar and spoons.

Sam was already at his normal place, immediately to the right of Richard's position at the end of the table. He was reading quickly through the management accounts prepared by Pat Simmons, the finance director and company secretary. These, true to form, had been produced so late that none of the directors would have had time to absorb them properly. Actually, only Richard, Sam, just one of the two joint-editorial directors, and Walter Lynne Thomas were capable of doing so anyway, and Walter only just.

Simmons, a comfortable-looking Lancastrian in his middle-fifties, concealed a plotting and devious character beneath a thick provincial accent and an assumed air of baffled wonderment at the ways of the wicked London world. He was much feared by the editorial staff for his ability to make or break a book at whim, and according to his relationship with the editor. It was all done by a mysterious process of allocating overheads, accruing work in progress, and ascribing something called 'net discounted cash-flow financing costs'. The fortune of editorial careers at Lilley & Chase was largely decided by Pat Simmons. He knew it, and he made sure that everybody else did too. He held his position by ensuring that books close to the heart of either Richard or Sam, particularly those that they personally edited, were accounted for in the most flattering light possible, and shown to be models of profitability to the ranks of the junior editors, whom Pat so despised. In recent months only the Lord Harper memoirs had defied his touch, and that was not for want of trying.

Simmons was at the coffee tray, Richard noticing with distaste that he was now eating his second doughnut, and that there was sugar liberally sprinkled on his chin and a spot of raspberry jam on his tie. Richard, who was a most physically fastidious man, loathed the doughnut tradition and wished he could find a way of discontinuing it.

Simmons had turned his back away from a junior editor who had been invited to the meeting to present his proposals for the new list, and was trying quite desperately to understand how the margin contribution forecasts on them, circulated by Pat but five minutes before, and showing them in a very poor light, had actually been calculated.

With the half-eaten doughnut held high in his left hand, and a slopping coffee cup in his right, Pat had trapped in the corner the pert twenty-nine-year-old figure of Birdie Jones, the newly appointed publicity director, and the object of Hazel's vehement dislike. Simmons greatly fancied her, and had played his first card in what was likely to be a long process of attempted seduction by preparing a schedule for the board meeting demonstrating the extraordinary financial success and acumen of her promotional campaign for a rather good first novel published the previous week.

The directors started to settle at the table as soon as Arthur Hill had made his arrival, which was of course ten minutes late. He looked unusually subdued, and Sam and Richard noted from old experience the evidence on his ravaged features of a prodigious hangover. He slumped down in the first seat he could get to. Pat Simmons, as always, sat beside Sam. Walter Lynne Thomas sat at the foot of the table. The others sat according to their current alliances.

The Minutes of the previous meeting were read and agreed to be a fair record. Absurdly so, actually, as this was exactly what they were not. Simmons's Minutes writing was always an act of pure fiction, reporting quite mythical statements of sycophantic delight in response to every proposal that Richard, Sam or Lynne Thomas made. Simmons was deeply in awe of Walter Lynne Thomas. Where approval had to be recorded for a proposal of anyone else's, it was done in a way which made clear Simmons's deep and weighty concern for its financial implications.

Today, Birdie Jones sat on Simmons's other side, then opposite each other sat the joint editorial directors: Ben Jackson, whose department published the Lilley & Chase fiction, poetry and children's lists, and Robert St John Simpson, whose team was responsible for all non-fiction publishing, including the small scholarly and academic lists. Jackson, who was in his mid-thirties, was a bespectacled, minor-public-school, slim, slightly unkempt man, who affected roll-up cigarettes and a plaid shoulder-bag. He was clever, student-like, manipulative and effective, a very good chooser of fiction, and generally thought to be amongst the best publishers of his age in London. He understood business finance rather well, but pretended an elegant incomprehension.

St John Simpson understood business finance not at all, but pretended an effortless expertise. A few years older than Ben, he had made his reputation some years earlier at a rival house, with the publishing of a number of major-selling memoirs and biographies. The firm had later gone bankrupt, largely because the advances St John Simpson had paid bore no relation to the financial potential of the books he contracted. If he wanted a book he bought it. If the publishers down the road offered an advance of two hundred thousand pounds, he offered two hundred and fifty thousand pounds. He was never beaten at auction. Because of some successes very early in his career, he had developed by the age of thirty a reputation as the brightest star in the London publishing firmament. This was aided by his charm, which was particularly effective with lady authors of a certain age and class. He himself wrote delicious little vignettes on Italy, spoke the language with the most delicate and refined Venetian accent, married a pretty and well-connected wife, and was featured possibly rather over-frequently in the Style and Life sections of the better broadsheet magazines.

St John Simpson was the darling of the London literary agents in this early part of his career. Not only did he pay unlimited amounts for their authors' books, but he lunched with them continually, always as host on his apparently unlimited expense account, and never upset anybody by an excess of zeal for editorial interference or activity.

He had joined Lilley & Chase just before his first publisher went into liquidation, and because Richard thought he saw in him a counterbalance to Sam's increasing dominance of the real management control of the firm. Richard told Sam that he would personally control St John Simpson's spending. He explained that he considered that the problems with St John Simpson in the past were that no one had been strong enough or clever enough to dominate him, that he was a potential source of unusually original new contacts and avenues for Lilley & Chase, and that it would be madness to let him go to one of their rivals.

Sam agreed, but with deep misgivings, and only on the basis that Richard prepared and agreed with Sam formal limits of authority for St John Simpson that he would be made to sign. These tied him down to the procedures he must follow in the buying of books and particularly the payment of advances. Also in the formal agreement were specific ceilings on his personal expenses.

There was suspicion between Richard and Sam for a while but Richard kept his word, and made every attempt to keep St John Simpson under close surveillance. The results, of course, were predictable. The literary agents were aghast to find books almost modelled for St John Simpson being offered for at advances perhaps one-third of his previous levels – Simmons and Sam between them made sure of this – and although many were still sold to Lilley & Chase, some went now to other publishers, and Sam and Simmons observed their loss with a feeling of a job well done.

Walter Lynne Thomas had begun to ask questions about the publishing schedule for a book by an American economist and guru by the name of Michael Brown. There was a tradition at Lilley & Chase that at least every two years they should have an apocalypse title in their Christmas list, and they had seldom failed to make money on them. Their first was the undoubted saviour of the firm at a time when printers were threatening to work for them only if cash was put up in advance; when the booksellers' credit was already being squeezed to a point where they were paying for books virtually before they ordered them; and when the bank manager was beginning to make some decidedly threatening noises about the December payroll.

This first apocalypse book was titled *Sprint for Cash Before Market Meltdown* by an Egyptian financier called Abdul El-Din, who made a pleasing sum of money personally from the bear market that followed. From the same author, writing this time under the name Jake Bartley, Lilley & Chase followed two years later with *The Death of Cash: The Market Will Win*, which led to the same result, but in reverse. Less successful was a book aimed at the ecological disaster called *Too Late Now – The End of Oxygen*, written in a moment of total impoverishment by Ben Jackson's niece, but Lilley & Chase came back to form subsequently with *The Honeycombs of Hell*, a book by an ex-head of East German Central Intelligence, which described a system of tunnels running between Leipzig, Hamburg and Potsdam, stuffed full of chemical weapons, and controlled by a man of lunatic and criminal tendencies.

The manuscript of the Michael Brown book, commissioned for the financial-apocalypse niche, had proved to be not at all what Lilley & Chase had hoped for. A dull work of moderate scholarship, it painted a mild vision of the redemption of the world by a return to spiritual and moral values. It bore no relation whatsoever to the shock-horror billing the book had already received in the catalogue, and having now seen the manuscript, the general opinion in the firm was that they would be lucky to sell two thousand copies in hardcover, which was not at all what Sam and Simmons had in mind. There was some literary publishing to be paid for, and this was decidedly not going to do it.

Lynne Thomas, who had also read the manuscript, made the familar gesture of stroking his Adam's apple in delicious anticipation of his elegant little remark to follow, a habit which always profoundly irritated Arthur Hill.

'I have to say that I find the book uneven. There is a confusion, I think, between moral dilemma and economic pragmatism, particularly in his chapter on Islamic sociology and its parallels in Confucian social-layering and the subsequent effects on consumer credit and deficit budgeting. I do believe—'

'I think I'm going to pass out,' said Hill, and certainly he looked more than a little grey in the face, sweat pouring down his forehead. 'Is there any water?'

He groaned. Birdie Jones shot to her feet, rushed out, and came back with a glass from the kitchen which he gulped down, then gestured for another, his hands shaking violently. He started to feel for his cigarettes.

'Something I ate. God, it's stuffy in here. Thanks, darling. Go on, Walter.'

'Perhaps a little later in the agenda, actually, Walter,' said Richard. 'When Robert presents. Ben first. Your overview, Ben?'

Sam watched and listened as Ben talked, and in doing so thought to himself that he was fonder of him really than anyone else in the firm. Excluding Richard, of course, but that was rather a different thing. Richard and he had shared so many years of struggle together, and if, during that time, there had been only rare moments of genuine personal warmth, there had been a considerable amount of dogged comradeship and unstated mutual loyalty.

But Ben was largely Sam's protégé, and he was extremely attached to him. He enjoyed his look of owlish adolescence, as he blinked behind his modish granny glasses. And he was greatly amused by his waspish, schoolboy wit. The mannerisms and affectations could be irritating – the campness, despite his evident enthusiasm for women, the rolling of eyes when finance was discussed, the studied air of the nineteen-sixties' student fresh from the Woodstock Festival. But he was so bright, so sound a judge of what worked and what didn't work, such a perceptive and detailed editor when that was needed, so sensible about money and advances, for all his affectations of ignorance.

And he was sometimes so surprisingly right. There had been a novel last year from a writer, now in his sixties, who all his life had held a reputation as a stylish and cerebral but rather obscure experimentalist. Lilley & Chase had been steeling themselves to refuse his next novel and allow his work to drop out of print, but he was a sensitive, intelligent, generous man, and somehow Sam could never quite face it. Catching Sam's position, Simmons always tactfully massaged the net-margin contribution of his books in the management accounts.

But then along came the manuscript of his new novel, and Sam found Ben in his office one morning when he arrived; unusually for Ben, because he bicycled in each day from his house in Brixton, plaid shoulder-bag in the handle-basket, and earliness in the office was not normally a feature of his life.

He had the manuscript in his hands, handed it over excitedly to Sam and said, 'Read it, Sam. It's absolutely marvellous. By far the best thing he's ever done. Quite unrecognisable. It's the best novel we've published since I've been here. God knows if we can get anyone to believe us, and we've never sold more than two thousand copies of anything he's done for years. But it's blinding. I'm not going to rest until we all know that here, and give him the success of his life with it.'

It was of course, as Ben said, a novel of very great quality indeed, and Lilley & Chase, after some early snubs by literary editors who refused to believe what they took to be hype, had one of the most satisfying professional successes either Richard or Sam had ever experienced, breaking down prejudices, knocking on doors, shouting from the rooftops.

The novel narrowly failed to win the Whitbread Prize, but had been favourite to do so. It was greatly acclaimed in the United States – the *Washington Post* described it as one of the most distinguished works of fiction of the century – and made the shy, reclusive, perceptive, wholly delightful man who wrote it something of a cult hero. Ben found the book, thought Sam, and in doing so made the man's life. That one could have got lost very easily indeed.

Having made some optimistic and, in Sam's view, possibly foolhardy predictions about the success of Mark Ryder's new novel, Ben had nearly finished his presentation, and had started to mimic the author of the final novel on his list, Callum Kelly. Kelly was an Irish writer of great fame and reputation and success, but traditionally a butt of office mimicry at Lilley & Chase, with Ben being decidedly the most talented performer.

'Shut up, Ben,' said Richard. 'He's the best writer we've got and God knows where we'd be without him. Right, Pat?' Simmons rolled his eyes. 'I don't want Birdie to have any idea we don't take the man seriously. Sam and I want to hear of extremely aggressive promotional plans from her in a moment, and all that elfin cynicism of yours is going to put her off. So shut up. But well done. Such a good list. Pleased, Sam?'

'Of course I'm pleased. Really good list, Ben. Let's hope we can sell it.'

The junior editor spoke next, his nervousness not helped by catching sight of Pat Simmons slipping a piece of paper in front of Sam, whispering to him, and tapping it meaningfully as he was halfway through his presentation. Notoriously in the firm, this was Pat Simmons's favourite boardroom ploy in the subjugation of those he perceived to be his inferiors; a means of destroying by innuendo the validity of whatever point was being made.

Robert St John Simpson followed. He's a good presenter, thought Sam, whatever else he's not. And he does believe in his books in his own way. It's interesting to listen to the different weight he places on those he bought and the ones I bought. Jealous little sod, really. He's not absolutely behind Celia Smith's book, though he should be because it will make more money for his division this autumn than anything else he's had for years. But he never thinks that way. He is actually less financially sharp than anyone else in the firm. Only thinks of how many he's printed and sold in, and whether he's in *The Sunday Times*'s bestseller list, and whether he's got the Waterwell's Book of the Month. Never thinks of the margin, and even less of the write-off on his damned advances.

As was customary, Robert finished his presentation with a superficially courteous but waspishly precise attack on Lorraine Dinkins, the production director. Good thinking this, as Lorraine was always blamed for everything, defended herself badly, and in her attempts to do so always succeeded in alienating everyone else and unifying them against her. Her very appearance somehow made her the more vulnerable to attack. She was a strikingly plain woman of indeterminate age. Dressed habitually in twin-set and pleated skirt, she was in her style and presentation a relic of the immediate post-war years. Even her glasses were of the period. Short-sighted, full-bosomed, full-thighed, mousey-haired, with poor skin and an erratic approach to the application of make-up, Lorraine had apparently abandoned early in life any attempt whatsoever at feminine glamour or allure. This made her all the more appealing to Sam, who always suspected that behind this lay a story of human tragedy – an unrequited love affair, or a sexual rejection, or something of that kind – so painful that it had branded Lorraine's heart for ever. He longed to know what it was. For the others, however, less sentimental than Sam, the temptation to bully her was quite overwhelming. She was indeed absurdly easy to bully, and in doing so as a group, and with a common enemy, everyone else felt themselves to be satisfactorily loyal members of a united and cohesive team.

Robert's technique was to attack Lorraine on behalf of Ben's list rather than his own. The purpose of this was to have Ben on his side for the rest of the board meeting, and avoid what he most dreaded, an attack from Ben that had all Pat Simmons's financial comprehension with publishing nous as well. Ben had the ear of all the agents, was closer to the street than even Sam was and, as Robert knew, was aware of precisely what Robert should have paid for each book, and where he had allowed himself to be talked up.

'Not really my affair, Lorraine, but I've got to say that I'm not entirely happy with some of the printing and binding costs I see you've negotiated for some of Ben's list. Mine I'm reasonably happy with, though I think we could do better. But there's better print-buying than this is, going on around town at the moment, quite honestly, Lorraine. Ben's done a marvellous job for us making money on good literary fiction, and God knows who else does . . .' He smiled and nodded at Ben. ' . . . And I'm not happy that we're working hard enough in the engine room for him. As I say, it's not my parish really, but I do think we've all got to buckle to for him. He deserves it.'

'Well, I must say . . .' Lorraine flushed, and to Robert's immense satisfaction started picking away at a costume brooch of an elephant that she habitually pinned to her bosom, a familiar action of hers, signalling that she was sharply in retreat. 'I do think, Robert, that there are times and places for those sort of opinions, and I don't think this is one of them.'

'Steady on, Lorraine. We're all directors here and we all have responsibility. We mustn't try to hide anything from Richard and Sam.'

'Nor me,' said Arthur Hill. 'God, it's stuffy. Love some more water, Birdie. Heavens, is that the time? I'm supposed to be at the Beeb at twelve-fifteen. Thanks, darling. Tell you what, Lorraine, just go back and tell those effing printers that we want ten per cent off everything or we won't pay. Or we won't use them again. Or we'll ravish their women. Or something.' Arthur was waving his left hand with the first sign of vigour he had shown all morning, some cigarette ash falling straight on to Lynne Thomas's papers, which he brushed off deliberately, his face curled with disgust. Arthur pushed his chair back and clambered to his feet.

'Bye, Richard. Bye, Sam. Great publishing. Too good for the punters. Egg-heads, that's us. Ciao, Walter. Hugs everybody.'

And with much banging of the door, and an obscenity as he tripped, as he always did, on the stair carpet, Arthur Hill set off for Bush House for his World Service broadcast, a monograph on minority Islamic sects in Britain and the sociological implications of their potential demographics. From there he would go to lunch at the Athenaeum Club with the Permanent Secretary of the Treasury. After lunch there was a meeting of the trustees of the British Museum, which he would leave in good time to get to White Hart Lane for the evening game, Arthur having been a director of one of the London clubs for a number of years. And then, certainly tight and probably asleep, he would be delivered by a chauffeur-driven car back to Cambridge.

Tomorrow he flew to Moscow to do a television programme for Channel Four, and next week to Harvard to give the annual Feidelberg Lecture on Contemporary Affairs. From there to Princeton, where he was hoping to succeed in getting into the bed of a certain Professor Helen Wilson, on to New York to speak at the Economics Club luncheon, and then back to Cambridge to work for a few days on his new book, already overdue for delivery.

As the BBC car took him through the traffic to Bush House, Arthur grinned happily to himself at the thought of the speech he was planning to make at Harvard. He was lecturing on Sino-Soviet economic interdependence over the decade 1980–1990, and had decided to do a complete about-turn on the position he had persuaded American mainstream academic opinion to adopt, after a quite furious debate over several months in the columns of *Foreign Affairs*. Nothing like a good U-turn to leave all the wankers floundering. But God, his hangover was awful. Never again. Never again.

Arthur's departure from the boardroom had happened with its normal chaos of dropped papers and false alarms, but, unwisely, Lorraine had not used the diversion to steady herself.

'That's not what I mean, Robert. What I mean is that you never brought this up before when you saw the costings, and you've had them a week. You could have said then.'

'This is an open firm, Lorraine. No secrets . . .' Robert was beginning to enjoy himself. 'If I think something is wrong, I feel I should say it. You should do the same.'

'Well, since you mention it—' Lorraine by this time was quite puce, and Sam rescued her.

'Let's move on. Thanks, Lorraine. I'll help you and we'll see what we can do. We'll report back jointly at the next board meeting. I think you've done some very good work. Let's move on, Richard.'

Birdie Jones's publicity report was rather quickly dispatched. She was too new to the firm to have positioned herself in any particular alliances. But she had done some bold things at Secker & Warburg, and most authors seemed to like her, as she returned telephone calls, came to all the functions and places where they had to go, and seemed sympathetic to all their likes and dislikes. She clearly had good contacts and favours to call in at 'The South Bank Show' and 'The Late Show'. She was quite remarkably attractive in a rather unpretty way, and she seemed to everyone to be reasonably bright and, so far, industrious.

Lilley & Chase corporately was as yet undecided about her, however. But Ben had a suspicion, as yet unfounded but growing, that she might try to do a hop to the new publishing firm Zephyr to join its founder Anthony Robham, taking some of his authors with her. Either that, or to the other new firm, Bedford Square. She was too attractive and too self-confident. Ben preferred his women plain. Too much of the Secker & Warburg gloss on Birdie. God knows what she was up to.

Sam spoke as she finished. 'I think we have a tendency as a firm – not your fault, Birdie, before your time – to be rather silly about what we ask authors to do. I will never forget, to my dying day, watching poor Zbigniew on Wogan. No English really, he thought he was on a programme to discuss Post-Modernism or Magical Realism, or something, and the poor man found himself facing the toupee and the twinkle being asked questions about whether Polish women liked sex. Also, that ghastly evening at Manchester for one of the Waterwell dinners, when Lord Harper tried to give a little talk on Mary Wollstonecraft, failing to grasp that the entire audience had come to hear that actor from 'Coronation Street' promote his *Saucy Crackers for Christmas* book, or whatever it was.'

Simmons orchestrated the laughter like a good servant.

'So let's think what we are doing, Birdie. The book-promotion circus is becoming a little obvious and stereotyped these days. We've got such a good list this year, let's really brood about how each author should be promoted, and what will be best for each one. Peter Hailey, for example, is someone I don't think we've ever made enough of. Twice short-listed for the Booker, and on at least one of those occasions he should have won it. He is so self-effacing, and I don't think we've ever really tried to help him out of it. I would like to see him do a lot more serious television, for example. He is very clever, he has got some good – though not necessarily fashionable – things to say, and he is very coherent and articulate. He was an actor, of course, in his early days. I know he does quite a lot of broadcasting on Radio Three, but it's television that will make him, and we haven't really tried to pull enough strings on his behalf.'

'I agree, Sam.' Richard was doodling on the pad in front of him. 'I might have a word in an ear or two.'

'That's good, Richard, and please do, but Birdie will have to go for it as well. It's her peer group that is really at the heart of this sort of thing at the BBC and the commercial television companies. I give that to you, Birdie. It's a real challenge. He really does write extremely well, he's very loyal to us, and I want him better known.'

Birdie scribbled a few notes, and Richard called for Pat Simmons to present the management accounts. These, unusually, had been put at the end of the Agenda because this was the meeting at which Robert and Ben traditionally made their first presentations of their next season's lists.

Simmons was at pains to demonstrate, as always, that the company was teetering on the edge of insolvency, but to Sam's weathered eye it looked as if, despite himself, Simmons's cash-flow schedule for the twelve months ahead was marginally more healthy than usual. Sam always ignored the profit and loss account and went straight to the cash flow, and by doing so, and by thus being ahead of events, he had averted disaster after disaster over the twenty-eight years of Lilley & Chase's life.

'Thanks, everybody,' said Richard. 'Sorry, Walter, I rather shut you up earlier. Do you want to come back on anything?'

'Well, Chairman, I would appreciate a chance, perhaps at the next meeting, to discuss whether we've allowed the firm to become too eclectic and too unfocused in our publishing. I wonder if we still have a "view" as such. Does the world know what we stand for? Do we know what we stand for? Do we still care? Do we believe? What do we believe? And so on and so on.'

'Fascinating,' said Sam. 'Could you write us a guidance paper, do you think, Walter? Laying down some thoughts on the ground rules? On the boundaries? How we fix our parameters, that sort of thing?'

Walter nodded graciously, Sam saw a ghost of a smile flit across Ben's face, and the meeting broke up.

As they left the room, Sam felt a hand on his shoulder, and to his surprise found that it was Richard's. They had barely touched each other physically in twenty-eight years.

'Do you ever feel that you and I are on a sort of treadmill, Sam? Is there anything new which either of us could possibly find to say at these things?'

Sam touched Richard lightly on the back; again, an almost unprecedented gesture in their long acquaintanceship. 'Well – like Adele Hall or whoever it was – We're Still Here. Thank God. See you, Richard.'

As Sam climbed up the staircase to his own office, his mind went back to the previous evening and the memory of Annabel walking up the street away from his house, her feet at that absurd angle, her body so like Hilary's, thrust forward, arms oddly motionless.

'Christ's sakes, Bells,' he muttered to himself for no particular reason, and raised his hand to Hazel, who smiled back at him from her desk.

Chapter Six

Christopher had told Mark some of the truth about his visit to Dr Morgan, but very far from all of it. To say that Morgan had confirmed that neither his heart nor his blood pressure was good was true as far as it went. After two mild heart attacks in the last five or six years, none of that was a surprise.

What Christopher did not tell Mark was that he had asked Morgan on this occasion for a frank assessment of what lay ahead for him. Morgan had said in response that he would live perhaps twelve months, and that it was very unlikely to be more and perhaps a little less. The problem, as Christopher already knew, but had not been open about with Mark, was the developing kidney failure; there was now not only hypertension but widespread arteriosclerosis. Morgan showed Christopher the X-ray films, demonstrating that he had an aneurysm and narrowing of the renal arteries, all due to the arteriosclerosis. He explained to Christopher that, in a man of his age, an operation to repair the aneurysm and to improve the circulation would be an enormous undertaking, and extremely dangerous.

'Christopher – as I told you, there's really not an awful lot we can do. I wish there was. Obviously we'll go on with drugs to control the blood pressure, and I'm sure you'll be careful with your diet. I suppose we could put you on a kidney machine if your renal failure worsened, but given your other problems it would not extend your life by much, and, knowing you, I somehow doubt you will want to bother at this stage with anything so miserable. Life won't be too uncomfortable, and we'll make absolutely sure that it isn't. You'll feel tired most of the time, but you have been anyway. The only other bore is that you may feel a bit of pain when you walk. But it won't be too bad. The end shouldn't be too hard; either another heart attack or, if the aneurysm bleeds, it will be very sudden. Make sure you see me every seven days until we get the blood pressure properly under control, and then every four weeks or so, depending on how you feel.'

Christopher had shrugged and smiled. 'Well, I'm eighty in three months' time. I have no right to live any longer than that. And I don't feel particularly unwell, really. I sleep rather a lot, and increasingly find it an effort to get out of the flat. I have Mark. I'm very lucky. Thank you for telling me so frankly.'

'Christopher, if you're feeling too uncomfortable at any time, just get Mark to call me, and we'll get somebody around as fast as light. Just call. Any time, day or night. There's no need to worry. We know where we are, and everything's under control. Be as active as you want to be. See your friends. Tidy up what needs to be tidied up. There's not much either of us can do apart from ensuring that you are peaceful and content and, as far as possible, free from any physical discomfort.'

They looked at each other with affection. They were not intimates, but had known each other on and off for many years in a professional capacity, ever since Morgan, as a very young Harley Street practitioner, had been unusually helpful to Christopher's father in the period of illness before his death.

'Goodbye, Rory. You're a good friend. I'm very glad I've got you. Thank you for looking after me.'

Morgan took Christopher down in the lift, and they walked together to the front door leading on to Harley Street. They shook hands at the door, Morgan turned back into the building, then stopped and called after Christopher and came up to him again.

'Christopher – you're the priest, and I'm not, and I don't want to be impertinent, but please allow me to say to you what I always want to say to everybody when I have to give the sort of news I've just given you.

'It's just this; be glad that with any luck you will have a period in which to plan. At least I think you do. Let's hope so. Use the time you have got to reconcile whatever has to be reconciled. Don't die with a quarrel still in the air. Or a relationship ruined by an act of cruelty or pride or whatever. Thank the people you want to thank. Apologise where you need to apologise. There's plenty of time for God. Leave this world with all the human bits tidied up and squared off. Don't brood about success or failure. Or opportunities that have been wasted, or things you might have done. Just accept it all, be grateful for it, be proud of it, and just tidy it up.'

He smiled, turned away again, then called after Christopher, 'Reconciliation, Christopher. The longing for reconciliation is at the heart of us all.'

When Christopher had got home to Camellia Mansions, his first action was to call his sister Norah at her Yorkshire home. She took the news entirely calmly, and asked if he was feeling strong enough to come to stay for a day or two the following week. She said there were hurricanes at the moment – which in Norah's language probably meant a steady drizzle – but the forecast was better, and the lilac was out, and the wallflowers lovely, and she hadn't seen him for ages, and a year sounded to her quite a long time, and she wanted to have a good talk with him about it, and lovely Sam Lilley would be there for one of the nights, and he was such a poppet and it was a good thing because his presence would stop her and Christopher from getting too maudlin.

He told Mark the morning after the dinner with the Rankins that he thought he would go up to Yorkshire for a night or two to see Norah, and Mark, who loved her very much, immediately started to think of some presents to send up to her with Christopher. Buying presents for Norah was not easy. Mark had once bought her an expensive seed-pearl brooch. She had thanked him immediately and warmly, and the last time Mark stayed with her he had found it back in its box, wrapped neatly in tissue paper, and rather evidently never worn. A double basket for the retrievers was much more successful. A special large-print *Ancient and Modern Hymns* – Norah played the harmonium at the village church – was a spectacular success. A first edition of *Oliver Twist*, in a lovely calf binding, clearly failed, and Mark found it holding up a leg of Norah's desk the following Christmas.

Now, what this time? The dogs were usually a good route in, but Mark had had his failures there too. The biggest – and Mark grinned to himself at the memory – had been a very fetching matching lead-and-collar set in maroon leather, which Mark subsequently found tying up the pigsty gate. Perhaps not the dogs this time. The garden? Some lily bulbs perhaps? No, too late in the season. A tree? Maybe a crab-apple? He decided in the end to send her a standard rose from her local nursery for delivery the next day, and made the arrangements by telephone.

Christopher arrived the following Tuesday at Harrogate station. The journey had seemed long, and there had been a rather disagreeable wait at Leeds for the change of trains, but he had taken with him Angus Wilson's *Hemlock and After*, together with an armful of newspapers, and had read happily most of the way, sleeping a little, too.

It was almost four o'clock when he arrived and, despite the bright sun of early May, it was cold and windy on the platform as he gathered up his suitcase and his various bundles. Norah was waiting by the ticket-gate, and the two old people hugged each other rather awkwardly; though the awkwardness was because of mutual physical stiffness rather than lack of ease, for all their lives the twins had been uninhibitedly affectionate with each other.

Christopher held Norah and looked at her. In the thinness of their eightieth year they had become quite ridiculously alike again, more so than in their middle years. Both were ascetic in appearance, their faces long and slender with noses just marginally greater than proportionate. Both were white-haired now, of course, and neither with very much of it, though the fact that Christopher had escaped baldness made their resemblance the more obvious. They had rather prominent ears, and this afternoon in the cold Yorkshire wind both had drops on the end of their pink, thin noses, a fact which Norah pointed out with her customary throaty chuckle.

'Hello, old Chris,' she said. 'Good to see you, dear heart. We look like a matching pair of wet scarecrows. You look a bit peaky. So do I, probably. Damned cold up here. I spend most of my time in the bath. Get down, darling.'

The latter remark was addressed to an elderly golden retriever, who was making arthritic attempts to place both front paws on

Christopher's white raincoat. Christopher leant down to hold and caress the dog's ears, and was given a look of slavish adoration in return.

'The dogs are as gaga as you and me now, as you can see. I didn't think either of them would survive the winter, actually. I should have put Lucy down ages ago, but I just couldn't face it.'

Lucy, a retriever bitch almost identical to the other dog, lay asleep across the back seat of Norah's Land Rover, snoring heavily. The car was full of dogs' hair and, as Christopher slammed the door, clouds of it rose in the air, then settled again, most of it on his corduroy trousers.

The Land Rover was completely filthy, covered in mud, and full of not only the dogs' hair but dogs' clutter too: a chewed red rubber ball on the floor, several leads, a selection of collars, a metal feeding dish with bits of caked biscuit around the rim, and a bundle of extremely dirty army blankets, on which the dogs were lying.

Norah had owned the car for at least twenty years, Christopher was calculating, and quite possibly longer. His knees were uncomfortably jammed against the heater, a large canister-shaped object about the size of a small refrigerator. The seats were torn, horsehair stuffing bulging out in places and in others crudely patched, and the engine had a rough, roaring quality about it, made the worse by Norah's attempts at changing gear, all scrunching and rasping of the metal teeth. Norah drove the car erratically, not fast exactly, but usually in the wrong gear and in a series of shudders and jolts, made the more frightening by her habit of spending much of the time turned around facing into the back, checking that the dogs were comfortable.

She was wearing a scarlet tweed coat, a moth-eaten black and yellow woollen scarf, and a startlingly clean lime-green bobble hat. Christopher knew them all. The coat had been previously owned by an aunt of theirs, who had died fifteen years before, the scarf he had bought for her at the village bring-and-buy sale perhaps five years ago, and the bobble hat Mark had put in her Christmas stocking just the previous winter.

She was hunched over the wheel, positioned firmly in the middle of the road, forcing the occasional oncoming tractors and cars right up into the banks of the lanes by which they approached her house. The gates at the end of her drive were jammed open and, as they drove through them, the Land Rover scattered the gravel on the long, curling driveway, overhung by massive rhododendron bushes, now bursting into flower.

They rounded the corner and there was the house, a solid late-Georgian stone rectory, pillared and with a thick-stemmed ancient wisteria, heavy with deep mauve flowers, clambering over the entrance portico and up the front elevation, the walls a faded pink, the stucco cracked and peeling.

Weeds had sprung up in the gravel, and Christopher noticed that the frames on the deep sash-windows of the ground-floor reception rooms were almost bare now of paint, and that the guttering was hanging down, cracked and broken, at one of the corners. Before they went inside he turned and looked at the great lawn in front of the house, with the ancient cedar tree still standing square in the south-west corner, the sprawling old camellias behind it and, as the ground dropped, the view opening up into a great sweeping vista of the Yorkshire hills, blue in the distance, patchwork green and brown in the foreground, the clouds now building again and the threat of rain in the air.

He wondered if he would ever see it again, and suddenly minded very much the thought that he might not. Norah had been there for so long; it must be almost thirty years now since Hetty had died, and Norah had bought it certainly ten years before that.

The house had been somewhere he had always been so happy to return to, such a place of calm and withdrawal. There was no television, newspapers only erratically, and Christopher doubted that Norah would even have bothered with a telephone had Sam Lilley not put one in at his own expense, and insisted that it remain there, at the time when Lilley & Chase was publishing that book of hers on the Himalayas four or five years ago.

Norah was now bodily lifting Lucy the retriever out of the back of the Land Rover and putting her gingerly on her four legs on the gravel drive. 'There's a girl. There's a girl. There's a girl.'

The ancient dog, head hanging, eyes drooping, saliva pouring, panting heavily, stood for a moment laboriously wagging her tail, and then very slowly walked towards the front door. This was now open and before it, in an old faded apron, stood Jane, Norah's maid and companion, who had been with Norah since she was a teenage girl, pregnant by a boy from the village, who was later killed on almost the final day of the war.

'Hello, Mr Christopher. It's lovely to see you again.' She took his bag from him, despite his attempts to keep it from her.

'There's tea on a tray in the study, Miss Norah. I've lit the fire in there. It may be May, but it's so chilly. I'll take this up to your bedroom, Mr Christopher, and I'm going to light a fire for you in there as well. Mark has just been on the telephone to tell me that I must look after you, or he won't be giving me a Christmas present this year.' She laughed, and set off up the stairs.

'He also told me to keep the dogs away from your bedroom as they give you asthma. I'll try to, but if old Henry knows there's a fire in there tonight you'll have a business keeping him out, I can tell you that.'

Norah threw her coat, scarf and hat on to the enormous mahogany coat-stand behind the front door, Christopher found room for his coat amongst the dozens of assorted raincoats and old cardigans, and they went together into the study. They looked at each other and smiled.

'Heavens, Christopher, what it is to be a twin. All these years looking like peas in a pod. I'm really sorry to hear your news. Though I suppose we've both been around long enough, really. I'll miss you quite dreadfully if you go before me, but there we are. After you rang I was thinking of all those childhood things we did together. Do you remember those photographs of us in that vast pram we used to sit in at either end? That was the time of that extraordinary Irish nanny, I think. The one who used to bend our hands back if we didn't eat. Remember her? And then there was that Scottish woman with a moustache who could never talk about anything except bowel movements. God knows where Mother got them all from.'

'I know exactly where she got them from. That terribly grand employment agency place off Belgrave Square. I went there with her once. I think it was the day I went off to prep school for the first time.'

Norah smiled at him. 'I always remember you going off to school, and feeling totally bereft when you'd left. You were so hopeless at looking after yourself. Even at home in the nursery you used to sit straight down as soon as our little eleven o'clock break came along, and wait for me to go and get your milk and biscuits. I never minded, of course. Do you remember I wanted to marry you?' She gave her old cackle of laughter.

'That just about sums you and me up, doesn't it? Not exactly suited to marriage, either of us, as it turned out. Hetty for me, and I adore your Mark, of course. Christopher, old love, I can't say much more. Thank you for telling me what Rory Morgan said, and thank you for coming up to see me. We'll have a lovely old gossip with Sam Lilley tonight. He said he'd get here by seven. I hope so. I'm always dead with hunger by eight.' She bent down to scratch the stomach of one of the dogs.

What an awkward pair we are, thought Christopher. Norah a famous eccentric. Me a notorious priest. There is love there between us, and there always has been, but neither of us has ever made much of a fuss over it. But we have genuinely helped each other in real crises. The Fall for me. That nightmare with Harrods and the shoplifting charge for Norah a little before. It's a good thing we've got each other. Thank heavens Jane's around. And thank heavens Norah's still writing.

The memory of the Harrods disaster now came fleeting back to Christopher. There had been an incident with a piece of silver of some sort. Was it a photograph frame? Norah had been staying with Christopher at Camellia Mansions, and he had been at the flat that afternoon, working on a paper he was delivering later that week to a conference at Lambeth Palace.

The police had called him, and he'd rushed around by taxi, after an interminable wait in the street to get one. Norah was being held at the little police station in Lucan Place. Christopher found her in a small side office, sitting on a plain wooden chair, leaning forward, head in hands. The police officer who showed Christopher into the room spoke to her gently, and she looked up and gazed at

Christopher quite expressionlessly, haggard, chalk-white, grey hair unkempt. There were no tears, just a face of traumatic blankness. When Christopher went over to the chair to help her to her feet, her fingers clutched at his elbows like a drowning woman struggling to get a grasp on her rescuer.

She was allowed to leave on Christopher's surety, returned with him to Camellia Mansions absolutely wordlessly, and when they reached the flat she went straight to her room and lay face downwards on her bed. Christopher shut her door, but stayed in the room with her. For some minutes she was silent, and then she started howling like a stricken animal. Christopher sat on the bed with her, stroking her and reassuring her as one would a child.

'There. There. There. There. It's all right, Norah. Hold on. Hold on.'

After a few moments she quietened, sobbed for a little, and then fell into a deep sleep. Christopher woke her at about eight o'clock, having run a deep, hot bath. He put her in it, washed her and sponged her face, wrapped her in a bathrobe and took her back to her bedroom. He had rung Rory Morgan earlier, knowing that Norah did not have a general practitioner in London, and Morgan had sent around some sleeping pills by special messenger, with a handwritten note to Christopher saying that he was to allow her two only that night, and was to keep the little bottle in his pocket, under no circumstances allowing Norah a chance of getting to it.

Christopher had put her to bed, brought some soup and toast and a large glass of whisky, given her the two sleeping pills, and left her alone. In all this time she had said nothing at all, nor he to her, apart from little calming words of comfort when she had been hysterical.

She appeared from her room at about eleven o'clock in the morning, by which time her solicitor had called Christopher to say that the court hearing would be the following day, and he would like to talk to Norah for at least forty-five minutes in advance of that, preferably that afternoon. When she came into the sitting room where Christopher was again working on his paper for the conference, he told her of her lawyer's call, and asked if she would like him to go with her. She shook her head, set off shortly afterwards, returned later that afternoon, and went out by herself that evening to a concert at the Wigmore Hall, again refusing Christopher's company.

The next day she went to court; this time, after a short argument, allowing Christopher to go with her. She pleaded guilty and was fined a hundred pounds. The magistrate began a homily, but there was something about the way she stood in the dock, appearing empty and drained, without fight or dissent or spirit, that made him pause, look at her for a moment, then quietly tell her to stand down.

She had driven back to Yorkshire that night, and neither Christopher nor she had ever spoken of the incident again. There was a small piece in one or two of the London papers, and a large piece in the *Yorkshire Post*. There was an unpleasant little incident at the village church, where she found an anonymous note in her pigeon-hole in the vestry, suggesting that she should resign as organist and from the PCC. She did neither. One or two people cut her in the street. A dinner party she had been asked to at the Lord Lieutenant's was cancelled a few days before.

Two months later her new novel was published. Sam Lilley called in every favour he could from every literary editor in town to try to get a helpful and generous Press. Reviews were good, and thoughtful and respectful of her status in the current literary scene. She did one or two quite delightful and, for those who knew her, reassuringly eccentric, radio interviews. There was a profile of her in the *Guardian* which was positive and well researched. Within a year, the incident had become positioned vaguely in people's minds as a typical bit of pottiness from a notoriously odd and lovable figure, and within two years it was forgotten.

It was said sometimes, by those who seem to know about these things, that she would have been made a DBE if all this had never happened. Christopher was comforted by the knowledge that Norah would have been totally indifferent as to whether she was a DBE or not.

Sam's car was heard coming up the drive at shortly before seven o'clock, and there were cracked old cries of delight from Norah as they hugged each other at the front door. Sam had come to bring Norah the galley proofs of her latest book, and with the express purpose of pinning her down to some sort of agreement over the promotional programme for it.

He had published her throughout her entire writing career, her first novel appearing when she was aged fifty-two and still at the Foreign Office. A celebrated success, it had been on one of Lilley & Chase's earliest lists. Every eighteen months or two years since then, a new title had appeared. There had been several collections of short stories, eight novels in all, some travel narratives, and a single play, which ran at the Fortune Theatre quite successfully one summer; there was talk now of a revival.

But in Christopher's private view nothing she had written since had been as good as her first book, the story of a Kensington schoolmistress and her obsessive but unrevealed sexual passion for her adopted brother, who was bleeding away her life in a series of manipulative acts. This had later made a very successful film, the central role of the schoolmistress providing a perfect opportunity for an emerging RSC player to make her name as a major screen actress, and it had put Norah into a position of status and respect amongst British writers of her generation.

There were some fair successes and some moderate failures in her subsequent books but, as her eightieth birthday approached, there began to be a wave of affection and adulation for her throughout the literary world. *The New Yorker* ran a six-thousand-word essay on her by Harold Brodkey, which positioned her somewhere in the rankings with Muriel Spark, Anita Brookner, Iris Murdoch and Penelope Fitzgerald amongst British women writers of her time. Sam, not entirely trusting Birdie Jones with the task, had persuaded the *London Review of Books*, the *Spectator* and the *TLS* to run eightieth-birthday features, *The Sunday Times* to carry an interview with Valerie Grove, and all the London broadsheets to carry little pieces of some sort. One of the reasons that Sam had come to Yorkshire that evening was to try to make her agree to give as much of her time as she could to all this. Penguin had her backlist in print in paperback, and sales were steady, but Sam was trying to persuade them to relaunch and repackage her novels and short stories, possibly with Marc cover illustrations, if suitable archive material could be found, and to run a 'Norah Howard at Eighty' promotion with Waterwell's, the booksellers, which would mean some sort of national tour for her.

Sam had often dined with Norah before at the Yorkshire house, and it had been a mixed experience over the years. The wine was always excellent and in continual flow, whilst the food was strictly English nursery, which Sam usually liked as a rule. But Norah's was bad English nursery, a caricature of English food at its most stodgy and poorly cooked.

It was quite obvious that Norah was sincerely fond of Sam. Their relationship, in its early days warm and amiable enough but only really operating on a professional level, had grown over a quarter of a century into a friendship of genuine intimacy. This was unusual for Sam particularly, who was a man of a great range of acquaintances but, as was probably little suspected, few real friends. Sam and Norah were solicitous of each other's needs and fiercely loyal about each other to other people. He looked after her, as her publisher, as well as these things can possibly be done. She repaid him by being unswervingly loyal to the firm, and openly affectionate to him, forever fussing over him, scolding him, getting him to repeat familiar and favourite anecdotes, and fretting over his comfort. He affected an irritation about all this, but the truth was he was amused and flattered by it.

With Christopher quite decidedly not interested in his father's magnificent cellar, it had been left to Norah on his death, and Sam was always sent down before dinner, clutching a glass of whisky, to choose the wine for the meal.

It had felt like a long drive that day, and Sam thought he might as well do them all proud, so he came up with a bottle of Puligny Montrachet '61 – it should have been drunk by now, of course, but was probably still pretty good, and with that lovely oaky taste of aged white burgundies; and, great excitement this, a bottle – no, on second thoughts, let's make it two bottles, thought Sam – of Château Haut-Brion '49. Sam had no idea what they were eating, but could resist neither wine, and reckoned he could switch the order of drinking around to make some sort of fit with whatever appeared.

The three of them made their way into the dining room, through which ran a draught so strong that the lilac-branch leaves in the big glass vase in the hearth were rustling perceptibly. Christopher dearly wished that the fire had been lit there as well.

The first course, when it arrived, and there was a considerable delay, turned out to be fish-cakes, warmish and just about half-cooked. These were served on lovely Wedgwood plates, on which Jane, ever genteel, had positioned a weary and yellowing sprig of parsley, together with a dollop of thick, creamy mayonnaise. Norah had inherited with her father's cellar some very good glass, china and silver, and both she in Yorkshire, and Christopher and Mark in London, always had their meals on and with exquisite things.

Christopher, who was extremely fastidious, looked at his plate in complete panic. Sam was triumphant with his selection of the Puligny Montrachet, and gave the three of them a generous helping – the Howard family wine-glasses were famously large quasi-beakers – then started to cut the two fish-cakes on his plate into small bits, pushing them around busily to give the impression of enthusiastic consumption.

Norah ate hers with a rapid nibbling action, which always made Sam think of the rabbits eating their carrots in the cartoon film of *Watership Down*. 'Delicious,' she said. 'Jane's such a marvellous cook. I wonder what's coming next.' Then: 'Poor old Chris. Do eat up, dear heart. Sam, darling, you know why Chris is here. He's had grim-reaper news rather, hardly a surprise at our age, and we're going to brood about it together a bit. You're family, of course, so there're no secrets.'

Christopher bit his lip with irritation. There was sometimes a booming, innocent openness about Norah which could lead to the most painful breaches of privacy. Christopher had told her the news first, even before he had told Mark, because they were twins, and had always felt like a split of the same embryo, even if they weren't. He was fond of Sam, of course, had got to know him quite well over the years through Norah, and through Mark too, as there was always a round of Lilley & Chase parties which he went to with Mark when the novels were published. No doubt he was discreet, and he was certainly a sensitive man, but it was still a breach of loyalty to Mark that they should be sitting together here in Yorkshire discussing his coming death at a point when he had not talked it through with Mark himself. But somehow Sam seemed sensitive to this, did no more than turn to Christopher with a look of sympathy and concern, pull a wry grimace, and let the matter drop. Christopher felt grateful to him for his tact.

Jane appeared again, this time with a chicken and rice dish of uncertain description. There was a floury-looking white sauce already poured over the chicken, crusted by having been kept warm under the grill, from which, Sam suspected, the fish-cakes had been prematurely ejected to make room. The rice was brownish, and had in it some mixed pieces of red, brown and grey, which Christopher made a point of not inspecting too closely.

Sam patted the two bottles of Château Haut-Brion standing in front of him, corks drawn. 'Perfect choice,' he said.

'Are these hens ours, Jane dear?' Norah asked, as the plates from the first course were being pushed into a dark hatch arrangement which connected with the kitchen. Norah's kitchen resembled a museum reproduction of the nineteen-twenties, and through the hatch Sam could see some familiar and favourite sights, not least the washing line strung above the old kitchen range, on which hung several pairs of thick pink knickers, some woolly vests, and a number of brown lisle stockings, pinned aloft at their banded thighs. He hoped they had not been dripping on the food cooking below.

'Yes, Miss Norah. I did two or three this morning.'

Christopher smiled and, copying Sam, made vigorous cutting and forking motions at his plate. Sam recognised his discomfort, enjoyed it, and turned to Norah. 'Norah, you will get the proofs back in ten days, won't you? Everything's nicely on schedule at the moment for our September publication date, and we mustn't run any risk of missing that.'

Actually the galley proofs were only sent to Norah out of a sense of decorum. Her corrections were always illegible, and full of corrections to the corrections, these marked with red arrows saying 'Sorry!!!', and the pages were regularly stained with coffee-mug rings, arrowed with 'Whoops!!!', or torn off across the bottom and used for shopping lists or notes for Jane. None of Norah's alterations was even so much as looked at by Lilley & Chase these days, and Sam suspected that she was fully aware of this, but treated the whole proof-reading process as an amusing diversion after a day of gardening, and as an alternative to *The Times* crossword or the *Spectator* competition.

If she treated these sort of tasks with something short of total reliability, this was certainly not true of her writing itself. The novels were of a virtually uniform length at around eighty-five thousand words, her first draft written at a rate of two sheets of foolscap a day, which in her tiny, spider-like hand gave her one thousand two hundred words. The draft took her therefore about twelve weeks to complete. The one hundred and fifty or so sheets of foolscap were put into a large box file and delivered to the vicar's wife, who returned a neat, double-spaced, typed-up draft manuscript three weeks later.

Unlike her performance with the galley proofs, Norah would then, with minute care and a clear hand, correct, add, delete, include new sections, expand, contract and – particularly – reduce and bleach the style of the first draft yet further, so that no vestiges of overwriting remained.

This process took a further six or seven weeks, and in that period Norah worked for five concentrated hours a day, from ten o'clock in the morning until twelve-thirty, and then from four-fifteen until a quarter-to-seven in the evening. The big box file went back to the vicarage, and three weeks later returned as a faultlessly typed manuscript, tidied and paginated and ready to be sent to Lilley & Chase. She never missed a deadline, nor ever needed reminding of a contractual delivery date.

Everything else in Norah's life was out of control. She had very little idea of how much money she had, took no interest in her business affairs, and bills were now sent directly to her lawyers for payment. This had been arranged in recent months by Sam, after numerous incidents of the electricity and telephone being cut off. Electricity was one thing, but to have the telephone cut off was a major inconvenience to Lilley & Chase, who needed to be in regular contact with her.

She was represented by a literary agent who was famed for her toughness and guile; actually rather pointlessly, as Norah would never dream of moving from Lilley & Chase, nor indeed from her New York publisher, Silas Rubinstein, who ran a tiny, exclusively literary list from offices of outstanding squalor in Greenwich Village. To her agent's rage, Silas paid royalties to Norah only when he had the money to do so, which was not very often, but he protected and cherished her name and reputation in the United States with obsessive zeal. The article by Brodkey in *The New Yorker* had been commissioned by the magazine after weeks of his incessant nagging, the *New York Review of Books* profile similarly, and each of Norah's books Rubinstein published by a technique of a barrage of direct telephone calls to every half-decent bookseller in North America, almost all of whom Rubinstein knew personally.

Norah's agent would tell her each time a new book was ready that advances of at least double what Sam and Silas would pay could be secured from any number of major publishers in both London and New York on the strength of one morning's telephone calls, but this was simply professional rhetoric, as she knew full well that Norah would never leave her two 'boys'. Indeed, given that Sam was a gentile and Silas a Jew, they were like a pair of brothers; physically surprisingly alike, both a little plump, a little dishevelled, buttons beginning to tug across shirt fronts, both with wiry, curly hair and round, good-humoured faces. Norah showered affection on them both, and the bonds of loyalty between them appeared unbreakable.

Neither Lilley & Chase nor Rubinstein had large sales teams or big marketing budgets, but both houses worked hard at ensuring that the publicity surrounding each new book was as strong and as favourable as they could manipulate – sometimes shamelessly manipulate – and that the most important, if not necessarily the biggest, booksellers were flattered into giving maximum support and exposure. She in her turn was reasonably prolific, reliable on delivery, and her books were good, if not major, sellers. They made money publishing her, and she had the comfort of knowing that both in Britain and in North America she was published by friends who cared for her, genuinely admired her work, and were determined to protect her reputation and status.

Both Sam and Silas separately did consider Norah to be as good as all but the very best of contemporary writers, and felt that her position and standing might very well survive her eventual death. Her world was an idiosyncratic and individual place, instantly familiar to her public. The geography of her novels changed, but the plots and the characters hardly at all. There was always a sense of spiritual dilemma, always a sacrifice for love, always a sense of bleak loneliness under a quite sheeny surface of articulate sociability. The books, invariably, were written around a single woman, generally of middle years, always intelligent, always in control of whatever route she has chosen, but usually at the point of terminal pain. The style was sparse and contained. The descriptive passages were tightly controlled, sentences short, adjectives few. All so different to how she lives her own life, thought Sam, as he watched her now talking to her twin, and so completely different to how, informally, she either writes or speaks.

Her letters were muddly, gushing, chaotic affairs, full of crossings out and asterisks and footnotes. Her conversation was warm and jumbled. Her clothes, of course, were notoriously odd, as indeed was much of her behaviour, with its frequent examples of absent-mindedness, such as walking down to the village and arriving back on a bicycle. Or, Sunday after Sunday, playing the wrong hymns at Matins. On one occasion she did it twice in the same service, and realising her mistake the second time halfway through, suddenly stopped, said quite clearly, if softly, 'shit', then started off again with the hymn she was supposed to have played in the first place.

She was actually a very bad organist indeed, and the vicar was at his wits' ends as to what to do about it. She had taken the job on some years before, when the previous volunteer died. She had answered an appeal from the vicar for someone to step into the breach at short notice, and her early efforts were reasonably dependable. As the years went on, however, and her eyesight and hearing deteriorated, her playing, with its long pauses, fudged notes, and muttered obscenities, became notorious in the neighbourhood. One of the reasons why attendance was always rather good of a Sunday was that her performances were beginning to be considered something of a cult event, house parties coming from some distance away to enjoy one of the more entertaining rituals of Yorkshire weekends.

The problem the vicar had, and he was not very good with problems, was that Norah was by far the biggest donor to his church's funds, and he was frightened at the prospect of threatening this flow of money. She traditionally, for example, paid for the choir and PCC outing to Scarborough each year, a most ambitious affair with hired bus, spending money for all, picnic hampers, champagne, beer, and a closing party at the Rose and Crown in the village when the bus returned. Perhaps it was worth some excruciating moments at Matins to preserve all that, though recent experiences had been so bad that the vicar was beginning to feel he would have to steel himself to take action of some kind.

Her professional style as a novelist, Sam concluded, had been dredged therefore from some quite separate part of her personality, a part that the rest of the time was submerged and sublimated. There was order in there really, thought Sam, but how strange that the only way one could find it displayed was in the ritualised form of her professional writing.

'Come on, loves. Bring the bottle, Sam. Let's get back to the study fire,' said Norah. As they left the room, Sam noticed that Christopher was looking drawn and tired. Sam smiled at him, and held him by the elbow for a moment as they crossed the hall. He had always been intrigued by the story of Christopher and Mark, particularly as there was something in the tone of Mark's novels – a melancholy, a loneliness, an alienation – that suggested to Sam that behind both Mark's charm and humour, and his constancy of affection for Christopher, there lay a subtler, more complex condition than the world would have suspected. Additionally, Sam had been an eyewitness to the first frantic hours after the story had broken in the media, as he had actually been staying with Norah in Yorkshire at the time. He was at the house when Christopher arrived that first night in flight from Hunstanton. Ever since he had been extremely curious as to how the relationship between the two of them had worked out.

'Sorry to hear that you're unwell, Christopher. It was such a nice surprise to find you here. I always wish we'd got to know each other better over the years. I hear so much about you through Mark, of course, let alone Norah, but we only seem to meet each other at their publication parties, and you know what those are like. I hope we will now.'

I'm not surprised Norah is so fond of Sam, thought Christopher. There's an unaffected warmth about him which is deeply attractive. No openness of course, though he pretends there is. Mark has it exactly right: Sam performs openness, like a reclusive actor playing a comic role. The warmth is real, though. It's the way the genuine warmth and the pretended openness work together that makes him so interesting and appealing. I wonder if anyone has ever really got inside him. I would think that Norah is probably as close to him as anyone.

'I hope so too,' Christopher said. 'I'm so glad that Mark and Annabel seem to be such good friends. I believe she is coming to dinner with us shortly, with that boyfriend of hers from the BBC. I hope Mark has reassured her that we won't muddle her up with one of Andrew Boot's PCC parties. That I would not inflict on the poor girl for anything.'

Sam laughed, though immediately he found himself reacting with a jolt of possessive anxiety to the reference to a boyfriend. Who was this boy? Why was it that Annabel would never let him see into her life? How was it that Christopher, of all people, had access to her in this way when he hadn't? But he smiled again at Christopher, touched his arm a second time, then turned to Norah, and engaged her with a question regarding the publishing plans for her new book that autumn.

He very much wanted to do some major promotional work around her eightieth birthday, and particularly television. 'The South Bank Show' had made quite specific proposals about including Norah in a short series of monographs for Channel Four entitled 'English Writers of Our Time'. The problem was that Norah had a terror about appearing on television, all dating from an interview of hers some years ago on a programme called 'Lives' which had been a distressing experience.

They had filmed her in Yorkshire, and encouraged her to dress in clothes that, even by Norah's standards, were unusually wild;

convincing her also, in her complete ignorance of the medium, that she would have to wear make-up of a grotesque vividness. Sam shuddered at the memory. Poor Norah had been totally disarmed by the sweetness of manner of the two young girl researchers who prepared most of the ground with her, particularly so as they had made the most extravagent fuss of the dogs, always the way to Norah's heart.

The interviewer had also been courteous and unthreatening in style, which had served to relax Norah's guard, but in an odd attempt to amuse she had made some completely inopportune comments about the British class system and the sadness of its demise, ludicrously out of character for someone who, as far as Sam and Christopher knew, was without any views on the subject whatsoever. The programme had closed with a sequence showing Norah at the village church harmonium, playing, as she always did, with a large fruit-crowned hat on her head, and with her tongue sticking straight out as she tried to concentrate on reading the music. It had, in fairness, made cruel but very funny television.

Norah had gone down to the vicarage to see the programme, having no set of her own. She recognised the disaster in dumb horror, the vicar making things worse by his frantic enthusiasm for her performance. She had appeared on television only once since, at the time of The Fall, when she read a short, bleak statement, looking saddened and elderly, and of course absurdly like a female version of Christopher, whose own fated appearance had been in the clip immediately before.

All other work on television had been refused. She was an eccentric figure in so many ways; her dress, the village organ, her carelessness over her affairs, her house, even the Harrods incident, and yet she was not a woman who drew deliberate pride from being an oddball. Had the 'Lives' programme been called 'English Eccentrics', or something similar, she would have seen the trap and run a mile from it. She was no exhibitionist, and absolutely no Sitwell, to whom the Howard family was distantly related. Norah would never have been carried prone on a litter down the Farm Street aisle, lilies strewn about her person. And yet, oddly, there was just a hint of Edith Sitwell in her face, and indeed in

Christopher's too. Just a touch of the Plantagenet in the nose and the cheekbones.

'No, Sam, I just won't. Certainly some radio if lovely Paul Bailey will do an interview with me again. Not only has he read every word I've ever written, but he knows what I'm trying to say. But no television. Ever, ever, *ever* again. Particularly not now. You know what I'm like. Totally batty and really looking it now I'm so old. I'd have no idea what to wear. Actually, I haven't got anything to wear.'

'Norah, I promise you we'll make it work. You're too significant a figure to be left out of this series, and I don't want to see that happen. Everyone will look after you. Let's try it. No more disasters, I absolutely promise you.'

Christopher knew exactly why Norah was so reluctant, and, with his memories of his own performance at the time of The Fall, was much in sympathy with her. But he did very much want Norah's career to be given the recognition which he believed it deserved. That first novel was a masterpiece, and if the later work had become a little sterile for Christopher's taste, a shade more bloodless than he could recognise in his experience of what human life was, then that was not an opinion which commentators generally seemed to share.

'Make a fuss of this birthday, Norah,' he said. 'Do it for me. It's my birthday, too, and I want all the vicarious pleasure of seeing it celebrated by everyone else.'

Nora laughed, clearly because she did not want to be forced to a decision, and started on a rather long story of a neighbour of hers who had shown her house on a programme called 'The Heritage of England'. Norah, again watching at the vicarage, had felt her to be not only wildly overdressed – she had appeared in a sort of Queen Mother outfit in lilac – but also given to suppressed histrionics, and, as an old television hand herself, had enjoyed a certain not unmalicious satisfaction in what she saw.

Then: 'Bed everybody,' addressed to include the dogs, who recognised the statement as being part of their nightly ritual, wagged their tales in a laboured, arthritic manner and started to make painful attempts to get to their feet. 'Sleep tight, boys. Take your shirt off,

Sam, and put it in the washing machine. It'll be clean and ironed for the morning.'

Quite possibly the worst-dressed woman in England herself, Norah always criticised Sam for the state of his apparel, making him take his socks off over drinks before dinner so that she could see if they needed darning (which they frequently did), and insisting on washing his clothes when he went to bed (this had happened once with a sweater Sam was fond of, which had re-emerged from the process the following day, shrunken and misshapen). He hoped his shirt would survive tonight's ordeal.

As Sam went to his room, he wondered if Norah would do as he had asked, and thought that she probably would. Norah, going into her own room, was thinking rather similarly. Christopher, delighted to find that Jane had made his bedroom warm and pleasant, with the fire glowing, the curtains drawn, and the bed turned down, reflected mostly that he was missing Mark, that he was tired, and that he envied Norah much of her life, including the rhythm and security and mutual trust of her relationship with Sam. She was lucky to have him, he thought.

Chapter Seven

When Christopher returned from Norah he braced himself to speak to Mark, and at supper that night he told him the news that Rory Morgan had given him. They sat quietly together until midnight. There were no moments of extravagant emotional outburst. Christopher had told him calmly and quietly and without fuss or emphasis. Mark responded in similar manner and sat holding Christopher's forearm, the room darkening as the summer night fell.

'I know it's child-like, Chris, but I've never been able to accept that you won't go on for ever. Somehow I've always told myself that in five years' time you'll still be here. Maybe Morgan's right. Maybe Morgan's wrong. God knows. I don't want to face up to anything, and as far as I'm concerned, I'm just going to go on planning ahead as I've always done. I can't manage anything else.'

Little more was said, but Mark slept very fitfully that night. When he woke with a start, at five o'clock, the light was already streaming through the window, and he was running with sweat. The memory of his previous night's conversation with Christopher suddenly hit him and, as he put his hands to his face, he remembered too that he would hear the results of his HIV test that day, and his stomach lurched a second time.

He had taken an HIV test one week before, as he had routinely every twelve months for the last four or five years.

The taking of these tests was not so much kept secret from Christopher as not spontaneously revealed to him. Mark had meant to, at the time of the first test, but had failed to do so, and once the omission had become institutionalised, he had never done so since.

He had no idea whether Christopher thought he was celibate or

91

not. Their own relationship had been only intermittently sexually active, even in its early stages, and now never so. There was no problem in this: no distaste, or lack of ordinary physical intimacies, or embarrassment at nakedness, or anything of that kind; just a natural waning and eventual extinguishing of an old man's sexual drive.

Mark was perhaps not unusually promiscuous by the standards of many of his age group in homosexual London, and indeed rarely took part overtly in the gay scene at all, but he never hid what he was, and inevitably there were encounters, sometimes actively sought, usually passively accepted. Christopher did not ask him about this aspect of his life; had he done so, Mark was by no means certain he would have told him the truth. The most important thing in Mark's heart was to give Christopher, whose life was so changed and broken by The Fall, as happy and peaceful and unstressful a final passage as possible. He wanted him to be comfortable and free of any concern or worry.

Mark's own young man's sexuality had nothing to do with his love for Christopher, and he was not going to let the casual unimportance of the former get in the way of what really mattered. When sexual encounters occurred, they were anonymous, brutish and short. There was no possibility of any form of emotional entanglement. That was Christopher's, and would remain Christopher's until he died.

Mark had his blood tests undertaken privately by a GP in Battersea who had become a personal friend since Mark had first seen him a few years before, having contracted severe bronchitis following 'flu over the Christmas holidays. The procedure was that the blood was taken, then sent away for testing, and Mark would come back to his surgery seven days later to hear the results.

The week of waiting was always a period of concentrated anxiety, made easier perhaps by the fact that at least the worry did not have to be shared with Christopher; although it was difficult to sustain a veneer of normality and customary good heart with the stress eating away inside. The moment of release, when the doctor smiled at Mark and told him all was well, was always like a sudden shaft of light.

He lay in bed until seven o'clock, then got up, shaved and bathed, and walked around the flat for a time in his bathrobe. He made coffee, took a cup to Christopher, dressed, went in again to his bedroom to wave him goodbye, and walked the half-mile or so to the doctor's surgery.

He had, as he always arranged, the first appointment of the day, and there was a certain amount of fussing around as the receptionist made a telephone call, and then another. After a few minutes he was sent into the surgery, and as Dr Hawker rose from his chair he knew instantly what the news was. Hawker beckoned him to sit opposite the desk, took his glasses off, started to polish them with his handkerchief, and looked at Mark with an expression that was partly a smile, partly a grimace. He put his glasses back on, clasped his hands together in front of him on the desk.

'I'm sorry, Mark. I'm really sorry. I don't have to spell it all out to you. Life can be so bloody awful. I am desperately sorry.'

There was a silence for some moments, and Mark realised that he felt practically nothing at all. He was completely numb. He felt no horror, no fear, no panic. If anything, he began to feel strength flowing into him. As always in his life, it was the unresolved situation, the issue that was not being faced up to that ate into him. Now he knew where he was, now that the enemy was there in the open, fully displayed, named and identified, there was a sense of relief. It was a question of courage and directness and tenacity, and Mark knew that he was good at all those things. No more bad news could come. Everything had happened that was going to happen. The nerve and spirit came pumping into him.

He said simply, 'That's OK.'

Hawker took a pen, and wrote for a moment on his pad, and then pushed the note across to Mark.

'That's what to do now, and who to go to. Who knows what will happen over the next few years? I believe there really is a prospect of a research breakthrough now, and none of us knows what drugs may come through their current testing programmes. You'll be told how to look after yourself, and it's very important that you do so. Good diet, good exercise, good mental attitude; if you can keep your underlying health and morale up to shape, we can all hope for happier news.'

He got up from his desk, went to the window, and looked out at the little gardens behind the surgery. After a moment or so he turned. He shrugged, and gave again his half-smile, half-grimace.

'Have courage, Mark. Go to these people and do what they say. Keep in touch with me here too. Good luck.'

They shook hands, Mark walked out through the door, and smiled and waved his hand at the receptionist. He walked into Battersea Park, and across it to the banks of the river. There he sat on the wall and stared down into the grey mud of low tide, studded with some dark stones and the occasional plastic bottle, a child's spade brightly fluorescent against the mud it sat on.

So – Christopher and me to die together, or pretty much so, he thought. Christopher probably within the year. And me? How much longer than that? Four years perhaps, or six if things go really well?

For the first time in months, perhaps longer, he suddenly found himself praying and, as he always had done, in a mixture of recited passages from the Book of Common Prayer, and very direct, very personal, very colloquial statements, rather as if he was talking to a colleague at Bush House. Initially, and without thinking very much about it, he said his favourite collect from the time of his rather devout adolescence, before his faith gradually evaporated.

'Almighty God, Who has prepared for those that love Thee such good things as pass Man's understanding, pour into our hearts such love towards Thee, that we, loving Thee above all things, may obtain Thy promises, which exceed all that we can desire.'

How odd it is, thought Mark, the memories that marvellous prayer brings back. It has been a sort of talisman for me all my life. Whenever something bad is happening to me, I find it comes straight into my mind. 'Such good things as pass Man's understanding.' Love, that's what it is. Human love. My love for Christopher. And all that goes with that. Peace, honour, truth, kindliness, trust, courage, forbearance, loyalty. All those wonderful things. Christopher has been a gift to me beyond anything I could have imagined. HIV and AIDS and everything that will follow is incidental to that. In all the years I've known him, I've never given love to anyone but him. I can't help all the sex. I've wanted that, and I've had it. And not always as wisely as I might have done, in the heat of the moment. But I never betrayed him. And what he's brought me does pass all understanding.

It's not so strange, perhaps, if faith comes back to me now. It was so real to me once. That prayer I made up as a boy, and used to say every day. Can I still remember it? The prayer of submission, that I suddenly realised was the key to everything. 'God, I give back to You everything I most wish to keep. Take from me anything You want. Leave me with everything or nothing. Lead me where You will. Amen.' Tough to say, that. It can be an almost impossible act of will. But one never knows peace until one has done it.

He got up from the wall, and walked along the river towards Chelsea Bridge. He thought of Christopher, and whether he should tell him what had happened. But why tell him anything at all? What was the point of hurting him? Why not just leave him alone? Why not let him have the last few months of his life simply absorbing affection from Norah and me? There are times when to be over-pedantic about the need to tell the truth simply causes pain.

Chris has always shied away from asking too many questions in the past about my sex life. He must have known that I was active. And yet he never asked me about it. Despite the fact that in every other area we have always been so open with each other about everything. Why tell him? There is nothing that he can do. Why cause him anxiety? He is so prone to worry and stress. He mustn't be made to worry about anything now. Particularly about things he can do nothing about.

Mark's mind went back to Hunstanton, and the dairy farm, and Christopher's awkward, intense, innocent, unstoppable declaration of love. He remembered his own initial sense of surprise and confusion, and how he had put his arms around him not so much as a gesture of attachment – for no thought of a relationship of this sort with Christopher had ever crossed Mark's mind – but one of simple affection and gratitude. And the accelerating pulse of excitement as the love affair sprang into life over the next few days and weeks, followed by Christopher's resignation and grotesquely immediate departure from his home of so many years in the

Hunstanton community. Then Mark's escape to France, and the solitary weeks of backpacking in the Auvergne, and the debate with himself over Christopher, and the determination to think the issue through with calmness and balance, and the decision – to be made once and for all, and with no latitude for second thoughts – to go with Christopher, and to make it work, and to hope that all the difficulties could be resolved. Though the difficulties had certainly appeared to be daunting, to say the least.

He had forced himself to concentrate on the huge difference in their ages, and not to pay lip service to the thought but to debate it thoroughly within himself, grasping the reality of Christopher's inevitable decline as the years progressed, and what this would mean in terms of Mark's responsibilities to him. He made himself consider the sexual aspects of the relationship as well, and particularly the recognition that his own sexual needs were not going to be satisfied within the relationship in the way that they would be in a more conventional partnership with someone of his own age. And it must be said that this problem did seem insuperable, and there was a moment when he was tempted to make a run for it before it was too late. He might well have done so, but there had been a message for him to ring Christopher when he got to his hotel, and when he had got through, and heard his voice, and sensed the urgency of the love being addressed to him, he knew that his mind was made up. And, having made his decision, he knew he would stick to it.

And, as the years rolled on, nothing had changed Mark's mind, though there had certainly been frequent periods of doubt. And as he walked through Battersea Park that morning, his hands thrust deep into his pockets, his eyes fixed on the path in front of him, it occurred to him that if he had lived a more conventional life, with a partner from his own peer group, the chances were that he would have escaped the HIV and AIDS threat altogether. Mark was driven to sexual pluralism by the celibacy of his relationship with Christopher, and it was a pluralism that ill suited the instinctive monogamy and fidelity of his personality. Too much guilt, he thought. Too many secrets. Too much sidling in through one's own front door, feeling like a bastard. It's painful when it's like that. But that's all in the past now.

Mark suddenly felt purposeful and confident. He hailed a taxi to Bush House, and as he settled in the back he told himself that one very practical step he could take for Christopher would be to help him reconcile some of the relationships that were ruined by The Fall. He knew some of the people, but certainly not all. Christopher's sense of privacy was such that it was very difficult to drag out from him an account of where the main wounds lay. But he would try harder now, pin Christopher down to some sort of frankness about which relationships mattered to him and which most needed repair, and then help him close those circles that could be closed.

And then there was the question of himself. He recognised that his current state of mind was an almost euphoric reaction to shock. That would wear off, and it would be replaced in all probability by fear, resentment, self-pity, anger and all sorts of other negative emotions. Those would be difficult to deal with. He wondered also if there was an obligation on him to tell the BBC that he was HIV positive. He would think about that too over the next few days, and might or might not risk a private word with Angie. It would feel good to share this with someone.

And then suddenly he remembered that he would have to face up to telling his parents.

'Oh *God* . . .' he said, speaking so loudly as he put his hands to his face that the taxi driver looked up into the mirror and asked him if he was all right. Mark grinned hastily, and made some little remark with a cheerful air. And then, this time silently, 'Oh God, not that.' His mother's face, with that pouting, over-painted mouth, in the cold, prissy Bedminster house, all repression and gentility and disappointment. And his father, a lifetime in that depressing insurance company, such a nice man, so sad that he had lost Mark, so eager to accept and understand but not knowing how to start. 'Oh God,' he mouthed for a third time, as the taxi turned up the Aldwych and stopped at the Bush House entrance.

Chapter Eight

There were cries from them both as they reached their orgasms, and then they collapsed slowly down on the bed and lay breathing heavily, their faces flushed. Sam opened his eyes and smiled at her. 'Thanks, Hazel . . .' he muttered, patted her vaguely on the back, and immediately went to sleep.

Hazel watched him with her head propped up, her right hand under her chin, occasionally running the fingers of her other hand very softly through his hair. One day, maybe, she thought, one day. But I've thought that for so long. Perhaps I don't really believe it any more. It no longer hurts quite as much as it did. He's mine now anyway. I love him so completely. He can't separate himself from that now. It's been going on for so many years; it's part of us both.

She turned her mind back to the early months of the relationship, and Sam's furious carnality, which she knew had softened quite quickly into a cosy warmth and a benign, perhaps sentimental attachment. When his passion was at its height she had been no more than nicely submissive to it, but her mild initial sexual excitement grew into affection, and affection grew into love, and then, sometime around the age of thirty-five, she found love had grown for her into a dependence and a devotion that completely dominated every aspect of her life.

From that time on she thought of very little but Sam. Her flat in Markham Square had small mementoes of him in every room, the fruits of over two decades of birthdays and Christmases. Photographs of him were tucked away in drawers in her bedroom, so that her callers – apart from her mother, almost invariably members of the numerous local clubs and societies of which she was an official or a member – would not intrude into her private emotional life.

The purpose and heart of her life was Sam, and she longed to marry him. At the beginning Sam had said that he did not want to marry again while his daughter Annabel was still a child. Then it was because Lilley & Chase was threatening to go into receivership, and this in itself was certainly true, as the firm had always been more frequently teetering on the edge of insolvency than the reverse. Then it was because Hazel's father was dying, and when he had died it was too soon to disturb her mother's mourning. Then her mother was seriously ill herself, and the moment had passed again.

It had all gone on for so long, and Hazel knew now that Sam had no present intention of marrying her, and that if she pressed it any further she would most likely lose him altogether. So she let it rest, at least until something else occurred which might change the situation, and accepted the positive elements of life as it was. She knew that he was fond of her, in his own fashion perhaps extremely fond, and she knew that she brought him a physical contentment in the mutual warmth and familiarity of their relationship.

She ran her hand gently over the back of his head, smoothing the hair as a mother would her child's. It's not absurd, she thought. It works in its own way. I'm in love with him, I can see him all the time, I don't have to share him physically with anyone, he's faithful to me, I'm quite certain that he's faithful to me, and he treats me with respect and gentleness and kindness and all the things that sound so dispassionate and unimportant in a love affair but which actually matter so much.

Sam stirred and opened his eyes and they looked at each other. Hazel bent over him and, stroking the side of his head, she kissed him softly on the mouth. 'I love you, my darling Sam. I'm always so frightened of losing you. Please don't leave me. Please don't let me lose you. I can't lose you now.' She kissed him again, and he stroked her too, his hands softly running down her naked back, caressing her and soothing her.

'I'm not going anywhere, Hazel. I never have been going anywhere. Couldn't lose you. You're much too precious for that.'

The half-truths of love, Hazel thought. He's right. I'm sure he's not going anywhere. I make him say it, because it's so wonderful to have it confirmed like that. But I'm not precious to him really. I'm important to him. But there are boundaries; areas in which I simply cannot tread. Hilary hangs over us like a dark shadow. A real relationship would be one in which we could discuss her. But we can't. The few times I've tried it's been a complete disaster. Sam just closes up on me. As he does if I try to talk about Annabel. Unless it's at the most banal level. If only we could get through that barrier. The relationship will never develop unless we do. It's so difficult to accept that it has to stay where it is. We could be real lovers. We very nearly are. How I wish we could break through that last gate. I do so wish that Sam would let me.

They lay there for a time with their bodies touching, the soft, warm bed so familiar and so pleasing to Sam, the intimate odours of Hazel's body on the sheets and on his hands, her arms around him, her fingers running gently through his hair. Hazel then spoke to him softly, still caressing him as she did so.

'Sam – try to tell me about Hilary.' Though she was nervous of his reaction, she knew she had to try to get him to talk, to reveal his emotions, even after all these years.

There was a slight tautening of Sam's body as he replied, 'I've told you everything, Hazel. We haven't spoken to each other about anything of consequence for years. She's married to a very pleasant husband. She's a good biochemist, as far as I know. She's got a very nice house down in Wiltshire. She's a solid mother. Nothing much else to say.'

He shrugged and smiled at Hazel, but the gentleness of the mood had passed.

'Please, Sam,' she persevered. 'It really would help me so much.'

And that's just the problem, Sam thought. The truth is that I don't mind if you are helped or not. I really don't care either way. Thank God I don't have to admit that. But it's true.

'OK, Hazel,' he said quietly. 'You know what happened. Hilary had an affair with someone. I wasn't all that nice about it. It hurt like hell at the time. I'm sure I hurt her like hell at the time as well. But – as I say – it was all a very long time ago.'

'I know all that, Sam. I wasn't asking the question you've

answered. I wanted to know much more than that. I wanted you to tell me why she had the affair, and why you weren't nice about it, and why you decided to leave her. Those things.'

Sam wondered how to reply. He had no desire whatsoever to talk about this, and he had to control how he displayed an immediate reaction of irritation with Hazel for her persistence. She continued to stroke him, and that too had become unwelcome and oddly intrusive. He forced a smile into his eyes, which enabled him to look at her without having to say anything.

'Please tell me, Sam. Also I want to know how you could cope with being split up from Annabel. You're such a natural father; it must have felt so difficult having your child brought up by another man. Tell me about that. Surely you must have been very jealous of him?'

She had asked the question in order to try to force a response. Sam was smiling gently at her and was now stroking her arm, but he was saying nothing, and there was a lack of warmth and spontaneity in his gestures that Hazel could sense. As had always happened on similar occasions, she found herself talking yet more, unnerved and flustered by Sam's silence. She knew it would be better to stop, but she was unable to make herself do so.

'And you say that Hilary has been a good mother? Do they get on well together? And does she still love you?'

God, that was a mistake, she thought. Asking if she still loved him. Why did I do that? I could see his eyes flinch the moment I said it.

'Lots of questions, Hazel.'

Again the smile, but only in the eyes, and this time Hazel was able to force herself to desist. Sam looked away from her, and out through the windows to the view he so loved, with the early summer breeze playing in the leaves of the plane trees. She was right, of course. He had never allowed himself to open up to her with the level of respect and equality and openness that he should have done. Whenever she asked for that sort of familiarity, he could feel himself tightening up inside. He was not proud of the fact, but it was true. Hilary and Annabel were locked away from her. Most other things he could share with her. But Hilary and Annabel were his alone. And that was why, he reflected, it would never be possible for them to marry. It wouldn't work. You couldn't have a marriage with that degree of failure of access and communication. It was unthinkable.

And she is such a good and generous woman. I would miss her so much if I lost her. I know I should have made her break with me years ago. She should have found someone else and married them and had children and had a normal life. She would have made such a good mother. I should have had the guts to break with her. I've never lied to her, but I've never told her the whole truth either. I've used her. I've used her because she has allowed me to. And now I've burnt up the two most important decades of her life. Jesus Christ.

Hazel had turned away from him now, and lay on her back gazing up at the ceiling. That wasn't a success, she thought. I was so stupid to witter on like that. But I can't accept for all time that I can never talk to him about these things. He must help me. How can I get him to just let his guard down a little? We can't go on like this for ever.

'I'm sorry, Hazel. Don't despair of me. I'm truly sorry.'

How strange it all is, he thought. I can lie here with her and have a peace of spirit and a calmness and a contentment that is quite wonderful. We have been lovers for over twenty years, and we caress each other and stroke each other and care for each other as if we were the closest couple in the world. In a way we are. But the truth is that I have only released to her one small part of what I am. Only one, small, limited, unimportant part. The major part of me lies in memories of Hilary and me as we were. And Annabel. And my childhood. Whereas Hazel has offered to me every part of her that I was prepared to accept. And I wouldn't even take much of that.

They lay together for some time longer, still stroking each other, but some degree of naturalness had now returned, and they were warm and gentle again in their comfortable physical world. They hugged each other as he left, and as Sam walked back through the Chelsea streets to the office he found himself singing a Gershwin song.

103

'Won't you tell him please to put on some speed, follow my lead, oh how I need, some one who'll watch over me. I'm a little lamb that's lost in the wood, I know I should, always be good, to one who'll watch over me . . .'

Christ, what crap! thought Sam. Asinine Gertrude Lawrence trilling away on Broadway, with her phoney upper-class English accent, and naughty little suppers at Sardi's. None of that is Hazel. Thank God. There's so much more to her than that. She's her own woman. She's got guts and she's got constancy and she's got determination. She took the situation for what it was and made something good out of it. 'Bless you, Hazel,' he muttered to himself as he turned into the Lilley & Chase courtyard. 'Bless you for accepting that I can only give you what I can give you. It's not enough for you, and it shouldn't be enough for you, but you've come to terms with it. You're a tough lady.'

In the entrance hallway there were boxes piled on the floor, mostly of advance copies going out to the major booksellers and literary editors. Sam picked over a box or two.

'Bloody awful jacket,' he said to no one in particular. 'Looks like an effing cornflakes packet.' And nodding at the switchboard lady as he went, he passed the little antiquated lift, and ran up the stairs to his office two by two.

Chapter Nine

Annabel had been dreading this particular Wednesday for fully three weeks, since the date had been set for their presentation to the McTavish whisky people.

Monk Grolsch Parsons was generally not enthusiastic about making speculative presentations for new accounts. But on this occasion Peter Grolsch had been asked if the agency would be prepared to present against just two others, both big American-owned agencies of high reputation but, in Peter's mind, of more arrogance than intelligence. Somehow he rather fancied the odds, and certainly McTavish would be a major feather in the MGP cap, with billings not far short of the Rothley grocery chain, which for some time had been consistently the largest account the agency represented.

Preparing for these competitive presentations was a time-consuming and expensive business. Consumer research had to be designed and commissioned, a team would have to do some desk research into the industry and the position of the brand in it, there would be telephone calls around the brand's competitors to get a feel of how it was regarded, and some preliminary ideas for press or television advertising would be prepared, sometimes to quite a finished state. All in all a lot of work was done for no very certain result.

But Peter, Matthew and Julian all felt that McTavish would be fun to go for. Julian had a vision of a campaign featuring a camp Scotsman, kilted, and wearing a sporran of clearly, but if necessary deniably, phallic angle and proportions. Once this vision had come to him, he was completely determined that they should win the account. He had had an intense dislike of the Scots and Scotland ever since some childhood holidays alone with his Inverness great-grandparents, a couple of great age, rectitude and moral fervour, who would strap him on the open palm if he was late for meals, or inattentive at prayers. The McTavish campaign he had in mind – and he knew just the male model he wanted to use, a middle-aged man from Shepherd's Bush of quite astonishing femininity – was his idea of a perfect revenge on the whole lot of them.

Peter was dispatched to be briefed by the McTavish people, and came back with gruesome stories of puce-faced figures, a bottle of whisky before each of them, thick with tweed, and speaking in unintelligible accents.

Julian was greatly cheered, considering this to be the perfect audience for his campaign proposals. He personally supervised the shooting of the photo sessions, taking particular care over the shape and positioning of the sporran. The copy was written, again personally by Julian, hinting at the astonishing restorative effects on a Highlander's virility that were secured by consumption of McTavish, 'Scotland's Ain Wee Drammie'.

Julian had the time of his life in the preparation of the proposed campaign. The male model was recalled, and the photo sessions done all over again, Julian having decided that none of the pictures from the first session showed quite the angle of sporran that he wanted. The pictures were cropped, the copy pasted up, the consumer research doctored to show the conclusions required, industry research likewise, and the presentation team fixed: Julian because no one could keep him out of it, Peter for good looks, worldliness and sincerity, Annabel to present the research and provide the feminine interest, and a very young account trainee called Philip as an alternative to Annabel should any of the tweeded ones prove to be gay. Peter had been asked about this, as the only member of the party who had had a sight of the enemy, and he confirmed that he had wondered about the finance director.

They left the agency bundled together in a taxi, Julian in his excitement irritating everybody by talking only in his highly inaccurate version of an Inverness accent. On arrival at the McTavish offices near Grosvenor Square they were shown upstairs to a very grand, panelled boardroom, where they were left on their own for a period of ten minutes or so. Then the door opened, and the McTavish party filed in. It was clear immediately that Peter had if anything rather underplayed his description. One glance at the finance director confirmed Peter's diagnosis, and Julian promptly sat Philip immediately opposite him. This was Philip's third week at the agency, having only recently come down from Exeter College, Oxford, where he had done a dissertation on Moral Philosophy. Julian had been mercilessly frank with him as to why he was part of the team for the presentation, and Philip was beginning to wonder if the advertising profession was quite the right field for him.

The McTavish chairman, a ferocious-looking man with ginger hair and a cropped ginger moustache, had shown immediate interest in Annabel's thighs, so, an old MGP hand, she positioned herself carefully to ensure they remained in sight. The marketing director, an irate-looking Glaswegian with rimless glasses, was unsmiling and abrupt, and Peter and Julian both separately decided to treat him as the principal point of enmity, probably under a bribe from one of the competing agencies. The McTavish team was completed by the sales director, sixtyish, purple, and apparently already drunk.

Annabel presented the consumer research, demonstrated the importance of a marginal redesign of the bottle shape to make it a little taller and more cylindrical, and suggested the introduction of a small knob around the cap, speaking of the ready subliminal association of the McTavish brand with all that is fertile in Scotland's green land. She emphasised the need to play this association back to the public in terms of an advertising style that celebrated the concept of nature's self-renewing and procreative functions, and showed research that poured scorn on the advertising campaign that the previous McTavish advertising agency had run (one advertisement featuring a Scottish terrier on the end of a lead, the other a kitten with a tartan ribbon around its neck).

At that point she handed over to Julian who, in a wild caricature of his Inverness great-grandfather, read out the copy, and at the closing line, 'Scotland's Ain Wee Drammie', produced with a flourish large blow-up boards depicting the Shepherd's Bush male model looking coy in his kilt, sporran primly between his legs at a half-erect angle, and his attempts at portraying a bluff Highlander giving his face a mincing sneer.

'Ain Wee Drammie indeed, Chairman!' cried Julian triumphantly. 'There's fertility for you! There's the spirit of Scotland! There's some Highland strength for all to see!'

The chairman rubbed the ginger moustache with a thick nicotine-stained finger, and said, after a pause, 'Aye. There is a certain male vigour about it.' He looked broodingly at Annabel's bosom. 'We cannae risk upsetting the ladies though, can we?'

Annabel jumped in quickly. 'Oh, Chairman, the campaign tested very well with women, I can assure you, particularly in the forty- to sixty-five-year-old groups, of medium to high income, tertiary education, and a semi-sedentary lifestyle. You need have no fear there. We tested for brand assurance, product compatibility, cross-merchandising parallels and psychometric interrelatives. We got very high readings – particularly for this one,' and she pointed to the final advertisement, Julian's *pièce de résistance*, with the Shepherd's Bush model's body in profile, the sporran at a saucy forty-five degrees, and the 'Scotland's Ain Wee Drammie' copy-line arranged in a curve around it.

The chairman looked across at the marketing director. 'What's your view, Hamish?'

Peter jumped in before the answer came, sensing that a negative word at this point might risk everything. 'May I call you Hamish? May I cut in first? Hamish, we have to position this, don't you think, as an opportunity for us to take the high ground, so to speak. Don't you agree? It's the moment to put our tent peg in the ground, to pin our colours to the mast, to say this is where we are, this is where we stand, we're number one, you come and get us, we're part of Scotland, we *are* Scotland, we're strength, we're manhood, we're vigour, we're *life*, Hamish. We're not a snivelling little dog' – a backhanded wave at one advertisement – 'nor a mincing little cat' – now at the other – 'we're men, Hamish. *Men*. That's what McTavish is. McTavish is the spirit of the Highlands. McTavish is the Calcutta Cup. McTavish is *Scotland*, Hamish. We should be proud.'

There was complete silence around the table. Christ, Peter, thought Julian. Not even I . . .

The finance director gave an almost imperceptible wink at Philip, and polished his glasses.

'Let's have a drink,' said the sales director, and bottles of McTavish appeared from the cupboard, and glasses too.

'Cheerio, Chairman,' said the sales director and raised his glass.

The McTavish team instantaneously downed their first glasses and poured their seconds, and the MGP people sipped delicately and with varying degrees of nausea at the taste of neat whisky at eleven o'clock in the morning.

'Most impressive, Mr Parsons. Thank you, Mr Grolsch. You're a clever lassie.' The chairman patted Annabel on the knee with a plump, freckly hand. He ignored Philip altogether.

'I'll be in touch,' he said, leaving a certain ambiguity as to whether it would be with Annabel for a dinner date, or the agency to tell them if they had succeeded in winning the account.

There were handshakes all round, and the finance director saw them out, pressing meaningfully against Philip as they all stood in the lift.

'A triumph,' cried Julian, when they were safely in the cab. 'God, how funny. What a tit you are, Peter. I haven't heard you in such form since the Kittikake days. Well done, Annabel. Masterly on the research. All well, Philip? Catch a sense of the underlying gravities of this great industry you are joining? The firm, manly handshake that seals the unspoken bond of trust and honour between agency and client?'

Annabel grinned across at Philip. 'Just remember that you're really going to be a high court judge, or a probation officer or a civil engineer or something, Philip, and that this is just an irresponsible interlude. I always do. I'm going to be a schoolteacher. I always have to say it twice, so that I really believe it. I'm going to be a schoolteacher. An underpaid, over-worked teacher. To impoverished children with learning difficulties. In Brixton. Soon.'

Peter said to her, 'We're perverters of the innocent in our own way, Annabel, but at least we're not pompous about it. You are a bit. You stay with us because you enjoy it. There's nothing wrong with that. Enjoy it.'

He smiled at her with a warmth that was clearly designed to take the edge off what he had said. As the taxi drew away, he and Julian said something to each other, both laughed, and they were still laughing as they swung through into the MGP entrance lobby.

Later that morning, Julian collected Matthew from his office, and they all three went off by taxi to the Bibendum restaurant above the Michelin building in the Brompton Road, which was where they were usually to be found lunching on a day of particular triumph. They had no reservation, and the room was almost full, but they were sat in due course at a table squeezed into a small space by the window, from where could be seen Peter Grolsch's old childhood house in the middle of Pelham Crescent, where the three of them had spent so many days together in the school holidays, the Monk family living close by in Chelsea Square.

Julian's mother had died when he was no more than seven or eight, and with his father absorbed in his career, and so often abroad, most of the happiest times of Julian's inadequate childhood were spent in this neighbourhood. And many of them in the house he was now gazing at, tucked behind the trees that shielded the elegant curving Regency crescent from the road. Peter no more than glanced across at the house before calling for the waiter and waving to an old girlfriend of his at the far end of the room, but for Julian, as always, the memories flooded back, and the gratitude too, and he drew away from the subsequent picture that came to him, of his father, now in the nursing home in Highgate, gibbering, senile, incontinent, alone, unloved and unlovable.

Matthew was speaking now, and it was a moment or two before Julian broke his thoughts away and followed what Matthew and Peter were saying.

'That approach to us from Interpublic was ludicrous, of course, but indicative of where we stand now. The question is, what we do next.'

'Why ludicrous? Our client list is strong, our productivity higher than almost any agency in London, we're extremely profitable, and our creative team wins every award going. Why ludicrous? I don't blame them for having a go. Of course we don't want to sell, but if we had wanted to, Interpublic would have got us as strong and focused as we have ever been. I'm proud of that, actually. We all three of us should be.'

Julian looked across at him. 'All that's true. And I am as proud of it as you are. I like very much the fact that we are as good as anyone in London. But we are an odd animal in some ways. We lack that sense of drive for growth and development and change that we probably need if we are to hold the agency's morale. We own the place, and we've always refused to let any of the staff get their hands on the shares. And I think that was sensible. But we've remained much the same size now for some time. And whilst that's fine for us, it's not necessarily what the people who work for us want to see.'

Peter said, 'I don't want growth for growth's sake, and neither of you do, of course. But there's too much cash in the company, and the staff know that, and it's not an entirely healthy thing.'

He gazed for a moment about the room, and then he noticed Richard Chase sitting with his back to him at a table at the far side, and he drew the other two's attention to him. All three looked across to try to catch his eye, but Richard remained facing away from them, so Peter got to his feet, and went across to put his hand on his shoulder. Richard looked up at him with a startled expression, and put his hand down to shield a piece of paper on which he and his lunch companion had scribbled some numbers, which he then pushed into his jacket pocket. Recovering himself, he got to his feet, smiled broadly, there was some laughing remark, Peter shook hands with them both, and then came back to join the others at their table.

'We've got too much cash, and Lilley & Chase have got too little. Or so I assume. They usually have. Good publishers no doubt. But broke. And Richard and Sam never seem to be quite going in the same direction. Because of Richard probably. A little economical in his loyalties. A little short of the scrubby little human affections and attachments that keep the rest of us going.'

Peter waved his arm, the bottle of champagne went over the tablecloth and on to Matthew's trousers, and there was a bellow of laughter from their table as waiters rushed over with napkins and mopped and fussed over them. In all the activity, they missed the hand that Richard raised to them as he left the restaurant.

Chapter Ten

Hilary was clattering around the Aga and the dishwasher, stacking glasses, piling plates, and mildly cursing the dogs. Annabel was sitting at the big beech kitchen table with its comfortable bright cushioned armchairs, the bottle of wine on the table, a glass in front of her, still a third full. One of the dogs wandered over wagging its tail, and Annabel squeezed its ears.

'I have a feeling I should be helping. I always feel like an adolescent when I'm down here. Leaving damp towels on the bathroom floor, and not helping to clear up unless I'm made to. I'm actually rather grown up when I'm away from you, would you believe? I don't know what it is about you that makes me regress. What is it, do you think?'

'Oh, I expect I'm too dominant or something. Jack says I order everybody around too much, including him, and that he knows he should feel emasculated by it, but is too passive to make the effort.'

Annabel laughed. 'I'm so glad he looks so fit and well again, after that heart attack. That must have been an awful time for you. I was very worried about him.'

'Oh, he's much better now, I think,' said Hilary. 'He's back in the office full time, or very nearly. Much the best thing for him. Don't you think he's the absolute stereotype of the country solicitor? He'd have been hopeless at anything else. All those wills, and disputes over garden boundaries and planning permissions and things. And little secrets with the widows. I can't really see Jack out in the real world, can you?'

Why do you do that? thought Annabel. Why do you always belittle everyone? Not much, not hysterically, but you just tug away at us all, knocking a little bit of gilt off here, a gleam of hope there.

'Go on, Mummy. You've been blissful with Jack. And he's been really good to you. And you admire him. Go on. Say it.'

'Blissful? I'm not sure I really believe in bliss in that sense. Jack has been good to me. Of course he has. And I've been good to Jack. I couldn't cope when your father left us. I needed someone with me to help bring you up, and it's worked out very well on the whole.'

Annabel put her face in her hands. Sam did leave, of course he left, of course it was his fault, of course it was everything, of course he should have forgiven Hilary, he should have understood it was just a silly aberration with that man, that marriage is more important than that; and didn't I bring you up wonderfully after that, and it was all very well for Sam, wasn't it, dipping in and out of your life, always there with the expensive present and the nice holiday, and the flowers on your birthday, and the trips to the theatre, and it was Jack and I who had all the nitty-gritty, wasn't it? Getting you back to school, and collecting you again, and putting up with a lot of rudeness from you, and that stage when you were so naughty all the time, and the shoplifting episode and the rest of it. That's what being a mother is. Being there. Being the rock. Not the lovely generous Daddy. The rock. That's what being a responsible woman is. It's all too easy to abandon everybody as soon as things go wrong. Sam abandoned us. Sam left us. I stayed because it was my duty to stay. Women stay. Men leave. Annabel looked up at Hilary, mopping down the kitchen surfaces, bending over the dishwasher.

'Mummy, don't always talk of Daddy leaving us. He never left me. He's always been there for me. Of course I wish your marriage had worked. But it didn't.'

'The marriage did work. It worked very well, and it was our duty to keep it together. I knew what was the right thing to do and I wanted to stay with the marriage. I never thought of anything else. A silly mistake with somebody. What's that? Marriage is for ever. Particularly when there're children. Sam is a weak man at the bottom of it all. He's self-indulgent and emotionally immature. At the heart of everything, he lacks courage. He walked out on a wife and child. He *left* us. What else do you want me to call it?'

'There's a resonance to the term "he left us" that I don't think is fair. You know exactly what I mean, Mummy.'

'It is completely fair. Sam would be a bigger man if he could come to terms with it. I know you love him, and I'm glad that you do. I have no doubt that he loves you too. Of course he does. But I do think there's a self-indulgence in his relationship with you. He has deliberately placed the whole thing at such an emotional pitch that it camouflages his original guilt. There's an aspect of him that can't face up to what actually happened between him and me. I was stupidly and trivially unfaithful to him, he went berserk with jealousy, and then he left. I wanted him to stay, and for us to make the marriage work. He left. He lacked the courage and the maturity to stay. I'm not saying that he left carelessly, and without pain. The depth of his unhappiness at the time was obvious. He was clearly totally devastated at the prospect of losing you. And I'm sure me too. But the fact remains that he didn't *try*. He should have stayed with us, and made the marriage work. He needed to show generosity and humanity and forgiveness and guts. He couldn't and he didn't. He left.'

'Mummy – do something for me. Please try. Say something nice about Sam. Something that you mean. You were in love with him, you had me. Tell me something good about him. Go on. Try.'

She smiled across at Hilary to try to reduce the threat of her remark, and Hilary crossed the kitchen to sit with her, putting her hand for a moment on Annabel's arm.

'Oh, Annabel. Don't let's fight over this. We've done it too often over the years. He's a very attractive man, and of course I loved him. There's no doubt about that. He and I were certainly in love with each other. Very much in love. That's the simple truth. And I'm glad you and he are such friends. You're his daughter, and I'm delighted that you're as close as you are. I don't mean to take anything away from that. He was wrong to leave the marriage, and I doubt he's ever been happy since. I think he's weak, and I think he lacks courage, and I think he's got a poor sense of moral judgement. But he's a loyal man in his own rather complex way, and . . .' She got up as she heard Jack's key turn in the front door, and the sound of his umbrella being dropped into the big china stand in the hall. '. . . I tell you something else, Annabel. I don't think he's got a drop of selfishness in him. Not a drop.'

As Hilary went into the hall, Annabel remained sitting at the table. She was astonished by Hilary's final remark, and made suddenly deeply happy by it. She thought to herself: that was quite wonderful. How odd it is that here I am, a woman of twenty-eight, and I can be given such joy by a little show of admiration of my father by my mother. One statement like that, and I feel overcome. What a child I still am. How I want her to be nice about him, to say good things about him, and to acknowledge him for what he is. Actually, how I want her to love him. She can't, of course. Not only because of Jack. Just because she can't. But that remark was so important to me. I wish she had said it before. Or anything, anything like it.

'Hello, Jack,' she smiled as he came into the kitchen.

'Hello, Primrose,' he said and came over to kiss her. Always 'Primrose'. Some memory of a Cornish holiday and gathering primroses from the hedgerows.

'How was the Constipational, Jack?'

'The Constitutional Club, Primrose, if it is that to which you are so vulgarly referring, tonight elected me president again, actually for a fourth term. I would have been damned angry if they hadn't. How's Sam? Book trade dying on its feet as usual? A country of illiterates? All Mrs Thatcher's fault? Or is it Major's?'

Annabel grinned. What a very nice man you are, she thought. How fastidious you are to ensure I know that you acknowledge Sam is my father and you just a friend. Bless you, Jack.

'I'm just going for a walk, Mummy,' Annabel said and left them chatting companionably in the kitchen as she went outside.

Hilary's was a very pretty Queen Anne house of good long proportions, pink lime-washed, and set by a long, curving carriage drive, which when Annabel was a child had had an avenue of huge old elms up its full length. As she walked down the drive, she remembered the time when she was at preparatory school as an eight-year-old and had come back at half term to find Dutch elm disease beginning to ravage the garden. First the trees nearest the house went sick, and these were burned in order to stop the disease spreading. But one by one the other trees in the avenue began to lose their leaves and fall ill, until in time all were lost.

One elm had been particularly mourned by Annabel. It was the largest of them all, and stood on the bend as the carriage drive turned to sweep in front of the house. Jack had built her a tree-house in it, reached by a rope ladder which Annabel could pull up behind her if she wanted to be alone. From the tree-house she could look down between the branches to the lawn which stood in front of the house, a long rectangle bordered by stone balustrades, always meticulously mowed by Jack into regular, orderly stripes. In the summer, when the elm was fully leafed, Annabel was invisible to those sitting on the lawn below. She looked now at the spot where it had stood, and she remembered it as she would a lost childhood friend.

As she lay in bed that night, Annabel was remembering back to that early period of childhood, when Sam's departure from them was still a raw wound for her; when Jack, newly in her life and anxious to please her, had just finished building her the tree-house, and when all the elms were alive.

She learned to count by walking up the avenue, numbering the elms off as she went. She gave them all names, which were secret to her, and she invented personalities and lives for them. Dora at the end of the drive was married to Ben six trees up, whose brother was Simon, next to him, who was really a pirate. Angela was Dora's friend, and she was a princess, who had been turned into a tree by a witch's curse. She could only be released back into being a princess by Sam, under some complex set of actions which Annabel could no longer recall.

What she could remember most vividly however was sitting up in her tree-house one day when Sam came to collect her to stay in London with him for a few days. He came up the carriage drive in his car, Annabel crouching as still as she could so that he could not see her. Later, she planned to jump down and surprise him. Sam parked his car and walked over to talk to Hilary, who was weeding the border that ran along one of the yew hedges bounding the small side lawn.

Annabel heard them first exchange greetings, shyly and without warmth. Sam sat on the wall and asked where Annabel was, and

Hilary said she thought she was up in her bedroom, packing. And there was talk of something else, perhaps money, or the arrangements to return Annabel the following week, or some other matter between them. Then their voices began to rise, there were clear sounds of anger and quarrelling, and Annabel stayed crouching in the tree-house in fear now, hands held down over her ears, whimpering.

The grown-up Annabel, remembering that single incident of so many years ago, hugged her arms across her chest, and squeezed her eyes shut in a tight grimace. And despite what she had said to Sam at supper in his garden last week, she could of course remember every detail of what Hilary had told her on the day he had left.

'Daddy has decided to leave us, darling. I know it's sad. We'll both have to be very brave, won't we? Now we're a special little team of two. Mummy and Annabel. We'll be happy soon. We really will. I promise. You'll see.'

Annabel had total recall of the whole conversation, even the exact phraseology Hilary had adopted to communicate with her, barely five years old and an only child. She could remember not only every word, she could remember every sliver of the pain. Annabel did not want to be a team of two. She wanted to be a threesome. It must be because of her that Daddy had left. Why was she always so naughty at bedtime? If only she had been good, and helped more, and tidied her bedroom better, Daddy would have stayed.

And going to school the following day Hilary had telephoned in advance to warn the head teacher what had happened. Annabel had been greeted with great solemnity and heavy consideration, and given a glass of milk and a biscuit in the head teacher's study at breaktime, when really all she wanted was to be with the other children racing around the cedar tree as she always did. She didn't want to be treated with all this kindness.

And that ghastly English teacher. Miss Fellows? Bellows? God knows. All her class being sat down to write essays on their mummies and daddies, and the woman – Beddows, that was it, Miss Beddows – coming over and putting her hand on Annabel's shoulder and saying, 'You write about your mummy, Annabel. You haven't got a daddy any more, have you?'

118

Oh Christ, thought Annabel, lying in the same bedroom that she had had as a child, all those years ago. Oh Christ. Did anything ever since hurt as much as that one sentence from that one stupid woman? The numbness. Her tears had dropped down on to the paper in front of her, which she tried to hide by leaning forward and cupping her hand over her brow. And then she had said loudly, 'Yes, I have. Of course I have, Miss Beddows. He's just gone to London on business, that's all. I spoke to him this morning. He's coming back tomorrow.' And then she'd turned, smiling brightly around the class.

Annabel got out of bed, and went across to the window, sat in the window seat and looked down over the garden, now with the light of early dawn showing the balustrades around the lawn and the yew hedges beyond. Why are these early-morning memories and worries always so bloody awful, she thought. I'll feel better out of bed. Thank heavens dawn is breaking, and there's some light. She felt calmer now.

That Christmas – God, that Christmas when Sam came down to join us. That must have been the winter before Jack and Hilary met. Her excitement when Hilary told her that Sam was coming. Her running around the house, shouting with joy. Sam arriving sometime after tea on Christmas Eve. Annabel rushing into the hall, and leaping up into his arms, and hugging him, and calling to Hilary and laughing and crying both together.

Then Sam sleeping in the spare room, the stilted formality and politeness between him and Hilary, the careful little presents to each other, the joy at being all together again, and then the deadening, cold horror of Boxing Day, with Sam's car going off down the carriage drive, and Hilary saying, 'Wasn't that a lovely Christmas, Annabel? And now it's just Annabel and Mummy together again. We're both going to be really brave. Aren't we, Annabel? Really brave and sensible.'

All that stuff about bravery and pain, bravery and pain. Oh, Sam. What did you do to us all? All that damned love. All those partings, and the screaming need to hold you and to hug you, and Hilary being brave, or whatever she was doing.

Thank God Jack came along. Thank God for the normality he

brought. Thank God he stayed, even though Hilary was never particularly nice to him. It always seemed that she had a compulsion to make him feel dull. And to make him feel privileged to live in her house. Perhaps it wasn't like that. But he did help very much by the respect he showed me about Sam. Never any stuff from him about Sam 'leaving' us. Just respect. And no attempt to become my father. Just a good friend, and a strong hand, and someone to build a tree-house. The best tree-house in the village.

Annabel suddenly grinned to herself, imagining a tree-house built by Sam. Three old planks, a Jolly Roger, and a rope ladder that would collapse the first time anyone tried to climb it. Plus Sam in a rage having hit his thumb with a hammer.

Feeling much better, Annabel got up from the window seat, stretched, yawned, rolled her shoulders, touched her toes, looked at her watch, put on her dressing gown, and went down to the kitchen to make herself a cup of tea. There were snores from Jack as she passed their bedroom, and a growl and a whimper of pleasure from one of the dogs as she opened the kitchen door.

Back to London this evening, she thought. She anticipated with a sudden shot of pleasure the slightly scruffy but deeply familiar Hammersmith Grove flat that Sam had helped her to buy when she first came down from Oxford, and where she had so contentedly lived ever since. She'd recently redecorated her bedroom, and in it now were a newly upholstered armchair, duvet covers from Peter Jones, and fresh pillowcases. I've become deeply urban, and genteelly domesticated, she thought. And distinctly spinster-like. For all the Groucho Club parties and the glitz, I'm actually a frustratedly homely and maternal woman. Just right for a schoolmistress. Dear God, I must get on with that. Twelve months more at Monk Grolsch Parsons and I'm there for life. They'll put me on the board or something, and then I'll feel grateful and spoilt and used to the money, and that will be it.

She had already become an icon for women in the advertising profession. That obsequious profile in *Campaign*, and the piece in the *Guardian* – Christ, she thought, this was absolutely not what I intended when I started out with MGP. I have to teach. I never want to entertain another client at the Savoy Grill again. I want to earn a rotten salary and be poor and never be able to go out because I'm correcting third-form essays. And teach netball, run the drama club, and be very wise and understanding with muddled and unhappy adolescents. And retire at sixty, clutching my leaving present, and bound for my cottage at Littlehampton. Perhaps not quite that. Not Littlehampton anyway. But something like that.

'Resolve, resolve, resolve,' said Annabel, and she drank her tea and went upstairs to her bath. Annabel the spinster, she thought as she climbed the stairs. And then she stopped, and gazed down at the stair carpet in front of her. It's not really Littlehampton I want, or netball, or the drama club, or any of those things. It's children. My own children. And a husband. And a domesticated, secure, conventional home. That's what all this teaching stuff is really about.

Chapter Eleven

Hilary's incident of infidelity, always dismissed by her in these occasional scenes with Annabel as a trivial affair, was in a sense just that. It was true that the adultery was short-lived, as was the emotional attachment behind it. To that extent it was an indiscretion of relative insignificance. But the reality was something a little different to that. The incident did not stand alone and in isolation. It had sprung from an earlier, and in some respects a more significant connection, and for Sam much of the resonance of it all, and the pain of it all, lay in that.

Hilary had first seen Dan Galetti at a Footlights Smoking Concert. It was her first term up, and she was in awe of Cambridge, which she found to be so unlike what she was expecting. Her mother's two brothers, who had been up together at Magdalene in the nineteen-thirties, had painted for her such a different picture; all very public school, with picnics on the Backs, and Girton girls in by nine, and elegant little supper parties in one's rooms, and Varsity men in striped blazers, and little red sports cars, and running down to London for dancing at the Empress Club.

The Cambridge that Hilary discovered when she arrived at Newnham in October 1962 was to her very much more interesting than this. Surprising to her was a comparative classlessness about the place, and that she liked very much indeed. There was the Pitt Club, of course, and an array of old public school ties worn with the uniform of the time: bold check shirts, duffel coats, pipes, and green corduroy trousers. But running parallel to this, and by no means subordinated to it, was a second stream of social layering in this still predominantly male world; boys from grammar schools in tweed jackets and drip-dry shirts and sleek hair and rimless glasses, mixing perhaps mostly with each other, but self-confidently so, by no means oppressed by the residual aura of upper-middle-class England that Cambridge still exuded.

And more than this: here were boys of eighteen, decidedly the first generation of their families to go to university at all, who took one look at the place and, joyfully, ecstatically, fell in love with it. They bicycled around in their gowns, they dominated the sports teams, they sang in the college choir, they organised the rag days, they drank their beer and, with a full weight of family expectation behind them, they worked with diligence, and they obtained their degrees. Or, tragically, they broke down when that full weight of family expectation became a burden too heavy to carry.

Newnham was much like this. Hilary had been to Wycombe Abbey, but very few other girls from socially comparable schools went up to the college in her year, and she found herself in the company of an eclectic group. Rooming on her staircase were a miner's daughter from Nottingham High School, a Punjabi girl on a Commonwealth scholarship, two South London Grammar School girls – who in the early weeks clung to each other until their confidence built, and then hardly spoke to each other again – a congregational minister's daughter from Swansea, and one of the Guinness heiresses.

Hilary's family background – military, upper-middle class, socially and politically prejudiced, tight with social ritual and convention – had been for her an increasingly unwelcome legacy. Her appearance was exactly fitting to her family background, with her pleasantly waving auburn hair, and pretty face, and her country girl's healthy complexion, and her wide smile and sensibly undemonstrative clothes and bearing. Her voice, manners, her lack of stridency – all these suggested someone of straightforwardly conventional leanings. Yet the truth was that Hilary's instincts were much more in the direction of the egalitarian and the meritocratic, and Cambridge – beautiful, clever, vibrant, bustling, funny, liberal Cambridge – was to her like finding her true home for the first time.

Dan Galetti was in his last year at Jesus, and had become a famous figure in the more light-hearted and cheerfully louche undergraduate circles. The son of a bottom-of-the-bill music-hall song-and-dance man, he was one of the stars of the Footlights at a time when the Footlights was full of great stars. He was a prodigiously funny mimic, and a competent and versatile actor in whatever guise he was cast to appear. His Bottom in *A Midsummer Night's Dream* was as good as those who saw it were ever to see. His Archie Rice in *The Entertainer* was a definitive performance.

He was just sufficiently attentive to the formal academic requirements of undergraduate life to have been allowed to stay up for his third and final year, but only because his tutor made special dispensation for him. His life at Cambridge was crowded and busy, but very little of it was spent at his desk. He performed with the Footlights at private smokers and in the cabarets of college balls and London parties. He played Regency beaux for the Marlowe Society and Russian peasants for the Cambridge University Dramatic Society. He drew a weekly cartoon strip for *Varsity*. He sang in his very good tenor voice in the Jesus College choir (which he always said gave him his only available hour of the day for planning and contemplation). He was always at parties. He bedded as many women as he could.

He was by no means a socially vindictive or revengeful man, but it has to be said that the main aim of his sexual targeting was upper-middle-class girls exactly of Hilary's type, and preferably virgins. No points of inverted class prejudice were being scored thereby, no scores being paid off against the oppressors of British society, no Jimmy Porter cries of rage and pain. Dan would not have passed the time of day with Jimmy Porter if they had been marooned together alone on a desert island. It was simply that he found upper-middle-class girls, with their accents, and their delicious red woollen tights and their white thighs, quite overwhelmingly alluring.

And there was self-mockery there too, of course. Dan was delighted with the humour of his situation – prematurely balding, by no stretch of the imagination conventionally handsome, the child of impoverished working-class Italian immigrants – he was in his own way one of the most successful undergraduates of his time at Cambridge, and that to Dan was a considerable joke. He did not come to Cambridge set to conquer. It was just that, when he got there, he found it so personally congenial, and so easy to use it as a stage for all the things that he was best at, the place just seemed to fall at his feet. And, most satisfactorily of all, the women particularly. Not the barmaids and Woolworth girls he was used to at home in Holloway. Real pearl-like, English-rose, public-school-educated, county-mothered women. Rows of them, and all of them honeys. Not for Dan the joys of Cambridge in its emergent egalitarian form. To hell with the working classes.

Hilary had gone to the Footlights Smoker to accompany a friend from Wycombe Abbey, who had gone up to Girton that same term. This friend had been invited to do an audition piece in a John Osborne pastiche that Dan had scribbled off in less than ten minutes specifically to try her out, together with another young aspiring Footlights member from Caius.

Dan had spotted Hilary from the stage in the middle of the packed little audience as he was halfway though a C. S. Lewis monologue – always one of his most popular party pieces – and he was so struck by her that he suddenly curtailed it, and went over to approach her. His self-confidence was something she had never met to this degree before. It emerged not as cockiness, not brashness, but sheer, cheerful certainty of his position in life; an ugly, vastly talented, theatrical Italian, with a future that looked at that time to have apparently limitless potential, and whose success with the women of Newnham, Girton and New Hall was unmatched in his generation.

Hilary fell, of course, as they all did. She had never made love before; most eighteen-year-old Wycombe Abbey girls of that time had not. She was completely terrified, totally passive, and extremely aroused. Soon it was done, and Dan went on his way, leaving her with a parting impersonation of Harold Macmillan replacing his trousers after a moment of connubial bliss with Lady Dorothy. Funny or not, given the gravitas of the situation this was not perhaps tactful.

For Hilary was at first very proud of herself, then immediately full of remorse. She had made no efforts whatsoever to protect her virtue. This was exactly the sort of thing that her mother had warned her against. And exactly the sort of thing that she had been angry with her mother for even thinking of warning her against. She had now done – and it had taken barely five minutes – what she had spent the greater part of her late adolescence imagining. And the fact that Dan had made a charming but undeniably immediate exit had done very little to help her sense of decorum.

For the next two days Hilary spent almost all her time in her rooms, so that she should be there when Dan came round. She missed dinners in Hall, a drinks party at the Principal's Lodge, and two whole days of lectures. But he never appeared, of course, nor sent any sort of message, and the longer Hilary sat alone the more unhappy she became over what had happened.

She was angry with herself for her lack of control and her lack of dignity; all her life she had carried with her an idealistic and romantic conception of love, and the first giving of her body was something she had cherished as an act of supreme importance. And it had in the event been given for nothing. Nothing. To someone who clearly had no perception whatsoever of what he had done. Who had not even troubled to stay with her, or talk to her, or cherish her. Or be in any sort of contact with her afterwards. It was not that she blamed him for the fact that they had made love together. It had happened very quickly, and with very little of what Hilary had always imagined would be a delicate and intricate period of preparation and persuasion. But she knew that he would have stopped if she had asked him to, and she was deeply aware that she was far from having done that. What hurt her was the empty void of it all. She had been trivially and swiftly seduced, and it had meant nothing to the man who had done it. Nothing. And now her virginity had gone. And her childhood and her expectation were gone. For nothing.

On the third day she went over to Jesus, and found him in his rooms. He was friendly enough, and gave her an affectionate hug and a loud kiss on the cheek, but told her he had to work all afternoon on an essay which was already two days late, and that he would be in touch in a day or so. She had meant to say all sorts of things to him about love and responsibility and care, and had rehearsed them as she walked across from Newnham, but in the event had said nothing.

A week later he left a message at the Newnham Porter's Lodge that she should meet him that evening at a party at someone's rooms at Christ's. When she arrived there, she found a room full of people she had never before met, and Dan surrounded by a crowd of admirers. He waved her over, put his arm around her back, and continued telling his story. She laughed with the rest of them at its conclusion, although having missed its introduction she was unsure of its point, and then found Dan's arm disengaged as he turned away to greet someone else. She stayed for perhaps forty-five minutes, grew increasingly miserable, then went over to him to say that she had to leave. He made a little fuss of her, again put his arm around her back, kissed her on the cheek, and said that he would contact her soon.

The Christmas vacation came, and she heard nothing. She chose him a Christmas present with quite painful care, and sent it to his parents' Holloway home, together with an affectionate little letter. Neither the present nor the letter were acknowledged.

She was there in his rooms at Jesus on the first day of the Lent term. Indeed she had been there some hours before he arrived, finding the door unlocked and waiting with increasing tension for him to come, sitting awkwardly at his desk, picking up books and putting them down again. She had been so anxious all over the Christmas period to get back to Cambridge to see him, and talk to him, and make another attempt to establish a relationship with him, but now she was there she was taut and tense and sweating with nerves.

She was about to abandon her wait and, not without relief, escape back to Newnham. Then she heard laughter and shouting in the corridor, and there he was, kicking open the doors, clutching bags and bundles, surrounded by a gang of noisy, happy friends, very few of whom she recognised. He was clearly taken aback to see her there and, although he made an obvious effort to conceal it, she could see his irritation with her and her persistence, and she was uncomfortable and embarrassed. She had a sudden perception that she was in the wrong place, with the wrong people, wearing the wrong clothes, and saying the wrong things, and she fled as soon as she could back to the safety of her rather suburban little college, tucked away in the meadows on the far side of the town.

And so Hilary's first Cambridge love affair, if it could be described as that, faded away. Dan made no effort to contact her, and she no longer had the courage to approach him. In fact she got to the stage where she was frightened at the prospect of even seeing him, and gave Jesus Lane, and all the other places where she felt at risk, as wide a berth as possible.

He passed her on his bicycle once in King's Parade, and a second time in Trinity Street, both times waving vigorously but failing to stop. On another occasion, much against her judgement, she found herself included in a group who made up a party to see him play Algernon Moncrieffe at the Arts' Theatre. They all went backstage to congratulate him afterwards, but there were throngs of people around him, and he did no more than kiss her on the cheek, take her by the arm, and introduce her to the assistant stage manager, with whom he left her.

She knew many more people in Cambridge now, she was working hard for her summer prelims, and she had busied herself with all sorts of activities at Newnham, including playing in the college lacrosse team, which was a sport at which she had been something of a star at Wycombe Abbey. There were parties, May Balls, long intense evenings sitting on the floor in the miner's daughter's rooms, curries at the Gungha Dhin in Trinity Yard, debates at the Union, tennis matches, and punting trips to Grantchester. It was a good and happy first year, and Hilary went off to walk and backpack in Tuscany and Umbria that long vacation feeling that all was well in her world, though the memory of Dan Galetti was still painfully raw for her.

Apart from anything else, Dan had awakened in her an acute sexual curiosity. There had been other boyfriends at Cambridge that year, but in the way of those times intimate contact with them had been limited to some boisterous and inexpert groping, and Hilary took with her to Italy that summer some mildly disagreeable if not unamusing memories of fumbled clothing and beery breath.

Hilary first saw Sam at a Poetry Society party in the first week of her second year, and she thought he looked cherubic and delightful with his rumpled clothes and his unruly curly hair and his beaming, open smile. She watched him across the room as he was telling some story to a girl from Girton whom she knew slightly. As he got to the end of the story, she could see he was quite unable to finish it for his laughter, hugging his arms across his chest and bending double at the waist rather like a mime artist or a character in a comic strip, then wiping the tears from his eyes with the back of his hand in a gesture of appealing childishness and innocence.

She crossed the room and joined them. The Girton girl introduced her, and Sam shook her hand with the sort of grip that her father would have considered to be suitably and desirably manly, looking down at her with a cheerful, crinkly-eyed smile. She loved him immediately and, absurdly as these things happen, he loved her.

He arranged to come the next morning to pick her up at Newnham. They went wandering together through Cambridge, first a little shyly, and then Hilary took and held his hand, and they walked together quite dazed by that certain delicate ecstasy which this simple physical touch brings in the first moments of love. They sat on a bench in the Trinity Hall gardens, talked together for some three or four hours, kissed, first in an exploratory way, then with growing excitement, and that afternoon went to bed together in Sam's rooms at Queens'. They stayed there until two minutes to ten, Hilary leaping out and dressing with frantic speed so that she should be out and safely through the Porter's Lodge before the witching hour of ten o'clock.

The next morning they were back in bed again before eleven, that afternoon they spent hand in hand walking through the water meadows to Grantchester, and days passed in this way, before the relationship began to soften just a little and the first raw sensuality gave way to a mutual but physically calmer state of love.

For the rest of their Cambridge careers Sam and Hilary were seen by all to be a couple; forever with their arms around each other's shoulders, always together at parties, sharing the same friends, eating curries in shouting, happy groups at the Taj Mahal, bicycling side by side down Trumpington Street, or walking with linked arms along the Backs. They were famously content with each other, and the relationship was so patently happy, and her future with the lovely, crumpled, cheerful, beaming Sam so obviously bright, that Hilary was the envy of her generation at Newnham.

She became pregnant during their final Lent term, and her mother, most anxious to have the ceremony out of the way before it 'showed', or more particularly before Hilary's father noticed anything, arranged for an early July wedding at the Chewton Mendip parish church.

They had very little money of course. The legacy from Sam's parents went into the initial share capital of Lilley & Chase, and that was all Sam had. Hilary had a small amount of capital from a family trust, just sufficient for a down-payment on a little flat they took off Parsons Green. But her pregnancy was now advanced, and although ICI gave her the research trainee job that she had set her sights on, they did so only on an initial twelve-week trial basis, with the understanding that if her work was of a high enough standard they would take her on again the following summer on a full contract.

The Parsons Green flat was extremely small, but they were delighted to have it, and they loved the whole adventure of being in London together and starting on their careers. But strains appeared rather quickly. Annabel's birth that December meant that the flat became for them not so much delightfully intimate as most impossibly cramped, and Hilary, who was an anxious and responsible mother, crammed into the tiny rooms what appeared to Sam to be the complete inventory of the John Lewis baby department, to the point that he could hardly find space to put his briefcase down when he got home in the evening. Annabel had been a little premature and was consequently fretful and noisy at night. Sam was going through the first of the long line of Lilley & Chase cash crises and was worried, irritable and uncharacteristically short-tempered. Hilary thought that he was insufficiently helpful with the baby, particularly in the small hours, and annoyingly chauvinistic about taking his share of the nappy-changing and bottle-washing and the other endless little chores of parenthood.

And there was another issue of which she was a little ashamed, but nonetheless naggingly consumed by, and that was a resentment that Sam was getting on with his career – indeed appeared to think at the moment of little else – whilst she had been obliged to give up her precious research job at ICI, which had been precisely what she had hoped for when she had come down from Cambridge. And it now seemed so much less likely that she would be able to go back there again as soon as the summer, with Annabel such a poor feeder, and no one very obvious to leave her with, and her tendency to get hysterical with her indigestion all the time.

Their lack of money became a problem too. In their first weeks of marriage all that had, if anything, added to the fun; hilarious trips to the supermarket working out on scraps of paper the cheapest loo rolls in terms of cost per inch, negotiating discounts for bruised fruit with the people in the corner shop, eating at home practically nothing but pasta salad, which they calculated cost them rather under two shillings a meal, and enabled them to save enough money to buy an occasional bottle of Frascati.

But the shortage of money was becoming much more acute now that Hilary was no longer able to work. Everything to do with looking after the baby seemed so very expensive. The clothes, the cot, the pram, the baby food; it all added up to much more than either of them had expected, the overdraft was mounting, and for reasons of economy paper nappies were abandoned for cotton ones, so that when Sam came home each evening he would always find half a dozen or so drying on wooden racks in the little hallway, and buckets of dirty ones soaking in the bathroom. They quarrelled a little now as the physical discomfort of their lives grew. They talked of finding somewhere bigger to live, but there was no possibility of this being realistically within their means.

The summer came, and it was clear that Hilary was not going to be able to go back to work for a time yet. This was bad enough, but in addition she was beginning to feel overweight and unattractive and poorly dressed, and as her physical self-confidence waned, so did her general sense of contentment and well-being. She missed her friends too. She alone of all their Cambridge group had married early and had a child, and although she loved Annabel dearly, there was a part of her that resented the freedom and fun everyone else seemed to be having in their first jobs and flats in London. For them it seemed that Cambridge had never come to an end. For

Hilary, life had become uncomfortable, confined and joyless, with a husband whom she loved, but who was totally absorbed in a working life in which she had no part, and who was increasingly preoccupied and uncommunicative.

The turn of events came when ICI wrote to her a most warm and complimentary letter suggesting that she should apply for a senior research assistant post at their new facility being opened near Bath. She was not expecting contact from them, and, with her present lack of self-confidence, she was delighted that they had thought of doing so, and that they had been flattering to her about her work the previous autumn. She immediately made an appointment to see them; they were friendly and enthusiastic; they made her an offer, and she and Sam sat down that evening to talk the whole issue through and to plan what was to be done.

It was not really a very difficult decision. Hilary was desperately keen to work. She was a good biochemist, ICI were the best people in the field, and an opportunity to be in at the beginning of a new department in a new facility with a firm of international stature that was at pains to express interest in her really did seem too good to turn down. They had not been happy together crammed in with Annabel in the little Parsons Green flat, and the Bath area was particularly convenient as there were several members of Hilary's family living nearby, including her parents at Chewton Mendip. Indeed there was a family house which, apart from a housekeeper, was lying completely empty at that moment, Hilary's great-aunt, who was crippled with osteoarthritis, having been forced to move into a nursing home.

So Hilary accepted her new job, she and Annabel moved down to live in the great-aunt's rather crumbling but very pretty Queen Anne house, which she subsequently inherited and was to live in for the rest of her days, and Sam stayed in the little Parsons Green flat on his own.

It all worked well enough in its own way. Sam was working very long hours at Lilley & Chase and, guiltily perhaps, was not sorry to have some solitude in the evenings and time on his own. Hilary had her new job, and all the excitement of that, and she had the convenience of having her great-aunt's housekeeper, whom she had known since she was herself a child, to look after Annabel when she was at work.

Sam came down every Saturday and Sunday, they rang each other at least twice a day and often more, and the strain and minor quarrelling of the last six or nine months sank away into the past. It would not be right perhaps to say that they were in love in quite the same way as before, but they were happy when they were together, Annabel gave them a common bond, and both of them, rather than Sam alone, were now absorbed in their careers. The marriage felt secure and comfortable and important to them both.

And so it continued for the next four years or so. It was not ideal to have Sam almost entirely in London, and Hilary and Annabel in Wiltshire, but they coped. Occasionally Hilary would come up to London on her own, and they would have dinner at a little Italian restaurant they used to go to sometimes before Annabel was born, and spend the night together afterwards at Parsons Green before Hilary would catch the seven o'clock train back to Bath. These evenings were always happy, nostalgic affairs, and the more so if they met up with old Cambridge friends, and drank a little too much wine, and told familiar old stories, and pretended that they were all undergraduates again, and single, and that all responsibility and care and real adult life lay ahead in the future. Sam was well content with Hilary, and she perhaps with him, and if a little of the sexual passion had ebbed away, then there was the mutual security and warmth of a relationship that had grown and matured over five or six years of their young lives.

It was a great pity therefore that Dan Galetti came back into Hilary's life, and given the chaos that followed, ironic that it was all so casually done. He was appearing at the Theatre Royal in Bath, playing on alternate nights Bassanio in *The Merchant of Venice* and Biff in *Death of a Salesman*, and knowing from mutual Cambridge acquaintances that Hilary was now living in the area, and having brooded on the information as the four-week engagement at the theatre progressed, he had found her number and rung her. It was not exactly that he intended to try to start anything with her again, but he did have a strong nostalgia for Cambridge and Cambridge people, and he had amused and pleasantly erotic memories of what he regarded to be his trivial little encounter with Hilary.

He invited Hilary to come to the play one night and have a meal with him afterwards. He asked courteously after Sam, and Hilary felt sufficiently reassured by this to accept the invitation. She told herself that she would tell Sam of it when next they spoke on the telephone, but when the time came she did not. Her position, in truth, was not unlike Dan's. She certainly did not have any specific intention of allowing anything significant to occur, and she had her own nostalgia for Cambridge and Cambridge people. And certainly her own erotic memories of Dan Galetti, though she hardly regarded their encounter together as being trivial.

And so it happened all over again. Only this time, and on the succeeding times over the next two or three weeks, she was no longer either terrified or passive, though she was certainly again aroused. Her guilt was painfully acute, of course, and it manifested itself in her being gratuitously aggressive to Sam when he was down at her house for the weekends. He was confused by this, but took it to be some sort of strain arising from her job at ICI, and let it pass without too much complaint, though he did express a certain puzzled irritation.

When Dan's four-week engagement at the Theatre Royal came to an end, and he set off from Bath to join the rep. company at Leicester where he was contracted for the next six months, there was a harsh little crisis of parting between him and Hilary. She was certainly much attracted to him, perhaps even in love with him, and, surprising as it was to him, he felt much the same about her. There were muttered words at the railway station about plans for future meetings, but both knew in their hearts that the affair, which had sprung into such passionate intensity over such a brief period, was over, and for both of them that knowledge brought a certain unstated but unmistakable relief.

But the damage was done, and the die cast, and Sam and Hilary's marriage was at an end. The little affair had lasted no more than nineteen days, and became for both the protagonists within twelve months nothing much more than a vaguely persistent memory. But from it sprang consequences of such importance in so many lives. Annabel and Miss Beddows. Hazel and her bedroom in

Markham Square, her hidden mementoes and her life without husband and children. Jack, and the tree-house, and the Cornish holidays and his marriage to Hilary. And for Sam a lifetime without the girl he fell in love with that October evening at the Poetry Society party, and whose loss he could never replace.

Chapter Twelve

Hilary did as much as she could in the weeks that followed the confession of her adultery to heal the quarrel with Sam, but he would allow her nothing.

She telephoned and asked him to spend a week or so in the country with her, so that they could walk and garden and cook meals together, and sit and talk as they had not done since before Annabel was born. First he said he would, and then he rang down from London later to say that he was too busy with various problems at Lilley & Chase.

She then wrote to him at Parsons Green. It was a long, affectionate letter; apologetic, calm, and free of any attempt at excuse or self-justification. She asked for his forgiveness, and told him that the marriage was at the heart of her life, and that she loved him, and that she wanted above all else to put the whole incident behind them both. But he never replied or responded to this letter, nor to another she sent to him the following week, which said much the same thing, but struck a more desperate note to convey to him her guilt and her longing for their marriage to be unharmed, and for them to build from this an even better future for both them and Annabel. She suggested that she should try to persuade ICI to transfer her to their London Research Centre, so that they could sell the Wiltshire house and buy something in London big enough for them to have as their family home. But Sam would accept nothing and give nothing back.

They did not see each other for four weeks or so, and then he came down to Wiltshire unexpectedly on a Sunday afternoon. Annabel was out at a birthday party in the village, and Sam found Hilary in the drawing room with the Sunday papers. She flushed when he walked into the room, and got to her feet, uncertain whether to rush over to kiss him, as she would normally have done, or to stay where she was. Sam was white and drawn, and sat down immediately in an armchair without making any greeting or gesture of familiarity.

'I've come down to say that I think it would be better if we called it a day now, Hilary. It's all been blown by that Dan Galetti business. Can't get it back from there. I wish we could. Too far to go.'

'Oh, Sam.' Hilary came over and squatted on the carpet before him, holding out her hands in a familiar gesture of hers. 'That's simply not true. Of course we can get it back from there.' Dear God, let me heal him of all this, she thought. I caused such dreadful things to happen to him.

As she looked up at him, she could hardly believe it had all taken place. He looked just as he always had done, with his open, uncomplicated face and expression; so child-like, so lacking in guile or worldliness. She remembered again that first time she had seen him. The way he had crossed his arms and hugged himself when he was telling that story to Stella Richardson. That heartbreaking appearance of innocence he had. And not just an appearance. There really is innocence there. I can't let him destroy himself over this. Or me. Or Annabel. That insane jealousy. And that extraordinary dark, violent sexuality it seemed to unleash.

'Sam, my love. I was stupid. It'll never happen again. You're too important to me. I could never be so asinine as to risk our marriage again. *Please* believe me, Sam.'

'Too easy to say that. Too easy to do that sort of thing and then dismiss it as a silly little aberration. When you've finished saying that you're so sorry and you'll never do it again. Getting all sanctimonious about the family. Marriage vows and all that. Like a bog Catholic having a nice sin and then rushing off to old Father Paddy for confession.'

This is like some ludicrous play, thought Hilary. This doesn't feel or sound like Sam at all. But then neither did that extraordinary scene in our bedroom. Shouting at me, abusing me, wrenching at my clothes. We have both behaved so completely out of character. Or rather so completely out of the character that we have always presented to the other person. If there is irrational self-destruction in Sam, then it's always been there, and I've accidentally released it. And that odd, dark voyeurism too. If there is sexual irresponsibility in me, then I certainly produced it when Dan appeared. Actually, without a second thought. Sam is right about that. What I'm asking for is for everything to be hidden away again. And I don't care how hypocritical that is. I want Sam back as he was. And I want to be back myself where I was. And I want us married.

'It's done, Hilary. You did it. It's a big adult world. You did what you wanted to do. You thought about it and you did it. This is the result. Face up to it.'

Hilary got up from her squatting position in front of Sam, and went back to her chair. She sat on the edge of the seat, leaning forward with her arms crossed in front of her chest.

'For heaven's sake, stop being so pompous, Sam. You're a bigger man than that. Stop being so stupidly lacking in charity and compassion and forgiveness and everything else. Grow up, Sam. For God's sake – grow up. I'm not a little bog Catholic, as you put it. I know perfectly well I behaved as badly as I could have done. I have no idea how I could have done what I did.'

And I don't know how you could have done what you did either, she thought. But you did it, and I still want you. It's not difficult to put marriages together again in these sorts of circumstances. We got on so well before it happened. Our marriage was never in trouble. People staying together when everything has died is a desecration of life. But we weren't like that. We both love Annabel. We're both bright people, and we like much the same things. We still make love to each other. We don't quarrel really. We share lots of friends. That's one of the most important things of all. So many people would be astounded if we broke up. We shouldn't break up. I made a shameful mistake. Sam reacted in a cruel and evil way. It's over. It's happened. Now we should just both forget it, and make friends again, and make our marriage again, and just get on with it.

'Sam – please, please. For God's sake, let's try. This is the most absurd nonsense. Let's just try.'

139

'I told you that I wish we could get it all back. But we can't. You might be able to put the whole thing behind you. I just can't. The whole thing was so deliberate. He arrives here one week and you are in bed with him the next. How could you just throw it away? Why couldn't you have the guts to tell him to leave you alone? Or perhaps that's the wrong question. Why the hell couldn't you leave him alone? The whole world knows he is an irresponsible shit. He'll spend his life like that. He'll never take responsibility for anyone or anything. He'll spend his life pissing around with other people's wives. I'd like to say that you're too good for him. Except to find myself sitting here telling my wife that she is too good for her new boyfriend is too grotesque a conversation even for me.'

Hilary looked across at him. There is a real insanity about this, she thought. He has a determination to break with me that has a sort of crazed quality about it. Every time I give him the opening to drop his guard, he rejects it. He is trying to maintain the pressure all the time, but it's artificial. What is he doing? This is just pure self-destruction. He is in love with me. I've never had the slightest doubt about that. He has a total devotion for Annabel. If he leaves home it will be an irrational, perverse act of cruelty upon himself. More than cruelty. Destruction. Terminal destruction.

'Sam. Sam. It's not so important. It's really not so important.'

Sam's face flushed an angry red, and he leaned back in his chair, his hands gripping the two arms. 'What do you mean, it's not important? You let him fuck you. You wanted him to fuck you. You probably asked him to fuck you.'

She shouted at him now, and tears were running down her face. 'For heaven's sake, Sam. Stop all that. That's just filth. Stop it. Stop insulting me like that. Stop talking like that. I want my marriage again. I want Annabel. I want clean things. I want my home. I'm asking you to help me. Help me. Help me. Stop talking filth. Just help me.'

She started to sob, uncontrollably, noisily, like a child. It was a moment or two before she could speak, and when she did it was in a soft, quiet, flat voice. 'You're my husband, Sam. You're my husband.'

Sam watched her as she sat, head bowed, arms crossed, silent

140

now, tears running down her cheeks and dropping down into her lap. He got up and knelt in front of her, and took her hands in his.

'I'm so sorry, Hils. I can't make it. I don't know why not. I just can't make it. These things happen. Some people can cope with these things. I find I can't. It would be better if I could. But I can't.'

She remained as she was, still with her head bowed. For a minute or so neither of them said more, then, very quietly, Hilary said, 'You'll have to tell Annabel. Be gentle with her. Tell her the best you can. She's at the Harrisons. Go now.'

Sam got to his feet, went to the door, turned and they looked at each other.

'Other people might have coped, Hils. I can't.'

Sam stood for some moments looking at her, but her head was now in her hands. In time she heard the front door slam, and she folded her arms across her eyes, and let the pain come.

Chapter Thirteen

Sam drove the mile or so down to the village, and for ten minutes waited in his car outside the house where Annabel was at her party. With the engine and heater switched off it soon grew cold, and Sam sat deep in the driver's seat, the collar of his overcoat turned up around his ears, his hands thrust into his trouser pockets.

The curtains of the house were undrawn, and Sam could see directly into the downstairs room where the children were running around with their balloons and jumping and dancing to music. He sat gazing through the windows, catching a glimpse every now and then of Annabel as she ran and played with the others, and then he saw her, for a moment ecstatic in her laughter, hug her arms across her chest and bend double at the waist in a mime artist's gesture that he knew was his.

Jesus Christ, he thought. How can this be happening? How can this be happening to me?

He got out of his car, and walked up the path to the front door, which opened as he approached it, and a woman he knew slightly came out with her daughter. Sam forced a smile on to his face, put his hand on the little girl's head, and made some word of greeting before going on into the house, and into the room where the remaining children were still playing and shouting to each other. Sam kept his smile in place, standing at the side of the room, his hand again in his pockets, his overcoat open and pulled back across his chest.

He watched Annabel at the other side of the room, talking and laughing with a friend from her school. Sam's heart went out to his child in a rush of love as he watched her. Such a plain little girl, and so pleased with her pink party dress that Hilary had just bought her, now running across the room to him with her arms out-stretched, and hugging him around the legs. He reached his hands down to her and smoothed and stroked her hair. I will never forget this, he thought. Never.

'Come on, Bells,' he said. 'Come on, my lovely.' Smiling stiffly now and waving to the hosts of the party, he buttoned Annabel's coat, knowing as he did so that his eyes were full of tears, then steered her out of the house and down to the car.

He started on the drive back to the house, and Annabel stood on the floor of the car behind his seat, both her arms around his neck, and chattered to him about the party, and school, and the things she had done. He stopped the car, and turned to her.

'Bells, my darling. Bells . . .'

He tried to hold himself in control, but the tears were running freely from his eyes now, and Annabel was staring at him, all the chatter gone, her face taut with anxiety. Sam made a desperate attempt to pull himself together, but waited for some moments before he risked speech, lest his voice should choke on him and frighten her the more. Then he tried again, and to his relief his voice held, and the initial words sounded calm and controlled.

'Bells. I've got something to tell you. It's not so bad. But I do have something to tell you. But first of all this. The great thing is to love each other. And I love you more than anyone in the world.'

Annabel stared at him still, her face solemn and adult, and full of concentration.

'But you love Mummy too. You love us both.'

'Yes. Of course. Of course I love Mummy. But, Bells . . . Bells, when you're grown up you make such a mess of things sometimes. And Mummy and I . . . Oh Christ.'

Sam pushed the heels of his hands up into his eyes and waited for the rawness of the pain to abate sufficiently for him to speak again. For Christ's sake hold yourself, he thought. This child's too young to watch you do this. You've got to hold yourself. She's too young. For Christ's sake hold yourself.

'Bells. Bells, my darling.' He reached for her again, smoothing her hair with his hand, rhythmically and slowly, looking at her now, his eyes trying to beam into hers all the love he could muster, calming her, calming her, his voice as soft and as controlled and as gentle as he could make it.

'Bells. I'm going to live in London all the time now. And you and Mummy are going to live down here in Mummy's house. I'll be on my own in London, but you and I will see each other as often as we can, and we'll love each other always. And everything will be all right, Bells. And you'll be safe with Mummy. And everything will be all right.'

She stared at him, and he could see that she too was crying, but there was no sound from her as the tears ran down her face. He waited for her to say something in response, but no words at first came. Then:

'What do you mean? What do you mean?'

For a moment Sam was tempted to tell a half truth, a sop, a lie, anything to avoid having to hurt this child any further. But then she said:

'Are you going to be divorced? Like Emma's parents?'

He tried to put an expression of gentleness and reassurance into his eyes as they looked at each other, seeing in her a depth of pain that he knew she was too young to bear.

'Yes. Yes. But don't worry, Bells. Don't worry,' and as he said this he continued all the while in the stroking of her hair. 'Everybody loves you. Mummy and I love you so much. Everything will be all right.'

They remained looking at each other for some moments, then he switched the car engine on again, and, so slowly that he barely overtook a pedestrian, drove back the few hundred yards to the long drive of Hilary's house. As he turned the car through the gate, he reached back across his chest with his right hand again and held Annabel's hand in his. Then they were there, and he drew the car up at the front entrance porch, turned around in his seat, and looked at her, forcing back for her into his eyes and mouth a smile of reassurance and possession.

He reached to her to wipe the tears from her face, and as he did so she remained staring at him, her chin puckering and twitching, her hands clenched. Then she turned abruptly away, got out of the car, and hurried the few feet across the gravel to the house. The door opened for her as she approached it, and she ran into Hilary's arms. And they went into the house together, the door shutting quietly behind them.

Chapter Fourteen

Jack Benson had somehow always thought that Freshfields or Herbert Smith or Linklaters or another great London law firm would be where he would spend his career. But his degree in the end was a little disappointing, his father had a sudden heart attack and died just as Jack was beginning his round of interviews, and it was obvious to anybody who knew the little Wiltshire firm of Benson & Co. that the surviving junior partner was clearly inadequate to take it forward on his own.

His mother, whom Jack had always in the end obeyed, gave a bravura performance as the heroic but stricken widow imploring her boy to honour his father's memory, and, really before Jack was conscious of having taken any decision at all, he was sitting at his father's desk, sifting through his father's papers and dealing with his father's affairs. And, as he discovered before the first month was out, these were affairs in both senses of the word.

Jack had wondered vaguely at the time about the rather surprising little woman at his father's funeral, whom nobody afterwards could quite place. She was tucked away on her own in a rear side pew, dressed in a shaped, buttoned overcoat with a fox-fur collar, a cloche hat which was perhaps thirty years out of conventional fashion, and a little wisp of veil over her pert, pretty face. She had wept without restraint as the service progressed, and thereby greatly irritated Jack's imposing mother, who herself was maintaining a rigid, military dignity in keeping with her training as the Field Marshal's daughter. Mrs Benson stood by the door as the mourners left the church, standing ram-rod straight, shaking hands majestically, her gaze unwavering, her features composed, her expression unsmiling, her grasp firm and manly. 'Pleased to meet you,' sobbed the unknown lady as she went. 'Such a lovely man . . . He was such a gentleman . . . so kind . . .' She choked, tears running, tiny hankie pressed to her cheek.

She had called at Jack's office before long. There was the nice little annuity that she had been promised would be in the will: she wanted to know about that, and also what was to happen to the little bedroom and sitting room that Jack's father had provided for her in a nearby village, tucked cosily away above a baker's shop. Jack made discreet inquiries, her story appeared as far as he could tell to be entirely accurate, and suitable provision was made for her out of a family discretionary fund that Jack administered as a trustee. All well out of his mother's view, Jack very much hoped.

He settled down happily enough to the life of a country solicitor. The firm had built quite a decent little practice over the years, more business seemed to appear without too much effort being expended in looking for it, and Jack's genial manner and reliable competence served his clients well. Benson & Co. grew to the point when another partner was required, then another, then two more, and by the age of thirty-five Jack had a country practice as good as any in the attractive part of England in which he lived.

He was a popular man in the community, a member of every local committee and a supporter of every worthwhile local cause. He was a very tall, pleasant-looking man in glasses, possibly a little pedantically fussy about his clothes, which were always emphatically pressed and laundered, but his appearance overall was impressive; he held himself sternly erect, he was a generous and easy conversationalist and his demeanour was most courteous and civil to everyone he met. He shot a bit, fished a bit, and played rather good golf. He was a governor of the local grammar school, president of the Wiltshire Hospital League, and treasurer of the High Sheriff's Benevolent Society.

He lived alone in a handsome Tudor cottage near his mother, to whom he was a dutiful if somewhat subjugated son. He was not a particularly lonely man, however. He was too busy with his solicitor's practice and his various local activities for very much introspection of that sort, though he was of a romantic disposition, liked women, and had a considerable longing for a family. He knew he would enjoy parenthood, welcomed the company of children, and was certain that, given the chance, he would make a participative and affectionate father.

It was not loneliness that led him to Hilary, and it was certainly not lack of prospective partners, for there had been a number of attachments which for one reason or another had not come to fruition, and there were bound to be more. It was quite simply that Jack thought Hilary the most attractive and interesting woman he had ever met, and from the moment that he first made her acquaintance he hoped that she would become his wife.

They met perhaps thirty months or so after Sam had left home, at a dinner party given by one of the local doctors and her husband. Hilary had been intelligent and lively and amusing and articulate, and Jack suffered something of a *coup de foudre* as he watched her and listened to her across the table. Now just past her thirtieth birthday, she had developed physically into a handsome, striking woman, the auburn hair cut a little shorter than in her Cambridge days, her bright youthful complexion still uncoarsened, her pretty, unremarkable features perhaps more regularly in balance now as she had matured and softened. Jack could barely take his eyes from her then, nor subsequently the following week, when he had dinner with her alone. But he was uncertain how to take the relationship further, for she gave him limited initial encouragement, and appeared to have very little available time, with her developing career at ICI to work on, and with Annabel to fetch and carry for in the evenings and at weekends.

But he persevered, they had dinner together once or twice, they were increasingly in each other's company, and slowly and pleasantly the relationship grew. He was in love with her, and told her so repeatedly. She was not in love with him, and told him that too. He minded the imbalance of the relationship, but not to the point of despair. He was a mature man, in emotional experience as much as in years, and there was in him a certain wry wisdom of how these things can work out from the most apparently unlikely of starts. And he was right in a way, for although Hilary never suggested that she was in love with him – and indeed never once did through the long years of their subsequent marriage – they

149

quite quickly became lovers, rather successfully so, they became friends, and in due course they became husband and wife.

Jack sold his Tudor cottage, and moved into Hilary's house. He built Annabel her tree-house, he gave her a pony, he taught her to ride her bicycle, and to swim, and to dive from the springboard, and to abseil down Cornish cliffs. He bought her a cello, and drove her into Bath every Saturday morning for her lessons. He took her to her ballet classes, and read to her every night in bed. He was indeed the model stepfather. He was not a substitute for Sam, but he was an affectionate, amusing, responsible man, and his presence very quickly added a feeling of security and shelter to Annabel's life. All this was done for Annabel without any strain or effort of will. Jack found, as he knew he would, that he enjoyed being with children, and enjoyed bringing them up; and Annabel, who was a bright, lively, questioning child, was particular fun to be with.

It was all the more a blow therefore that no children of his own appeared. After a year or so of living together, Hilary went through the whole process of smears and tests, but it was clear that there was nothing whatsoever untoward with her, and Jack then went to be tested himself. Problems were indicated with his sperm-count readings, and his general fertility levels, and although the specialist was at pains not to rule out the possibility of successful conception, Jack was told that the odds were very much against it.

As he sat opposite the doctor listening to the quiet, unemotional presentation of the diagnosis, almost irritatingly technical and detailed, Jack felt a void in his stomach. He found himself maintaining an air of phlegmatic calm and detachment, but he could feel the familiar signs of panic: a shallowness in his breathing, sweat on his back and brow, and a heightened, tight concentration. He had tried to prepare himself for bad news from the time he had started undertaking the tests, but his natural optimism was too strong, and somehow he could not stop himself from thinking that there was going to be some easy explanation, and some obvious and speedy cure. As the doctor spoke he found, despite the bleak precision of what he was being told, that he was still waiting for the comforting little disclaimer, the note of dismissal of the evidence, the anecdote of other cases where the whole thing had proved to be nonsense. But none came, of course, and it was not until Jack was sitting in the car afterwards, trying to steady down before he started his homeward journey, that he was able to get himself to absorb the whole truth.

The long drive back home to Wiltshire gave him some time to rationalise the situation through, but he was still severely shaken when he arrived, and he immediately tried to find Hilary to share the news with her. She was in the garden picking some Victoria plums for supper, and he felt immediate pleasure and relief at seeing her.

He went up and hugged her and, with his arms still around her, he started to tell her what he had been told.

'I'm really sorry, Hilary. It seems that it's all my fault. If that's how one puts it. Sperm-count lousy, fertility readings poor. I've got the piece of paper in my bag. Read it. It will mean more to you than to me.'

'Oh, Jack. Don't fret. Don't worry. These things often work out.'

'He didn't give much hope, frankly. I feel embarrassed and inadequate, to be quite honest. I really am very sorry.'

'That's absurd. It's not your fault. I wouldn't have blamed myself if the situation had been reversed. I'm sorry too. But it's just bad luck.'

Hilary felt nothing, except possibly a sense of relief. She could see Jack's distress, but she couldn't relate to it. In fact, the more she got used to the news, the more cheerful she felt. She recognised the incongruity of this, and the unkindness, but it was there all the same. She told herself that she must be careful how she presented herself to Jack, but she knew she had always been a poor prevaricator.

'We can go on trying, of course. Obviously we can't do much else but go on trying. Maybe something will happen quite unexpectedly. It would be so wonderful if that happens.'

'Of course we can. Just forget about it all, Jack. Everything is fine. Just forget about it.'

She gathered up the plums she had picked, put them in a basket, and started to walk back towards the house, whistling a tune from a Disney film that she had been to with Annabel the previous weekend. She stopped and pointed out to him a mature old Moss rose which was in full, luxuriant flower. She walked on, and asked Jack about a planning application that a nearby farmer had made for some building over which there had been a public dispute.

'Hilary – for heaven's sake. This is inconsequential chatter. We were talking about something which really matters. We want to have a family. We have just been told that it's very unlikely that we can have one. That is a very important statement for us to hear. We have to talk about it and think about it.'

Hilary stopped, laid the back of her hand against Jack's cheek and looked at him, trying to read his face to gauge what she should say.

'I'm not sure that we should spend too much time brooding over it, actually. As I said, it's not your fault and it's not my fault. It has just happened. The world doesn't come to an end because of it. We'll just have to carry on as we are. We're perfectly happy. I think it would be quite wrong to let this build up into a huge issue. Let's put it behind us.'

'I don't want us to put it behind us. I think it's far too important for that. I think we should see another man perhaps. Get some more advice. Maybe there's some sort of treatment I could be getting. Perhaps we'll need to watch over you more carefully. Plot your cycle accurately. Check for the moment of peak fertility each month. That sort of thing.'

Hilary laughed. 'Do you remember meeting that friend of mine from Cambridge a few months ago? Janice Jenkins? She claimed that she and Henry practically had to do it in front of the doctor on his surgery couch before he was satisfied that they knew what they were up to.' She laughed again, then shuddered, turned to Jack and put her two hands on his shoulders. 'None of that, thanks, Jack. Don't worry about anything. Everything's fine.'

He moved back from her so that her touch fell away. 'Everything is not fine. This matters to me very much indeed. I want my own children. I want this marriage to be a real marriage. This is my only marriage. It's not like that for you, and I recognise that. I don't mind about that. I do mind for myself. I want children. The news I had today was very bad news. I realised it was probably coming,

152

but it was still very bad news. I don't want to be morbid about it. Or self-pitying. But I do want us to take the thing seriously. Both of us.'

'Jack . . . Jack. We've got Annabel. We've got a beautiful house. We're both happy and successful in our jobs. We live in a lovely part of England. We're very lucky people.'

They sat down together on the long red brick wall that bounded one of the side lawns, Jack with his hands in his pockets gazing out across the fields that stretched away down to the river at the bottom of the valley.

'I don't have Annabel, Hilary. You do. I don't have a beautiful house. You do. I'm very happy to live in your house, and I'm very happy to be married to you. But I don't envy you what you own. Perhaps that's not quite accurate. I do envy you Annabel. She is not my daughter, and she doesn't feel like my daughter. But I'm very fond of her indeed, and I wish she was mine. And I wish other children were mine as well. That's what we're supposed to be addressing. We've been told today that we are not going to have children, or are very unlikely to have children. What do we do about that? Do we try to solve the medical problems? Or do we think of something else? Should we think of adopting, for example? That might be a very good thing to do. Why don't we talk to one of the adoption agencies and see what is possible?'

There was a silence for a minute or so.

'Jack, I have to be honest with you. I have no intention of adopting children, or even thinking of adopting children. Not now, and not ever. Nothing could be further from what I want to do.'

'Do you actually want to have any more children at all?'

Hilary put her hand inside the basket on her lap, and shuffled the plums around. She bit her lower lip, and frowned, then looked at Jack.

'Oh, Jack. Not much. I'm so sorry. I don't want to hurt you. But perhaps it's better to face up to it. If children come along, that will be fine, I suppose. Though I'm not absolutely sure even of that. My maternal instinct seems to have got rather burnt out in Annabel. Perhaps I'm just not a very motherly woman.'

'Or perhaps you just shouldn't have married me. Perhaps you

have never got over Sam. Perhaps you never will get over Sam. Perhaps I did neither of us a favour by being so persistent with you. All a bit late to worry about that now. But I did very much want to marry you. Maybe that was not very realistic of me.'

'We married, Jack. Everything's all right. We get along fine. Neither of us were children. You knew where I came from. You knew that I never wanted to break up with Sam. I have always been absolutely honest with you about that. It was an appalling blow when he left. And it still feels like that. He shouldn't have gone. You know that I think that. And you know that I was the guilty party. Except that I wasn't. We were both the guilty party. I had that ludicrous fortnight with Dan Galetti. Sam was morbidly cruel. And sexually psychotic, in some odd sort of way. The real failure was Sam's. He couldn't find the strength or the courage to show me forgiveness. I wanted to put the whole squalid little incident behind us, and throw everything into making the marriage work again. He couldn't do it. Or wouldn't do it. It ruined both our lives. It's not a very nice thing to say to you, but I am afraid it's true. The break-up of my marriage ruined my life.'

Jack's body seemed to slump, his head dropped, and his face grimaced. Not now, he thought. For Christ's sake, not now. This is not the time for yet another re-run on why she broke up with Sam. That persistent self-justification. Endlessly replaying versions of why they split. It's always on her mind. I need her now. At this moment it's me that needs help. She has no idea of the pain that awful news gave me today.

'So – no children with me, then. No natural children, and it seems no adopted children either. No real family together. I'm here as a lodger or something. That's rather tougher than I think I can manage.'

Hilary got to her feet, and they walked slowly in unison back to the house.

'Perhaps I shouldn't have said all that to you in quite that way. The truth is sometimes too hard to hear. That may have been a gratuitously cruel act. I'm sorry if I've hurt you, but I do think that this is a moment for looking facts squarely in the face. This issue of children does need to be confronted. It's too big a point to muddle around with.'

'And it is all tied up with Sam,' said Jack, in a flat, dead voice.

'Yes. Of course it is. You know that. We can't allow ourselves to have a relationship based on a complete falsehood. But, Jack . . .' She stopped, came in front of him, put both her hands again on his shoulders, and looked at him straight in the eyes. This time he did not move away.

'Jack . . . there are all sorts of marriages. Let's make this one work. We can really make it work. In its own way.'

Jack smiled at her, and they went into the house through the kitchen door. My marriage. The only one that I'm going to have. Limited to working in its own way. With no children from it, and with the shadow of my wife's first husband hanging over it. Actually, my wife's only husband. For her, that marriage was the only one that she has had. Sam has been her only husband. If he was dead she could mourn him. But he's alive, and he's there for her all the time.

He poured her a glass of wine, and she touched his arm for a moment, smiled, and turned to address Annabel, who had just come into the room. He ran a hand through Annabel's hair, then went up to his bedroom and sat down on the bed, his head in his hands. This is going to be a long journey, he thought. One hell of a long journey.

Chapter Fifteen

Mark at last got himself to pick up the telephone and dial his parents' number. The telephone rang eight times and Mark, delighted that they were out, was about to put the receiver down when his mother came on the line.

'Hello. Mrs Ryder speaking.'

Mark recognised that upward-curving extended final syllable, very much her telephone voice, slightly plummy, deeply suburban and respectable.

'Mum, it's Mark.'

'Well. Hello, stranger.' The accent adjusted immediately to its natural intonation. 'Fancy you. What brings you to the land of the living?'

'Nothing really, Mum. Just ringing to see how you both are. How are you? Is Dad OK?'

'Well, he would like to hear from his precious son a bit more, I can tell you that. But he's all right. He's playing bowls this evening at the Conservative Club, so he'll be going there straight from work, I expect. He'll be glad you rang. You might try again tonight at about nine-thirty. He'll be home by then.'

'Hold on, Mum.' Christ. She can't wait to get me off the telephone. 'Hold on. I wanted to speak to you too. We haven't spoken for ages.'

'Well, that's not our fault, dear, is it? We've hardly heard hide nor hair of you since Christmas.'

Seen hide nor hair, thought Mark. Not bloody *heard* hide nor hair.

'And you know we don't like to ring you in your flat. We might disturb the bishop.'

Mark sat with the receiver away from his ear, his hand on his forehead. She bloody knows Chris is not a bishop. Just let it run. Don't rise, don't rise.

'Mum – I'd love to see you both. Could I come down to Bristol soon to have a chat and spend the night? Maybe this Saturday or something?'

'Good heavens – whatever's up? Yes, I suppose that's all right. We've got a bring-and-buy sale at the church, but we'll be home at tea-time, I expect. See you then. Don't be later than five o'clock. And you'll have to sleep in the back room as the front guest is under dustsheets. There won't be anything very grand to eat. Dad can't manage much now anyway with his digestion. He'll die of surprise when I tell him you're coming. See you on Saturday, dear.'

Dear God, thought Mark. Why am I totally incapable of handling her? Has there ever been a time when we've said anything to each other which has meant anything at all? Is she capable of it? Or am I capable of it? Maybe it's my fault. Maybe I should have grown out of all this adolescent revolt bit. Perhaps I need to grow up, and show more compassion. And stop being ashamed of where I come from.

But I'm not ashamed of Dad in any way whatsoever. I love him, and I'm genuinely proud of him. Not as a Bush House arrogant patronising his dear old working-class father. I'm proud of him because he is a good man. I've never met anyone so bleached of malice. His whole life has been punctuated by acts of pure kindness. Considered, positive, decisive acts of pure human goodness.

Mark went into Angie Morris's little office, and started fidgeting irritably with her stapler, knocking some papers on the floor as he did so. She was on the telephone, and leaned across with her ruler to smack him on the back of his hand. He clasped his hands behind his neck, and gazed out of the grimy window at the rain which had now started to fall. 'Bloody English summers . . .' he muttered aloud, and then wondered why he didn't simply write his parents a letter. It all seemed so pointlessly painful for all of them to have to grind out the whole dismal story together. But he had telephoned, and now it was too late.

'Do you ever dread facing up to things?' he said.

Angie was picking up her papers from the floor, and looked up at him. 'No. But I'm one of the new breed of super women who are going to run the nation's broadcasting. You're just a man. Get off my desk, and put my stapler down.'

Mark told Christopher that evening that he would be away in Bedminster on Saturday night. No questions were asked, Christopher simply expressing mild pleasure that he was going. He had met Mark's parents just once, when they had called for tea at Camellia Mansions at the end of an annual shopping trip to London. The memory of that occasion still filled Christopher with remorse and shame. He was at his most awkward and shy, and had got involved with Mark's mother in a stupidly heated conversation about Roman Catholicism.

Her bigotry was of a level that Christopher had never before met and, very rarely for him, he had allowed this to rattle him. The result was that he had said practically nothing to Mark's father, who had sat the whole painful hour smiling awkwardly, saying little, and continually offering to do the washing-up.

Mark had not helped by being himself extremely taciturn, impatiently correcting his mother's more outrageous statements, but doing and saying little else. It had been a nightmarish afternoon, and after his parents had left, Mark and Christopher had one of the extremely rare quarrels of their life together. They both were left guilty and remorseful about a situation they had both handled badly. There was a flare of anger from each. Mark walked out of the flat, petulantly slamming the door behind him, there was silence when he returned, and it was fully a day before they were able to talk together normally again.

Christopher had always wanted a little of this damage healed, but recognised the chasm between Mark and his mother. Whenever Mark did contact his parents, and it had been on very few occasions indeed in the last three or four years, Christopher had always expressed pleasure that he had done so. But there was an embarrassment between them both on the whole subject and, apart from Mark's anecdotes of his childhood, most of them extremely funny, his relationship with his parents was not discussed. They had never come to Camellia Mansions again, nor had they ever issued Christopher an invitation to visit them in Bedminster.

Mark drove down shortly after lunch, arriving, as his mother had told him to, punctually at five o'clock. His father was in the little front garden when he arrived, clipping the beech hedge. He flushed with pleasure as Mark got out of the car, and stood rather awkwardly, uncertain whether to shake hands, or wave, or put his hand on Mark's shoulder, or do what he really wanted to do, which was to take him in his arms and hug him. It was Mark who resolved the situation. He walked straight up to him, put his arms around him, then stood back and smiled.

'How much longer is it then?' Mark asked.

'My retirement? Six weeks yesterday, and I absolutely cannot wait. Forty years of it, and I'm only forty-one days from being free. Couldn't be happier. They can keep their rotten gold watch, though I expect I'll take it politely. But the pension's all there, and I'm free. Or very nearly. Bloody marvellous!'

'Dad – you shouldn't have spent your life doing something you loathed so much. Why didn't you leave years ago?'

'Because I was never clever enough, or brave enough, or free enough. Thank God you're all three of those. Some of us are only good for the sort of stuff I have lived my life doing.'

'That's not true, Dad. You could have done all sorts of things.' Mark bent down and started to pick up some of the clippings, while his father began to snip away again.

'I've had some pleasure from doing a decent job, and not letting my colleagues down. And I've met some nice people and made good friendships. But still it's been a waste of forty years in many ways. Not entirely, though. It's paid for the house. It's given your mother the things she wanted, or most of them. It's brought you up. Those are all worthwhile things. I should be grateful for them.'

And so should I, thought Mark. I should be able to be grateful for all the things that I actually despise. He worked all his life to pay for this house, partly so that he could house me through my childhood. And I hate the place. And I hate the things that my mother wanted, for which the poor man struggled all those years.

'Is Mum in the house?'

'Yes – she's just getting tea, I think. Go in and say hello.'

Mark picked up his little lightweight zip bag, and walked along the few yards of neat front path, roses on both sides, and two large hydrangea bushes either side of the front door. The door was unlocked, and he entered the narrow little hall leading into the kitchen at the end. His mother was chopping vegetables on a marble slab.

'So you've come, then.' She turned her face away as Mark kissed her on her cheek. 'Quite a stranger you are. I'm surprised you could remember the way. Did you see your dad outside?'

'Yes. He's so excited about his retirement. Will he have enough to do, do you think?'

His mother laughed indignantly. 'Enough to do? He's got his bowls, and his gardening, and his fishing, and his books. And he's secretary or treasurer or something of the Rotary. He runs the Hiking Club. He's certainly got enough to do. It's me you should be worried about. Having him here all the time. And the pension's not going to be enough. You ought to be thinking more about us, you know. You've no family of your own to support; you earn more money at the BBC and from your writing than your father has done all his life, I dare say, and it's time you started to think about your parents a bit more.'

Mark made his way up the stairs to the back bedroom, which overlooked some small gardens behind the houses. Beyond these lay the local public playing fields, on which this summer evening groups of boys were kicking footballs about, and the odd young couple sat or walked together hand in hand.

Those playing fields had been at the centre of his life when he had been a small boy. He had learned to bicycle there, he flew kites, played little tennis-ball cricket games and, at the far end, where the rough grass bordering the fields ran down to the river, he used to lie in his teenage years, reading and reading, desperate to get to university and away from what he considered, in the smug cruelty of adolescence, to be the dead philistinism of the life around him.

And then university had come, and the excitement of it; the frantic joining of every club and society he came across, most of which had proved to be the wrong ones; and the sex and the friendships and the reading and the writing and the arguments and the fun and all the good things that had followed that. And now back to this tonight. I hated growing up here. I hated the lives around me. I hated my mother, I pitied my father, I longed to be free. And now how on earth am I going to tell them what's happened to me? Why didn't I just write them a letter? What's it to do with them, really? I'm thirty-five, I'm independent of them, I have my career, I write my books, I have Chris, I'm free of all this in every way. Just let it all go. I can't help them, and they can't help me.

There was a knock on the door, and his father put his head around.

'Can I come in? Looking at the view? Do you see how all the gardens have come on over the last few years? Everybody tries hard. It's a lovely view from this room, I always think.' And then, 'Why have you come, Mark? There's something you want to say, isn't there? It might be better to say it. Things are always worse in anticipation. For both of us. Tell me what it is.' His father had sat on the edge of the bed, and Mark was standing by the window. There was quite a long silence.

'Yes, there is something I have to tell you. It's not great news, I'm afraid. I'm . . .' He hesitated, looking down at his father, who had taken off his glasses and was looking up at him calmly, but with total concentration. ' . . . I'm . . . HIV positive. You know what that means. It means AIDS almost certainly in due course, and five or six years to go perhaps. Perhaps a bit longer, but not much. I feel perfectly well at the moment. Maybe some new drug will appear or something.' He shrugged, and looked at his father with an attempt at a smile.

'It's not so bad. I'm one of so many hundreds and hundreds of thousands. The great thing is to face up to it, and then go back and attack one's life all over again. And that's what I'm doing. Or trying to do.'

He turned back towards the window, and listened to the whirring of the little lawnmower being pushed up and down in the tiny garden across the wall. His father sat on the bed, his shoulders hunched, his arms across his chest, hugging himself, his head down. They were both silent for a matter of two or three minutes. Then:

'What's your first memory, Mark? Do you remember the house in Leigh Road where you were born? You must have been two when we moved here. I wanted to have another child so that you wouldn't be alone, but your mother had such a hard time having you, and we never did. That was a pity, looking back at it. You seemed to be so lonely, even when you were very young indeed. Do you remember that?'

Mark did not reply.

'I used to do as much with you as I could. I carried you in my backpack even when you were three or so. We went down to the river to fish some Sundays, and spent all day there. You used to sit there and chatter away to me. Always questions, questions. Why does the wind blow? What do the clouds do? Where does rain come from? Why is the sun hot? You loved talking to me. You seemed to like the answers I gave to all the questions you asked me. You never made friends very much. You gave the impression of liking school, but the teachers told me that you were alone there too, much of the time. You were always clever, and you loved working hard. You played football and cricket and all the games, and you looked as if you were joining in with everybody, but I knew that inside you were lonely. I wanted to help you with that, but I didn't know how to. But you and I together were so happy. It was the best thing of my life. Nothing has been so important to me as that, ever.

'And that's what I wanted to say to you. All that was real. The happiness was just as real as any of the unhappiness there may have been since. The bad things don't cancel out the good things. The happiness you and I had together is a fact, just like this HIV thing is a fact. But it's not cancelled out. It's real. And I carry it in my heart. Always.'

Mark moved from the window, and sat in the only chair in the room. 'Yes – I do remember lots of those things. Without you my childhood would have been completely hopeless. You made it all bearable. Thank you for that.'

After a moment his father got up and left the room. Mark could hear them talking in the kitchen, first quietly, then he could hear his mother's voice raised, and then quietly again.

Mark went downstairs and saw them there, sitting opposite each other at the kitchen table. His father's face was pale and drawn, and his mother's was puffy with crying. She got up as Mark came in.

'Tea's ready. We may as well have it,' she said, and there was an awkward silence as the table was laid and the food served.

'Your father has told me your news. I've been waiting for something like this, and I'm not really surprised. Let me ask you one thing. Are you going to make all this public, or can we keep it to ourselves?'

Mark looked across at her, and found himself reddening. 'It's a private affair of mine alone. I haven't made up my mind whom I shall tell, or when.'

'Well, for heaven's sake don't tell anyone around here,' said his mother. 'It's better for all of us if we keep this private to ourselves. There's no point in washing our dirty linen in public, is there? I don't want your dad and me to feel like that Mrs Taylor in the end house when her son went to prison. And I'm sure you wouldn't want that either.'

Mark watched her, but said nothing.

'If it does get out,' his mother continued, 'the best thing we can say is that you got it from a blood transfusion. I wonder if we should say that anyway. You haven't had a blood transfusion, have you?' She looked at him hopefully. Mark shook his head. 'How you could live the life you do, I shall never know. I can't understand it. Pansies – that's what we used to call your sort of people. All those disgusting things you do to each other.' She shuddered.

'Where did you catch it, then? Don't tell me from the bishop.' She made a sort of indignant snorting noise, and pushed her plate away.

'Stop, Mum. Please stop,' said Mark. 'Let's try to control everything. I know how you feel. I know what a shock it is to you.'

His mother's voice rose to a shrill shout. 'I've already told you it's no shock at all. No shock whatsoever. I've been expecting it. Every time I see a television programme on pansies and AIDS, I wonder if you've got it. And . . . oh God . . .' and she suddenly broke down into uncontrollable weeping, heaving and sobbing and choking out, 'Oh God. Oh God. Oh my God.'

Mark's father put his hand on her shoulder, then gently drew her towards him, cupping her head and smoothing her hair. 'There, Pearl. There. There. There.'

After a period the sobbing quietened, and she still wept, but softly, and with little chokes and whimpers, like a small child. To Mark's astonishment, she pushed her hand across the table and laid it on his, the first time in his memory that she had made an unritualised gesture of physical affection to him.

'I'm sorry, Mark. It's all so awful. We're such strangers, you and I. I so wish you were normal. You're my only child. I'd like to be proud of you. Having a wife and small children and a nice house somewhere.'

She started to weep again, but this time she was sufficiently in control to be able to calm herself.

'I often thought you might stop all that . . . homosexuality one day, and just be like everyone else. But it's too late now . . .'

Her voice dropped away to a bare whisper, and she sat at the table with her head in her hands. Mark watched her, and the nearest thing to love he ever remembered feeling for her crept over him. If not love, then at least a feeling of connection and, however unwelcome in a way, of physical bonding. But with that, a realisation again of how apart they were. I'd like to be proud of you, she'd said. As if no radio programme had ever been made, no novel ever written.

'It hasn't worked between us,' she said. 'It's my fault, I think. You never felt like mine when you were small. All that screaming when you were a baby. I never seemed able to give you what you wanted. And I couldn't when you got bigger, either. Your father could, perhaps. I couldn't. You always wanted to talk to him. Those questions of yours. Why is the world round? Why do leaves fall in autumn? Why is the sea salty? I never knew the answers. Your father always did. You knew that. You turned to him for everything. Even the things mothers are supposed to do. He mended your socks. He took you to the dentist. He ironed your school shirts. He did your homework with you. He read to you in bed. He said your prayers with you. He sat up with you when you were ill. I don't know what happened, really. The less I coped as a mother, the less I was able to cope. By the time you were five, even, it had gone too far. I told myself it didn't matter. Your father was good with you, you didn't want for anything. I don't think it did matter for you. It may have done, but I don't think so. But it certainly mattered for me. I longed to be a mother. I wanted to do all the things that other mothers did. I wanted to have a child who clung to me. Who thought the world began and ended with me. Who wouldn't go to sleep without being tucked in by me. But the child I had never spoke to me. Treated me like a stranger. Never touched me. Never wanted me. Never came to me. Never loved me. I don't know how that could happen.'

'Pearl. Pearl,' said Mark's father. 'Don't fret yourself like this, my dear. You are a good mother and a good wife, and you mustn't think otherwise.'

'No. It's not true. I wish it was. It's all too late now. It's been too late for a very long time. I'm glad you came down, Mark. We haven't made it easy for you. I don't know what your dad said to you upstairs. But I know I haven't made it easy for you. You'll go away tomorrow, back to London, and you'll deal with this the best you can. You've got friends, and your job, and you write your books, and you're strong in your own way. I'm not. I haven't got friends, and I'm not strong. Not in my own way, nor in anyone else's way. And you'll grow weaker and you'll die, and I'll still not have reached you.'

There was a long silence, and then Mark broke it. 'We've both failed each other, Mum. You're right, it is too late. We would both be sentimentalising the situation if we pretended otherwise. I don't know whose fault it was. I'm not at all sure these things ever break down in that way. Neither of us tried very hard. I know I didn't. I gave up too easily. I decided too early that we didn't get along. I think you did too. As the years went by, we neither of us made any attempt at all to mend the relationship. But there were some good things. I don't know what memories you have of me. But I'll tell you, I've got one very strong memory of you. I often think about it. It's very clear to me, and it's been important to me all my life.

'It's not a big story. It's just one moment of my childhood when everything was right. It was a Christmas when I was – what – six? Dad had made a little sledge thing on wheels. It was painted scarlet and had white seats. He made it for me to run down Leigh Hill on. As with everything Dad made, it didn't work properly. I sneaked it out on Christmas Eve when he was at his office party or something, and it wouldn't go because the wheels weren't set straight. You took it into the workshed, dismantled the wheels, straightened the axle, put it all together again, and of course it worked perfectly. And you said to me – don't tell Dad I've made it work. He's spent so many evenings on it after you'd gone to bed. We'll just keep this as our little secret. I've always remembered that.'

Mark's father laughed. 'I remember that little cart. I thought it went rather better than I was expecting.' He laughed again, and went over to put the kettle on for coffee.

'You were too clever for us, Mark. It made an embarrassment between us. As you grew older, we never felt good enough for you. We were right in that, actually. We weren't good enough for you. That's a difficult thing for a parent to face up to. We were both so proud of you. I think perhaps I was a little better in conveying that to you than your mother was. But we were both as delighted as each other. You know you were the first person from either of our families to go to university. Or even think of going to university. We couldn't quite believe it when you got there. And then when you joined the BBC, and you started to make those wonderful radio programmes. "Produced by Mark Ryder." We hear that read out on the air, and we see it printed there in the *Radio Times*, and we're so proud. And your novels. Every week I'm in George's in Park Street, or that bookshop on Blackboy Hill, just to make sure that the books are still there, and I look at them on the shelves and I pick them up and I see your name on them and I just can't believe it. Still can't. I've never got used to it. So proud. Both your mum and me. Both of us. Not just me. Although you only seemed to want to hear that sort of thing from me. Both of us.'

His father went over to the other side of the kitchen, and came back with coffee for the three of them. Mark looked at him as he sat down again, and noticed how stiffly he was carrying himself, and how much he had aged. With his hair combed back in a style forever time-locked in a Denis Compton quiff, and his bright, alert manner, and his pink, scrubbed complexion, he had looked for many years much younger than he really was. But tonight he was old and tired and devoid of energy or spirit, and Mark had a sudden fear that the news he had brought would end his life. He looked small now, and so bent, with his head slumped forward on his shoulders, and his movements slow and awkward and painful.

'I'm glad you came down. It can't have been easy for you to tell us your news. It wasn't a shock really. Your mother was upset and she didn't put it the way she would have liked to, I know. But she was right. It wasn't a shock. It's almost a relief to know the truth. Now that you have told us, we must treat this as a bit of a turning point. Don't let's lose each other again. Now that we've broken the spell. Let's stay together now. We've all hurt each other enough. Let's stay together now.'

Mark looked across at him and smiled, and they all three sat in silence now for a little, the pain and the tension drained from them, the stress and the emotion gone.

They went upstairs, and later that night Mark lay in bed, looking up at the light with its British Home Stores shade hung dead centre in the ceiling. So that's over, he thought. Thank heavens it's done. It didn't turn out as I thought. I unearthed good things, and I mustn't underestimate the importance of those.

Now I must go home and look after Chris, and keep myself as well as possible, and enjoy myself at work as much as possible, and do a great 'Africa' with Angie, and finish the new novel on time for Ben Jackson, and not waste a single day that's left. It's no good looking back. It's happened now. I am as I am.

Suddenly full of sleep, Mark flicked the bedside lamp off and turned on his side. It's all just destiny. Nothing that can happen to one really matters. There are so many good things to remember. And so many good things still left to do.

Chapter Sixteen

The Boots had asked Christopher persistently to preach at St Barnabas's on the Sunday of his eightieth birthday. At first he was absolutely determined not to do so, but it was Mark who changed his mind. Mark considered that the Boots had largely been responsible for Christopher surviving the ten years in London since he had left Hunstanton without serious mishap, and he was extremely grateful for that. They kept him as busy as he would allow, and Mark recognised the kindness. In the end Mark simply insisted that Christopher should accept the invitation, so he did so, but on the basis that this would be the last time he would ever preach.

Mark and Andrew took considerable trouble to plan the service. St Barnabas's was famed for its music, and the big Victorian church had acoustics as good as anything in London. The choir, all full- or semi-professionals, was inclined to truculence, but on a good day could sing like angels. The Willis organ, now itself eighty years old, was in continual need of minor repair, but was still a notably good instrument.

For Christopher's service, Andrew and Mark arranged with the choirmaster that the choir should be increased to its full complement of twenty, and a small chamber ensemble from the Royal Academy of Music was engaged to perform with the choir the Mozart Credomesse, which Christopher had loved all his life.

Lizzie Boot risked a lifetime of hurt feelings with the Flower and Music Committee by herself doing the flowers for the service; in doing so – admittedly with the most complete abandon – spending at least half of the budget for the whole year. The church was decorated by her under Mark's detailed and strict supervision, who – himself under daily nagging by telephone from Norah – requested that the church should be full to bursting with all the flowers that Christopher loved most, and he was a man who much loved flowers.

It wasn't a question of deciding simply on a theme of white roses and lilies, and lilac delphiniums. Mark and Norah insisted that Christopher should have the exact varieties that he most admired – so there were no 'Iceberg' or 'Virgo' amongst the roses, but dozens of 'Pascali', which Mark remembered Christopher had planted in a special bed he had prepared at Hunstanton. The delphiniums were either 'Cascade' or 'Purple Showers', the lilies Regal or 'Black Dragon'.

The church looked at its very best that early September morning. It was a breezy, blue day; warm enough for the church doors to be thrown open, and for the earlier arrivals to gather and greet each other outside in the gardens that Lizzie tended so devotedly.

The tubs in front of the church were bright with dahlias, packed tight together with petunias which tumbled over the sides, a little straggly so late in the season, but good enough, Lizzie thought, for one last Sunday.

The normal congregation on a Sunday was sometimes as low as fifty – and looked much less in a church the size of St Barnabas's – and, apart from Easter or Christmas, was almost never more than a hundred. But by sitting together in the vicarage office four evenings consecutively, and using both of the available telephone lines, Mark and Andrew had ensured that the congregation for Christopher's birthday would be at least two hundred and fifty.

Mark had prepared a list of people whom he thought Christopher would have most liked to be there if he had been given his own choice, and he was determined to ignore the residual embarrassment of The Fall, making a point of calling a number of people who had been out of contact with Christopher for the decade that had followed.

He had found and collected together almost thirty of Christopher's ex-pupils, a few of the Hunstanton staff, though sadly not by any means the majority, and perhaps half a dozen of his undergraduate friends from Oxford, which was as many as Mark could find still alive, and physically fit enough to come.

Every member of the parish was personally dragooned by Andrew, who also spoke to a number of academics and churchmen whom he knew Christopher felt warmly about. There was a cousin or two, and Norah of course, who brought down with her Jane and her middle-aged daughter. She now ran the little village grocery shop and post office with her husband, and Christopher had been most attached to her when she was a small child running round Norah's house and garden. He still made a point of calling on her in the shop whenever he was up there to stay. Also in Norah's party were one or two other people whom Christopher had got to know over the years from Norah's village and she had herself called Sam Lilley who was there as well, Norah sitting beside him and fussing over whether he was comfortable.

Andrew and Lizzie had issued invitations for everybody to drink champagne after the service in the vicarage garden, securing from Veuve Clicquot the champagne free of charge, and in very large quantities, as an act of 'sponsorship', encouraged by the fact that their sales director was currently sleeping with Andrew's sister.

Mark drove Christopher to the church in sufficient time for him not to get flustered, but not so early that he would lose his nerve. He had known nothing of the preparations for this service, and was quite unaware that so many people he knew would be there. Mark knew that he was not really a man for surprises of this sort. Catch him in the wrong mood, and he was quite likely to be so thrown by the surprise that he would turn tail. Mark dropped him at the vicarage garden door at the back of the church, having arranged that Andrew should collect him there and busy him inside.

When in time the clergy and the choir processed in, the big congregation standing as they came, Christopher's face suddenly assumed an expression of great puzzlement as he recognised so many unexpected people. He smiled and nodded as he went, caught Mark's eye and grinned. When he was in his place, he looked at the service sheet and saw what care had been taken. His favourite hymn – 'Lord of All Holiness, Lord of All Might' – was at that time being sung with great verve by the choir, strengthened by the added numbers. He saw that they were to have the Mozart Credomesse, and viewed with delight the chamber ensemble who were to accompany it. And then he read that the anthem was to be 'Jesus Christ, the Apple Tree', and chuckled delightedly to himself; Christopher and Mark had heard this simple and lovely English anthem absolutely butchered by Norah's church choir the previous summer, to the extent that even Norah's customary attempt to drown the lot of them at the harmonium – the piece demanded no more than a whisper of an accompaniment, if that – was on that occasion possibly a good thing.

The Introit, the early prayers, the Mozart mass, confession, absolution, all followed in easy, practised expertise, the church looking lovely, the music perfect, the congregation confident and happy and affectionately anticipating Christopher's sermon.

When the time came, he climbed the pulpit steps stiffly and awkwardly. When he had reached the top of the little circular staircase, he stood for a moment fumbling for his glasses, this process being sufficiently protracted for Mark to feel a clench of worry as to whether he had brought them at all. But after much patting of his surplice, he found them, put them on, placed a single postcard in front of him containing a few ringed words and a jotting or two and, lifting his right hand, quickly sketched the outline of the Cross.

'In the name of the Father, and of the Son, and of the Holy Spirit. Amen.'

The congregation sat. Christopher stood there looking down at them, and for a few moments said nothing at all.

'Totally gaga,' whispered Mr Rankin to Mrs Rankin. 'Has no idea where he is or what he's doing.'

Not a bad sense of theatre, the old boy, thought Sam Lilley. Bad as old Celia Smith at the memorial service for her third husband. Loved that bit of business with his glasses.

Dear God, he's beginning to look so frail, thought Mark. But I think he's loving it. You can never quite tell, but I think he is.

Suddenly, Christopher began. 'For reasons that I shall explain later, the text is from Isaiah six: verse eight. "I heard the voice of the Lord saying, 'Whom shall I send, and who will go for us?' Then I said, 'Here am I, send me!' "

'This will be the last time that I shall ever preach. Eighty today . . .'

He looked down for a moment at Norah, who nodded and smiled up at him. ' . . . and I'm really no longer able to build arguments and sustain good theology. I hate reading from a prepared text. For years I've preached like this – ' he waved his little postcard for a moment, then put it back '– and whereas even a few years ago I was able to hold a good coherent intellectual density, if you will, from five or six heading words, I now just reminisce and tell anecdotes. Maybe it doesn't matter. Go to any one of ten or fifteen churches within a radius of two or three miles from here, and you'll hear better theology than I ever knew. It's there for you every week. Do go and hear it.

'But I'm going to preach an entirely self-indulgent sermon, and it's going to be as simple as can be. I'm just going to talk to you of the things I care about most.

'I have taught theology all my life, rather as I might have taught economics, and know nothing about it. I accept the Resurrection in an unthinking sort of way. The Immaculate Conception is absolutely all right by me. God is so clearly capable of doing whatever He wants to do, I see no reason why He should not impregnate a virgin's womb if He so wishes. In so far that the Trinity is a concept that I have ever been able to fully grasp, I wholeheartedly believe in it; I certainly have based my life on an instinctive faith in the concept of God the Holy Spirit. I have a passionate and total certainty about the after-life, but no sense at all about what it could entail. I am completely unable to articulate anything helpful on the subject at all.

'I profoundly believe in Sin, but I have no idea what Original Sin could possibly be about. I cannot understand the fuss over Transubstantiation. I believe in Saints. I believe in Miracles. I don't believe in Papal Infallibility. I think I'm probably rather Marian.

'Bits of Christianity I would die for. But some of the metaphor eludes me. I am embarrassed, to be quite truthful, by all that pastoral imagery about sheep and shepherds. And, God forgive me, the Lamb. I am perfectly fond and respectful of sheep, but personally I'm not one. Neither actually, nor figuratively. And I don't believe many of you are either. And I particularly dislike the extension of the point that any or all of us are part of the Bishop of London's flock. The thought of us all trotting around going baa-baa while he smacks us on the bottom with a stick with a bend in the end is not quite in my line.'

'Disgraceful business this,' breathed Mr Rankin to Mrs Rankin. 'Thank God the bishop's not present to hear it.'

What an old trouper, thought Sam. Marvellous stuff. I wonder if there's a book in it.

'I find the sheep imagery particularly difficult because of the emphasis it places on passivity. Passivity becomes too easily caricatured into a sort of wetness. An inability to stand up for oneself, or a cowardice under attack. If you go boo to a sheep it runs away. Sheep are barely brave enough to protect their young from attack by a wolf or a bear. Rams will, but for some reason there is no extension of the metaphor to rams. Are rams the less dear to God because they will protect themselves and their families? Most unpleasantly aggressively, if needs be?

'It is the docility of it that offends me, and it's not my experience of life. Great men and women don't run away from anything. From physical danger, from an enemy's attack, from the cruelties of life, from illness, from bankruptcy, from protection of what is theirs. They don't turn the other cheek. They turn face on and stand their ground. They fight their own fight. We all know this. There are no difficult areas of spiritual judgement here. It's a simple observation of how the world is.

'And the pity of the imagery is that somehow it generates an obfuscation of what I believe is the greatest truth of life. And that is the Islamic perception that the source of peace in a man's soul is the act of yielding, of surrendering to God. The obfuscation comes from the failure of the metaphor. The yielding is not a passive act – a sheep-like cowering away into frightened subservience. Peace comes from an active, positive decision to offer back all that one has been given. That is a brave thing to do. It's not sheep-like at all. It requires more bravery than most of us can find. But the search for that bravery brings more happiness in its wake than one could imagine.

'Don't worry about Transubstantiation. Don't worry about Immaculate Conception. Don't worry about the Coptic Heresies.

176

We don't have to work God out. We're not going to find God by reading Theology at Balliol. God is not a mathematical formula that can be explained and taught. God cannot be proven. But He is endlessly demonstrated to all of us in our simple experience of what goes on inside our minds. We all have certain, unmistakable experience of the presence of the human soul. All of us. I wonder if there is really any such thing as an atheist, except at the level of the student maverick. Like being a paid-up member of the Flat Earth Society. All of us, and from an extremely early age, know about, and long for, the presence of God.

'We may not think about it very much. Indeed, the older I get I wonder if we *should* think about it very much. Perhaps it is better just to accept it. We may profoundly dislike the Church of England. We may have an instinctive and probably justifiable contempt for clergymen. We may . . .'

'If the bishop were here, this would be a major scandal. Quite unforgivable,' said Mr Rankin to Mrs Rankin, this time audibly.

' . . . but none of this matters. None of it has the slightest relevance to God. Or our understanding of God. And the wonderful, precious truth is this. We have things we own. Our gifts. Our families. Our lovers. Our money. Our health. Our good looks. Our reputation. Our standing in the world. Every day – every few hours – offer these back to God. And genuinely offer these back to God. Tell God to take what He wants. This is not sheep running around the Bishop of London's ankles. It's the strength to stand four-square to the world. It's the opposite of passivity. It's the act of fighting one's way through life. Using every moment to join the fray. Being afraid of nothing and nobody. Continually stretching oneself to new dangers, new adventures, new experiences. But recognising the central truth, that despite the best efforts of the Church of England to conceal it, despite the superstitions of the Church of Rome, or the cruelties of Islam, or the prejudices of the Jews, or the nonsenses of any of the organised religions, the God we all know, and all of us long to draw near to, owns everything. We have no privacy from that. It is simply not possible to separate ourselves from that.

'And I want to link this into my second point, which is that although sheep may not have the sensitivity or the intelligence to look at the world, men have. My eightieth birthday present back to you is to suggest that you never cease to observe and to marvel in the brilliance, and the creative power, and the generosity and the intelligence and the *goodness* of man. Selfishness, deceit, greed, disloyalty, dishonesty – given the rawness of the physical peril of the world, all these things seem to me to be perfectly understandable. What is inexplicable, however, is the other side of the coin. The overwhelming goodness of man. The heroism, the loyalty, the moral courage, the disinterested kindliness. Not passive goodness, not sheep-like goodness, but positive, active, deliberate, selfless goodness.

'Watch mankind. Not church-going, pious, overtly religious mankind. Sit at your street-café table and watch mankind. All of it. Marvel in it. It's not mine, and I wish it was, but I remember somebody saying that to be alive and not to marvel in and absorb oneself in life is quite simply bad manners. Rather like going to a dinner party and refusing to eat the food. And that brings me to human love. Believe in it. Treasure it. Absorb yourself in all its aspects – sexual, romantic, parental, familial, protective. Combine it with generosity and selflessness and you have the greatest thing God has given us.'

Christopher stopped at that, and looked down at the people sitting before him. The business with the glasses, as Sam would put it, had continued throughout the sermon. They had been put on, taken off, waved and polished. They were now put on again.

'But remember that, when you have it, offer it back.'

He picked up his postcard, and stuffed it away in a recess of his surplice.

'One last thing, and the final sermon of my life is over. Never regret anything. When you have a failure, accept it. When you have a success, accept it. Be at peace with yourself. I have had what the world would consider to be an ambiguous life. I can tell you that I am completely at peace with it. I regret nothing whatsoever.

'And the text? Why the Isaiah text: "Whom shall I send, and who will go for us?" Because it has the ring of Bunyan, and Mr Valiant-For-Truth. And I wanted the very last words of my preaching life to have the ring of Bunyan. And Mr Valiant-For-Truth.'

Christopher made a vague sign of blessing, muttered without enthusiasm something appropriate about majesty, might, dominion and power and, with painful caution, made his way down the six or seven steps from the pulpit.

Sam grinned at him. The Hunstanton ex-pupils whispered amongst themselves. Mr Rankin raised his eyes to the ceiling in response to a shrug from one of his allies. Mark sat completely still. Norah dropped her handbag. The service continued.

Chapter Seventeen

There are those whose childhoods are as anecdotalised and exposed to their friends and children as any part of their lives. For others, the memories are held in extreme privacy, most often perhaps to conceal a pain too acute to be laid bare, but at other times because those memories contain a glimpse of a perfection and a loveliness that no experience in subsequent adult life has come near to matching.

For Sam, those childhood years had been spent in his parents' comfortable if modestly sized house at Hadlow in Kent. It was a typically pretty, tile-hung converted farmhouse in an area where there were many houses of the type. White railings bordered the close-cut lawn that ran down to the lane on which the house stood, the garden most scrupulously tended and presented. It was a fine sight at most times of year, but best of all perhaps in the spring, when bright clumps of daffodils burst out from the longer grass by the side hedges and under the apple trees, and the borders were aflame with massed wallflowers and tulips.

Sam's father held a modest position in the City – at his death he was junior partner in a small commodity-broking firm in Mincing Lane – but his physical appearance, his manner and his style of dress suggested something much grander than this. He cut a fine dash on the eight-fifteen to Charing Cross each morning, his bowler hat at just the right angle of jauntiness for a military man in mufti, his umbrella tightly furled, his regimental tie puffed out above his waistcoat and held by a pearl pin and, in their season, a single red rose, picked each morning fresh from the garden, displayed proudly in his buttonhole.

It was something in Christopher's comments in his sermon about

181

familial love that turned Sam's mind back to him. His father, Sam reflected, had not been, by any standards, a remarkable man. His achievements were extremely modest. He had neither striven for great goals, nor fought any famous battles for conscience's sake or for honour. It could be said that he had left no mark on the world of any sort. He had attempted little, and done little. But there was in him something of the innocence and the nobility of the absolutely ordinary man, and Sam, as he thought of Christopher's plea for the observation of the transcendent in the most worldly manifestations of humankind, suddenly had a pang of longing for him, and loss, and regret.

He had called himself Major Lilley; a mistake perhaps in such a neighbourhood, where the niceties of social proprieties were most strictly observed and remarked upon, for his rank was only that of a temporary officer called up for the war, and his commission had been in a regiment as markedly undistinguished as the Royal Army Service Corps.

But he and Mrs Lilley were a handsome couple, and were as active as any in the local social life, which centred around the golf club, the tennis club, and cocktail parties and bridge games in the houses of any one of a dozen families of their class and type. And although the 'Major' affectation cost them a sneer or two in their circle of friends, they were a popular enough couple on the whole, and indeed there was no reason why they should not have been, as the life that Johnny and Priscilla led exactly conformed to the aspirations and style of the people with whom they mixed. They were an identikit couple for the peer group they represented: philistine, unread, loyally Tory, socially prejudiced, moderately affluent, minor-public-school people, usually most pleasantly housed in the English fashion, but without a decent picture or a serious book in sight, and without a thought in their heads for art or culture, and not a pretension for it either.

Sam's parents had first met dancing at the Empire League Ball in Limpsfield Chart, which was entirely in keeping with what their lives together were to hold.

Johnny was thirty, and a departmental manager in the little Mincing Lane broking house that his father had managed to smuggle him into as a junior, a sixteen-year-old school-leaver fresh from Lewes Grammar School. Priscilla was twenty-six, and rather well off. Both were quite unusually handsome, and both had an eye for style and dress, though Johnny was without the means to do much more than ensure that his tiny wardrobe was always pressed and clean, immaculately so, and as gaily presented to the world as possible, with his collars boldly cut and fiercely starched, and his ties perfectly – if caddishly – tied and pinned.

Priscilla, who was a genuine beauty, worked in a fur shop in Knightsbridge, and was spoilt by her father, a retired and wealthy draper, who gave her a generous dress allowance, and watched her with pride and possession as she spent it.

Having first met dancing, they danced most nights thereafter through the months of their courtship and almost immediate secret engagement, largely financed by judicious siphoning of funds from Priscilla's dress allowance. They were as content with each other as any couple could be. Their tastes, interests, humour and aspirations were as one. They were in love from the moment they met, they were in bed together within the week – no easy logistical task this in those times in their class and circle – and they stayed in love, passionately and overtly, for the rest of their lives.

Three years later, Priscilla's father died, and she was left quite comfortably off. They had been married then for a year, and the pretty house they bought in the affluent little commuter village to London was a statement of a certain upward mobility in the family's social position. But the facts of Johnny Lilley's schooling cast a little ambiguity over their rank, if predominantly perhaps in their own eyes. Paddock Wood railway station of a morning was a sea of minor-public-school ties on the up-train platform, and poor Johnny, lacking by a distance the self-regard that would have made the detail of his childhood circumstances irrelevant, clung to his bowler hat and his pearl tie-pin as a talisman of his status. His dread was that he would one day be hailed there by a fellow, and socially unsuitable, old pupil of his grammar school. It once had happened, but mercifully in the comparative privacy of a crowded corridor on the five-fifteen down-train, which Johnny had never since taken again lest the occasion be repeated.

His unease was apparent to all, though he never fully sensed this, and the perceived opinion of Johnny and Priscilla in the village was that they were good sorts, of course, but, frankly, a little bit common. There was a touch of the home counties in the vowels perhaps, and they were both sometimes just a little too anxious to position their status by the things they said and did.

Two children had come from the marriage. First born was a daughter, three years older than Sam, who died of meningitis when she was thirteen, and effectively left her younger brother orphaned. There were those of his family who would say that her death was a blow from which Sam never fully recovered. Perhaps they were right. It had at all times been difficult to gauge the degree of solitude and shyness that had been there beneath the cherubic, always smiling, always beautiful face of the little boy with the chestnut-coloured curly hair and the anxious, anxious eyes. Certainly his whole life seemed to revolve around his sister, and hers around him.

Sally and Sam loved their parents of course, and uncritically, as most children will; it was only when Sam had reached maturity that he rationalised in hindsight those features of his parents' lives that were most at odds with him and Sally. Most of the relationship had been unremarkable enough and, at worst, the children were aware that their parents carried a certain dissociation and detachment from them, broken by the occasional moments of awkward attempts at communication. But they did realise that they were a bore when they got in the way of the bridge arrangements, or the golf-club foursomes, or the tennis-club dance; their education was tiresomely expensive; and they knew that it was an irritant to their parents that they never seemed to want to do anything but be with each other, and play their odd, private games, read their books, and stage their plays in the so-called theatre they made for themselves in the outhouse.

Sally and Sam were in some ways surprising children for their parents to have produced. Neither Johnny nor Priscilla would have claimed to be clever, and nor did they aspire to be. But their children clearly were, and if their parents never articulated their pride in this to them, no doubt it was there. What was certainly articulated, however, was their pride in the children's looks, in Sally particularly, who showed every promise of being as pretty as her mother. In fact they were both the pleasantest-looking children imaginable, very alike with their curly hair, and their wide, crinkly-eyed smiles. Johnny and Priscilla were strong on manners and appearance, if distinctly vague about most else in the children's upbringing, and Sally and Sam were famously courteous, always taught to be straight to their feet when an adult came into the room, stiff-backed at table, good conversationalists when addressed, but only when addressed, and reliably schooled in their demeanour to Johnny's golf-club friends and Priscilla's afternoon bridge partners.

And although they did love their parents, it has to be said that neither of the children felt much connection with their lives. There was no infantile, child-like sense of smug judgementalism or precocious intellectualism, but merely an instinctive awareness that they were different. It was perhaps fairly generational, for Sally and Sam had no feeling of association at all with the agonies of debate over social nuance their parents went through, and it was certainly partly a matter of the respective levels of their intelligence. But whatever the reasons, there was undoubtedly a lack of full communication between them, and while Johnny was inclined to be rather sloppily tender with Sally, particularly with a whisky or so inside him, and, at times to a positively physical degree, he was prone to feel irritated by Sam.

The irritation sprung from what was clearly an instinctive inherent sense of dissimilarity: Sam was not a son with whom Johnny could find any point of contact. If Johnny had wanted to have a son at all – and in point of fact he hadn't particularly – it would have been a cricket-playing, scrum-half, not-too-clever, uncomplicated sort of a chap, who would carry one's golf clubs for one, and worship the ground one walked on, and want a berth in the same firm one day when he was older. Sam was always smiling, always respectful, but Johnny found him to be at the heart of things withdrawn, unresponsive and, he suspected, wholly unimpressed by his father.

Johnny could never quite get to grips with him. He was not effeminate exactly – Johnny was very decided about poofs, as he called them, and he would certainly knock any nonsense like that out of him if he had need to – but he was so damned, well, sensitive for lack of a better word. Too much with his sister. Too keen on his damned books and stories. Too quiet when he wasn't with her. An odd little cove. Don't know what he's got going on in his mind most of the time.

Sam was slapped occasionally, and usually inconsequentially, by both his parents, but beaten by his father, in a curious, ritualised way, and far too savagely, perhaps half a dozen times over the course of his childhood.

There was a dreadful Sunday afternoon one summer when Sam was eight or nine; Johnny came home full of pink gin after the monthly foursomes at the golf club in which he had played uncharacteristically badly – and in front of another member's wife he rather had his eye on – to find that Sam had broken the toolshed window. The boy was shouted at, and taken up to his bedroom, and bent over and beaten with the cricket bat which Sam kept hidden in his bed as a means of protection against robbers.

Priscilla wept loudly downstairs, though Sam recognised this as not so much a mother's fear for her child as a general wail of disappointment for the fact that her Sunday had turned into a distressingly disruptive occasion, and it was such a pity to have Johnny in a mood when she had been looking forward to a set or two of mixed doubles after tea, followed by the drinks party at Mark and Pinkie's, and some bridge somewhere afterwards, no doubt.

Johnny came down to lunch still looking red and angry, Sam followed with his eyes puffy with crying, and then Sally started to cry as well. No one spoke very much at lunch after all that, but worse was to follow, for Priscilla and Johnny had gone up to bed after the meal was over for their 'rest', as they almost always did on Sunday afternoons, and Priscilla had immediately taken all her clothes off to cheer the old boy up a bit, and was lying on the bed waiting, and Johnny had come over to her, still dressed, thank heavens, but her legs were open and his hand was between them and her arms were around his neck, and horror upon horror, she had forgotten to turn the lock and there was Sam gazing fixedly at them both, standing in the doorway, his mouth open, his eyes staring.

Johnny had sprung away from her and shouted and shouted at the child, and Sam had run away down the stairs and into the garden, and Priscilla could hear Johnny bellowing, 'Get out. Get out. Get out, you little swine,' at the front door.

Sam went off on his bicycle and still had not returned by the time the drinks party was over and Johnny and Priscilla had arrived home. When night started to fall and the light was fading, Johnny had gone out in the car to try to find him. He saw him eventually, sitting on a bench by the side of the village green, his bicycle lying on the grass before him, his arms folded across his chest, his face pinched and frightened. Johnny walked up to him and Sam stood as he did so, perhaps waiting to be hit. But then Johnny put his hand on his shoulder, and made a little grimace of a smile, and smoothed the hair back from the little boy's eyes.

They said nothing further to each other then at all, but when they got home Priscilla was waiting for them in the hall, and as she started to speak Johnny held up his hand to stop her, and turned to Sam and said to him, 'I expect you'd like a hot drink, old man, and we must get you off to bed. Mum will take you up to your room, and I'll bring the cocoa in a moment. Up you run.'

That was the one great moment of closeness and connection with Johnny, and Sam never forgot it. And then, within a day or so, everything was much the same, and the events of that Sunday were buried away and certainly never mentioned again. But the irony was that Sam came out of it with, for the first time, something not far from a sort of rapturous love for his father, as if he had seen him in a moment of failure so abject that he had stepped beyond the conventional parameters of a child's dependent affection, into an area where a mature, entire love could be released, let go by the child's forgiveness.

In a similar way, it was pity – aware, responsive, comprehending pity – that released Sam's full love for his mother. It was in itself an absurd little incident. The Marquess of Aberystwyth was the leading figure of the area, and for Priscilla and her circle a man of overwhelmingly glamorous connections and social superiority; a friend and a frequent host and guest of the Royal Family, and an old Navy colleague of Lord Mountbatten's. The nearest that any of them had managed to get to him previously was through Harris, his chauffeur. A man of mischievously secure self-confidence, who was a very strong golfer, Harris had been observed on several occasions playing with Lord Aberystwyth, and had been rather emphatically successful in his playful pursuit of the secretary of the ladies' committee.

The club had been through agonies of indecision as to whether to invite Harris to be a member. In favour of the case was that he was an unusually good player, socially (and, the secretary of the ladies' committee would privately perhaps admit, sexually) quite extraordinarily self-confident and proficient, and he spoke with a secure and acceptable accent and intonation, with not a home-counties-flattened vowel in threat. Against the case was that he was, quite undeniably, a chauffeur; albeit a chauffeur to a marquess, and one with apparently free personal access to the Daimler.

But once you open the doors, where does it all end? There was Hooper the chemist's son, for one, who claimed to have been at Wellington College, and had asked Philpot to propose him for membership. One in, all in. One owes it to the ladies to be scrupulously careful. But Harris was such an amusing fellow, of course. And Lord Aberystwyth seemed to treat him almost as a friend.

Priscilla had spoken to Aberystwyth one evening at the local constituency Conservative Party ball. Indeed, for a heady if brief moment she had danced with him, and she had somehow thought that this connection would have left him with some sort of lingering memory of her. She had herself been overwhelmed by his practised courtesy and unheeding charm, but it was nothing to him, of course, and poor Priscilla had made no more impression on him than any other of the many unfamiliar middle-class women he had met at what he had considered to be a most thoroughly dreary evening.

The dénouement had been savage in its petty cruelty. Priscilla had seen the Daimler outside the chemist's shop in the village, barely one week after she had danced with the Marquess at the Conservative ball. Sam was with her, having volunteered to carry her bags of groceries home after her weekly shopping expedition. Priscilla crossed the road and asked Harris if Lord Aberystwyth was inside. As he was about to answer, the door of the shop opened and the Marquess came out. Priscilla put on her prettiest, most winsome smile, said something in greeting and held out her hand. Perhaps he did not see it or notice that it was Priscilla who stood there, perhaps he saw the hand and failed to recognise the owner of it, or perhaps he indeed meant to snub her; whatever the reason, Priscilla was left standing, hand now dropped to her side, as Aberystwyth brushed past her and climbed into the car and Harris drove away.

It was in itself a tiny thing. A stronger, more secure, more intelligent woman would have turned it into a story against herself, embroidered it yet further and enjoyed its telling as an example of the aristocracy's disdain for what they perceive as the social climbing of the middle class. Sam, child as he was, knew its total inconsequence, but recognised that to his mother it would represent a mortal blow to her pride and esteem. And so it was, and the ten-year-old little boy found in his horror at her humiliation a real, protective, familial love for her.

And those were the two real incidents of Sam's memory of his parents. The moment of his father's tenderness that night when he came to him on the village green, and then the pain at his mother's petty humiliation at the hands of Lord Aberystwyth.

But then there was Sally, of course. And it was his attachment for Sally which camouflaged from others the privacy and the solitude that was there in the rest of his life. Sally and Sam were so emphatically happy together, and looked the most content and cared-for children one could imagine. They shared a style of laughter that was impossibly infectious, their arms crossed across their stomachs, their bodies bent double at the waist, tears running down their faces as they whooped and choked with the joy of it all. They would laugh like this as they walked through the village High Street together, or on the bus that took them off to the woods, where they would picnic and play secret, private games, or together in their bedrooms, or as they played in the garden, or hid in the outhouse.

189

It was all so infectious and cheerful, and the people of the village would find themselves smiling at the sight of them coming down the street. 'Tweedledum and Tweedledee', the village people called them, and the baker would shake one of his long loaves at them in playful threat as they passed, and the milkman would pretend he needed help to push his float up the hill, and the admiral's widow in the gloomy old house behind the vicarage would ask them up to tea, and play with them a game called 'German Battleships', the rules of which she could never precisely recall, which led to much chaos and confusion and provided for the polite little children yet another reference point for more private hilarity when they were safely out of sight and on their own.

Johnny and Priscilla were not exactly church people, but the convention of the village was that the Easter house party in the vicarage was something that one's children went to whether they liked it or not, just as the parents themselves would all come to the little prayers-and-drinks-party ritual on the final evening, with absolutely no excuse acceptable.

Johnny was always quite patently uncomfortable in the presence of clergy, and particularly with the vicar himself, a grand and imposing man of late middle years. The vicar had been ordained after a career as a Lloyds' underwriter, and affected before Johnny a certain breezy men-of-the-city bonhomie, which always left Johnny almost convinced that the vicar knew personally the firm Johnny worked for, and thought decidedly little both of it and of Johnny's position within it.

But Johnny and Priscilla would come to the evening, of course, as all the parents did, and they would stand in a semi-circle around the grand piano in the vicar's drawing room, regimental and old-school ties firmly in place. The children would sit demurely on the floor, legs crossed, hair brushed, knees washed, and Johnny would join in the hymns in a suitably gruff and manly way, and Priscilla would look ravishing in her silk frock, and she would smile her lovely smile, and make bright little conversation with the vicar afterwards with that special drawled attempt at an upper-class accent she reserved for use in encounters such as this. Sally was a most proficient mimic of it in the safety of her bedroom alone with

Sam, where the two of them would re-enact for months afterwards some of their more cherished memories of the vicarage house party, their pièce de résistance being the moment when the vicar's wife inadvertently broke wind as she made strike at a ball in an afternoon rounders game.

The vicarage, and not just at house-party time, was the source in fact of several moments of amusement and colour in the two children's lives. In the latter years of the war, and for the quite extended period thereafter before repatriation, there was the Italian prisoner-of-war who worked at the vicarage as a gardener. He was on day-release from the local detention centre to work in the village, as were most of the other Italians in the camp. Sam, in later years, remembered him as a jolly, grinning, loose-limbed, shambling man, whom he and Sally would chatter with for hours as he potted and watered in the vast old greenhouses that stood in the walled kitchen garden hidden at the end of the vicarage grounds. The children were shooed away by the vicar's wife whenever she found them there, her personal contribution to the war effort being to extract the maximum labour from Mario, and any other prisoners-of-war she could secure for the vicarage, for the minimum possible reward. But Sally and Sam would hide in the rhododendrons, and return as soon as the coast was clear, and Mario would talk to them about his village outside Naples, and his sweetheart there, and his mother, and her cooking and the meals with all the family gathered, and the chickens that ran in the yard, and his brother who had died in combat defending the Sicily landings.

The day that sweet rationing ended, Sally and Sam were waiting outside the village sweet shop at least half an hour before it opened. They spent their entire savings on butterscotch and chocolate pennies and licorice allsorts and fruit drops and sherbert delight, then sat on the pavement steps of the shop, their bicycles beside them, and ate all they had bought. They had meant to keep some for Mario, but it was all too wonderful a treat after a childhood that had known nothing but ration books and monthly quotas. Everything was devoured, and by mid-morning both children were vomiting and crying with the pain of their stomach cramps. And little wonder, for children of their generation had been brought up

191

on nothing but the simple war years' diet of fruit and vegetables from the garden, home-made bread and biscuits, a sausage or two and perhaps a chop and a little bacon from the butcher each week, and just one egg per person, bought with the ration book each Monday morning, made to last for several meals by being mixed into milk and used as a dip for bread, then fried in dripping.

Every week of the war, the two children would be taken to the British Restaurant in Tonbridge. This was one of those clattering, sand-bagged, smoky, noisy, happy places that the Ministry of Food had established throughout the country to provide a good, hot meal at the cost of a food coupon or two. There they had waited to have the food slapped on their plates by the blowzy, scarlet-lipped women behind the serving tables, their hair wound up and knotted in headscarves, and cigarettes clamped in their mouths. Sam would be sat beside his mother and Sally, his hated gas-mask on the table before him, and be made to eat the meat loaf and mounds of mashed potato and gravy for which they had stood in the queue. The family would make the trip into Tonbridge by bus, and Sally and Sam would sit there watching out for disguised German paratroopers amongst their fellow passengers, whom they had been told by the baker's boy were invariably dressed as women, and could be identified by their hairy legs showing underneath their skirts.

Johnny was away for most of those wartime years, of course, but occasionally would be able to get home on leave, and would appear in the house looking handsome and gallant in his uniform and cap, every inch the military man. Priscilla would fly to him and hold him, and they would shout with laughter and Johnny would swing her round like a child whilst the two children stood shyly by and watched.

There had been a moment of total horror when Sam was just two and a half, and newly articulate. His father had arrived home for the first time for at least nine months. Sam, of course, could barely remember who he was, and was anyway perfectly content with his life at home with his pretty mother and his beloved sister and the kindly nanny who was with the family at that time. On watching his mother's joy at seeing him, and registering his own reduced status now that this man seemed to be monopolising everybody's attention, Sam turned to Johnny and told him that he wished he would go back to the war, as he was noisy and they were all much happier when he wasn't there.

Sally, who privately was not in total disagreement with Sam, but was old enough to know that his statement was an act of the gravest treachery, went bright red with dismay and embarrassment and took Sam away before anyone had time to respond. But she often thought of that moment as the next few years rolled out, and as it became clear that Johnny was uncomfortable with Sam, and seemingly rather unattached to him. And although the two children never discussed it again, Sally always believed that her father had been more hurt by the incident than would have been supposed, tiny child though Sam was, and that it had contributed to the subsequent difficulties they had together.

And perhaps she was right, for as Sam grew up it was only to Sally that he turned for simple, reliable, requited love, probably to a degree that stopped him from ever developing the range of friendships with other children that would have made him more able to cope with the horror of her death.

They were amiable enough with the other children they knew in the village, but they constructed around them an odd, private world, frequented not by a peer group, but carrying within it secret, intimate relationships with some adults who were strangers with the conventional world around them, and lived outside it. Mario, the Italian prisoner-of-war. Then Tony, the village idiot, who would sit all day by the village pond smiling vacantly and nodding incessantly, to whom Sally and Sam would give daily little treats of biscuits, and apples and greengages from Johnny's garden, and sometimes some of the cold Sunday joint carved surreptitiously as it stood in the back larder, the slices wrapped in old sheets of greaseproof paper and pressed into Tony's hands as he sat nodding on his bench, singing in his sweet, gentle, tuneless voice.

And, intensely for the first two or three months after they had first discovered him, Heinz Schumacher the German upholsterer, who had lost a leg as a boy of eighteen in the spring offensive of 1918, had been picked up and saved by a Quaker stretcher party, and in time had come to live in England with the nurse who had cared for him through his months in hospital, and whom he had subsequently married. Sally had found him and his wife when she was ten or eleven and Priscilla had sent her down to Heinz's little cottage to see if he had completed some work for her. She was so delighted by the discovery that she brought Sam down that same evening so that he could meet them too.

Heinz was a quiet, underweight, frail little man, who kept his artificial leg standing proudly in the corner of his workroom, but had never been seen to use it, and hopped around on his crutch like a tiny emaciated bird. His wife was a great, bosomy, booming, overpowering woman, and they lived entirely alone, without children, and apparently without family or friends, in what seemed to Sally and Sam to be the most perfect connubial happiness.

For a period the children would bicycle down almost daily to the Schumachers' cottage for tea. This was served in Heinz's workroom as they all four sat on the chairs and sofas which were with him for repair, and Heinz would tell them improbable stories about the trenches and his childhood in Ulm, and his father the butcher, and Mrs Schumacher would shake with laughter, and scold him for his exaggerations, and press chocolate cake on the children, which Sally was mature and sensible enough to know had been made especially for them, with ingredients which Heinz and his wife could by no means afford.

But there was some incident then with a disputed bill, or a quarrel about an overdue account, or something of the sort, and the children were forbidden by Priscilla to go down to the cottage ever again. And they never did so, through fear of punishment, nor ever smuggled the note to the Schumachers that they had meant to in explanation of their absence, and it was with a pang of real conscience that Sam heard many years later that Heinz and his wife were both now dead, and that it had been three weeks before their bodies, arms wrapped around each other, had been discovered in Heinz's gas-filled workroom.

With the war well behind them, all the family's summer holidays were at Woolacombe, and Sally and Sam would be organised into joining the games parties on the beach, whilst Johnny and Priscilla spent their days on the golf course or playing tennis, then dancing together every night in the hotel ballroom.

The children were greatly popular with the retired barrister whose beach group was acknowledged to be the established and unquestioned leader, the one that you hoped, with mounting anxiety as the summer holidays approached, that you would still be admitted to this year, despite the fact that last year's cherubic complexion had given way to incipient acne, and there were bands now on your teeth.

The Lilley children's elaborately correct manners and deportment were unrivalled by those of the other children, however, and the barrister was amused by them because of it, and enchanted by their appearance. At thirteen and ten, their fourth holiday in succession at Woolacombe – and, as it transpired, the last the two children would ever have together – they were easy candidates for selection. Sam was quite tiny, his head of curly hair hardly at shoulder height on Sally, and she was considered small for her age. The effect was made the more striking by the fact that the two children wore identical clothes of light blue Aertex shirts and dark blue shorts, which was Sally's games kit at school, Sam wearing items she had grown out of and had passed on to him. Priscilla, so well dressed herself, never appeared to notice that Sam suffered agonies of embarrassment over the fact that his shorts were cut for a girl, most obviously in their lack of fly buttons.

But they made an amusingly matched couple, and if both were ineffective at beach cricket, particularly Sam, who blushed a furious pink each time he flailed at the ball and missed, which was every time, they were so enthusiastic about everything they did, and so easy to please with their shrimping nets and their crab hooks and their sand castles and their laughter, that they were quite the barrister's favourites.

It was a very happy holiday that year. The children had been with their parents only occasionally, but Johnny and Priscilla seemed well content, too. There was a rush to get to the first tee in the morning, and there was always such a good crowd of people at Woolacombe, thank God the great unwashed haven't descended on it yet, though it won't be long, of course: may as well have a good time until the revolution, cheers Harry, my shout next I think.

The weather had been so lovely, and Sally sounded such an old moaner when she said she had a sore throat that last day of the holiday. They gave her an aspirin and told her to go out on to the beach and forget about it, and have a lovely last day shrimping or whatever she wanted to do, and it would be time enough to be unwell when they got home to Hadlow the next day, and this was Johnny's holiday after all, and he'd had such a hard year slaving away at the office to pay for school fees and lovely summer holidays and all the rest of it, and the last thing he wants to hear is a whining child.

They rushed her to the Kent and Sussex Hospital three days later, on the Monday night, but it was too late. Her temperature was uncontrollably high with the meningitis, and there was no time for the doctors to do anything else but pour into her every antibiotic available and hope that one of them would work in time. But, barely conscious, she drifted away a few hours after she had been admitted, Johnny and Priscilla at her side.

So Sam was on his own now. One afternoon a week or so after her death he moved his things into Sally's bedroom, and there he slept for the rest of his childhood and adolescence.

Priscilla was too distraught with her unhappiness to organise anything very much, or to take any of the practical steps that were needed to tidy up the last fragments of Sally's life, as was Johnny, who had declined into a lachrymose, maudlin despair.

So it was Sam – tiny, curly-haired, ten-year-old Sam – who did all that had to be done. He sorted her possessions, telephoned her two best friends from school, packed away her clothes and her books, and kept for himself just two small treasures that were with him for the rest of his life, and which he guarded from everybody. Not even Hilary or Annabel had ever known that the rabbit's foot and the Dumbo brooch, which Sam kept hidden in an old tin box holding a whole collection of his collar stiffeners and cufflinks and odd buttons, were Sally's. Sam was aware of them every day that he lived.

Perhaps it is too simple to look into a childhood for the roots of the adult's personality and character. Hilary would have said so for sure, and perhaps she would have been right. But whatever came to Sam in his later life, there was in him a disinclination to engage with unpleasantness and impurity and disloyalty and disenchanting things, and those who were puzzled with Sam and disappointed in him for this, might perhaps have found a clue to his life in the rabbit's foot and the Dumbo brooch in the ugly little tin box. Only Sally – and Annabel – had never let him down.

Chapter Eighteen

The September publishing season was always a frantic affair. The disappointments of the previous Christmas were long forgotten, and there were mutterings that the one to come would be 'good but late', which is what publishers have been telling each other since Chaucer, the truth of course being that Christmas as far as the publishing trade is concerned has always been late, and never as good as hoped for.

Sam believed in saving up some particularly promising titles for September which he might have published in June, and forcing some early which should have been published in November. All four times that Lilley & Chase had published Booker Prize short-listed novels they had been on the September list, and Sam had a decided superstitious attachment to the month.

This year their list was, by Lilley & Chase standards, most promisingly commercial. Celia Smith's book was to be promoted as one of the theatrical memoirs of the decade, and Anthony Ruges had written a sweeping, peripatetic novel that Sam anticipated would be moderately reviewed but enthusiastically received by the public, and a certainty for the bestseller lists. It had a good jacket, and Sam had arranged for it to be printed on particularly thick paper, so that it would bulk well, and enable a £15.99 price to be set. W.H. Smith would be important buyers of the book, and Sam's experience was that bulk and jackets were virtually their only selection criterion. Sam had been to their buying office in Swindon six months before with the autumn list, and after over twenty-eight years of selling to them, had decided to eliminate all other – particularly literary – considerations from his presentation.

Novel number one would be held up. Sam would say: 'Ellie

Wharton. You did well with her last one. Good jacket?' (Good jacket.) 'Just feel the bulk.' (Great bulk.) 'Four thousand to start with?' (Make it three.) And so on through the list. The meeting would be over in thirty-five minutes, and everybody would then go off to lunch.

The other major September title for the firm was the Callum Kelly novel, which Sam thought had a fair chance of getting on to the Booker Prize short list, with a possibility of winning it. Sam had been working The Ivy, Garrick Club, Groucho Club, Le Caprice word-of-mouth circuit most industriously on this one, Birdie Jones had charmed her way into securing profiles of Kelly in the *Guardian* and the *Independent On Sunday*, and victory was in the air.

Birdie was having a good run in her first few months, for she had also managed to secure Celia Smith as the subject of the September Foyle's literary lunch. Sam and Richard had been Celia's escorts, and she had swept into Grosvenor House with them on either arm, the hotel staff making a fuss of her as she went, Birdie having tipped them off in advance in both senses – extravagantly. The lunch had gone very well, and the audience of suburban ladies in hats peeked at and adored the theatre stars who sat on the top table, introduced camply and winningly by Ned Shirley, the accomplished chairman.

There was a quite extraordinary amount of kissing, and what seemed like several hundred books were signed for the Foyle's stock. ('A book signed is a book unreturnable,' murmured Sam to Celia, to keep her going.) Quite a number of books were actually bought, and the *Evening Standard* was fed by Birdie with a little piece for Londoner's Diary about one of Celia's earlier ex-husbands, who was at the lunch, but sat forlornly at a distant table. The book was on its way.

Next planned was a sweep through the North of England and Scotland, on which Celia was to be joined by Anthony Ruges and Callum Kelly, with either Ben Jackson or Sam in attendance, and Birdie as the minder.

They all met up in Edinburgh. Lilley & Chase had booked rooms at the Elizabeth Hotel at their normal, very sharp discount, Sam having promised the chairman of the Tudor Hotel Group, of which the Elizabeth was part, that Lilley & Chase would publish his memoirs when completed. They had failed to be completed in ten years, much to Lilley & Chase's corporate relief, but Sam's diligent and earnest enquiry by Christmas card each year as to how it was all going ensured continuing discounts for the company at Tudor Hotels throughout the land. When on the firm's business, staff and authors stayed nowhere else.

They had two engagements that first night. In the early part of the evening there was a signing and reading session for the three of them at Fettifer's, the old established and revered booksellers on Ainslie Bridge. This was to be followed by a Radio Scotland programme called 'North of the Border', at which they were to be joined by the ageing but legendary Scottish native broadcaster and journalist, Petrovic Johnson.

The three authors, accompanied by Ben Jackson and Birdie Jones – Sam had stayed in London – were at Fettifer's punctually at the agreed time of five-thirty, having walked across town from the Elizabeth Hotel. On arrival they were greeted by the chairman of the firm, Willy Fettifer, a ginger-moustached figure in a thick tweed suit and an Edinburgh Academy tie. He accompanied them upstairs to a section of the History department which Fettifer's used for 'socials and signings'. There were ten rows of twelve wooden chairs before a little rostrum where the three authors were to sit with Mr Fettifer. Eleven chairs were occupied, and each of the eleven people present was sitting as far away from the others as possible.

Ben and Birdie placed themselves at the front, attempting to beam encouragement up at the speakers. Mr Fettifer stood and drew from the inside pocket of his tweed jacket a sheet of paper, on which his office had typed his speech. He cleared his throat and read this verbatim in a tight, strangulated voice.

'Good evening. Thank you all for giving us such a good turn-out this evening for another of our "social and signing" events at Fettifer's. Tonight we welcome to literary Edinburgh three distinguished writers from Lilley & Chase. Dame Celia Smith . . .' Here had clearly been written PAUSE FOR APPLAUSE. There was none whatsoever until Ben and Birdie sat up and started to clap wildly. 'Anthony Ruges.' He pronounced this three times – first Rouge, then Roogs, then Roogis. Anthony flushed furiously, and mouthed angrily at Ben and Birdie, who were now applauding with the abandon of mothers at a kindergarten Christmas play, joined this time sporadically by one or two of the scattered eleven. 'And Callum Kelly.' The Irishman, who was a master of situation anecdote, and was clearly adoring the whole affair, beamed delightedly down from the rostrum.

Only nine of the eleven were still actively involved in the proceedings. One, a bag lady of apparently immense age but very few teeth, had taken from the shelves near her a £120 edition of *The Book of Kells*, which she had removed from its cellophane wrapping and was now turning over page by page, licking a filthy thumb each turn to give her better purchase. A second, a middle-aged man wearing a tartan cap, an old and filthy raincoat, tartan trousers and a pair of trainers, and clutching a paper bag from which protruded the capless neck of a whisky bottle, had fallen deeply asleep, chin on chest, snoring occasionally but heavily.

Ignoring them, Fettifer continued reading his speech. 'I now have the pleasure of asking each of our authors in turn to read extracts from their new book. We will then join the authors in a discussion on matters of literary interest, which I know many of you have so looked forward to.'

The nine had for all intents and purposes now become eight, a man at the rear having taken out a tabloid newspaper from the back pocket of his trousers which he was now engrossed in.

'First, Dame Celia Smith. A warm welcome again please, Ladies and Gentlemen.'

Celia stood, smiled sweetly, and told a charming little story of a small house she had played to in Great Yarmouth. The anecdote put a very earnest young woman in the second row into such paroxysms of prolonged and hysterical laughter, long after Ben and Birdie had abandoned their tactful light chuckling, that there was a whispered consultation between Fettifer and Ruges as to whether someone should slap her face. When the girl had eventually been quietened and helped from the room, Celia read a few paragraphs, and Ruges galloped furiously through another piece, apparently chosen completely at random, then sat down scowling, furiously waving away Birdie's attempts to start some applause.

Callum Kelly got to his feet next and read a complete short story about a country woman from County Clare, abandoned by a brutish farmer after two decades of expectation. This lasted for forty minutes, and a full hour had now elapsed since the proceedings had begun. As he finished it, Ben stood up to lead the clapping, and told Mr Fettifer that, sadly, they would have to postpone the literary discussion until another evening, to which they would all much look forward, as they were due shortly at the Radio Scotland studios.

The man with the tartan cap, now awake, asked if there would be any refreshments, and the authors were sat down by Ben and made to sign at high speed fifty copies each for the Fettifer's stock, Mr Fettifer making sporadic attempts to make them desist.

When released into the street and safely out of sight around the corner, the five of them dived into a small and filthy pub.

'Totally delightful,' said Kelly. 'What a success. So vital for us writers actually to meet our readers. Brings us back to earth. It couldn't have been more valuable. I'm determined we shall have just this sort of thing at O'Flaherty's in Cork.'

'God, I loathe the bloody Scots,' said Anthony Ruges. 'Prissy, cheap little buggers. I suppose Fettifer was too mean to do any publicity for the evening at all. No wonder no one was there.'

'I did check, Anthony,' said Birdie. 'I really did, and they said the town was literally plastered with posters.'

'Yes – I saw one of them.' Celia was now on her second large gin and tonic. 'One of those hand-drawn things with each letter in a different colour that children do for their school fêtes. There's one in the Ladies here. There's probably one in the Gents.'

'Probably *was* one in the Gents,' said Anthony. 'None of these pubs in bloody Scotland ever have bog rolls. If that's where the things have been put, I'm not surprised we had a small audience.'

They spent another thirty minutes or so in the dingy little bar, and then set off for the Radio Scotland studios by taxi. Celia was by this point slurred in speech and verging on aggressive in behaviour, having been particularly irritated by Callum Kelly, whom she had not met before.

'Your lovely short story – or was it a complete novel? – absolutely saved the evening, darling. So clever of you to realise that Anthony and I had been such awful old bores. It didn't seem too long at all the way you read it. So moving, too. I did think the farmer was such an old sweetie. I was terrified he was going to get himself trapped by that awful girl.'

Birdie thought wearily of the days ahead, when the party was due to move on to Glasgow, Aberdeen, Newcastle, Liverpool, Manchester, York and finally Brighton. Seven more Tudor Hotels to weather, and seven more days of signings, dinners, speeches, local radio and press. If Celia and Callum were going to quarrel, it would be a long haul. She decided to ring Sam at home tonight, and get some advice on how to handle all this.

In fact, had she realised what was awaiting the party at the hotel later that night, her nerve would have broken earlier. The radio programme had gone rather well. Each of the authors was allowed the chance to talk about their book in quite adequate detail. Johnson had told some familiar stories, but told them well, the presenter had been sympathetic and well briefed, and the atmosphere in the taxi back to the Elizabeth Hotel was positively jocular. And then the blow struck.

There were messages for each of them, and in Anthony's pile was a faxed copy of a review of his novel in that day's *Irish Times*. The reviewer was Callum Kelly. Initially mildly appreciative and generous about Ruges's narrative sense and drive, the final paragraphs took a savage turn. As Anthony read them he reddened and started to perspire.

'Ruges's career has been a long one, and he has his place amongst the minor craftsmen of the last three decades. But his books may soon be lost. There is an immaturity of mind beneath a veneer of worldly sophistication. His plots repeat. His ideas are not so much reworked as replayed. We tire of his narrow range of metaphor. There is a flaccid quality to the prose. No real issues are addressed. His books have neither advanced our understanding, nor sufficiently lightened our hours.

'Ruges stands in a long and not undistinguished line of authors who have done very well from their writing. We should be glad for him that he has made money, and enjoyed a good level of commercial success. He should be content with that. Perhaps he has written too much. Perhaps, with more self-discipline, a better writer would have emerged. He has had his triumphs, and he has certainly had his rewards. He is not without reputation. But the truth, I believe, is that the reputation exceeds the achievement. Substantially.'

When Anthony had finished reading this, he handed it to Birdie. Kelly was over on the other side of the lobby talking to the people at the reception desk, and Celia was looking through her post. Birdie read the review and handed it back to Ruges. Her expression was blanched and anguished. Without saying a further word to any of them, he took his bags in either hand and went on up to his room.

Chapter Nineteen

When Birdie rang, Sam had just got home from a launch party at the Groucho Club for a new publishing house, which had been named Bedford Square. Sam wished the new firm well, but anticipated disaster for it.

The founder and chairman was a plump, slightly balding man in his early forties, who could charm the sparrows from the trees, and was fiercely intelligent, but cheerfully improvident. In his immediate post-Oxford days he had worked at Lilley & Chase in the rights department, and Sam had been very fond of him.

Sam had met some of the founding investors at the party, and indeed had given carefully guarded but generous references on Steven to many of them over the telephone in the course of the preceding months. Talking to them at the party, he realised that they had swallowed the Bedford Square business plan hook, line and sinker. It was logical, intelligent, numerate, self-confident, persuasive and impossible to reject. To read it was to feel privileged that one might, if deeply fortunate, be allowed the opportunity of becoming an investor in this flawless and prestigious enterprise. In Sam's opinion every hypothesis on which it was built was marginally but significantly wrong. As one of the older hands in the desperate and losing game of trying to keep a literary publishing house solvent, he looked forward, with considerable and delicious anticipation, to seeing how Steven would cope.

He was always greatly warmed by the company of Steven, and enjoyed the party. Before leaving, Sam slipped his arm through his and wished him and his firm bon voyage, relating with amusement the conversation he had just had with an earnest young man from the City, who explained to Sam that the reason Steven's firm was going to revolutionise publishing was that Steven's returns rate was going to be under five per cent, whereas the rest of the industry was struggling at a rate of at least twenty per cent.

Steven grinned. 'So it will be, Sam. So it will be. You publish such crap that I'm surprised you don't invert the equation and look for five per cent solds.'

Sam laughed and said goodbye, kissed a Lilley & Chase author whom he passed on the way out, making a mental note to ensure that Ben gave her especially devoted treatment over the next few months, and caught a taxi in Old Compton Street to take him home.

Birdie's call did not entirely surprise him, but he promised to fly up to Scotland in time for the Waterwell's literary dinner in Glasgow on the Thursday night. He told Birdie that, if relationships had become too strained by that point, he would reorganise all the schedules, separate Callum Kelly from the other two, and accompany him on a special tour for him alone.

There was a part of Sam that actually rather agreed with what Kelly had said. Anthony had written too much too quickly. Twenty books were in print, and twenty-nine had been published in fewer years. He was very difficult to edit, impatient of criticism, and resentful of any attempt at amendment, save occasionally by Sam himself. He did have a strong and attractive sense of narrative, but he had found little new to say in the last six or seven books, and for those who knew his work well, there was more self-plagiarism than was comfortable. Not so much structured leitmotifs as sloppy repetition.

Anthony was in fact a frequently brutal reviewer himself, but the wounds tended to be slight because the blows were unfocused, and sometimes too overtly motivated by personal antagonism. Indeed, underlying Anthony's whole personality was a sense of understated, unreleased malice, and despite all the years of working together, Sam was never entirely comfortable that he knew and trusted him. But there was no doubt that the commercial success of his books had contributed greatly to the health and survival of Lilley & Chase, and Sam's instinctive protectiveness towards him was an acknowledgement of this.

'Jesus,' muttered Sam. 'I didn't know that Callum was reviewing

Anthony for them. The *Irish Times* have always been rather good to him in the past. Didn't Maeve do something nice for him last time? Hold the ring, Birdie. I'll see you at the Waterwell's dinner, and keep them apart as much as possible. Make sure that Celia doesn't know what's happened or she'll have a ball.'

'Jesus,' he said again as he put the telephone down. He went to the fridge, took out a packet of Philadelphia, spread the lot on one slice of wholemeal bread, and sat down at the kitchen table to eat it. This would be Sam's dinner. He was actually quite a competent cook, but when alone seldom did more than open a tin of soup, or scramble an egg. At one stage he had eaten an egg almost every night he was at home, but he had been greatly impressed by the Philadelphia advertising claim that it contained half the calories of butter, and for the last few weeks he had eaten practically nothing else. The fact that he had never much liked butter, and now ate Philadelphia at the rate of one packet a meal did not occur to him.

His mind turned to the Glasgow dinner on Thursday, and he wondered if Tom Waterwell would be there to chair it. He had read a recent profile of Waterwell in the *Guardian*, and smiled at the memory of it. It had been oddly, emphatically critical of Waterwell's appearance, which had never struck Sam as being anything else but the plain side of neutral. 'Jug ears,' Sam recalled happily. 'Gnome-faced. Weak-chinned.' And then he recalled that, positioning Waterwell as some sort of nightmare figure of High Victorian moralistic hypocrisy, the article had been accompanied by a caricature drawing reminiscent of Mr Squeers, with the caption: MR NICE DOES NICELY.

Sam laughed contentedly. Serves him right, the silly bugger, he thought. Never pays on time, and damned greedy for discount. And, whistling cheerfully, Sam went up to bed.

Chapter Twenty

Annabel set off from Hilary's at four o'clock, having had one of those Sunday afternoons in a country house that feel irritatingly wasted. Sunday lunch at Hilary's was a serious affair: roast lamb, mounds of roast potatoes, and apple crumble and cream. It always felt as if it was half-term and Annabel was being fattened up with home cooking before being returned to school to starve.

They had sat in armchairs afterwards, swapped pages of the Sunday papers, talked a little and dozed a little. Hilary arranged to come to London and stay with Annabel in a month or so, and chose a play she wanted to see. Jack took Annabel's car off and filled it with petrol, fussing around with the tyre pressures and oil. It was a pleasant, affectionate day. Nothing of any great meaning was discussed, no important decisions made, there were no revelations, no bursts of emotion, no tensions, no points of stress.

When Annabel left there were simple embraces and cheerful waves, quite unlike any occasion she left Priory Grove, when she felt every time she was making a fresh wound on Sam. She drove through the country roads to the motorway junction, looked at her watch, and calculated that if the traffic was reasonable she would be home before seven. The late afternoon was warm, the motorway monotonous, and several times Annabel felt herself at the point of falling asleep. She wound the window down, found the noise excessive, and wound the window up again. She thought of drawing off at a junction and finding a place where she could stop and rest for half an hour or so, but she did not want to waste the time.

She passed the Oxford turning, and told herself that she only had ninety minutes or so to go. Ten minutes later she fell asleep, and woke with the car crossing the hard shoulder and heading straight for the wooden fence that bounded the motorway, beyond which was a drop of twelve feet or so into a rough field. The car went straight through the fence, dropped, burst its tyres as it hit the ground, rolled over several times, and exploded into flames.

When the police got there about ten minutes later, the car was almost burnt out and Annabel was dead.

PART TWO

Prologue

'I know that my Redeemer liveth, And that He shall stand at the latter day upon the earth, And though this body be destroyed, yet shall I see God . . .'

Sam stood alone, hands straight down his sides, listening to Christopher as he led them quietly into Annabel's funeral service. Jack had motioned him to stand next to Hilary in his place, but he had smiled his refusal. They had asked for privacy and they had it. Just eight of them were in the church: Hilary, Sam, Jack, Hilary's sister Mollie, Norah, Mark and Andrew Boot inconspicuously at the very back, tucked away at the side with the four pallbearers.

Hilary stood with Jack and Mollie on her either side. She was ashen, and her face was only just held in composure, biting at her lower lip, her chin just on the move. Jack's head was bowed, and his hand nearest Hilary was open and ready to hold her arm. Mollie, as she could be depended to do, stood calm and resolute, gazing straight ahead, composed and courageous.

Sam's face was set and expressionless. He looked a little dishevelled, as he so often did, his thick wiry hair, now flecking with grey, rather cursorily brushed, his shirt collar curling up.

'For Christ's sake, just get me through this,' he muttered to himself, 'just get me through it.'

Christopher read the prayers in a gentle, rhythmic, practised voice. 'Oh God, whose mercies cannot be numbered: Accept our prayers on behalf of Thy servant, Annabel, and grant her an entrance into the land of light and joy, in the fellowship of the same.'

And it's true, thought Sam. I am praying for her. I do want her to be a servant of God. I do pray that she has her entrance into her land of light and joy. Whatever that is. That's all I want.

If I can hold that picture I can get through this, and I can get through the rest of my life. I've got to stop remembering her as she was. I've got to stop replaying her childhood, and the way she ran at me across the room the day I left Hilary. And watching her in the school play and . . . oh Christ . . . and although he managed to remain standing rock-still, the tears were pouring down his face, and he was biting his lip to stop himself from making any sound.

Christopher glanced up at him, but continued reading without break or pause, allowing the rhythmic, lean beat of the prose to anaesthetise the bleak, cold, devastated sorrow he could see on the faces before him.

'Like as the hart desireth the water brooks, so longeth my soul after Thee, O God.'

Got to put this behind me soon, thought Sam. Got to move forward. Can't bring her back. One day I'll face remembering things. But not now. Let all this stuff wash over me. Think of her in the land of light and joy. Don't go to pieces now. Keep going. Don't go to pieces now.

They were moving out into the graveyard now, and Sam was able to push his sleeve quickly over his face. Nearly through now. Nearly through.

'In the midst of life we are in death; of whom may we seek for succour but of Thee, O Lord . . .'

God, how I long for death, too. How I long for a closing of all this. I've got to find some strength. I've got to hold on. Must hold on.

'We commend to Almighty God our sister Annabel, and we commit her body to the ground. Earth to earth, ashes to ashes, dust to dust. The Lord bless her and keep her. The Lord make His face to shine upon her and be gracious unto her, the Lord lift up His countenance upon her and give her peace.'

'Peace, Bells. Peace,' muttered Sam, and suddenly and at last he felt an unexpected measure of calm and control come over him.

'Rest eternal grant to her, O Lord. And let light perpetual shine upon her. May her soul, and the souls of all the faithful departed, Through the grace of God, rest in peace.

'Amen,' said Christopher, and closed his prayer book, and looked up at the little group around him.

Sam shuffled his feet, smiled bleakly at him, briefly held and kissed Norah, waved a hand at Mollie and Mark, then walked over to Hilary, and put his arms around her. It was their first physical embrace since their marriage had ended twenty-three years before. She put her arms around his back, and they stood for a moment, motionless, holding tightly to each other.

'Goodbye, Hils. So many things we could say.'

He released her, nodded to Jack, and strode off quickly on his own to find the safety of his car, and the promise of the privacy and solitude of Priory Grove.

Chapter Twenty-One

They had traced the car ownership within a few minutes, had forced their way into Annabel's flat within an hour, and within two had paged Sam at Manchester airport as he came off a plane with Callum Kelly. The British Airways office had given him the London police number to call, and he was left in the privacy of a closed room while he did so. The police officer told him the news directly, calmly, and with a certain tender simplicity.

Callum Kelly had come into the room and found Sam sitting absolutely motionless at the desk, gazing in front of him with a face almost purged of any expression at all. He turned to look at Kelly, asked him to leave, and he went to wait outside.

After about twenty minutes Sam dialled Hilary's number in Wiltshire. Jack had answered the telephone, recognised his voice, started to make some friendly greeting, but sensed something was very wrong, and motioned Hilary to come over to take the call. Sam told her what had happened. He had kept his voice very low, and he tried to beam tenderness and gentleness to her so that she might hold herself together. They were on the telephone for an hour. There were minutes of silence, there was a bad moment of raised voices and a near quarrel, but there was a directness of communication between them of a sort they had not known for two decades.

Jack had pulled a chair up beside Hilary and sat stroking her hand. Sam wanted to keep her on the line until such time as he felt absolutely certain that she was calm enough to be released. After a time they had even become tender together, the grief numbing them, their voices almost at a whisper, Sam keeping up a gentle repetitive liturgy. 'Hold on, Hils. Hold on. Hold on.'

* * *

For three days after Annabel's death, Sam sat on the floor of the Priory Grove hall. He got up occasionally to get a slice of bread or a cup of tea, and, halfway through the second night, a bottle of whisky.

For most of the time he sat hugging himself, periodically muttering, 'Dear God' or 'Christ.' Once, having shouted 'Bells, Bells, Bells,' he broke into sobbing, and after that he slept, curled up on the carpet.

The telephone rang regularly, but he did not get up to answer it. On one occasion someone banged continuously on the front-door knocker and called his name, but he recognised the voice as Hazel's, and did not get off the floor. On the third day a police car drew up outside the house, and Sam saw the reflection of the revolving blue light and heard the chatter of the two-way radio system. There was a knock on the door, and Sam opened it. On the doorstep were two policemen and Jack.

The policemen asked Sam if he needed help, but before he could answer Jack spoke to them and they returned to the car and drove off.

Jack came into the house and put his hand on Sam's elbow. 'Come on, Sam. Come up for a bath.' He guided him up the two floors to Sam's bedroom and bathroom, turned on the taps and said, 'Get into that, Sam. I'll come up in a moment with a mug of tea, and then I'll fix you something to eat.'

Sam undressed and climbed into the bath, then Jack reappeared with the tea and put it in Sam's hands. He sat on the lavatory-seat lid, and for ten minutes or so neither of them said anything, though Sam drank his tea, and once or twice turned the hot tap on with his toe. Then Jack said:

'We've arranged a private funeral for Friday afternoon at St Barnabas's in the King's Road, and Hilary asked me to say that she hoped you would organise a memorial service there in four weeks or so. Christopher Howard has done the arrangements for the funeral with the vicar there. Norah Howard is coming down for it, incidentally. She sent a long message to Hilary yesterday by courier, and she said how worried she was about you, and that she's been trying to reach you on the telephone. She's travelling down to London tonight, I think. Everything is done, and there's nothing for you to worry about. I'm going down to Wiltshire again tonight, and I'll drive Hilary up on Friday morning.'

Jack went to the little dressing room, and came back with Sam's towelling bathrobe. 'Put it on, Sam. Then come down to the kitchen for something to eat.'

They sat at the kitchen table, and Sam half ate the omelette that Jack made him. He pushed with his fork at the rest of it. 'Sorry, Jack. I feel terribly sick. Thank you for doing this. I can't get myself going at all yet. I can't actually say that I want to very much. You must get back to Hilary.'

'She's gone walking all day with her sister. Mollie's come up from Cornwall to be with her. You know what friends they are. Mollie's more use to Hilary at the moment than I am, actually. I want to be with you now. I rang Christopher Howard earlier this morning and he's going to come around later. I hope you don't mind.'

'No one else, Jack. I don't want anyone else here. I don't want to be jollied. This all feels beyond jollying.'

There was a silence, then Sam's head went into his hands, his elbows on the table, and he sobbed quietly for some minutes. Jack sat still in his chair and said nothing. When the crying stopped, Sam remained in the same position for a time, then looked up.

'Sorry, Jack. Except I didn't ask you to come here. It helps when I can do that. I hope to hell I can do it a lot more. I wouldn't mind doing it for the rest of my life actually. Look – hop it now.'

Jack got to his feet, and started to move to the door. 'Before you go . . .' Sam called to him, and for a moment they looked at each other without speaking. 'Bless you, Jack. I know what you did for Annabel . . . oh Christ . . .' and he started weeping again, this time standing with his back to Jack, his arms hugged tight across his chest, his face, deliberately hidden, grimaced and puckered tight. In time the sobbing ceased, and Sam turned around again. He looked totally drained now. There was a degree of exhaustion in his face that Jack had never seen before in anyone. He was used to Sam as he normally looked: cheerful, rather battered, in recent years a little puffy around the cheeks and chin. Now his face had lost much of its weight and was drawn and white, his eyes red-rimmed and staring.

'Let's try that again. You did a hell of a lot for Annabel. Much more than any of us could have expected. You're a very good man. Now sod off. Call me tomorrow about the Friday thing.' And then, as Jack was opening the front door, 'Hold on to Hils, Jack. As if you wouldn't. And Jack . . .' Sam walked through the hall and stood with him, ' . . . thanks for coming.'

When Christopher arrived an hour or so later, Sam was looking tidier, and more in control. He had shaved and brushed his hair and had thrown on a blue cotton shirt, sleeves loose at the wrist, and a comfortably worn pair of khaki trousers. He opened the front door to Christopher, smiled at him, and showed him up to the first-floor drawing room. It was a wet, drizzling evening now, and Sam shivered.

'Bloody weather. Call this summer. Hello, Christopher.'

'I'm not going to be a nuisance, Sam. I'm not going to try to make you pray with me, or any of that, so don't worry. I'm here because Jack asked me to come. We both know there's nothing I can do. But it's better to have a fellow human to look at than to be alone all the time. Perhaps I can make you a cup of tea.'

'Everyone keeps on making me fucking cups of tea.' For the first time in four days, Sam laughed. He felt first better for it, and then immediately a shaft of pain went through him again. Christopher looked at him closely, and studied him for a few moments. He had an intimation of the danger Sam was in.

'Actually, I'm going to stay here longer than I thought I was going to. Including tonight. I'll call Mark in a moment and get him to throw some things in a bag for me.'

Sam did not reply. For a long time they sat silently, Christopher moving to a chair outside Sam's line of vision, so that he would not be disturbed by eye contact. Mark eventually arrived with the bag, handed it to Christopher, went up to the drawing room, dropped on his haunches before Sam, and for a few seconds held both his hands in his. He then got up and left without a word.

Christopher distrusted alcohol, but made a pot of coffee later in the evening and put some brandy in Sam's cup. They talked intermittently, and only when Sam led. There was no talk of religion or after-life, and no more reference to prayer. At one point Sam got up and played a record of the Elgar piano quintet. The longest period of talk was a reminiscence by Sam of some moments of Annabel's childhood. They talked a little of Hilary, and of broken marriages. Sam refused anything to eat, but drank some more coffee. The telephone rang frequently, Christopher took all the calls, and Sam refused to speak to anybody. At almost midnight Sam got up and said they should both go to bed.

Christopher awoke the next morning to find Sam standing at his bedside, fully dressed for the office, bathed and shaved, but looking grim and drawn, with his eyes bloodshot and red-rimmed.

'I'm feeling a lot better, Chris. I'm going to go into the office. Got to sell some books. Just let yourself out when you're ready. See you tomorrow.'

Later that morning, Christopher rang Hazel, saying he had Norah with him. She said that Sam would not take any calls or talk to anyone, bar a few simple words with her. He had signed some letters and cheques, scribbled out one or two handwritten notes to people, and made two telephone calls. She didn't know to whom. Three dozen white roses had arrived from Celia Smith, and letters marked 'Strictly Personal' were standing in piles on Hazel's desk.

Richard had rung through from his office, but Hazel had put him off. She had cancelled Sam's lunch appointment with a literary agent, and Sam did not emerge from his office all day until about four-thirty when he suddenly burst out, pulling on his raincoat at the same time.

'The funeral's tomorrow, Hazel, and I don't think I'll be in. Christ . . .' he said, as he saw the roses and the piles of letters. 'I'll tackle all that soon.'

He raised a hand and set off, and Hazel got up and hurried after him. 'Sam. Sam.'

He turned.

'Sam.' She looked at him and raised her arms in a shrugging

gesture of helplessness. 'I would so love to be able to say something to you that would mean anything. Oh, Sam.'

'Never mind, Hazel. It's all a bit private, this thing. You know what I'm like.' He smiled, and was gone.

Chapter Twenty-Two

Over the following weeks, a certain pattern evolved in Sam's life. He went to the office for an hour or two most days, but only that, and when there did little else but sit at his desk signing cheques and scribbling little handwritten letters.

The staff learnt to leave him alone, and only Ben Jackson made a point of coming to see him every time he was in, Hazel being instructed to call through to his office the moment Sam arrived. Sam made attempts to be affectionate and warm to Hazel, but there was complete withdrawal behind the smile, and she knew this of course.

Richard was now in the office every day, and there was always a stream of people coming in and out of his room as he took control of the daily management of the business. Sam would come and go at erratic times, each time just raising a hand at Hazel and smiling.

He spent long hours wandering around London, setting off with no particular route in mind, hands thrust in his pockets, and, with the onset of autumn, the collar of his old blue cashmere coat turned up, its buttons undone, a red silk scarf – a present from Annabel – untied at his neck.

He once walked from Chelsea to Hampstead without having really thought what he was doing and, finding himself near Celia Smith's house, called to see if she was there.

Her house was a pretty Regency villa, with mature gardens at the sides and rear, and open views down over Haverstock Hill and to London beyond. She had lived there ever since her fourth and final marriage had ended eight or nine years before.

Having knocked at the door with no result, Sam made his way around the side of the house and found Celia kneeling at the herbaceous border, her long green gardening apron tied at her waist, weeding and scraping with a sharp little hand-hoe.

'Oh, Sam!' She clambered rather arthritically to her feet, and hugged him hard, pressed against her. 'Oh, darling! I'm so glad you came. I've spoken to Hazel several times and I'm so worried about you.'

She held him away from her and studied his face. 'And you look pretty ghastly, darling. Settle down on the terrace here' – she put her arm through his and led him across the lawn – 'and we'll have some tea and a long talk. I won't be a second, and don't bolt again, darling, will you? I've got a good mind to lock the gate so you can't.'

When she returned, she poured Earl Grey into delicate porcelain cups, and passed Sam a thick slice of brown bread spread with butter. 'Eat that! And after that you are going to have a large slice of plum cake.'

She started to cut the dark brown cake beside her. 'Nanny's orders. I might well make you have two.'

She studied him closely again. 'You do look awful, Sam. You've got to pull yourself around. Tell me how you are. Tell me what I can do.'

God, this is a mistake, he thought. Celia's wonderful company when you're in the mood for all that stuff, but I just can't handle it at the moment. She's very kind and generous and warm but it's always such a production. She observes herself doing it. She is incapable of an unstudied gesture. She's now at centre-stage, performing as the adored mother-figure comforting and strengthening the tragic, bereaved friend. She'll suddenly break into a speech from *Mother Courage* without realising what she's doing. There is genuine kindness in her, but I need much simpler help than this.

He smiled at her, made a slight shrugging movement, then smiled again to indicate that there would be no fuller response from him than that. They looked at each other for a moment, then Sam said, 'Celia – I've no idea what's going on at the moment. I'm so sorry. I haven't even looked at your sales figures or read your reviews.'

'Sales excellent, reviews good,' said Celia. 'Except for that unspeakable bitch in the *Guardian*. My God, what a woman. Ralph was so sweet in *The Times*, and they got darling Sybil to review for the *Independent*. No, everything has been very successful really, though I never want to do another bookshop signing as long as I live. Dear God! Simper, simper, simper, scribble, scribble, scribble. Callum Kelly seemed to disappear after Glasgow, but Anthony was with me, of course. Quiet as a lamb, poor darling – most unlike him.'

'Look, Celia – it's been lovely to see you. Thanks for the tea. Long walk home. I'm so glad all's well.'

'Don't be ridiculous, Sam. You've only just arrived. Look, darling, would you do something for me? You know what I was like when Harry and I broke up. Or rather when I left him, or whatever I did. Elspeth got me to go to a psychiatrist. Dragged me there actually. His name was, is, Wilson-Smith, and he's at the top end of Harley Street, opposite the London Clinic. He was quite marvellous with me. Saw me at any time of day or night, was always there when I wanted him, and always so calm and wise and lovely. Perhaps he saved my life. Or perhaps I'm being over-dramatic. But he was so good with me. Look – let me scribble down his name for you.'

She went into the house, and came back with a little piece of paper. 'Call him, Sam. Do try. I'll ring Hazel in a few days to make sure you've done so.'

Sam stuffed the note in his pocket. 'OK, Celia. Lots of love. Thanks for everything. I'm so glad the book is doing well.'

They chatted for ten minutes or so more, they kissed, she laid her hand on his cheek, and with a wave he went out again the way he had come, through the garden. A hundred yards up the road he passed a bin, and dropped the piece of paper in it.

There is, he thought, a part of me that is incapable of open communication with people that I am genuinely close to. Particularly when it matters. Even with Annabel I could never allow myself the risk of treating her like an adult over anything of importance. Celia is barely more than an acquaintance. So I go to see her. I know she won't get near me, so I am content to play the game with her. When I am hurt I can only talk to acquaintances. Pretending a mutual confidence and familiarity that both sides know is not really there. There is only one person close enough to me to be of real help. Hilary. And with Hilary there is too much rawness of pain between us to face this together. Hazel would try. Quite desperately she would try. But she can't help. So I go to Celia. And Celia and I then play a luvvie game together of tragic grief and heroic friendship. Meaningless and empty. Christ. Annabel's death is too important for that. I'm the original emotional cripple. All love, and all inability to handle it maturely.

He shook his head. 'Witch-doctors, for Christ's sake,' he muttered, and walked on. By the underground station he turned down the High Street, saw the black-fronted Waterwell's branch and wandered in through the open door. Books stood heaped high on the tables, and in smaller piles on the floor. The bookseller at the till, a young, cheerful boy in jeans and a sweatshirt, was arguing good-naturedly with an older man whom Sam recognised, with a slight start of dread, as a Lilley & Chase salesman. Sam began to move towards the door again, when his name was called.

'Sam! Sam!' Sam turned, put a grin on his face, and walked up to the till.

'Hello, Ted. Hello!' He shook hands with the bookseller. 'Delighted to see so many of our books here. Everything selling?'

'You know us,' said the bookseller. 'We sell books by the yard. Even your stuff.' Sam smiled, said there was fifty quid in it for him for every Bedford Square title he returned, and, reluctantly, but unwilling to be impolite, accepted an offer of a lift back to Chelsea from Ted the salesman.

He was fond of Ted, and always enjoyed his caustic, ritualised cynicism at sales conferences, his best performances being reserved for bright-eyed young editors presenting their lists with what Ted and the other old lags considered to be unseemly enthusiasm.

Sam hoped very much that the fifteen-minute journey would pass with no more than a banal exchange of Lilley & Chase gossip. So it did, until Ted had drawn into The Boltons to drop Sam off at the top of Gilston Road. Then, 'Sam – do you mind if I'm a little bit personal for a moment? Watch how you go, Sam. You know how it is. We've all got so used to having you as the great autocrat. I'm sorry about all your awful news. But don't leave it too long before you get back into the saddle. There's a little bit of talk going on about what's happening. You know what publishing houses are like. One or two enemies are beginning to come out of the woodwork. It's just . . . well, come back to us as soon as you can, Sam. Let's just leave it like that.'

Sam patted him on the knee, got out of the car, slammed the door and, with a wave, walked the hundred yards or so back to Priory Grove. 'Witch-doctors,' he muttered. 'Enemies in the woodwork . . . Christ!'

Rather too many days passed in this way. He walked to Richmond Park and back along the river. All the way down the Embankment one Sunday, around the deserted streets of the City of London, with the great office buildings and banks empty and still. Again up to Hampstead, but this time he kept well away from Celia's house, and looped across the Heath to Highgate, then down through Parliament Hill and Primrose Hill.

He saw nobody, and left his telephone on answerphone even when in the house. He returned calls only very selectively and occasionally. He once went to church, having a sudden longing to hear good sacred music. He chose a small, very high-Anglican church he had been to sometimes over the years, but left rather noisily after ten minutes or so, having taken a profound dislike to the vicar. He drank a bit, read a bit, grew careless over his meal-times, went to bed late, got up late, left mail lying unopened and unread.

There was no more weeping, and the edge of the pain had blunted, but what was left was a dull, dark melancholy, remorseless and without relief. After a time he stopped going to the office at all, having written a note to Richard saying that he was going to be away for exactly four weeks more, that he would be returning then fully restored and eager for work, and apologising for his absence. He did this in a moment of energy, and had the wit to know he should seize it before it passed.

He recognised Richard's handwriting on a reply that came by messenger the following day, but by that time the melancholy had returned, there was a dark listlessness hanging over him, and the letter lay unopened. That night he rang Hilary, but when she picked up the telephone he found himself able only to make a brief greeting before lapsing into silence. She held on and waited for him. Then in time, 'Hils . . .'

'Sam?'

Again a wait. 'Bit of a haul, isn't it?'

'Get some help, Sam. There's nothing to be ashamed of. Get some help.'

'Hils . . .'

'Sam?'

'Sorry it all happened.'

'It's so many years ago, Sam. I was at fault. You were at fault. It was one of those things. We were very young. It just happened. I'm sorry too, Sam. It's taken twenty-three years for us to say that to each other. I'm glad we've done it now.'

There was a silence again. Then, 'Hils . . .'

'Sam?'

'There were some good things. Some wonderful things. I still think of them all the time.'

'I do too, Sam.'

'Goodnight, Hils.'

'Goodnight, Sam. Get some help. Please get some help.'

Chapter Twenty-Three

Hazel struggled with her bags as the up-escalator discharged her on to the first floor at Peter Jones. One more department – she needed some buttons and thread and the Peter Jones' haberdashery department seemed to be about the last one left in London – and then up to the top floor for coffee and a croissant in the restaurant or, if that was too crowded, round the corner to the General Trading Company and their nice, leafy, basement-garden coffee shop.

In fact, come to think about it, she would go there anyway, and while there she could try to replace that plate she had broken the other night. Except they always made you buy them in packs of six these days, and she really did not want to spend eighty pounds or whatever that would be.

I come to Peter Jones every Saturday morning of my life, she thought. It really is extraordinary how a single woman like me, living alone, with moderate tastes and a small flat, can find the need to come here every seven days. But I do. I'm at the moment clutching four bags, just as I did last week, and will do next week, and no doubt the week after that as well.

And the contents of the bags followed much in her normal pattern as well. A new jersey for Sam. Navy blue, round-necked and lambswool, the only colour, style and wool he would ever wear. She had found this out by observing the fate of any variant jersey she had ever bought him; invariably affectionately received, but never seen again. A lampshade for her mother. It was her birthday in a month, and Hazel hated the stress of leaving birthday-present-buying until the last moment. A new tie for Sam. Exactly as always: red paisley silk of medium width. Sam's ties needed replacing at least once every three months, as they bore the stains of three or

231

four publishing lunches a week. Though of course there had not been any publishing lunches recently. But she was anxious to keep the rhythms of her life going, and one of the most precious rhythms of all was the weekly purchase of presents for Sam. A large blue bath towel for her mother. Her mother rang every week with something that was needed; for her, for Hazel's grandmother, or her aunt, or for the head dairyman, or for someone or other. The purchases sat in Hazel's second bedroom and were delivered or collected monthly.

Sam and her mother. That was pretty well her life. Although there were other bits that mattered, like the local Christian Aid group of which she was treasurer, and the Meals on Wheels committee of which she was secretary, and the tennis club, where she had been captain, and was still an occasional member of the team. And then there was old Mrs Harris next door to shop for and take to the clinic, and Mrs Rogers on the corner who was so frail and lonely and loved their weekly talk and the look through her old family photographs, and there was the Conservative Association, and the Chelsea Residents' Association where she was chairman of the Gardening committee.

Her cappuccino and her croissant stood before her on the little table with its gingham tablecloth, and she pushed the plate backwards and forwards in a pensive, unconscious gesture. Perhaps I do too much, she thought. But she knew so many people and kept so busy and all that stopped her from too much brooding about Sam, although there was certainly enough of that.

She thought about their love-making together and its almost absurd regularity. Except for when she had her short summer holiday with her mother, or when Sam was in New York or in Europe visiting publishers there, or at the Frankfurt Book Fair, they went to bed with each other every seven days, usually Tuesdays, and always at her flat.

Quite apart from his marrying her, or even living with her, she would have been so happy if he had spent nights with her more frequently than the five or six times a year it happened. But he hadn't, and he wouldn't now, except . . . perhaps now with Annabel dead? She would bring him so much love if he would accept it. And they got on well physically. Their love-making was always extremely pleasurable, entirely assured, always affectionate.

His happy lack of physical self-doubt had initially been good for Hazel; when she met him in her early twenties she had had fairly frequent but consistently unsuccessful little escapades with a variety of men her own age, these leaving her full of self-doubt and uncertain of her physical attractiveness.

Sam approached her with an intense and expert carnality, and this persuaded her of her physical appeal in a way that a more tentative, softer approach might never have done. And for all those years she had never slept with anyone else, or ever been mildly tempted to sleep with anyone else. Sam was all she ever wanted or needed. She was aroused and fulfilled by him, and although she knew there were parts of his life she could never reach, and darknesses of which she could only catch just the shadows, she had of him as much as he would allow. She was faithful quite instinctively and without any desire to be anything else. More than that: an act of infidelity to Sam would be like an act of violation against what was most dear to her.

It was an irony in a way that this side of their relationship was so without strain or difficulty. It would have been the perfect physical base for marriage. And indeed in so many other ways, Hazel felt, a marriage between them would have been entirely successful, even given Sam's profound sense of privacy over Annabel and Hilary. There was an intellectual imbalance between them perhaps, but this did not seriously intrude. Indeed, although Sam was much better read than she was, and possessed a much stronger historical and political grasp, she was certainly the better linguist, and an unusually experienced and knowledgeable theatre- and ballet-goer. He was the more adventurous conversationalist, but she was by no means poor company. In all, she was sure an observer would have concluded that they were as well suited to be married as most people who marry are.

The last few weeks, since Annabel's death, had been such a nightmare. She had become stricken with anxiety about Sam. They had seen each other only in that first week or so when he was making his short little visits, sitting in his office and signing cheques and writing his notes.

She was desperate to speak to him, but did not know the way to approach it. She went home for lunch each Tuesday as before, hoping that he would come. She heard from Richard Chase that he was to be away completely for a month and would then return full time, but she had no letter from him herself, and the daily notes she sent around to Priory Grove were never answered. She left messages on his answerphone that were not returned.

And yet – she took the blue jersey out of the Peter Jones bag and looked at it again – she did not feel that she had lost him. There were the physical bonds between them. There were the habits and familiarities of over twenty years. There was the humour and the friendship. She had drawn short of insisting on marriage because she knew that if she did so she ran the risk of losing him. So would she now be careful not to be so insistent on seeing him over this period lest she frighten him away.

It could well be that he would never get rid of his grief unless he was allowed to burn it up in solitude. It might be that he was nearly there. She looked at her bill and took money from her purse. She would go back home now, give the flat a really good clean and tidy, and make sure that the drinks cupboard was full and that there were plenty of good things in the refrigerator. She smiled to herself. And some mulligatawny soup, of which she had known him eat two cans at a sitting. And she would send him another short little letter this afternoon, with the new CD of Mahler 5 with Tennstedt and The London Philharmonic. She would take a taxi now to the big HMV store in Oxford Street to get that, then walk down to the Algerian Coffee Stores in Old Compton Street to buy a pound of his favourite Gourmet Noir blend, and then another taxi home.

She stepped out into Sloane Street. She thought: do I know anyone else like me? I wonder what I look like to other people? Childless, neurotically hyperactive in my local community, unmarried and a mistress for over twenty years to a man that I am one-sidedly and hopelessly in love with. Reasonable looks, reasonable intelligence, reasonable job. On the verge of fifty. Retiring in ten years. Not much money, and only a Lilley & Chase pension to look forward to, though I suppose there'll be something in due course from Mother.

Quite a number of friends, the aggregate perhaps growing rather than declining as women of my age lose their husbands and turn to people like me, for human contact and friendship. 'A gutsy girl', is what I imagine they say of me. I must say I rather encourage that sort of description by the way I dress and look. All a bit Betjeman-like and plucky. Slightly Brown Owl. Is that what people see in me? Always one to help is Hazel. First person to put her hand up when she's needed. A grand woman.

I know what I'm like, she thought. I'm like one of those spinster women who organise all the families together for beach cricket at Frinton. I behave exactly like that at the tennis club. All brave little backhands and scampering after lobs and, 'Just out, Major!'

She climbed into the taxi. I would have had a wonderful war. I'd have been a lieutenant in the Wrens or something. All the girls would have had crushes on me, and the men would have thought I was a jolly good sort.

It's a strange thing that my personality has got itself fixed in this way in other people's eyes. It doesn't feel like me. The public perception of me is that I behave like a scout mistress or something. And for some reason I allow that image to be the one that is perpetuated. Actually I encourage it. I suppose I feel more secure if the world caricatures me into some sort of clear identity, even if it's the wrong one. And it is the wrong one. I don't feel that way inside at all. I'm someone completely different.

She looked out of the window of the taxi as it turned into Cadogan Place. You'll come back, darling Sam, she thought. If only for the familiarity and comfort of what I can give you. But what if he didn't? A cold grasp of fear hit Hazel. She had felt it so many times in the last few weeks, but had been less stressed today until that moment. Oh dear God. Oh dear God. Don't even think about that. Blank your mind out. Blank it out. Blank it out.

There is a level of fear through which I cannot force myself, she thought. Everyone's got that somewhere. Sam met it with Annabel. I've got it with the fear of losing Sam. It's there in all of us. Much better not to attempt to face that wall until it's there in front of me. I'll be able to deal with it when it comes, or I won't be able to deal with it when it comes. Leave it until then. Don't worry about it now. Now is too soon.

She would keep herself busy. Ben had got so much on at the moment. She could help him out, and work with him every evening for as long as he wanted. And she had a meeting to call of the Gardening committee, and the membership data needed so much work on it, and it was time she got immersed in the Christian Aid AGM arrangements. And Mrs Rogers's flat could do with a thoroughly good clean-out, and the poor woman's television set needed an engineer to come to look at it. She would arrange that, and she would also get around now to see if she could find some means of tracing that sister of Mrs Rogers in Gateshead or Grimsby or wherever it was she lived. And her mother's farmhouse could do with a good going-over as well. She would arrange for Mrs Foster from the village to go in to do five days consecutively with her. Though the trouble was that the pair of them spent most of the time gossiping.

That farmhouse is getting far too big for Mother. Dear God, I suppose I'll have it when she dies. I know she is determined to leave it to me. What on earth will I do with it? Maybe Sam will be with me. He might enjoy some of the year in the country when he grows older. What a wonderful thought: Sam growing older. I do so hope I can be with him and look after him. He will be a sweet old man. Perhaps he will let me brush his hair, like Winston Churchill and Clementine.

We could have Ben and his family to stay, and Callum Kelly could come and do some writing there. And we could make the garden smaller, leave some of it to grow wild and plant all the things Sam likes in the rest. We could make the old walled kitchen garden into a rose garden like that one at Hampton Court which Sam loves so much. And if he died before me I could plant a rose tree for him there. A Mermaid like the one he treasures so at Priory Grove, and I'll mulch it so that it's strong and grows right up into that old pear tree by the far end of the greenhouse.

She paid her fare, and went into the HMV store to buy the CD, wincing at the blast of pop music that hit her as she hurried through the store to reach the peace of the classical section in the basement.

What I need to do, she thought, is to keep calm and to keep busy. And show some guts. Sam's having to find courage. So can I. That's what I'm good at.

Chapter Twenty-Four

Richard Chase's flat was on the north side of Onslow Square, looking down on the big gardens in the middle of the square, which were always so immaculately tended and kempt. It was the home of a man who knew what he was. It presented to the world exactly that projection of Richard's personality that he wanted.

The centre point of the flat was the large drawing room on the first floor, which stretched across its whole width. The room had two deep sash-windows that gave full view of the gardens below. Mahogany bookcases lined most of the wall-space, packed solid with Richard's collection of modern first editions, but there was space for a few very good pictures – a large William Orpen above the fireplace, two Gwen Johns elsewhere, a Patrick Heron in the alcove – and an exquisite Giacometti figure, slender and lovely, standing on a plinth in a corner, lit by a pencil-thin beam of light from some hidden source behind a pillar.

The chairs were comfortable, the lighting discreet and subtle, the curtains gathered *à la mode* in French folds above the windows, the carpets, dove grey and close fitted, were of the finest Wilton, and there was a great Persian rug lying across the centre of the room.

To one side of the drawing room was a small study, with a Hepplewhite desk, some comfortable leather chairs, a good engraving or two, and some photographs of Richard with the famous. There was a pretty dining room, a minimalist and icy-white kitchen, and Richard's bedroom, with its cool green ensuite bathroom, thick-carpeted and lined with marble. A hallway, an immaculate and tiny lavatory off it, with piled editions of John Julius Norwich's *Christmas Crackers* on a little ledge, and that was the full extent of it.

No child had ever trod its boards, no woman's influence had been allowed to diffuse its personality. A cleaner came daily for two hours to spruce and polish it. A florist changed the flowers twice a week. Small dinner parties were held every two weeks, the food cooked and prepared expertly by Richard himself, the wine sparsely provided but of famously good quality.

There were no family photographs, no tennis racquets abandoned on the bedroom floor, no papers piled high in the study, no jackets thrown across chairs. The flat was beautiful, but the perfection was a chilly one.

There were three of them there that December evening. The curtains were drawn, the wood fire alight, and the silver drinks tray on the walnut corner table held a bottle of champagne, whisky, and some crystal flutes and tumblers.

Both of the Lilley & Chase non-executive directors were in the drawing room with Richard. Arthur Hill sat with a glass of whisky in one hand and a cigarette in the other, his jacket looking a little too tight, his face slightly flushed. Walter Lynne Thomas was on the other side of the fireplace, a flute of champagne on the table by his side, his suit finely tailored and sharply pressed, his Old Wykehamist tie worn against a striped Jermyn Street shirt. Richard sat across from him on the sofa, legs crossed, one arm thrown over the back, champagne glass in his hand.

Arthur drew on his cigarette and threw the butt into the fire. 'I'm a Sam Lilley man, Richard. You know that. I'm not looking to be offensive, but he made the firm, in my view. Everything about it carries his stamp. The people, the list, the humour of the place. Everything. Walter and I are outsiders, of course, but our view would be that of most people, I should think. This is not a damned great international corporation. It's a small, broke publishing house, doing good things and publishing good books and enjoying a lot of prestige, and employing some very nice people. Sam made it like it is. It's his. He needs loyalty from us. In fact, we owe him as much loyalty as we can possibly muster.'

'You said *our* view, I think, Arthur,' said Walter Lynne Thomas. 'I don't want to be pedantic, but I would like my position to stand in isolation.'

Arthur bared his yellow teeth in a broad smile, and waved Lynne Thomas on.

'Of course I agree that Sam's contribution to Lilley & Chase has been extraordinary. No one could sensibly deny that. In all senses he has been an excellent publisher.'

'And a lovely man,' muttered Arthur.

'And a reliable and capable manager. Of course I agree with that. But we have to look at the facts as they are. We have a responsibility to the staff, and we have a responsibility to our authors. And to our shareholders.'

Arthur flushed. 'You're not thinking, Walter. We don't have any shareholders to be responsible to. The firm is owned by Sam, Richard, the staff, and you and me. We've kept this thing for ourselves. It's ours. One of us has got hurt. We should look after him.'

'I do think we must try to look at this dispassionately, Arthur,' said Richard, getting up from his chair and walking over to the hearth to put another little log on the fire. 'Lilley & Chase is a business and, as Walter says, we have financial and professional obligations to all sorts of people. Cultural obligations too. We have become one of the country's leading literary publishers. We have a responsibility to preserve that position.

'You are very concerned about Sam. That's quite right. We all should be. Of course he made the business. I would be absolutely the first person to say that, and if I wasn't, I would be self-deluding. He made the business. But he's now an ill man. He's lost his daughter, and he's finding it beyond his strength to pull himself out of his grief.

'I'm told by my friends in the psychiatric profession that he will never be the same man again. He's in the throes of a very severe breakdown. He may well make a superficial recovery in perhaps nine months or a year, but he will be prone to breakdown thereafter for the rest of his life.

'Arthur – if you feel that we should hear this formally from an expert, then of course we should do so. But I assure you that I am right. Sam's condition is beyond that of conventional grief. He is deeply unwell. What we have to address is what we should do about that.'

Richard went to the drinks tray, took the bottles in both hands and refilled their three glasses. Walter Lynne Thomas sipped at his champagne with a prissiness that Arthur found extremely irritating, and he deliberately made an audible sucking noise as he drank from his whisky.

Walter looked across at Richard and Arthur.

'I think we should try to make some progress. The point that Richard has made to us is that, although he is happy to take full executive control for a period, he does not want to extend that period indefinitely, and certainly for no more than another two months at the outside. He has broadcasting and other commitments that he is not willing to put to one side longer than that.

'He has also told us that, in his view, neither Ben Jackson nor Robert St John Simpson has the capacity to assume the managing director's role, even on a temporary basis. None of the other directors is a feasible candidate.

'We thus have two alternatives. The first is that we allow the managing director position to lie vacant for such weeks or months as it takes for Sam to get himself well enough to come back to work. In this, we would have to depend on Richard to oversee the firm's management, but essentially on Ben and Robert and the others to run their divisions themselves.

'The second alternative is that we look now for a replacement for Sam, who on Richard's advice will have to be from another publishing house.

'There we have it, I think. Wait for him, and trust that when he does eventually return he is fit enough to do the job, or move now to find a successor.'

There was a silence. Then Arthur said, 'I want to wait for him. I definitely want to wait for him. Of course we should wait for him. For at least another month. It's virtually Christmas now. We should certainly give him until well into the New Year.'

'I'm afraid I would find it difficult to recommend to Richard that we wait that long,' said Walter. 'Sam wrote to Richard nine weeks ago or more to say that he would be back in a month. He is now at least five weeks overdue from that, and in that time he has replied to no letters and returned no telephone calls. Certainly not to me. If we leave it until the end of January it may well take five or six months after that before we have found the right candidate and got him or her into place. That will be June or July of next year. I think that is an unacceptable timescale. And irresponsible and dangerous for the firm.'

There was a silence for a little while, and then Richard said, 'I'm afraid I agree, Arthur. I hope you can understand why we take the view we do. I think you must accept that Walter and I will propose to the working directors that Sam's employment contract is terminated – there's a health and incapacity clause in it, just as there is in mine, so there won't be any difficulty in that – and that we start the search immediately for a successor.

'If we are indecisive over this, we will do more harm than has already been done. This isn't British Telecom or Unilever. We don't have cadres of management ready and trained to step into the breach. We are simply too small to rub along without a managing director for more than a few weeks.'

Arthur went over to the drinks tray, poured himself another large whisky, and stood there looking down at Richard and Walter. 'I don't agree. I won't go along with this, and if you force it through I shall make a public fuss about it. And I won't make it easy for you by resigning. I shall be very interested also in hearing the views of the working directors, Ben in particular. I'm certain they could not bring themselves to do this to Sam, whatever the temporary inconveniences of his current condition.'

He gulped his whisky down, put the glass back on the tray, and started to leave, saying as he did so, 'And in any case, win or lose, he'll still have his shares. He will still have one-third of the company, and he will keep that.'

Richard straightened himself, and faced Arthur head on. 'Arthur, you must know that will not be the case. There's a clause in the company's Articles which you surely remember? You're a director, you must be aware of what's in the Articles. You have read them, haven't you?'

'Of course I haven't read the fucking Articles. How do you think I spend my spare time?'

'The Articles were changed after the experience of the MegaMedia business. Shares can only be held by working directors and staff.'

'What the fuck are you talking about?' Arthur's language was lapsing into that of his notorious departmental meetings at Cambridge. 'I've got shares, and bloody Walter has got fucking shares. If we can have them, why can't he?'

'You had them by special dispensation at the time the Articles were changed. The Shareholders' Agreement specifically states that when you and Walter retire from the board, your shares will be bought back by the working directors and staff shareholders at a special formula price, as will the shares of any director who ceases to work for the company. And that after you and Walter, no non-executive directors will hold any shares at all. You must know all this. You were a signatory to it all at the time.'

Arthur came back into the room and stood in front of them. 'It won't work anyway. Apart from you, Richard, the others haven't got the money. And the company can't buy Sam's shares in because it hasn't got the reserves. And anyway, a thirty per cent holding is too large for the company to buy back, whether the reserves are there or not. So it's only you who could do it. And I tell you what I do remember from those papers. That no single director can hold more than a third of the company.

'You can't have them even if you were allowed to, because you're too fucking poor,' pointing to Walter Lynne Thomas, who had never in human recall been spoken to in this manner, 'the staff can't have them because on Lilley & Chase salaries they're too poor as well, poor sods, and you can't have them,' pointing now at Richard, 'because the Articles say you can't. So game, set and match. Sam keeps them.'

'Again, Arthur, actually no,' said Richard. 'You're right, of course. I can't buy them. But Walter and the working directors and staff can. I've arranged for them to be lent the money. You too, of course, if you would like to join the others.'

Arthur had by this time managed to calm himself, though his anger was raw. 'I don't have to tell you that I am insulted by that suggestion. If you lend the others the money, and secure the debt on the shares, it would be tantamount to holding the shares yourself. If you lend them the money for that purpose even without the security, then I'll get a lawyer to stop you.'

'I'm not lending them the money.'

'Then who is? This is not a sound proposition for a bank. A lousy little arty publisher, paying lousy little arty dividends. With a lousy phoney little balance sheet, and a lousy great mountain of debt. And the money is not inconsiderable. I do remember some of the papers now. If I have it correctly the formula price is net book value plus twenty per cent. That would make Sam's shares worth about four hundred thousand.'

'Five hundred thousand,' said Richard, 'and it's not a bank. It's Monk Grolsch Parsons.'

Arthur sat down heavily. 'What? What on earth are you saying? Those three old poofs? Why? What on earth is there in it for them? They wouldn't do that. Sam's daughter worked for them, for heaven's sake. What do they think they are doing?'

Walter cleared his throat.

'Arthur, Richard and I think this would be a very good strategic move. It may be that sometime in the future Monk Grolsch Parsons would like to acquire the company outright.'

He looked across at Richard for a moment, and then continued. 'Actually, to be a little more frank perhaps, they have already suggested to Richard and me that they would. And they have suggested a valuation that is by any standards very tempting. They have also agreed to make a loan to the Company of three million pounds at six per cent annual interest, which puts us in a very strong position indeed to build the business. We could not sell, of course, without a change to the Articles, and to change them we would need a unanimous board.'

'As I've told you, I won't resign,' said Arthur. But then, suddenly realising the position, 'I see. I come up for re-election at the next AGM. Of course.'

There was silence.

'Quite,' said Walter eventually. Arthur went again to the drinks tray, found his glass, and poured himself more whisky. He lit a cigarette and stood facing them, glass in hand, a look of cold fury on his face. 'So Sam gets half a million for one-third of the company, having built it from nothing and given it his entire life, energy and concentration for twenty-eight years. I will guarantee that the queens are offering you a valuation of at least three times that. Right? Right?'

Richard nodded, shrugged, and looked up at Arthur, holding his gaze.

'That means that you will be getting let's say one and a half million for your third, and Sam five hundred thousand for his. And Sam has done the lot.'

The whisky was downed again, and Arthur wiped his mouth with the back of his hand. 'Nice one, Richard. I'll see myself out. I'll certainly be there at next week's board meeting. I want to hear it from the others myself. Particularly Ben.'

He nodded at Walter, and clumped off down the stairs to his car. As soon as he got back to his club there was telephoning to do.

Chapter Twenty-Five

The following evening, Arthur was at the Monk Grolsch Parsons offices, having been on the telephone to one or other of the three directors several times that morning, insisting that they should meet that day.

The four of them sat in the boardroom, drinks on the table. They were all of virtually identical age; they had been at Eton together but had seen very little of each other since.

Arthur had gone to Oxford, which was his base and home for so long; first as an undergraduate, then a junior lecturer, and then a Fellow of Balliol before becoming Professor of Modern History at Cambridge. The others of course were together at Cambridge, and started the advertising agency immediately afterwards.

Arthur had not been a particular friend of the other three at school, but they had all four moved in a similar set, and Arthur remembered that Matthew Monk and Julian Parsons had been considered intellectually precocious, even amongst a memorably clever peer group.

Although Arthur was himself the supreme iconoclast, and a most enthusiastic destroyer of academic pomposity and conceit, he found the way Monk Grolsch Parsons presented themselves to be irritating, carrying in his view an inverted intellectual snobbery and a speciousness that mocked the genuine cleverness of the three founders. Arthur had no objection whatsoever to empty people of empty minds doing empty things together and growing rich from the proceeds, and indeed amongst his fellows at the London football club where he was a director he found some very good examples of people who had done exactly that, and he liked most of them very much indeed. What he did object to was three clever men mocking what they were doing, and, by doing so, mocking others less gifted who made their livings in that same profession. And whilst mocking, growing extremely rich in the process. The riddles ladder was in Arthur's mind the last straw; an exercise in pure preening self-regard and sterile, plaything intellectualism. He recognised there was a joke somewhere in the Monk Grolsch Parsons story, but he was damned if he would laugh at it.

Julian Parsons was saying, 'We're dancing on nobody's grave, Arthur. I have been very fond of Sam' – he spread his arms – 'we have all three been very fond of Sam for many years, and we all of us absolutely adored Annabel as I am sure you realise.

'It's true certainly that she joined us largely because she was Sam's daughter. But once here, her career was what she made it, and she was actually very good at it. She would have joined us on the board next year, and she would have been running the agency herself within five years. At that point we three would have thrown in the towel and retired to that monastery up behind Grenoble we've had our eye on for years. A quite wonderful chef, compulsory total silence until drinks time, and all day blissfully spent gathering herbs in the mountains.'

Oh piss off, thought Arthur. Piss off, you self-admiring old queen.

'And time to write,' Julian was continuing. 'Hours to write on our own lovely little bare oak desks in our cells.'

Arthur thought to himself that this could run for some time, and cut in. 'Julian, I'm not saying that you are dancing on Sam's grave. What I am saying is that you are allowing, perhaps unwittingly, something very unpleasant to happen. Perhaps you don't realise what is going on. Richard is taking the opportunity to dump Sam while he is ill. There is a health and incapacity clause in his employment contract which means they can fire him. Once his contract is terminated, under the Lilley & Chase's Articles of Association and the Shareholders' Agreement his shares are bought compulsorily from him by the other directors at one-third the price you are subsequently paying for them.

'Lilley & Chase would not have existed without Sam. His energy and imagination have made it what it is. He has given everything to it for twenty-eight years. To have him dumped and destroyed like this is an outrage. Richard gets the senior staff and the other directors on his side by arranging for them to be the people who buy the shares off Sam at this savage undervalue, putting in place a deal which enables them to sell them on to you at three times what they have just paid for them. Using borrowed money, also thoughtfully supplied by you. Or – to put it more brutally – they are not actually paying for Sam's shares at all, because you three are popping the money into their wallets first. Did you realise the whole story? Did you understand how Richard has arranged the whole thing?'

The three looked at each other, and it was Matthew Monk who replied. 'Look, we're not complete innocents, and you know we're not. We've been looking out over the last year or so for something additional to do. The agency is extremely profitable, even after the fact that the three of us take out as much as we want. So what do we do with the cash? Buy another agency?'

Matthew shrugged, and pulled a wry little face. 'Perhaps. But we are not exactly orthodox advertising men, as you may have noticed, and we have got quite enough advertising going on here. We've looked at buying out an art dealer whom we all three know, who has got himself squeezed for cash. We might well do that. We've brooded about publishing, and there are plenty of publishers for sale, but rather few who publish the sort of books we would want to be involved with. You're quite right. Sam has built up a marvellous house there over the years. Lilley & Chase don't make any money, really, but it publishes a very interesting list. And incidentally, with us owning it, it will not only publish an interesting list, but also make money. It's undercapitalised; has too little working capital availability to give proper cover of its overheads. We're going to give it the funding that it needs.

'Richard brought us the idea, and we jumped at it, quite frankly. We have offered to invest very heavily into the firm immediately, and this means that it will be in a very good position to grow the list substantially next season. So good news for authors, good news for agents, good news for Richard, good news for the other directors, good news for the staff. Not such good news for Sam. But he is an ill man now, demonstrably, and he would probably never have been able to get back there and lead it again. Without Sam, Lilley & Chase needs owners like Julian, Peter and me to push it on and make it work. Richard is too busy being a star. Coming to us was a very sensible and practical thing for him to do.'

There was a silence, then Peter Grolsch got up, went across to the window, looked out for a moment, then turned and half sat on the sill behind him. 'You are an academic, Arthur. A famous and extremely successful academic. You are not a business man, and I hardly blame you for that. Whatever we may appear to you, we are. If you heard us talking together in private you would realise that we can be extremely serious about what we do. If this was to be our life, then we decided to be very good at it. Some say that we do here better advertising than anyone else in London. I think that is true. We have supremely good staff. We pay high salaries. We run a very good advertising agency. And we are tight business managers because we think that life is simply more fun that way.

'This is an absolutely conventional business deal. A willing seller and a willing buyer. There is no fraud, no little arrangements around the back, no misrepresentation, no naughtiness of any kind. It's all absolutely straightforward. It makes sense for us to do the deal, and we are going to do it. Sorry, Arthur, but that's where it is.'

Arthur looked up at him. 'Sam's been your friend for years. Of all three of you. That's why Annabel was here, as Julian said earlier. I couldn't do this to a friend. How could you?'

Julian stared across at him, and there was a look of contempt on his face. 'We didn't write the Lilley & Chase Articles, or the Shareholders' Agreement. You did. Frankly, we were astounded by their naïveté when we saw them. You were a director – did you think what you were doing when you signed them? Or did you never even read them? Always the English amateur!'

Arthur flushed, and stubbed out his cigarette. 'You haven't answered my point. We were talking about friendship.'

Julian answered. 'Yes – as I have said already, we were, are, all three of us very fond of Sam. Always have been. It would be difficult not to be. He is an appealing man. But . . . we three hunt in a pack a bit. Like Mr Marks and Mr Spencer. Or Mr Gilbert and Mr Sullivan. You've probably noticed.'

Arthur got up to go. 'Thanks for seeing me. Thanks for the drink.' He shrugged and turned away. Then turned again.

'One thing more. Would you have the courage to tell Sam to his face all that you have said to me over the last half-hour?'

Peter Grolsch answered. 'Absolutely, Arthur. We have our own honour, you know. And telling people the truth is an important part of it.'

Chapter Twenty-Six

Arthur eventually found Sam through Hilary, whom he rang on Hazel's suggestion. Sam had been telephoning her apparently at least four or five times a day for the last several weeks. She told him that Sam had been living in a small seaside hotel where he and she had spent a holiday in the early months of their marriage.

Hilary would not say where the hotel was, as she had promised Sam she would not do so, but agreed to ensure that Sam telephoned Arthur that day. To Arthur's surprise, he did so. Arthur told Sam simply and directly what was happening and implored him to get back to London and Lilley & Chase and protect his position.

Sam refused. Arthur tried again, this time with a coarse, abusive profanity that he hoped would shock Sam into activity.

'You're being too fucking self-pitying, Sam. For God's sake, jolt yourself back into life. You're not a child. Show some guts. Come and fight the buggers. Stop rolling over like a spaniel. Come and fight.'

There was a long silence.

'You've got one besetting fault in life, Sam. You're a coward. Life kicks you in the crutch sometimes, but it does that to us all. I repeat: you're a coward.'

That's not it actually, thought Arthur. That's not it, but it will do if it will shake him into life. He's not a coward so much as terminally self-indulgent. He did exactly the same thing over his break-up with Hilary. The grief is genuine enough. But what he then does is observe it. He stands back from it and studies it. Until in the end he's completely lost control of the situation.

Waiting for a response from Sam, Arthur fumbled around for his cigarettes, propping the receiver under his chin. It's as if he's

253

fascinated by what he's seeing, thought Arthur, and he has to watch it through to its conclusion. And squeeze from it every last delicious sliver of pain. He does feel the pain. He felt it with Hilary, and he felt it with Annabel. All that is totally genuine. The problem is that he won't let it go. The real grief over Annabel's death probably lasted – what? – four weeks? Thereafter he's been going into an exploration of personal pain. It fascinates him. He even has to go back to his honeymoon hotel, or wherever he is. Just for a further source of grief to tap into if the first lot shows any sign of easing up a bit.

'Sod off, Arthur.'

Thank God for that. He sounded almost human again. Much less heaviness and self-conscious melancholy in the voice. Maybe he really is on the mend. Perhaps I can heave him over the top.

'Yes. Maybe I should sod off. I've wasted too much time on this already. This is my last telephone call, and my last attempt.'

There was a silence, and then Sam said, 'What do you want me to do then?'

'I've just told you. You've got to come back to London and fight your corner. You're about to lose your company. It may well be too late anyway. But it's well worth coming back and going for the lot of them.'

'Where does Ben stand in all this? He's a good friend. He won't let me down.'

'That's exactly why you need to come back. I don't know where he stands. I don't know whether he's made up his mind or what he's doing. Perhaps he's hoping against hope that you will give him a lead. God knows. Let's find out.'

Perhaps it isn't too late, thought Arthur. Perhaps Sam coming back will turn everybody around again. And what we haven't done yet is try to get support from the other authors. If I feel so loyal to Sam, probably the others do too. I'm sure they do. Me, Kelly, Ruges, Celia Smith, Hailey, Norah Howard, Mark Ryder even – Christ, between us we pretty well run the place. If we all stood together they couldn't proceed. Surely they couldn't proceed. Julian and the others would take fright and run.

'I'll give you a call tomorrow, Arthur. I'll be at Priory Grove.'

Thank God, thought Arthur. Thank God. The important thing is that he is now going to give it a go. At least I assume he is. One can never quite tell what he'll do in his present state. Maybe he was just trying to get me off the phone. But what I can do this evening is to try to get the authors together. Or at least get some soundings from them. I can't believe they won't support us. All of them owe him so much. I must get through to them tonight. It may be better coming from me than from Sam direct. He can always follow up on them afterwards.

Arthur telephoned Hazel, who gave him all their numbers, and also that of Aubrey Giles, the freelance reader and editor, who she said had been wanting to speak to him urgently.

He called Norah first, and found her very anxious for news as to what was happening. She had returned to Yorkshire from Annabel's funeral extremely worried about Sam, and had left messages at least daily on his answerphone for him to contact her. She had telephoned Mark to send him around to the house, but although he had made several trips there, he had never found Sam at home. And although everyone she could think of had been left with instructions to tell Sam to be in contact with her if they saw him, no word had come from him.

Arthur had never met or spoken to her before and, wary of her reputation as a notorious eccentric, addressed her initially in a courtly, pedantic manner until he could get a feel of her competence and interest. He was quickly reassured.

'Mr Hill, I am enormously relieved to get the sense that Sam has such a champion. As for me, I am simply one hundred per cent supportive of Sam in this affair and everything else. If he decides that the right thing for Lilley & Chase to do is to sell to these advertising people, then that would be fine with me. If he feels the reverse, then that's fine with me as well. But what is really concerning me at the moment is his state of health and mind. And his whereabouts.'

'It's more complicated than that, Miss Howard. I mean about the state of the company. I have been in contact with him, and I will be seeing him shortly. I'll make certain he calls you. But on the other matter, I'm not sure I made myself clear. What the others are saying is that they want him out of the company to ensure that the sale goes through. They think they can do that because his mental condition could be said to trigger off the health and incapacity clause in his contract. If they can terminate his contract, then they are able to buy his shares at a third of their resale value.'

There was a silence for a little as Norah absorbed this. I feel so out of step with the world, she thought. It's not that I imagine myself to be too superior to know anything about money or business or how things like that work. It's just an ignorance and an ineptitude that I have allowed to become part of my persona. And because of it I am unable to do very much to help Sam at a time when he could quite clearly do with a considerable amount of help.

'So – what can we do in a practical sense to help him? You're a director of the company, but I'm simply one of their authors.'

As she said this, she found to her surprise that she felt a certain amount of irritation with Sam building up inside her. She would support him, of course, to her dying breath, but he was silly to have allowed himself to be put in this position. He was so much in control of that firm. So much the dominant and admired leader. How could he have allowed himself to be outmanoeuvred by everybody in this absurd fashion? His grief must have been dreadful when Annabel was killed. Quite dreadful. But having said that . . . and Norah's mind turned to one of her childhood memories; her mother losing two of her brothers within three weeks of each other towards the end of the First World War, and her raw, distraught, stupefied pain, which was quickly collected up into a gathered fortitude and dignity. People do have to cope. It's very easy to say it, but people do cope.

'What I would like to do is come back to you on that. I am going to speak to one or two of the other authors and collect some views together. If enough of us are willing to put up a strong enough fight, the board will have to take notice, of course. I'll talk to you again if I may. Perhaps I could telephone you again tomorrow?'

Norah thanked Arthur again, and assured him of her support. But there was a piece of her that remained unhappy with Sam. Such a good man. Always kind and persuasive with her. Without him she doubted very much whether her literary career would have developed in the way that it had. Her agent would say otherwise of course but . . . no, I'm sure that's right. I wouldn't have done so well. He is an excellent editor; bright and perceptive. I've always loved him so much that I've never been able to bear the thought of letting him down. Silas too, of course, but Sam has always been special.

How could he have been so feeble? How could he have allowed these people to do these things to him? People cope. Sam should have coped. She would do all she could to help him now, of course. Though, despite what Arthur had said, she was very unclear as to how any contribution from her was going to make very much difference in the end. But she would do whatever she was asked. But how silly Sam had been. And how late all this was in her career. To leave Lilley & Chase now, and start all over again . . . it really was so late for that sort of thing.

Some of Norah's unspoken hesitancy had got through to Arthur, although his call later that night, to Callum Kelly, was straightforward and entirely clear. Kelly had apparently already written to his agent that afternoon, with a copy to Richard Chase, saying that, in the event of Sam leaving the firm, his instructions were that his next novel, still uncontracted, was to be published by a different house, and that he would invoke a specially negotiated clause in his contract that his backlist would consequently be removed from Lilley & Chase.

Arthur then called Mark, who was anxious to be supportive of Sam, because, as he made clear to Arthur, of his affection for Annabel, but he took pains to emphasise his concern that anything he said should not be construed as being disloyal to Ben Jackson, who had edited him since the earliest drafts of his first novel eight years before. He asked for confirmation of where Ben stood in the affair, which put Arthur in an awkward position, as he himself was uncertain as to whether Sam could influence him at this stage to come down irrevocably on his side.

Arthur prevaricated in his response, and then telephoned Anthony Ruges, but could only reach his answerphone, on which he left a detailed description of what had happened, and asked that Anthony should contact him as soon as possible.

The call that came back at nine-thirty the next morning was from Anthony's agent, who told Arthur that Richard Chase had kept Anthony closely informed of the situation over the previous weeks, and that Anthony's view – and he was to confirm it in writing to the Lilley & Chase board later that day – was that the firm had always been underfunded, and that they should accept the MGP offer without hesitation. The agent also told Arthur that Anthony was to say in his letter that he would only continue being published by Lilley & Chase on the basis that he would be given guarantees of advances for his next three novels of over double those that the firm had previously paid him and, given that, he suggested that the board should take particular heed of the funding implications that a rejection of the MGP offer would bring in its wake.

Later in the morning, Celia Smith also replied to a message that Arthur had left the previous evening on her answerphone. She expressed her devastation about all that had happened, said that she would do whatever Arthur asked to make her position known, but pointed out that her ground for bargaining was limited as she had no plans to write any further books. She said much more, and all of it passionately in defence of Sam, but as Arthur listened to her he reflected that she would not prove to be as valuable an ally as he had thought; he had assumed that a second volume of memoirs was to be written, but it was clear there would be nothing further, and she was anyway a little too garrulous, a little too theatrical and unfocused to be of effect. She would try instinctively to convert the situation to a cameo role for herself – all desperate loyalty and plucky concern for a tragic, tragic friend.

When Arthur called him at Priory Grove later in the morning, Sam sounded relatively vigorous, and said that he was just in the process of sorting out a mountain of letters that was lying in the hall. Arthur went straight around there by taxi, and they sat down together at the kitchen table to plan what was to be done. He described to Sam the conversations he had held with Norah, Callum Kelly, and Celia, and did so with pedantic emphasis so that he could be sure that Sam had a clear understanding that the situation with them was helpful, but could not be assumed to deal a terminal blow to Sam's opponents. Sam immediately asked about Anthony

Ruges, and Arthur, with some initial hesitancy, told him what he had heard from his agent.

Sam gazed out into the garden, the grass uncut, the borders overgrown and unkempt, the tall dahlias and hollyhocks and delphiniums bent and broken. Jesus Christ, he thought. So it is slipping away. There was a sharp moment of pain as he absorbed again what Anthony Ruges had done. He tipped back his chair, locked his fingers together behind his head, and turned to study Arthur. So Arthur turns out to be a true friend. And Callum I suppose, but it's Arthur who has really fought for me. Not Norah, and before all this I would have thought she was certain to do anything for me that I needed. But for whatever reason, I'm sure she'll stay where she is at Lilley & Chase when this is all over. Mark Ryder too, I would guess. To be with Ben. So Arthur is my champion. Who would have believed it? I didn't know that he thought of himself as being as close as that.

'What about Peter Hailey, Arthur? He's important to the firm. Shall we call him?'

Sam looked through his diary, found Hailey's number in Notting Hill Gate, and picked up the telephone. While waiting for the call to be answered, Sam pictured the house, where he had been a guest occasionally over the years. Peter Hailey had been an actor before writing his first novel in his late twenties – a very funny semi-autobiographical work about growing up as a homosexual in South London. A string of further novels followed, together with two very well received biographies, several plays for television, and a considerable body of greatly respected reviews and articles, mostly for the *TLS* and the *New York Review of Books*.

Hailey became a frequent presence on Radio Three and the BBC World Service, and a respected figure in literary London. He was a shy, reclusive man, and stayed within a fairly narrow circle of familiar, mostly left-wing friends. He was a well-known supporter of the Labour Party, and it had been at a buffet supper party at his house that Sam had met Lord Harper, author of the ill-fated memoirs. Richard had been a more frequent guest at the house, particularly after his media career had started to develop so strongly in the mid to late nineteen-eighties.

When Peter at last answered the telephone there was an awkward exchange of pleasantries before Sam told him why he was calling, although he had guessed by Peter's tone of voice, more reserved even than usual, that he knew what was coming.

'Sam – I can't help. Richard has told me what is happening. I'm not so close to you two that I can really say that I know who is right and who is wrong. Though I have to say that Richard did make his views sound pretty convincing to me.'

I'm too late, thought Sam. It's all too late. Richard has already been round them all. Except for one or two like Norah and Callum who he knew would never desert me. Although I'm not at all sure he's right about Norah. If 'desert' is a fair word to use. This is not going to work. It's also humiliating.

'Look, Sam. I'd rather be left out of this. Let me just write the books. You and Richard can make up your minds between you what you want to do. I'm sorry not to be more helpful. But I'm really not keen to interfere.'

Sam looked across at Arthur, and neither of them spoke for a little. Arthur gazed out of the window at the grey autumn day, and wondered to himself what the next step should be. The calls to the authors had not got them very far, and it was beginning to feel that they were rather washing their dirty linen in public. Maybe that didn't matter. There were plenty more authors he could talk to. But so far it hadn't been encouraging, and he didn't want to do more harm than good. Richard had undoubtedly done an effective job in covering the ground first. Callum and Celia and Norah Howard were all very well, but there wasn't enough there to mount a large-scale attack on the board.

And the fact did remain that the board meeting had been called for the following Tuesday, and that one of the agenda items was a resolution to terminate Sam's service contract. Arthur could see the large envelope containing the board papers sitting in the pile of correspondence on the kitchen table, and wondered if he should show Sam this or not. Perhaps he hadn't yet read it. He picked up the envelope, saw that it had not been opened, and pushed it across to Sam.

'Open it, Sam. And turn to the agenda for Tuesday. You can see it all laid out. They vote you out of office, and then they agree to accept the offer for the company.'

Sam read the papers several times, but Arthur saw that there was an aura of lethargy and indifference about his actions, and a little of the spirit went out of Arthur as he observed it.

In due course, Sam looked up at Arthur. 'What happens if I simply turn up? And say that I want to continue? And, having established that, to say that I am managing director of the company, and that I don't want the deal to go through.'

Arthur gazed across at him. 'I don't know. If they all want to sell, I suppose they will vote you out of office and continue with the sale.'

'But they can't simply vote me out of office. I have my contract to protect me.'

'Sam – I've explained the situation to you. They will invoke the health and incapacity clause.'

'But I can say that I'm well and that I want to carry on.'

'It hasn't looked that way, Sam. For those who want to get you out there's plenty of evidence to use. Surely you realise that?'

Sam looked down at his hands, and picked at his fingernails in thought. 'I'd like to speak to Ben. I want to hear from Ben what he wants. And what the others want. When I've heard that, I'll know what to do.'

There's no fight in him really, thought Arthur, but at least he's here with me in this last period and to some extent in control of his own destiny. There's more dignity for him in this. If he's lost his hold on his firm, at least he's here to see the final chapter for himself. And it's possible perhaps that Ben and the others will change their tack. They were always so dependent on him for everything. Now that he's back, even in this condition, they may decide to stick with him. But the trouble is they are all going to make money out of deserting him. And, thought Arthur, with the experience of many years of dealing with people – rational, intelligent, highly educated, apparently loyal and honourable and decent people – put money in large enough quantities in front of those who haven't got the stuff, and who need it, and you won't be able to move for the stampede. Whatever their loyalties.

Rather than call the office, Sam telephoned Ben's home in Brixton, and to his surprise Ben himself answered. His reaction on hearing Sam's voice was theatrically enthusiastic, but beneath the surface there was a distinct tension, and Sam could sense it. Sam asked if he could come straight down to Brixton to see him – Ben had apparently stayed away from the office that day to catch up on some work at home – and he was there less than an hour later.

Sam had never been to Ben's house before, and found it with difficulty. The house was in a long street of Victorian terraced houses. There were bicycles in varying states of repair chained to front railings and lamp-posts, and elderly and mostly rather battered cars parked at irregular intervals. There were some very well-presented houses, and some very shabby ones. The best had brightly painted front doors, gleaming brass knockers, and well-tended little front gardens, but these were intermixed with others in severe disrepair: dustbins overflowing, the occasional window broken and boarded up with hardboard, and dead plants in cracked and broken tubs littering the doorsteps.

Ben's house was at the end of the terrace, and was painted and maintained, if less obviously gentrified than others in the street. He came to the door as soon as Sam pressed the bell, smiled at him warmly enough, and showed him into the crowded little sitting room on the ground floor, clearing a pile of manuscripts and other clutter off the sofa so that he could sit down.

There was an awkward conversation while they felt each other out, then Sam asked him what his plans were and how he was going to vote at the board meeting. Ben hesitated before he replied, and Sam spoke again.

'Ben, I'm sorry to embarrass you, but I do want to hear the truth. It does seem so odd that I'm here as the supplicant. But I need to know what your view is about all this.'

Ben looked across at him, and thought how different Sam appeared in the context in which he was now presented. Rather like an ex-government minister a month or so out of office, he looked curiously belittled in his physical state; with the power gone, he looked smaller, older, less commanding. For the first time ever in their relationship Ben felt at least Sam's equal.

'It's been a bad time for us all with you away, Sam. We were all sad at what happened to you. But you know what corporate life is like. Everything has to continue. There's the next month's list to publish, and manuscripts to edit, and telephone calls to return, and copy-editing to supervise, and books being auctioned, and salesmen being pinched, and all the things that happen all the time. There was your tragedy on one side, and absolute normality on the other. It's been a strange situation.'

He half smiled at Sam, and they looked at each other in a pensive, guarded way. Ben had been dreading Sam's arrival ever since he had received his call, but now he was actually with him he felt confident and dominant. Sam was sitting low in his chair, his elbows on the armrests, his hands interlocked in front of his face, as if shielding himself from attack. Ben fiddled with a book on the table beside his chair, then spoke again.

'When Richard told us about his talks with Monk Grolsch Parsons, we were all completely taken aback, as you can imagine. But he was very persuasive about it. We've never had enough money behind us, really, and as you well know it's been a tough battle to hang on to some of our authors with all the big conglomerates now able to offer such huge advances if they want to. That extra three million pounds coming in is really going to be a godsend.'

'So you've already got used to the idea.'

Sam's voice was quietly interrogative and passive, and his expression as he looked across at Ben was without aggression or challenge.

Ben hesitated again before continuing, feeling somehow cheapened by his previous remark. Then, now with more emphasis and strength, 'Sam. Sam. It's sort of a *fait accompli* now. I think it would be much better for you and for all of us if you would accept that.'

Again there was a silence for a moment or so. Then Sam smiled. 'And you are all going to make yourselves a nice lot of money! That's good news for you as well.'

'Yes. Of course that's right. It's better to put the point on the table. We are going to make some money. And for all of us that is certainly very good news.' He gestured around him. 'You can see that is hardly going to come amiss for me, or, I expect, any of us. I didn't go into Lilley & Chase expecting to grow rich. But there's a mortgage to pay, and the kids' clothes to buy, and the kitchen to build on to, and family holidays, and . . .' He shrugged, and again looked at Sam with that same half-smile he had shown before; an expression of nervousness and of defiant guilt, Sam thought, as he looked across at him.

'People like me don't have too many opportunities to make some capital. For all of us, this was probably going to be the only opportunity of our career. There are family loyalties for us all as well as corporate loyalties. And it looked to me, and it seems to most of the others, that on all scores this was a good deal.'

'You talk of the others. You said most of the others thought like you. Who did?'

'Just accept it, Sam. I don't want to have to grind through a whole list. Just accept it.'

'I asked you. What do the others think?'

'OK. I'll tell you. If there were waverers after Richard first talked about it with us, then Pat Simmons certainly did his bit to persuade them. Birdie Jones was immediately in favour, and so was Robert. Fairly predictably, given the fact that he can now up all his advances. Lorraine was very loyal to you indeed, if you want to know. She hesitated for a long time. But I think we were all persuaded in the end, even Lorraine possibly, by the fact that the firm desperately needed more capital if we were going to be able to compete. It has been tough, Sam. You know that.'

'You say Lorraine was loyal to me. What does that mean?'

'Sam – you know what it means, for Christ's sake. It meant refusing to make a decision about your company without you there in person to have your own say. It meant refusing to accept that you are ill and that you will have to leave us.'

'Here I am sitting in front of you. Who says I'm ill? I'm not ill. I'm the managing director. Who says I can't come to the board meeting next week and simply vote against the proposition?'

'Sam. It's too late. Don't do that to us. Richard has explained to us the health and incapacity clause in your contract. And in his, for that matter. You've been away too long. We're too small a firm to be able to cope with that. It's a great pity you wrote that note saying that you would be back in a month, and then making no further contact and never appearing. It's too late now, Sam. I wish it wasn't. And I'm very happy you seem to be fit enough to be with me now like this. But it is too late. The firm needs the money, the Monk Grolsch Parsons people sound ideal for us in many ways, certainly considerably better than us being swallowed up by some conglomerate, and – yes, let's face it – we are all very relieved that we are going to make a little bit for ourselves. It is too late. Please accept it, Sam.'

'And you know about my shares? You do understand the position on those? That I have to sell them to all of you at a price much less than you are then going to sell them on at? You do realise that?'

Ben sat completely still in his chair, and as he looked at Sam there was now an overt tautness and strain to his expression. But then it suddenly came to him. The odd thing in all this conversation, he thought, is that Sam is acting. He's going through the motions because he feels he has to. Arthur Hill or somebody has shamed him into it. But actually he doesn't care. About the price he gets for his shares, or anything else. At the heart of him he actually wants to lose the business now. It was probably like that with his wife all those years ago. He decided to lose her too. Because she let him down. Because she had gone with someone else than him. Like Lilley & Chase is doing now. We've cuckolded him, and he can't wait to be rid of us. But meanwhile, to satisfy Arthur, or whoever it is he feels he has to perform to, we have to go through the scene.

'Yes. I do understand about your shares. We all do. It's a very unfortunate thing. But it's the arrangement that's specified in the Articles and the Shareholders' Agreement. And those were written before my day. And all the rest of the working directors. They were written by you and Richard. And I suppose Walter and Arthur. It's a tough deal for you, we all know that. But it's the one laid down by you.'

Sam watched Ben as he was saying this, and, as Ben had suspected, almost because he felt that the situation demanded it of him, he responded in a raised, angry voice.

265

'I'm being driven out of the company. By you, actually. Of all the people there, I trusted you more than anybody. I'm glad to hear that Lorraine had some vestiges of conscience. I didn't hear that you did. Why couldn't you . . .?' He put his head in his hands and paused for a few moments. 'Oh, for fuck's sake . . .'

And suddenly Sam had lost interest and stamina. It was too late. To go through the processes of battle against people he was as fond of as this, and with whom he had worked for so long, didn't feel a game worth playing. He looked across at Ben, and it was an effort to continue to play the role of the injured party.

'Forget it, Ben. Good luck.' He looked at him with affection. His attempts at anger had melted away, and Ben's child-like, red-faced expression of guilt suddenly amused him a great deal.

'Good luck. Maybe I'll start a new publishing house. Maybe I'll take over fucking Monk Grolsch Parsons. God knows. Ciao, Ben. Publish well.'

He had got out of his seat, and was already trying to work the lock on the front door to escape to the street. Ben reached across him and turned the latch.

'Sam. Look after yourself. The firm continues. Your name is still there. It's been a huge achievement for you. You're one of the best-known publishers in London. You'll find what you want to do.'

Sam was at the door of his car, and fumbling in his pockets for his key.

'And Sam . . . Sam.' But as Ben walked towards him, his hand outstretched, the engine started, and the car drew away from the kerb.

Chapter Twenty-Seven

Arthur's taxi drew up outside 113 Sharpe Street; a large, five-storey house that had been divided into several bed-sitting rooms and tiny flats. He studied the nameplates beside the six or seven bells to identify which belonged to Aubrey Giles. Some of the names had been removed, but Arthur's instinct was that Aubrey would live in the basement, and sure enough when he rang that bell it was Aubrey's feminine, soft voice that answered.

Arthur found that Hazel was already there, sitting on a corner sofa with an enormous Persian cat lying across her knee. Arthur went over to kiss her on the cheek, a gesture he had never made before in all the ten years or so that they had been acquainted; she seemed rather taken aback by it.

Both she and Aubrey were drinking orange-coloured, thick-looking drinks with cocktail cherries floating in them, and Arthur was relieved on seeing these to be offered whisky, which he instantly accepted. It arrived in a notably dirty glass, which felt greasy and sticky to the touch, and had on one part of its rim a deposit of dried food, which Arthur scraped off with his thumb when he saw Aubrey was not looking.

The basement room was large, piled everywhere with books, and contained a large quantity of furniture, mostly rather bulky, heavy Victorian pieces cluttered with *objets d'art* and kitsch little mementoes of Aubrey's life. A grand piano stood in the corner with the lid open, and large piles of sheet music and scores sat on the stool and on the floor beside it.

Against a wall was a very good eighteenth-century writing table, on which were manuscripts, ink pots, and a walnut travelling chest, out of which tumbled stamps, envelopes, writing paper, rubber bands, paper clips, and various pens and pencils. A leather chair, cracked and holed, was against this, and the carpet beneath it was worn and threadbare and stained with what looked to be variously ink, coffee and soup.

There was one large picture over the fireplace, depicting a mythological scene of quite overwhelming heroics and grandeur. Hung together on the wall above the grand piano was a pair of oils, crudely and garishly painted, each depicting naked children with little pink bodies and dimpled bottoms, in one of the pictures running together on a beach, holding kites and being chased by naughty little dogs, and in the other getting ready for bed in a chintzy bedroom, one of the children sitting demurely on a potty.

Dust and debris was everywhere. From where Arthur was sitting he could see through into a dark kitchen which was piled with the remains of what Arthur assumed initially was last night's supper party, but which he then conjectured might actually be the aggregate of the week's meals awaiting its eventual wash. On a piece of newspaper near Arthur's feet stood a dish containing the congealed remains of the cat's dinner, and under the chair in which Aubrey had now sat Arthur thought he could see a dead mouse, though when he put on his glasses to have a better look this, rather to his disappointment, turned out to be a single sock, presumably unwashed.

Arthur thought the room was a delight, and warmed to Aubrey even more than he had on the one or two occasions he had met him previously, always at Lilley & Chase office parties. He smiled happily across at Hazel, who several times had made attempts to get the cat off her knee and on to the floor.

'So, Hazel. You look very much at home. Do you and Aubrey see much of each other?'

'Well – we live so close that we do, I'm glad to say. Aubrey's friends are much more glamorous than mine, and I do love coming here. He gives the most wonderful supper parties. I usually feel completely out of place, but Aubrey makes such a fuss of me that I always enjoy myself.'

The banality of both his question and Hazel's response acted as a ritualistic, formulaic opening to an uneasy situation. Arthur was not at all sure why he was there, and it was not difficult to detect in Hazel a sense of strain and awkwardness.

Aubrey got up to remove the cat from her lap and, now that he was standing more directly in the light, Arthur could see that the front of his trousers carried a ring of yellow urine stain down the right leg. The more Arthur studied him, the more spectacularly unkempt the man appeared. Arthur took another sip of his whisky, having taken the opportunity to wipe the rim of the glass with his handkerchief while Aubrey was picking up the cat.

'It's very good of you to come round here tonight, Arthur,' said Aubrey. 'I do appreciate it. It's just that I have so hated being on the sidelines with all these things going on over Sam, and I did very much want to have the chance of talking to you. I'm not going to say very nice things, I'm afraid, but then we're not in a very nice position. Sam has been incredibly kind to me over the years. I've always thought that Lilley & Chase was the pleasantest of all the independent publishing houses to work for and, as you know, I do work for most of them.'

This is fun, thought Arthur, but it's not going to get us anywhere. One more whisky and I'll be on my way. I want to get back and do some more telephoning. I wonder why Hazel was so keen that I should come here. How typical of her that she should be friends with Aubrey. I bet she is absolutely the first person watching over him when he needs it. Which I imagine is most of the time.

He looked across at her and was able to study her silently for a moment as she sat with her head down, twisting her glass in her hands. Aubrey had limped his way into the kitchen, where he was delving for something in the fridge. The bright manner Hazel had assumed for Arthur's arrival had now given way to an expression of fatigue and frowning anxiety, and he reflected how traumatic the last few weeks must have been for her. She was in reality rather remote from the debate. There were only limited ways in which she could fight the battle on Sam's behalf. Arthur knew of their relationship, as everybody did, and had always regarded it as a bit of a joke. But watching her now he could sense, in a way that he had never before done, the degree of devotion that she had for Sam. He was an old-fashioned man in many ways; he liked his women to stand by their men, and he was moved by this.

'Hazel?' She looked up and smiled rather wanly at him. 'Why am I here?'

Hazel looked across at Aubrey, who was now back in his seat, and then at Arthur. Aubrey said nothing, and she turned to Arthur.

'This is such a dreadful period, Arthur. I can't just sit and watch Sam's life being destroyed like this. Decisions are being taken as if he didn't exist. Everybody at Lilley & Chase owes Sam such a debt. Even Richard. He has given us all many years of work and achievement. As perhaps you may know, I have a special relationship with him. So obviously I have a particular interest in looking after him. And for me it has been such a total nightmare. I don't have any power. I'm just a secretary at the end of the day, despite all those years I've been there. I'm not a director, and I don't have many shares. Because of that it has been very difficult for me to help him over the last few weeks in the way that I would have liked to. But I did want you to hear from me how I felt. Aubrey asked you to come here tonight because he wants to say something of his own to you. I don't know what it is, but I do know what I wanted to say for myself.'

Hazel's mind raced on as she was speaking. She wanted to keep the tone of the conversation as unemotional and as focused as possible, and she was determined not to waste this time with Arthur by bursting into tears and having to be comforted and mopped up, though in the privacy of her own flat she could weep as much as she wanted, and there had been a good deal of that. But to witness people who owed Sam so much abandoning him bit by bit was a horror. The dreadful Pat Simmons, who had been appallingly sycophantic to Sam all the time in the past. To watch him now scurrying after Richard, feeding him with titbits, and whispering in his ear like some sort of Dickensian fat boy currying favour from the beadle. And Birdie. The woman had only been in the firm five minutes and here she was in a position to make a personal act that would destroy Sam's life.

'Hazel. As you know, I agree with every word you've said. I'm still trying to save the situation. Though I have to say that time is running out, and it is proving very difficult. I've tried to get all the main authors to make a stand with me, but that has been only partially successful. I had thought that Sam might be able to persuade Ben to change his mind, but he's been with him this afternoon, as I'm sure you know, and apparently that hasn't happened. I had thought that . . .'

No, thought Hazel. I didn't know. So Sam is back in London. Thank God for that. Maybe he'll come around tonight to the flat. God, I would like to make love with him again. And to hold him, and cherish him, and love him and make him feel better and healed and with me again. He must be better. Thank God. He must be mending now. I must get back there in case he calls. I must get back for him. She realised that Arthur was still speaking.

'. . . but somehow it hasn't worked out that way. I'm going to fight on, of course. But it isn't easy.'

Aubrey moved in his chair, and got up to offer Arthur another whisky, which he accepted. As he limped off again into the kitchen, he said over his shoulder, 'Did Sam feel that Ben would change his mind if he put more pressure on him?'

Arthur wondered how to reply. He was clear from what Sam had told him that Ben was determined in his stance, though Arthur hung on to a slight hope that he would change his mind when he had reflected over the weekend on their conversation together.

'I'm not sure, Aubrey. I suspect that the answer is that Ben has made up his mind.'

How could Ben do that to Sam? thought Hazel. How could he do it? But then those sort of people often let you down. There is such an air of openness and friendliness about him. And he puts himself forward as a radical, anti-bourgeois sort of person. And yet here he is backing off at the one moment when he could show true loyalty and true courage. Because he had the chance of making some money for himself. And Sam had always shown him so much support. Almost favouritism really. He was devoted to Ben. Saw in him something of himself, perhaps. And yet in the end, the only one of those working directors who is prepared to stand up for Sam is Lorraine. And Sam probably knew her less well than any of them.

'Arthur, there is a reason why I suggested that you should come round here tonight.' Aubrey's quiet, soft voice had an edge of

271

tension in it now. 'I haven't told Hazel about this, though I did ask that she should come too, to hear what I had to say. I know she wanted to see you anyway, and I asked her to make the arrangements with you. It's been difficult for us, and some of the others who don't have shares and don't have a place on the board, or any way of making our views felt. Worst most of all for Hazel, but many of us do feel that a great injustice is about to happen, and Sam is such a special man . . .'

Aubrey continued talking on in his gentle, unemphatic voice, and Arthur's concentration wandered away. It's no good us all sitting around saying what a nice man Sam is, he thought, and how badly he has been treated. Of course he's nice, and of course he's been badly treated, but he should have fought harder for himself. He should never have got himself into the position where it was necessary to have to make supplicatory trips to Brixton and whingeing telephone calls to Peter Hailey. If that's what was in Norah's voice when I spoke to her, then she's right. This is fun sitting here with old Aubrey, and Hazel breaks my heart, but what the hell I'm doing here when I ought to be working on God knows how many things, I really don't know.

'. . . So I'm not suggesting anything threatening at all, but if all is really lost it might be worth this final effort. It sounds distasteful, but it needn't be, and I know Cameron well enough to be sure that he would not pitch the conversation too strongly.'

'Who's Cameron? Pitch what? Sorry, Aubrey, I've lost track.'

Hazel got up from her chair, searching for her handbag and clearly in preparation to leave immediately. Looking across at her as he too instinctively rose, Arthur saw that she was flushed in the face. Aubrey was clearly embarrassed, there was a difficult little moment while Hazel's umbrella was searched for and found, then Arthur too looked at his watch and told Aubrey that he would have to leave. While Aubrey was getting his coat out of the little closet by the front door, Arthur asked him again what he had been saying. But it was Hazel who replied.

'No, Arthur. Let's leave it now. Aubrey was telling us that Walter Lynne Thomas and he share some friends in common. And that a particular friend might have a talk with Walter to suggest he change his mind. I'm sure that's not a good idea. And I'm quite sure you wouldn't think so either. I certainly have to go now. Thank you, Aubrey.'

Arthur went with her up the outside stairs that led to the street, Aubrey standing forlornly in the half-light that fed out from the basement into the stairwell. They both waved at him, then bustled away in the drizzle that had begun to fall, hoping for a taxi when they reached Exhibition Road at the intersection at the end of the street.

'I'm so sorry about that, Arthur. I hadn't realised what Aubrey wanted to say, and I would certainly have stopped him if I had. But he is genuinely horrified by what is happening to Sam. It's just that his suggestion was not something which either you or I would have wanted to have anything to do with.'

They waited for a moment for a taxi but none came, and Hazel took the opportunity to break away from Arthur and walk the half-mile or so back to Markham Square. He kissed her again, and watched her as she set off up the street, clutching her umbrella, holding her raincoat collar clasped tight around her neck.

She's hurrying back in case Sam is waiting for her, he thought. He's lucky to have her. What Sam could do with is some of her strength. We all could.

A taxi stopped and discharged a passenger, and Arthur clambered in. As he dropped his umbrella on the floor, he thought of Aubrey, and chuckled as he did so. The thought of blackmailing Walter Lynne Thomas or whatever he was proposing was not exactly what they all needed at this time. Poor old Walter. He chuckled again.

Chapter Twenty-Eight

Arthur went to his lawyer, who sent him to another lawyer, to find out if he could force a postponement of the board meeting on the grounds of Sam's incapacity. The second lawyer advised that they should take counsel's opinion, but to arrange this he needed to write an instruction to counsel, and to do this he needed to study the company's Memorandum and Articles of Association and the Shareholders' Agreement. Arthur had some years before thrown away his copies of both.

By this time it was Friday evening, and the Lilley & Chase offices were closed until Monday morning. Arthur telephoned Richard's flat, but there was no reply. He tried several times more, but with no success. He reached Ben at his home in Brixton, and discovered from him that all the relevant documents were in the company safe, and that apart from Richard and Sam, the only other key holder was Pat Simmons. He rang Pat Simmons, but a stranger answered the telephone and told him that Pat had gone to Ireland for the weekend to see his daughter. Lilley & Chase's solicitors' offices were closed until Monday. Finally, Arthur decided to abandon the attempt to get the board meeting postponed. He accepted that it would go ahead on the Tuesday, and that all he could do was to be there, and fight for Sam the best he could.

On Monday he had various committee meetings to attend during the morning and afternoon, and in the evening he was a speaker at a City dinner. The day had been too full for him to make any further telephone calls, or to attempt any lobbying of the Lilley & Chase staff, which was what he had hoped to be able to find time to do.

The meeting convened on Tuesday morning, and Arthur, for the first time ever in his years as a director, was there early. Richard had brought with him to the meeting the company's lawyer, Alan Jamieson, who had acted for the firm ever since its birth. He was, as Arthur would have conceded, an impartial man, strictly professional, and on a personal basis closer to neither Richard nor Sam.

Richard simply and clearly laid out the decisions the board had to make, and Jamieson gave a summary of the resolutions that had been tabled, and the legal considerations of each, all with relevance to the Memorandum and Articles of Association and the Shareholders' Agreement.

Further tabled was the offer letter from Monk Grolsch Parsons, and Jamieson reported that the MGP lawyers were standing by their telephones to confirm or discuss any points of issue arising from this.

The meeting was technical, unemotional and efficient. Arthur asked for confirmation that a single negative vote from him against the resolutions would be sufficient to defeat them. Jamieson confirmed that this was so under the Articles of the company, but said he felt bound to table at that point a letter signed by six of the directors, that, in the event of Arthur voting to defeat the resolutions, then they would bind themselves to vote against his re-election as a director at the company's Annual General Meeting, to be held the following week.

Arthur started to demand that in these circumstances the meeting should be paused until he could bring his personal lawyer to it, but caught Jamieson's eye, and the little shake of his head. He slumped in his chair, put his hands up in a gesture of surrender, and waited for the next move.

The resolutions were formally read, proposed for adoption by Richard, and seconded by Walter Lynne Thomas. Lorraine Dinkins suddenly shot her hand up, before anyone was called to vote, and asked Jamieson if an abstention would defeat the resolutions under the company's Articles. Jamieson said not. The voting then proceeded, and on each resolution seven directors voted in favour, Lorraine abstained, and Arthur voted against. The resolutions were therefore defeated by Arthur's single negative vote.

Jamieson then asked to speak to Arthur privately. When they were alone he smiled at Arthur, told him that there was nothing that Arthur could do further, that he very much appreciated his position, that he admired him for it, but that his advice now was that Arthur should resign, so that the meeting could be reconvened and the resolutions re-presented. He was emphatic on the binding nature of the letter that the six directors had signed committing them to vote Arthur out of office at the AGM the following week, and told him that, in his opinion, a resignation now would save embarrassment and the probability of pointlessly adverse publicity for Lilley & Chase.

They went back into the meeting, and Arthur resigned his directorship, quietly signing a handwritten confirmation that Jamieson had written out whilst Arthur was speaking. Richard acknowledged his resignation, the meeting was reconvened, the resolutions were again voted on, and all directors voted in favour, except for Lorraine, who again abstained.

Richard closed the meeting, and there was a silence. Richard pushed his pen into its cap, clipped it into his inside pocket, and said, 'Two things, now that it is all over. Firstly, when Sam is better, I shall see him and tell him that Lilley & Chase was his creation, and his creation alone, and it has been a magnificent achievement. Secondly, I would like to thank Arthur for being with us for almost ten years. And to say that I admire him and respect him for his stand for Sam. Meeting closed.'

'One moment, Chairman . . .' Walter Lynne Thomas had his finger raised and was starting to speak.

'No,' said Richard, and got up and left the room.

The others slowly gathered their papers, and left one by one. Jamieson shook hands with Arthur and Walter, nodded at whomever would take any notice, then left himself, no one showing him out. There was no conversation. Arthur sat in his chair, hands behind his neck, watching them leave. Ben tried to talk to him, but Arthur put his hand up, saying, 'You did your thing, Ben. Whatever it was.' When Ben tried again to say something, Arthur shook his head and put his finger to his lips. Finally, it was just Arthur and Walter left.

'My car and driver are outside, Arthur. Can we drive you somewhere?'

Arthur shook his head, made no reply, but he got to his feet, put his hand out to Walter, who shook it in an oddly yielding, feminine way, and then Arthur went out through the door. There was just the usual profanity when he tripped on the stair carpet, and he was gone.

Chapter Twenty-Nine

Christopher died on a grey drizzling night, late in January. The end had come suddenly. There had been weeks of increasing fatigue, and latterly there had been few days when he came out of his bedroom at all.

Mark was with him every minute he was able, but he was in the middle of working on his 'Africa' series, and found it very difficult to be away from Bush House for too much of the working week. There were agonies of conscience for him over this, but he found it next to impossible to let Angie down. She felt that they were on the edge of producing something memorably good, and was working away at it for twelve or fifteen hours a day: editing, writing copy, revising; determined to bring the programmes in precisely on schedule and as good as she and Mark could make them.

Christopher had grown frailer as the autumn progressed, but seemed a little stronger as Christmas approached. He went to morning service at St Barnabas's on Christmas Day, but there was a raw and biting wind, and although he was wrapped up by Mark in a thick overcoat and woollen scarf, he looked grey and cold and shrunken.

Mark had prepared Christmas lunch at Camellia Mansions for Christopher and an old Oxford friend of his who had been recently widowed, but Christopher's tiredness was such that he spoke very little, went to his room immediately afterwards, and barely rose from his bed again until he died four weeks later.

He never complained much over this period and appeared to be in no very great discomfort; what pain there was Rory Morgan monitored carefully and kept under control. He just seemed to fade, each day talking a little less, eating less, sleeping more. Norah came for a little, but Christopher seemed more comfortable with a Jamaican nurse that Rory Morgan had acquired for him, and she returned to Yorkshire, with instructions to Mark to send a car for her the moment she was needed.

Mark sat with him all the time he could get away from Bush House, setting up a camp bed in Christopher's bedroom so that he could watch over him at night. Christopher listened to some music sometimes, but could not read. He prayed, but Mark never saw or heard him do so. He had always been the most reticent of public worshippers, but Mark wanted very much that, with the end so clearly near, he would be allowed to bring Andrew Boot in from St Barnabas's to hear Christopher's confession, or whatever would bring him peace.

But Christopher expressed no great interest in this, or in seeing anybody very much, particularly when Mark tried to persuade him that he should be allowed to arrange for some of the Hunstanton people to come.

'I don't want unfinished business left in your life, Chris. You know how important it is to reconcile all the things that have to be reconciled. It's important for the others as well as you. There's a number of the Hunstanton people who want to see you. Donald Graham has called. Ken Harris has called. There's a pile of letters that I would so much like you to read. Try, Chris. Please try. I won't allow anyone to stay more than a brief moment, and I'll make absolutely sure no one tires you.'

'It really isn't a matter of reconciliation. I feel no bitterness towards anybody. They never betrayed me because they weren't my friends. Acquaintances can't betray you. They can reject you, but they can't betray you.'

Mark went to the window, and looked out at the dark outline of the trees in Battersea Park, and the cars as they drove along Prince of Wales Drive. When he turned, Christopher was already drifting away back into sleep, and Mark quietly left the room, telling the nurse that he would be back within two hours.

He ran down the stairs of the mansion block, hailed a taxi, and told the driver to go to Lambeth Palace. He spoke to a security guard, and asked to see one of the archbishop's chaplains, whom he knew slightly through a mutual friend in the BBC. The chaplain was there, they talked, he took Mark to a waiting room, and came back ten minutes later to show him into the archbishop's study. A few minutes later the study door opened, and Archbishop Gurney came in, smiling his greeting to Mark and holding out his hand.

He was a tall man, almost seventy years old, but with brown curly hair only barely touched with grey. His face had a cherubic, beaming, open quality about it, and he fussed over Mark before settling down opposite him, offering coffee and tea and whisky, all of which Mark refused.

'I haven't seen Christopher for ten years. As of course you know. He taught me at Hunstanton years and years ago, as of course you know as well. We formed a very close bond at that time, and remained correspondents and friends for many years after. I loved him very much. As a young man he struck me as being one of the very few wholly good people I had ever met. Actually, I still think that. He was a fair to middling teacher perhaps – too dismissive of certain things, too accepting of others – and he lacked in some ways a certain vitality of intellect. But he was disarmingly good. And loved by many of the people who came into contact with him. Which was at least part of the reason why the outcry was so great when . . .'

He tailed off in embarrassment, and looked across at Mark with a wry grin on his face.

'Chris and I call it The Fall,' Mark said. 'The Fall. After all that nightmare of making a departure from Hunstanton, I went off to Europe for a month or so, and Christopher sent me a postcard which simply carried a quote from *Paradise Lost*:

> . . . freely we serve,
> Because we freely love, as in our will
> To love or not; in this we stand or fall . . .

'We've referred to it as The Fall ever since. It somehow reduces the pain of the memory to familiarise it like that.'

'The Fall.'

Gurney looked across at Mark, and his cherubic expression had grown unexpectedly distanced and cold. 'That's well named. You

281

talk about reducing the pain of the memory. I'm not sure you should do that. It might well have been healthier for you both to have looked at the incident with greater frankness and realism than that. It really was a period of complete horror for all his friends. I'm sure you realise that. We were all critical of Christopher and, looking back, even with the softening of time, I am sure we were right to be so. This was the one great crisis of his life – his comfortable, stressless, painless life – and we felt that he had failed it. He realised the harm he was doing – he simply must have realised the harm he was doing to himself and to us and to Hunstanton and to so many people – but he appeared to make no effort at all to withstand the temptation. And I'm afraid that's how it appeared to us. Simple temptation. Just straightforward, common-or-garden, squalid sexual temptation. And Christopher met it for the first time in his life, and wasn't man enough to stand up against it. Or even to *try* to stand up against it. He failed quite utterly. And that made a lot of us very angry indeed.'

As Mark listened to Gurney he felt his skin tighten and his breathing shallow. He had been taken quite by surprise, and he was at first aghast at what he would have to face, and then oddly relieved. This was absolutely not what he had thought he was going to hear when he had come to Lambeth Palace. If there was an assumption at all in his mind, it was that there would be a scene between him and Gurney of lachrymose regret and nostalgia, followed by a deathbed reconciliation scene at Camellia Mansions. Gurney's attack was the first time in ten years that Mark had faced articulate and informed antagonism over his relationship with Christopher, and, after the shock of surprise, it was a not unpleasant dose of realism. Gurney's coldness to the facetious semantics of The Fall met an acknowledgement in Mark of a point well scored.

'And I cannot allow myself the dishonour of not being brave enough to say to you, now that we've at last met, what I think has to be said. And that is that you personally should have known better.' Gurney was looking at him firmly, and his voice was low and calm. 'You had an elderly and distinguished man at your mercy. He was suffering from what seemed to the rest of us like an absurd and perhaps senile sexual aberration; you simply took advantage of him. If you had any sense of propriety or decency at all, you should have helped him. As it is, you destroyed him. And you also dealt a very heavy blow to an institution that it is very easy to make look ridiculous. I resent that.'

Gurney's gaze shifted from Mark, and he sat silently for a moment, his fingers playing with a notebook and pencil that sat on the table beside him. He then looked up at Mark again.

'I appreciate your action in coming to see me. I'm afraid I haven't been very nice to you, or made any great attempt to be tactful. But I believe you did all of us, and most of all of course poor Christopher, a considerable disservice. To put it mildly. I have to tell you that.'

And although he then smiled at Mark, it was a mechanical gesture without warmth or meaning, and Mark found himself growing angry. What right does this preening ass have to judge me or to judge Christopher? he thought. The bastard. Here am I trapped with him in this flatulent place listening to a lot of bullying nonsense that is a travesty of what the truth actually is. But bite the lip and take it. A quarrel here will exactly serve to ruin what I'm trying to do for Chris. Don't lose your temper. Keep calm. Keep calm.

'What you say is untrue. Or most of what you say is untrue. We gave each other our lives because we loved each other. And we still do. And we have had considerable happiness for ten years. It's not a question of me knowing better, or Christopher knowing better. We made a brave decision. It's very easy to make homophobic noises about . . .'

'Don't insult me. I am not homophobic, and nor were my remarks. I am not going to insult you in return by saying that I would have felt just the same if Christopher had taken up with a young girl, but actually I would have done. Or very nearly the same, if I am absolutely scrupulously honest about it. What you and Christopher did was devastatingly damaging.'

Mark looked across at him, and although his voice remained calm he made no attempt to conceal the anger in his eyes. 'Maybe I should rephrase what I was trying to say. I accept the sincerity of your view. I don't agree with it. I don't think you realise how happy we have been.'

'I'm glad to hear it. I'm glad for both your sakes. I'm sorry if I sound to you to be cruel or vindictive. But I cannot allow you to leave here with any sort of muddled impression of where I stand on all this. It's possible we should all of us have handled the event differently. Christopher's reaction to the snub from the Hunstanton people was, I suppose, understandable, but still quite ludicrously insensitive. The public statement I made could well have been better expressed. There was a considerable amount of bitterness, and I'm afraid it showed. I'm glad you've been happy. But I must tell you that I think your happiness has got nothing to do with the issue at all. As I said earlier, this was the one and only moment in Christopher's sheltered life for him to show courage and fortitude and plain Christian guts. The qualities a lot of people have to show all the time. He failed. So did you.'

They fell silent, and remained looking at each other. Then Mark said, 'Where do we go from here? Is there anything more to say?'

This time Gurney smiled, and he did so now with what appeared to be a genuine attempt at good humour and warmth, though this served to make Mark the angrier with him.

'Yes. There is something else to say. I'm not at all convinced that Christopher would want to see me anyway. Neither of us actually knows. But I can tell you that I would deeply appreciate the opportunity of saying goodbye to him. Despite everything I have said to you tonight, I can assure you that I love him. It's really up to you now. If you still want me to come then I not only will, but I will do so with considerable joy. But I'm not going to come under false pretences. It's up to you.'

Mark hesitated. He had found Gurney's whole conversation with him a travesty and an insult. Why should he meekly agree to him coming around to Camellia Mansions? Why not just tell him to keep his own opinions and leave them both alone? But . . . he had come here not for his own purposes but to give something important to Christopher. Don't spoil that now.

He told the archbishop he could come, there was a call through to a chaplain, the diary was rearranged, and it was confirmed that he would be at Camellia Mansions at six o'clock the following evening.

Mark left Christopher asleep at ten o'clock in the morning,

departing for Bush House with the usual instructions to the nurse as to where he could be reached, and was back at Camellia Mansions at half-past five. Having released the nurse for the evening, he went straight to Christopher's bedroom and looked at him as he slept, the breathing a little too deep, the face ashen-white, the cheeks sunken in. He reminded himself that he must not leave it too late before he called Norah and brought her back to London.

After a few minutes he put his hand on Christopher's shoulder, and gently shook him until he awoke. He got a basin of warm water, and sponged his hands and face. They talked a little, though Christopher was beginning to lose awareness of time and day, and mostly he lay watching and listening whilst Mark spoke.

The doorbell rang, Mark got up and went to the front door, and came back into the bedroom with Gurney. He pulled up a chair for Gurney beside the bed, and himself withdrew over to the window. Gurney sat and, leaning forward, took Christopher's hand.

'Hello, my old friend. Mark said that I could come, and I very much hope you don't mind.'

Mark wondered for a moment if Christopher recognised him. For some time he made no response at all, but then looked intently into Gurney's eyes, and when he spoke it was so softly that Mark could only just hear his voice.

'Hello, Alec.'

Gurney smiled, and said no more, but simply sat holding one of Christopher's hands in both of his. Christopher appeared to try to speak further, but couldn't, and just lay propped up on his pillows, looking at Gurney and across at Mark. After a time, Mark walked over to the bed.

Gurney stood, looked down at Christopher and said, 'You hate the public display of this sort of thing, Chris, but you are too weak to stop me, and I'm going to do it anyway.'

He leant across, and made the Sign of the Cross over Christopher. 'Almighty God, look on this Your servant, lying in great weakness, and comfort him with the promise of life everlasting . . .'

Christopher's eyes were open but expressionless. As Mark watched him, he muttered a prayer that Christopher should have sufficient awareness to know what was happening, for looking at him it was impossible to know whether he was conscious of the proceedings or not.

'Deliver Your servant Christopher from all evil . . .'

Gurney's hand was lying softly on Christopher's head as he spoke, and Mark felt a shiver run through him as he watched them together in the extraordinary personal intimacy of the ancient prayers.

' . . . And set him free from every bond, that he may rest with all Your saints in the eternal habitations, where with the Father, and the Holy Spirit, You live and reign, Oh God, for ever and ever . . .'

Is Christopher really to leave me? Mark felt a surge of panic run through him. I can't be without him. I can't be without him.

'I lay my hands upon you in the Name of our Lord Saviour Jesus Christ, beseeching Him to uphold you and feed you with His grace, that you may know the healing power of His love.'

Mark watched Gurney as he bent over Christopher, his thumb, glistening now with the holy oil, sketching the Cross again on Christopher's forehead.

'I anoint you with oil in the name of the Father, and of the Son, and of the Holy Spirit. Amen.'

And then, as Christopher's eyes closed again, and he appeared to drift back into sleep, 'Into Your hands, O merciful Saviour, we commend Your servant Christopher . . . Receive him into the arms of Your mercy, into the blessed rest of everlasting peace, and into the glorious company of the souls in light . . . May his soul and the souls of all the faithful departed, through the mercy of God, rest in peace. Amen.'

As Gurney finished, he sat again and watched Christopher for a few moments. Then he got to his feet, and went quietly with Mark to the door.

'You've done me a great service, Mark. Thank you. And –' he looked at Mark and hesitated for a moment – 'thank you for all you've done for Christopher.'

As Gurney went down the stairs, Mark went straight to the telephone to call Norah, who wanted to come down that night. He called Harrogate to arrange for a driver and car to collect her straight away, and rang Norah again, who said she would pack immediately.

As he was putting down the telephone, he heard a sudden cry of pain from Christopher's room. He rushed in, and found Christopher doubled over on the floor, arms crossed over his stomach. There was another long cry, followed by moaning, first sharp with pain, then dull and soft.

In a minute or so he was dead, locked hard in Mark's arms, his white head on Mark's shoulder, his eyes open and staring. Mark closed them gently, stroked his head, and prayed for his soul. Goodbye, Chris, he thought. Everything worked out for us. Everything worked out. Everything worked out.

Chapter Thirty

By late the following summer, Norah had finally got around to selling the Camellia Mansions flat, after it had been sitting empty for over seven months.

She wanted Mark to stay there as a free tenant but he had refused. She offered to give him the flat, but he refused that too. He moved out within five weeks of Christopher's death, on the day after the memorial service. Norah came to say goodbye to him as he packed up the last of his boxes, the little self-drive removal van standing outside in Prince of Wales Drive.

Christopher had left Mark everything he possessed: the deposit account, the Marks and Spencer shares his mother had left him, and the books. Mark sold the shares, took the money from the deposit account, and gave the combined sum to Hunstanton in the form of a bursary in Christopher's name. The books were to go to the neat little flat he had rented for himself just off the Portobello Road, and he was packing them into boxes as Norah was talking to him.

He left Camellia Mansions scrubbed and clean and stripped of everything: curtains, blankets, chair covers all laundered and cleaned and folded into neat piles on the beds; the carpets shampooed, the windows cleaned, the paintwork washed down. He wanted the end of his time there to be symbolically and actually pristine, this to mark the closure of what had been the single happiness in the whole of his personal and emotional life.

Norah hesitated to sell the flat because to do so was an affirmation of her twin's death, but the village church needed money: the roof was leaking, the kneelers threadbare, the hymn books falling apart, the paint peeling, the vestments holed and filthy. She decided to use the money from the sale of the flat entirely on the church's restoration. She hoped that in its unaccustomed brightness, it too could act as a memorial for Christopher, for whom she arranged that a small plaque should be squeezed into a quiet place on the north side of the transept.

By the end of March, Mark had decorated his new flat with fresh wallpaper, new curtains, new carpets, and white-painted bookshelves. He had stripped out a shabby kitchen and made from it one of glistening modernity with its white walls, bleached pine floors and cupboards, a glass table and marble working surfaces. He was determined that AIDS, if it came to that, was not going to mean a descent into physical and moral collapse. He would die in due course no doubt. But for the present he was in his beautiful flat, amongst clean and polished things, with his books on his shelves, his study set up with his word processor and printer, his kitchen sparkling, fresh flowers everywhere, and the sun shining through the deep sash-windows with their bright new yellow curtains. There was to be purpose and bustle and freshness to the last period of his life. No darkness, no guilt, no pain.

He completed two last programme projects at Bush House, and gave to them both a concentrated and focused commitment. He counted his savings, calculated that he had just enough to spare to help set up a counselling service for AIDS victims, arranged with Andrew Boot at St Barnabas's that he would do it in financial partnership with his team at the church, and resigned from the BBC in July.

By the end of August, he and Andrew had raised enough money from various sources to think of doing the project on a much larger scale than Mark had first planned, with four volunteers to help man the telephones. Like Mark, these were all people in their thirties: an actor; a Welshman who had worked in one of the smaller merchant banks; an ex-builder's mate; and a hospital nurse.

The actor worked when he could, and was at AIDSLINE the rest of the time, his self-deprecating humour and persistent cheerfulness greatly valuable to the people who called. The Welshman, dressed as if he was still at the bank, was at the centre from breakfast time until late at night, busying himself with the administration and the money-raising. The builder's mate attended erratically but, when there, gave cheerfully direct and unsentimental advice to all, usually accompanied by cackles of laughter, and punctuated always by pauses and curses as he opened cans of lager. The hospital nurse was ill and weak – he died only six months later – but gave the team a professional medical proficiency and a calm expertise that were invaluable, though he grew tired quickly, and his appearances at AIDSLINE were seldom of more than two hours' duration.

Mark was there seven days a week, twelve hours a day, taking calls, writing letters, organising medical appointments, forming lobbying groups, writing articles for the press, and somehow finding time in all this to finish the first draft of his novel, and to get it in the hands of Ben Jackson a month earlier than scheduled.

As money started to appear from new sources, more telephone lines were put in, and more helpers were taken on. They moved to some offices above a dry cleaner's, Mark succeeding in getting sponsorship from a large drug company for the rent of this, together with the cost of the telephone system, including their monthly telephone bill, which now ran well into five figures. An article on AIDSLINE appeared in the *Guardian*, and another in the *Independent*. Mark appeared on a discussion programme on Channel Four.

They started to widen their scope from just telephone counselling to forming links with hospices, organising home-help groups, and providing some form of financial assistance for the terminally ill. They were efficient, structured and organised. They matched expenditure with income, and increased both by means of tight budgetary control. They only took on helpers whom they judged to have the balance and intelligence to provide genuine help. And they only took on helpers who were either HIV positive or AIDS confirmed.

Mark worked, saw some friends once or twice for dinner, exercised, dieted according to the precise regime laid down by his clinic, and felt very well. He assumed that in due course the AIDS confirmation would come, and feared it not at all.

He spoke to his parents each week now; cordial, almost affectionate telephone conversations, with Mark and his parents trying as best they could to communicate with each other. They were solicitous about him, and he about them.

He thought of Christopher many times a day, but preserved in his new flat only a handful of mementoes: two photographs, both taken by Mark on an occasion when they had driven down to Salzburg one summer for the music festival and to do some walking; a single letter; his books, of course; and a pair of jade cufflinks.

One of his radio series was short-listed for an award, and he went with Angie Morris and the controller of the BBC World Service to the dinner, where he was fêted by his friends and his old colleagues. He failed to win the award, and he minded not in the least. It was an affectionate, happy evening and he felt surrounded by goodwill and friendship.

When he arrived home, there was a call on his answerphone from Norah, and he returned it the following morning as he was having his breakfast. Norah sounded breathless, and her voice had a fatigue to it that made Mark wonder how long it would be before she too died. She sounded as if she had aged years since he had last spoken to her.

'Mark, darling, find Sam for me, will you? He's gone from Lilley & Chase now, as you well know, of course, and I would like to know how he is, and what we can all do for him. Though, to be quite honest, the main thing on my mind at the moment is that I'm delivering a new novel in six months, and I need to know who will be editing it for me, and who to talk to, and all the rest of it. I don't really want to talk to Ben Jackson, whom I hardly know, until I am quite certain I am going to stay with the firm now that they've sold out to these advertising people.'

'Of course I will, Norah. Is there anything you want me to mention to him before he speaks to you?'

'I don't know, darling, I'm just feeling rather wet and isolated and tired out. I would love one final talk with Sam somehow, before I make up my mind. I'm so sad about what's happened between us. We were devoted to each other. He must think I've let him down so badly. Perhaps I have. Perhaps I should have fought for him more. But it's a little late in my life for fights. And he wouldn't look after himself, and one does have to look after oneself. And show resilience when things go wrong. And courage. But whatever happened, or didn't happen, I've been with him for all these years, and I feel lost without him there with me. I can't imagine I shall be able to face another book after this one, and it's ghastly having to go through with it all without Sam. Am I being very selfish? Would you mind?'

Mark eventually found Sam at Priory Grove, though it was a week before his message on the answerphone was returned. Sam asked him around there for a drink, and when Mark arrived, he found Sam up in the drawing room on his own, fire lit, elderly black leather slippers on his feet, and a Schumann piano sonata playing on the record player. Sam poured him a drink, and sat him down in a deep armchair.

'I don't know what I can say to Norah, but the obvious. It's far too late for her to move to another publishing house at this stage of her life. Quite apart from the fact that she would have to negotiate herself out of her contract, Ben Jackson is as good an editor as there is around, now that the conglomerates have fired everyone else. He'll look after her fine. He looks after you very happily, doesn't he? What's the problem?'

He shrugged over-expansively, and stared across at Mark with an expression which Mark interpreted as a deliberate statement of disinterest. A slight feeling of irritation came over Mark, but then he reminded himself that there was no reason why Sam should feel obliged to be helpful, or indeed why he should be expected still to be interested. But there was nevertheless an immaturity about it all. A quite unmistakable immaturity, actually; the spoilt child who has lost his toy. Norah and he had been friends for so long. He owed her more than that damned shrug.

'I think she would just like your hand on her shoulder, actually, Sam. I'm not sure how well she is. She's certainly worried and stressed over it all. She sounds much older than she did. Call her for me, anyway. Maybe call Ben Jackson as well.'

'You call Ben Jackson.' The voice was languid, but there was an aggressive edge to it.

'Fine. I'll call him.' Jesus Christ, Mark thought. This is verging on the insulting. But I mustn't let this drift into a quarrel. Try something else for a few moments, finish my drink and leave pleasantly.

Then Sam smiled at him, perhaps himself looking for a way to defuse the threat. He smiled again, and then spoke in a much gentler tone. 'Stay where you are, Mark. I'd like to show you a private thing. I'll be down in a moment.'

Mark heard him climb the stairs up to his bedroom, and when he came back into the drawing room he had in his hands an ugly little tin box. He put it on the upholstered ottoman in front of Mark, opened it, and from amongst all the collection of studs and links and buttons he took a rabbit's foot and a Dumbo brooch, and laid them down side by side.

'I've never forgotten her. She's with me every day. They're my sister's. She died when she was thirteen. I was ten. One of the two people of my life. Sally, and Annabel. Perhaps three. Add Hilary.'

Mark looked at him, and wondered how to respond. He was pleased to have been paid the compliment of this sort of intimacy, but he was taken aback by it. He knew Sam moderately well, but not more than that, and what he had always been struck by before was his amiability, certainly, but predominantly his personal reticence, cloaked by an assumed air of gregarious openness. It was odd that he should be choosing this moment for this sort of intimacy. And with him.

'Not healthy possibly, but true. It's a statement, not a cry for sympathy. It doesn't add up to a balanced life perhaps. But it's what life has brought me. Sally was the perfect sister. We were friends in a way I have never been friends with anyone since. She never let me down. Nor did Annabel. Never once in her life. Both lives were far too short. In aggregate they didn't add up to a single lifespan. But between them those two lives have been all that I have ever really had. I nearly achieved the same with Hilary. I wish I had.'

Mark started to mumble something conventionally appropriate, then grew irritated with himself for doing so. There was an aspect of Sam's approach of which he didn't approve. Too much emphasis on people letting him down. Too much saintliness attached to those who didn't. Too much on what other people had done to him. Too much passivity. Not enough on what he had done, or not done, for others. Too little respect for everybody else's loyalty to him. From people whom he doesn't count as being on the saintly team. Loyalty which may not have been asked for, nor particularly wanted, but important to the person who had given it.

Mark knew of Sam's relationship with Hazel through his many evenings talking with Ben Jackson in the Brixton kitchen, and he had never really approved of it. Not for reasons of prudery, for, given Mark's own sexual history, that would have been absurd. Nor specifically because Sam had not married her, for it could have been that he had continued the relationship for so long out of a sense of kindness and response to Hazel's devotion.

Mark's disapproval was because he had a sense that the relationship was continued simply as a physical convenience for Sam. If he had begun to find Hazel sexually uninteresting, then Mark suspected Sam would have dropped her promptly. If this were true, Mark by no means admired it. Indeed, Hazel's story was one that occupied his novelist's mind a good deal. On one level it was a classic story of a woman's constancy in love. On another it was a story of an obsessive relationship that made void the life of the perpetrator. Perhaps it could be interpreted as a parable of human goodness operating in an unconventional morality. Or a metaphor for woman's subjugation to man. Or alternatively a straightforward story of a man behaving like an old-fashioned shit. Whatever the analysis of the relationship, Mark wanted Hazel honoured for her loyalty, and admired for her capacity for love, and he wanted to hear that from Sam.

'Forgive me, Sam. I don't know you well enough for this . . . but . . . Hazel, too. I would doubt she ever let you down.'

Sam coloured and turned away. 'She doesn't quite mean—'

Mark's vague irritation with Sam was suddenly switching to anger, but he made a concentrated attempt to hold it back and conceal it. He was glad Sam had not finished the sentence, for he feared what he guessed was about to be said. He talks all the time of loyalty. Where is his loyalty to Hazel? That affair, or liaison, or however it should be described, should never have been allowed to go on for year upon year without a resolution.

Mark knew about matters being brought to resolution. He'd had experience of that with Chris. He had hesitated initially and, looking at the trouble his young man's sexual needs had brought him subsequently, he had been right to hesitate, but he had made a decision, and when he did so it was a considered moment, and he stuck to it. He accepted Chris's love, and he gave him back everything he could give, and he made everything work out for them. Despite some of the frustrations about it all. But he had not given him his celibacy. Nor even attempted to give him his celibacy. Or, to put it less delicately, his sexual fidelity. Whatever the age difference was.

Perhaps, he thought, Sam could turn the tables on my disapproval of his treatment of Hazel and make me face up to that. But it would have been impossible. I couldn't have led a celibate life. I'm just not strong enough for that. So maybe one shouldn't judge too easily what went on between Sam and Hazel. Or indeed what goes on between anybody. But to hell with that. Whatever I have been, Sam has been a bastard to Hazel, and for too many years. It's an odd thing, because he's by no means like that in the rest of his life. Though I've never got to grips with that Hilary story, I've got to say that there's a piece of me that considers it a lot of sanctimonious bullshit.

Sam was speaking again. 'Look, Mark. Of course I don't admire myself for what I've done to Hazel. I can only explain it to you by saying that for years I have been very fond of her, that I am by nature a monogamous man, that I was faithful to her throughout our entire relationship, and that I never misled her. She wanted me, even on those terms.'

So it's over, thought Mark. I wonder if he's told Hazel that. He never could quite take her seriously. It would not be at all untypical if he was telling me, virtually a stranger, before he'd got around to telling her. Sam despised Hazel in a way. He sentimentalised her, but he despised her. He had these two figures of what he considered to be visionary purity: Annabel, and his sister Sally. Something for his wife, but then she went off the rails. Nothing for his mistress. If one has to trivialise poor Hazel by calling her that.

Mark tried to pull himself together, and in doing so he

remembered that he had not expressed sufficient interest or sympathy with Sam a moment ago. 'I hadn't realised that you had lost a sister, Sam.'

Sam picked up the Dumbo brooch, looked at it, then laid it back. 'A bit more than that, really. I seemed to lose my childhood when she died, together with more of my soul than should have been lost at that age. She was the closest friend I ever had. We were isolated together in a home where our parents were like people with whom we had been inexplicably boarded. Not in the least unhappily boarded, just inaccurately so. I'm sorry if I'm embarrassing you with all this. Annabel's death is an echo to me of what happened forty years ago when Sally died. I seem to put the finger of death on those I love most. Perhaps Hilary did well to escape me. At least it can't happen to me again. There's no one left now.'

Mark looked across at him, and had no idea what to say. He felt he wanted to give Sam a lead to help him restore himself, but that to do so he would first have to encourage him out from his current perspective.

'Sam, that's a maudlin way of looking at things. You know that. Grief and loss are part of life for us all.'

'It may sound maudlin. It may sound sentimental. I'm not sure if I care very much if it does or not. It's true, and that's what matters to me. I've had too much pain to care very much about other people's reactions. I'm not sure why I'm telling you. Except to say that I don't want to quarrel with you, and I thought we nearly were quarrelling a moment ago. I'm sharing with you an intimacy that I have never shared with anybody else. As a peace offering. In memory of Chris. Or something like that.'

Sam got up from his chair, and drew the curtains across the north window, which faced the garden and the back of The Boltons' houses beyond. He wandered back to his chair, and sat for a moment gazing into the fire.

'I fall in love with purity. I don't mean sexual purity. I mean constancy. That's why my life has been so dominated by Sally and Annabel. The first a child. The second a child too in my eyes. I could never adjust my vision of her to that of a grown woman.'

Mark thought back to a quite recent evening in Annabel's flat, when he had gone round there after supper one night to return some books he had borrowed from her earlier in the year. They had sat together until well past midnight on the floor in front of her gas fire, and Annabel had talked of her relationship with Sam, and how she couldn't have any conversation with him that addressed in any meaningful way her sexual and emotional life. It was at a time when Annabel was badly hurt. She had just broken up with the young BBC producer with whom she had been going out for some months. He had left for a trip to Norway to research some programme or other, and on his return had moved back to his own flat with no more contact with Annabel than a telephone call and a vague arrangement to meet her sometime for dinner. Before he had left, Annabel had begun to think of him as someone she could marry, and his loss was acutely painful to her. She had been to Priory Grove the evening before her talk with Mark, and she described to him how difficult she had found it, with Sam affectionate and jocular as he always was with her, and that had been the point; for the jocularity of Sam was that of a father to a child daughter: trivial, patronising, inherently uncommunicative. And this on an evening when Annabel had been deeply unhappy, and unable to share it or show it.

Sam was speaking again. 'I can't handle things that are close to me, when they turn sour. The moment I am presented with an impurity or a disloyalty to me I want to turn my back on it. Arthur Hill thinks I'm a coward. That's not really the truth. I have a disinclination to fight sometimes. That's not the same thing.'

'Why didn't you fight for Lilley & Chase? I find all that very difficult to understand.'

But the moment Mark said that, he did understand, just as Ben had before him. It was because Lilley & Chase had turned out to be like Hilary. Sam loved them both, but they both let him down. Neither was constant to him. Hilary had her affair. Lilley & Chase was seduced away by the Monk Grolsch Parsons people. Both were sullied. Sam turned his back on them both. But he had first engaged with them both. Fully engaged, as he never did with poor Hazel.

And he'll brood over them both for ever. He does now with Hilary. He will do in the future with Lilley & Chase. He'll be obsessed with what he will be imagining as their continuing treachery to him. Hilary's life of sexual and familial bliss with Jack. Which I've always gathered from Annabel's gossip was probably anything but that. Lilley & Chase's disloyal forays into publishing ventures of which Sam would never have approved. Richard stealing from him his friendships with his authors.

Sam was starting to speak in reply, but Mark held up his hand to stop him. 'Sam . . . let's forget it. For us to quarrel is quite absurd. We've both got enough to deal with without that. You've been through a hell of a lot. So have I, actually. But I tell you something, Sam. I never had a Sally in my childhood. I wish I had. Because I didn't have anything much to hang on to, I learnt to be detached, and deal with life as it came along, and not expect very much purity, as you put it, from anybody. One of the results of all that was I grew up a considerable little prick.'

Sam laughed, and got up to pour Mark another drink. He chuckled again when he was fumbling around with the bottles and the ice and the mineral water at the tray.

'Didn't we all?'

'Maybe not in the way I did. All that smug adolescent superiority about my parents. Particularly about my mother. Whom I rejected out of hand as being not good enough for me at the age of about three months. And a love for my father, but a certain cruelty in there as well. A touch of contempt, though this is the first time I have admitted that to myself, let alone anyone else. And an unforgivable egotism about whether they were sufficiently proud of me or not. The great intellectual of a son. The little prick. Though why my mother, poor woman, should have been required to be proud of me, God alone knows. I did something to her that is about as big a crime as I can think of, off-hand. I robbed her of her motherhood. I stole from her the right she had, as all women have, to experience requited maternal love. A positive right and expectation. Jesus Christ.'

Mark put his hands behind his head, and sprawled deep in the armchair. 'Jesus Christ.'

Sam said nothing, but watched across from where he was sitting. There was a long silence.

'And then Chris comes along, and that one I do get right. Thank God I can claim that to myself, anyway. I never realised I was going to come to love him the way I did. That's what made it work. I made a formal decision to go with him, certainly, and I knew that I had not chosen the easiest course in life by doing so. And indeed I didn't attempt some of the things for him that I should have attempted perhaps. Which is why I'm HIV positive. But what happened then was love. It defined my life. All very Philip Larkin.'

Mark looked over at Sam, and smiled. 'And I accused you of being maudlin.'

He got up from his chair, stretched, and started to make his preparations to leave. Sam too got to his feet, and he grimaced as he spoke. 'Mark . . . you said HIV positive. I hadn't heard. I didn't know. I'm so very—'

Mark interrupted him before he could go further.

'It's OK, Sam. I've known for some time. I can deal with it now. Or most of the time I can deal with it. On a pragmatic level at least.'

But he smiled his recognition to Sam for his concern, then, starting towards the stairs, he said, 'Maybe you could do with a bit of my pragmatism, Sam. You look back too much. Talking of which, what am I supposed to say to Norah?'

They were walking together through the hall, and Sam opened the latch on the front door to see Mark out into the dark and rainy street. Mark pulled up the collar of his coat and shivered. 'Promise you'll ring Norah, Sam. She loves you. A lot of people do.'

He walked away towards Fulham Road in search of a taxi. Sanctimonious bullshit, he thought. I'm hot on accusing Sam of that. Then ministering to him like I'm some sort of Angel of Light. The joke with Chris come true. There's a lot of sanctimonious bullshit in me at the moment, let alone Sam. My whole persona exudes too much of fairy-tale goodness. The AIDS world does that a bit at this stage of things. I've got myself too much positioned as the saintly figure of virtue. The fact is that I am neither virtuous nor unvirtuous. Sex is not like that. I've behaved neither well nor badly. I just don't want to come out of this as Mother Teresa. And all sorts of things happen inside me now that are full of resentment, and anger and self-pity and whingeing regret and all those things . . . and frustrations . . . and doubts sometimes whether the whole thing with Chris was worth it. And a longing at times to break out of the whole Andrew Boot and Lizzie Boot churchy closet, and its suffocating lack of worldly contact and realism . . . and fun. Maybe I've done enough. Maybe I should draw a line under it all and do some more things, and meet some more people before it's all too late. Real people.

He waved urgently at a taxi, which ignored him and drove on towards Brompton Cross.

And I feel bloody lonely as well, he thought. I want real life again.

Chapter Thirty-One

8 Priory Grove
London SW10

14 December

Dearest Hils

I haven't written you a letter since we were at Cambridge and we got split up in the vacs. You with your parents at Chewton Mendip most of the time, and me with Priscilla's sisters, usually. Except when I could escape with you to somewhere. Like Ireland, and that cycling holiday we had in the rain.

I do hope you can read my handwriting after all this time. No one else seems to be able to.

I woke up in the middle of the night, and I thought how unlucky we'd been. You probably only get one chance in life for real love. We had our chance, and we missed it. Mostly one just stumbles along from moment to moment. And then one is presented with a sudden point of time when there is a decision to make, or one of a choice of decisions to make, and it really is pretty much a lottery if you get it right or not. And if you happen to get it right, you never realise how near disaster you had been. And if you get it wrong, the consequences of that ruin your life.

There is not much doubt that what happened between us that ghastly autumn ruined my life for me. I still think we were both in the wrong. It was too easy for you to be so flippantly unfaithful and think that I would just accept it. It was wrong of me to be so cruelly aggressive in my response. We both made the wrong decisions. I was certainly punished for mine. I doubt you were for yours. Jack must have been a marvellous husband for you. But I still think of you as my wife. And even after all these years I want you with me. And I want you to make love with. And I hate the thought of you making love with someone else.

But at least you haven't had more children, though I have always wondered why not. Perhaps I might have been able to face it if you had. But I have always dreaded it. The stark evidence of your physical relationship with someone else. The appearance of the child. The inter-mixing of your bloodline with another man's.

I held you in my arms at Annabel's funeral. Just for the briefest of moments. And when I did so, the brush and feel and texture of your body was immediately familiar to me, even after twenty-five years. Mark Ryder told me this evening that I looked back too much. I need to look back. I need to hold in my memory our years together, and particularly our first undergraduate years. We were the happiest people in Cambridge. My parents' death in that car crash just as I was about to come up was not the blow to me that people must have assumed, though I certainly mourned them. But their death was a small thing to me against that of Sally's. And when I found you, it was the first time in a decade that I had been released from an obsessive pattern of brooding on her death. I loved you so much, Hils. Thank you for all those times.

As I said, we had our chance of love, and we let it slip away. And I've known that for so many years, and I wanted now to say it to you.

One's not supposed to write love letters to other people's wives. But this is a love letter. It's the first I've written to you since we were not much more than children. And I suppose it will have to be the last.

God bless you, Hils.

Sam.

304

Chapter Thirty-Two

Hilary lay on her bed, Sam's letter lying open beside her. She could hear Jack downstairs in the kitchen, whistling out of tune, clattering around with some boxes, talking to the dogs, slamming doors, as always making a quite mysterious amount of noise.

Yes, she thought. We missed our chance. There is only one chance. He's perfectly right. I've wanted him back ever since I lost him. And perhaps this letter is a cry for us to be with each other again. I want him too. I can't love Jack. I should love him, but I can't. I'm sure this letter means he wants me now. He's quite right. We should be together. We should have been together all along.

She got up from the bed, walked over to the window and looked out of it for a time, then went back to the bed and picked up the letter again. She read it through two or three times more, then sat, her head in her hands.

I'm fifty years old in a few months. I haven't known love for approaching twenty-five years. I've become withered and shrunken in my emotional life. What a teenager would call 'a dried-up old prune'. Annabel knew that. I wish she had known me as I really am. As I really was. Sam talks of us at Cambridge. We were children, of course, as Sam says, but there was a quality to me then of joy and love that I so wish Annabel could have seen. A vitality of life. My only child never saw it. Never saw what I really am. Never saw me loving Sam, and all the laughter there was, and all the trust, and all the life. I wish Annabel had seen it. I wish I had told her about it. I wish she had known.

My only child. My conduct towards Jack about that business must have seemed to him so heartless. But I had to tell him the truth. Or a part of the truth. It was a relief to me to hear that he

305

was infertile. I didn't want his children. But he never knew the real cruelty. That I despised him a little when I heard he was infertile. I had a sexual contempt for him. Despite the fact that I didn't want his children.

I closed my heart to life when Sam left. I married Jack because he so clearly wanted me to. I liked him, and I thought that liking might grow into love. It grew into affection at least. But not love. But it tidied up for me my physical life, and that was a lot of what I wanted. I didn't want any more mess. No affairs. No Dan Galettis. No horrors with other women's husbands. And all that physical side of it went well enough. But he knew I wanted Sam.

She looked down again at the letter, and thought how little his handwriting had changed since he was young. How little he had changed at all, really. She remembered telling Annabel that he was weak, and that he lacked moral judgement and courage. She still did think he was weak. He'd always lacked bravery, and moral sense. But she had thought that even when they were married, and she had still loved him. And she had mourned him from the moment he had left.

She put the letter in her handbag, and went into the bathroom to wash her face, and brush her hair, and steady herself to go down to the kitchen to talk to Jack. She must at least go to London to see Sam, and she would tell Jack that she was going. She could not tell him about the letter, or why she was going, but at least she would spare herself and him the indignity of a lie over whom she was going to see.

She called Sam from the privacy of her office the following day, and they arranged to meet for lunch later in the week. Sam was waiting at the table when she arrived; he stood as she approached, his face lit with the familiar, beaming smile, and they hugged and held each other before they sat. But they were awkward for some moments, and there was a shy exchange over what Hilary wanted to eat, and whether they would or would not drink wine, and an account of mutual acquaintances the two of them had or had not seen in recent years, and who was doing well, and who was not, and who was dead or divorced, and all the trivia of the sort that sustains a moment of this kind. They both spoke too fast and too eagerly, and it was some moments before the tension had eased and they could settle.

A pause came, and Sam could see Hilary's attention wander from the conversation as her face tensed. She then seemed to come to a decision. She reached into her handbag, and brought out Sam's letter. She read it, frowned, laid it on the table in front of them, and looked up at Sam.

'What happens, Sam? What do we do?'

Sam did not reply, but looked at her steadily, and with a slightly flushed face. She looked back at him, and in doing so she felt a sudden tightening of sexual tension and anticipation. Perhaps they should just go for it, she thought. Perhaps they still could.

'I'm glad you wrote. It was a nice letter. I'm glad you love me. I love you too. I always have.' She shrugged, and her face assumed a characteristic expression of part-smile, part-frown, that Sam had so often remembered in the years they had been apart.

Sam smiled back at her. 'Do? Happen? There's not very much that can happen, and not very much that we can do. I wish there was. I wish most of all that we had led our lives differently. I meant what I said in the letter. Losing you ruined my life.'

'Losing you ruined mine too. I've never forgotten you, and I've never stopped missing you. I've dried up inside. I never let Annabel see me as I really am. Probably I shouldn't have married Jack.'

There was a pause, and she looked at him very directly and steadily. Then: 'All because of Dan Galetti.'

Sam smiled at her, but with a pensive, rather withdrawn look in his eyes. 'All because of Dan Galetti,' he said.

And then, after a moment, he went on: 'But, Hils, as the years have gone by, I've understood more about that. It wasn't just an accident with Galetti. You went with him partly because you and he had unfinished business together, and partly because you were looking for something beyond me. I am what I am. For all sorts of reasons you and I are in a mood to romanticise our past together. We've lost Annabel and that's made us close. The horror and pain of all that has made both of us remember times in the past when there was nobody else in the world for either of us but each other. But I was never quite the man you wanted for yourself. You were always looking, in your heart, for someone more dangerous. I know you didn't want me to go. But you went with Dan partly because he was so damned exciting. Whatever I am, I'm not exciting. I'm just Sam. Cuddly old Sam. Sentimental old Sam. And I do love you, Hils, and leaving you ruined my life, and I have never even attempted to find someone who could replace you; but I left partly because I couldn't have stayed and held my pride. And then there was poor old Jack. The odd thing about that was you married in him almost a caricature of me at my weakest element. You wanted danger, Hils, but you kept on marrying safety, and then you blamed it for being safe.'

Hilary looked away from him, and neither spoke for a few minutes. Then Sam put his hand on hers. 'We married so young. We did have a chance of love. We threw it away. But even I am balanced enough to know that when these things have been lost, then they have been lost.'

There was another long pause, and Sam had now taken both her hands in his. He said, and he smiled to her as he did so in a way that signalled the completion of the conversation, 'I wish it had been different.'

He saw her to her station, they held each other as they had at Annabel's funeral, and he waved his hand once in farewell as the train drew away.

Epilogue

Sam and Hilary never saw each other again. The failed meeting in the London restaurant was the last they ever had. Each year though, on the anniversary of Annabel's death, he would send her flowers, and some small memento he had preserved of Annabel: a photograph of her on the beach with bucket and spade, a school report, a tiny doll. She sent him nothing.

Hilary's life wound its way on. The pink Queen Anne house with the long curved drive where Annabel's elm trees used to stand seemed so large and empty now that Annabel was no longer there to visit and stay in the big bedroom overlooking the lawn, which had always been hers. Hilary and Jack saw their lives through there though, and perhaps as the years went by it could be said that they grew a little closer and more responsive to each other. But Jack died only a year or so after he retired, a second heart attack killing him as he sat one summer evening alone in the walled rose garden. Then it was past the time for Hilary to give him any of the love that he so much craved, and she mourned him with all the despair that follows the loss of a partner that one has never in their lifetime reached. Jack never had his children, of course, and he never had his marriage either, and Hilary knew when he died the destruction she had wrought in him, now too late to repair.

Norah drifted away in her sleep one night, only a month or so after she had made the telephone call to Mark which had sent him around to Priory Grove. Jane found her when she brought in her breakfast tray, and when the vicar came rushing up to the house on receiving her call he found Jane rocking Norah's grey old head in her arms, tears running down her cheeks, singing to her a country lullaby. There had been, as far as anyone knew, no pain very much, nor any very obvious discomfort, and it had seemed that from the moment Christopher had died, she had simply willed herself to fade away. Her funeral was a tiny, quiet affair in her beloved village church, and the vicar laid her wreaths under her plaque beside Christopher's, on the north side of the transept.

Just the day before Norah died, she had received a long letter from Mark, and this was lying on her bed-cover when Jane found her in the morning. It was in a US airmail envelope from a San Francisco address, and it contained little in terms of news, but much in terms of unaffected affection and care. Beside the envelope on the bed was a sheet of Norah's writing paper, on which she had written just the date, and the opening words of a letter in reply to his. 'Darling little Mark,' she had said, then below that was just a smudge of ink, rather as if the letter was one of her galley proofs.

For Sam, life became increasingly remote and obscure each month that passed. He had a meeting with Jamieson, who had formalised the severance terms of his contract with Lilley & Chase. He wrote his will, had dinner at The Ivy with Callum Kelly, and lunched with Celia at Wilton's. He went once to Yorkshire and laid a garland for Norah in her village church. For a period he looked quite well, spoke rationally, and seemed oddly devoid of passion or strain.

He sent Hazel a long letter, full of warmth, perhaps even love, and a cheque for one hundred and forty-five thousand pounds, which represented half his entire proceeds after tax from the sale of Lilley & Chase to Monk Grolsch Parsons. She returned it. He sent it back again. She refused it again, and did so with a letter of cold, devastated bleakness that accepted his loss, and in doing so restated, as if on a memorial stone, her parting love for him.

Sam did a little reviewing, drank rather more than in the past perhaps, and forgot an appointment or two, though none of any great importance. He spoke to nobody at Lilley & Chase. He sold his Priory Grove house to discharge the mortgage, then in time rented some rooms somewhere up in North London, and moved in there. Ben saw him in a restaurant once, but Sam returned his wave without warmth and Ben did not go over to him.

He was said to be in New York at one time with Silas Rubinstein. There was a rumour a little later that he was to head the British

Council, but that appointment went to some unknown from the National Health Service. He spoke at a conference in Oslo, and another in Sri Lanka. He was a member of a cultural delegation to Lima. But months passed now between sightings of him, and no one seemed to know much of where he was, or what he was doing.

Within a year, the rumours had died away, and efforts to reach him were waning. Within two years he was spoken of barely at all. Within three years, even the name of Lilley & Chase was lost, as Monk Grolsch Parsons sold out to the Madison Avenue advertising agency, Crackett Kern, who closed the firm down.

New publishing houses started, new publishing houses closed, authors moved on, reputations came, reputations went, publishers were bought, publishers were sold, the Americans moved in, the Germans moved in, the Americans moved out, the Germans moved out.

Richard was now chairman of the National Gallery, a governor of the BBC, vice-chancellor of York University, and a member of the House of Lords.

Sam was forgotten, and Lilley & Chase was forgotten. He was seldom seen, and when he was he was said to appear subdued, passive and taciturn. He knew nobody and cared for nobody, and, if the song were true, nobody cared for him.

But Hazel cared of course, and the house she bought when her mother died was for Sam. She stayed there for the rest of her life, waiting, in case he should return.